Out There Again

Memoirs of an X-Serial Dater

By Sarah Jane Hush

For my husband,
who had me at hello,
and my mother,
the cock-eyed optimist.

Chapter 1 Let Me Introduce Myself

My name is Cherry Thomas. I know, I know, Cherry? I was named in homage to some very distant ancestors who had a wild cherry farm somewhere in the British Isles. My father was a romantic and he loved a good story. His mother told him something about his father's family coming from wild cherry farms and he was always intrigued by the story. So, here I am, named after a fruit. It's really ok, I mean, I like my name. It's definitely a conversation piece. I've always been very outgoing and an extrovert anyway, but imagine how easy it is for me to strike up a conversation with a stranger with a name like that. People I meet are destined to instantly be engaged by just my name alone. For example; if a man walks up to me at a pub and says, "Hello, my name is Jeff." extends his hand to shake mine and I say, "Hi there, I'm Cherry." one of two things always happens. Sometimes it's a good solid laugh and a tighter grip on that handshake. Other times it's a raised brow, surprised look to the left and then the right while they think to themselves, "is she a hooker?" or, "am I on camera?" and they immediately release the handshake. No matter which reaction I get, the conversation is always sure to continue.

I have never had a problem talking to the opposite sex. In school, I could not have been less interested in boys, and I was always so disappointed in all of them because the boys in movies were much more worldly and entertaining. What I am saying is that I was looking for a Mark Hunter, played by Christian

Slater in "Pump Up the Volume" type, and all I could find were guys like Fred O'Bannion, played by Ben Affleck in "Dazed and Confused". To each their own, but needless to say, I spent my teen years as a "Single White Female".

I specifically remember being a teenager in the 90s watching "When Harry Met Sally". That movie came out in 1989, but I didn't see it until I heard the Meg Ryan fake orgasm deli scene dubbed into a rap song and I had to watch it. That movie is a classic to me and such an accurate portrayal of what dating was like pre-internet as well as the complexities of male and female relationships. When I watched it I felt both excited to be an adult who was dating, and completely freaked out. There are so many memorable dialogues that I love from that movie but the one that has stuck with me all this time, like a guiding light on the dark road to find a husband, was spoken by Marie, played by the amazing Carrie Fisher. After she and her serious boyfriend, Jess, hear from their friends, Harry and Sally, who are up to their ears in a "single and dating" frenzy, Marie takes a deep breath and says, "Tell me I never have to be **out there again**." Jess replies by calmly saying, "You never have to be **out there again**." Jess and Marie promptly get engaged. I think it freaked me out a little more than I like to usually admit. I didn't want to be "out there" at all. Have you ever needed something in the refrigerator but you couldn't be bothered to move stuff around to find it so you just stand there and stand there leaning in like it was going to just

—

jump into your hand? That's how I wanted to find the man I would marry. He would just jump right into my lap like a stripper with bills.

It's a tale as old as time, as they say, a girl on the hunt for a husband. The one thing I wanted more than anything was to find the most wonderful husband a girl could ask for. Mr. Perfect. We all have different reasons for wanting to find that special someone. Some of us want babies, some of us want a red-hot romance, some of us want stability and commitment, some of us want a partner in life to share adventures with, some of us are trying to fill a void or a husband shaped hole in our hearts, as I have always said, and some of us want all of the above. No matter what the primary reason might be, we honestly start looking at about 16. We meet the opposite sex and subconsciously think to ourselves, "He's cool...could he be...nah." My mother, who just prayed that I didn't become a pregnant teenager, would be happy to know that I was basically Jerry Seinfeld back then. There was something unacceptable about every male I came into contact with. Remember "man hands" girl, or the one who ate her peas one at a time, or the one who thought Jerry talked "too dirty", or the one who always wore the same dress? I related to the overly critical, Jerry Seinfeld. I literally became disinterested in a guy because he said "but" at the end of all of his sentences like a nervous tick. I know you know what I mean. "I'm going to the store...but." But what? I never could figure that out. I also could not date a guy if he listened to NickelBack. So, I spent my twenties the same way I spent my teens, single and judgmental.

My best friend, Shaun, is not like me. She is outgoing like me and we have a lot in common, but what I mean is that she has been with the same guy since she was 19. She met him at a party when we were in college. It's like they "saw each other and knew" she always says. Well, back then I just thought she was lucky. She is Irish after all, you should have guessed, with a name like Shaun. She's a tough broad, as my father always said, so it works. The truth is her parents wanted a son and she has spent her entire life making sure they know that she doesn't care what they want. She is all woman and when she drinks, she can drink most men under the table and look good doing it. That is one of the many reasons why her man loves her. We grew up together in New York. Shaun's beau is from Boulder, Colorado, so after they pledged their commitment to each other she went back to Colorado with him. They were living in Denver when I visited for the first time and if you have ever seen Colorado you must understand why I immediately wanted to move there too. So, I did. Shaun and I still love New York and visit every single year, but Denver; Denver is a great town. You can just feel the energy there. It rejuvenates you. We knew it just had to be our destiny.

I have always been pretty sure I wanted kids one day, though when I was a kid, I always said no kids past age 28. That's the cut off so there is no generation gap. Well, what the hell did I know? My affinity toward the idea of having babies has changed so many times, but Shaun? She has always said the very same thing since she first heard how babies are born, "Kids are a bad plan." Maybe they are, who knows, but what I do know is that having babies has never been number 1 on my list of reasons to hurry up and find a husband, like some people. I would put it at about number 3 right after 1. Travel the world and 2. Make a million dollars. I have been through the regular motions that led me to believe that I always did want children like choosing names for them, having ideas on parenting styles, and imagining the "I will just live with my kid" retirement plan. I can't say that I ever felt the ticking of my biological clock. I figured that one day, when I met the one, I would get caught somehow in a whirlwind of aggressive baby making. It was something to look forward to, that's for sure.

My brother, Blayne, is ahead of me a little on the subject of making a fortune and traveling the world. He has always been very focused on what he wants personally and professionally, but struggles on the love front. He had a different girlfriend every year since he broke up with his high school sweetheart, Amanda, before college. I wish I were kidding when I tell you that six of them were named Brittany. It's like he seeks them out. I picture him walking into a party or a bar and yelling, "Can I have everyone's attention? Are there any Brittanys in the house?" Then, like they are leased cars, he trades them in every year in January. He claims it isn't on purpose. They share an entire year together in passionate bliss, take at least one trip together, he takes them home for the holidays and then right after New Years Day, the party is over- literally and figuratively. At this point it's just funny and I no longer try to remember their names. Let's be honest, the odds are on my side that it's Brittany anyway. Blayne still lives in New York exactly where he always wanted to live, in a deluxe apartment in the sky. Manhattan specifically, he's kind of a cliche, but I love him dearly. Some of the best friends are siblings.

On the subject of love, the example my parents set for me was profound. They met, fell in love in an hour, and got married a few months later. They lived in wedded bliss until the day my father passed away. Mom still lives in the house Blayne and I grew up in Roslyn, New York, on the North Shore of Long Island. It was a cool place to grow up. My father's parents, who bought it for twenty dollars or something from my great grandfather, originally owned the house. They started a successful real estate agency together and when dad graduated high school he started working for the family business. That is where my parent's met. Mom got a job at "Thomas Realty" and on day two she met dad and fell madly in love. The rest is history. Thomas Realty is just my mom and her assistant now. She loves it and won't ever retire. She says it keeps her young. I have no reason to argue. My mother hasn't dated since dad died but she was never closed off to the idea, it's just that he would have to look like Tom Selleck or Colin Firth so her options are limited. I think she might actually want to date *the* Colin Firth, so I assume she will remain single. I inherited my love of movies from my mother. She won't miss anything with a love story in it whether it is comedy or drama and loves guys with English accents. She also watches "The Ref" everything single December because she thinks, "It's a good Christmas movie." Mom had three great loves at three different periods of time in her life. My father was her last and the only one she married and had children with. They are all gone now and though it is sad, she doesn't dwell on the loss but rather on the happiness she shared with all of them. One reason I spent so many years being lackadaisical about settling down and having children is because my parents were in their thirties when they met. They broke the rules in a way. I always looked up to that. Because of her experiences, she was never the kind of mother who calls every Sunday and whines about giving her some grand kids or who constantly gives the "when are you going to settle down" speech. So many people have mothers or in-laws like that. Your twenties should be about finding your true self, learning from your mistakes, and figuring out your dreams. Maybe indulge yourself a little, you know, with a little too much drinking and staying out late. Maybe kiss a few frogs. The trick is to KNOW they are a frog and be ok with it for the moment. That way you always have the upper hand. Say to yourself, "I am going to kiss this frog and tomorrow morning he will still be a frog and I will go get pancakes." That is to say, let your 20s be spent indulging yourself. Let your 30s be for raising babies. You know, if that's what you're into.

It wasn't until I was in my early 30s that my life turned into a shopping spree for men and I turned into a Serial Dater.

Chapter 2 Grooming?

It's not as if I woke up on my 30th birthday and said, "Ok, I'm ready to find a husband now." It was more like I had spent the last several years since about my 16th birthday figuring out who I was and I felt like I finally knew. I had done what my mother and all of her friends told me to do which was, "find yourself, before you worry about finding a man". It's a classic metaphor, find yourself, because I had never been lost, but I think that the more time you spend alone in your own head learning and experiencing things by yourself, the more confident and self-reliant you may become. I mean no offense to those women who find love right away because, of course, many of those women, like Shaun, are quite confident and independent as well. I can only speak from my own personal experience, which was that I was sure that I was fully aware of who I was by the time I was 30 and there had never been anyone but me in my head since I became an adult, except my mother. I was truly ready to share myself with a man. By "myself" I mean my heart, mind, and soul. I had already shared my bed and so far I wasn't all that impressed.

I decided, from then on when I went out I was going to be on high alert. I was going to be diligent and I was going to be fearless! My next move was to condition myself to truly be the perfect catch to the opposite sex. I was going to be charming, agreeable, witty and funny as always, as well as fully available. So available that I made sure that at some point in every conversation I would bring up the fact that I was "single and looking". There was nothing legal and within my moral compass that I wouldn't do. No fear. No shame. My first step was to make a list called "Things men look for in a woman." Based on what I knew to be true my list started as follows:

1. A Good Job
2. A Good Appearance
3. Intelligence
4. A Car
5. Confidence
6. A Good Attitude.

I'm a list maker and this one was especially fun because I could immediately cross off Job, Intelligence, Car, Confidence, and Attitude. Done, done, done, done, and done. So, I went to work on my appearance.

I took a long hard look into my closet and what I found was, I'm sure a common problem in many women's closets, quantity outweighing quality. I changed my entire clothes shopping strategy, so when I went shopping for clothes I made sure I was genuinely devoted to the task. For example, I used to suddenly realize that I needed a black top or something so on my lunch break I would go to the closest store and grab whatever I could find that worked. That kind of laissez-fair attitude about clothes shopping would no longer be acceptable. There was no way in a million years that at any given time I was not going to look "perfectly squared away". My outfits would need to consist of shirts and blouses with a little bit of cleavage, more skirts and a lot of leg, and definitely more of a sense of fashion. Have you ever been on a certain kind of budget that allows for periodic new clothes shopping but only if the clothes are appropriate for play AND work? I have, and at this point I was adding, "must be sexy" to that rule of thumb. I had a long talk with myself and decided that a woman can't afford to not look good in public. It doesn't matter what the reason is but the most important reason is out of respect for herself. Don't go everywhere in a messy bun and sweats, ladies, put a little effort into it and just see the difference it makes. The truth is that wearing pajamas in public is just straight up unacceptable. I decided I was going to be a textbook over-dresser. I was always in heels and I always had on dramatic earrings. Every outfit I wore was carefully planned and put together.

The next area of importance was my makeup choices and skincare. I started wearing more eye makeup and what was really funny when I think about it now is that I started caring about my skin. Can you imagine? Moisturizing is very important and often ignored by poreless 20 something's. Skin is a living organ and should be treated as such. I had always been a sunblock wearer but realizing that spending a little more money on what you put on your face, neck and elsewhere was life changing. Furthermore, never again would I miss a pedicure or manicure. My fingernails are not qualified to be left to their own devices. I had cuticles for days and though I kept a regular presence in a pedicure chair, I often neglected my fingernails.

I did have a hard time *not* getting my hair done at Super Cuts or Cost Cutters anymore though. I have long, straight, dark brown hair, not exactly high maintenance, but every time I got a trim the next person who cut my hair would always say something like, "Girl, where did you get your hair cut last?" with a horrified look on their face. I would always smile and say, "Uh, here." and sit the rest of the time in an awkward silence. I just know some of you have heard that before. So, never again, I would only get 50 dollar or more haircuts from then on. It would be worth the money, I just knew it.

Finally and most importantly, I decided I would stop shaving and start waxing my bikini line. That is until I could afford laser hair removal. I never met a single woman on earth who said, "I love getting waxed, it's so fun." But, that doesn't mean you don't do it. Beauty is pain sometimes. It's just the way it is. When a girl has unruly eyebrows I automatically have a secret and small amount of judgment of them because I wonder what *must* be going on with their bikini zone. If women think that way, you know men just have to.

I became a warrior. A hunter. Hell on heels. A dignified, semi-feminist, totally in control, knows exactly what she wants, I's dotted, T's crossed, single woman looking for long-term commitment. I felt like I was absolutely ready for the right guy to come in and steal my heart like a thief in the night. I was prepared and ahead of the game. I thought the game was my middle name. I thought I had all of the answers. Turns out, I had no idea what the hell I was doing.

Chapter 3 Where are the Men?

I admit that I was looking really good. I could have even left "good attitude" on the list and then crossed it off later because after giving myself this mini-makeover, I really did feel better. I had an even better outlook on life. I don't think it is too materialistic to believe that looking good helps one to feel good. It's the truth. My confidence level was even higher than before and people noticed. My boss, who is one of the busiest human beings on the planet and didn't notice when I dyed my hair blonde for a month when I was about 26, kept saying, "Cherry, you look great, what's different?" I would just smile and tell him he was so funny. That's my go-to response when I don't know what to say. "You're so funny." It's terrible. I literally say it all the time. My boss is Benjamin Goldwitz, a prominent Denver attorney specializing in corporate law and I am his paralegal, or legal assistant, or let me just tell you the truth I am his assistant. Sometimes I pick up his dry cleaning. I wanted to be a lawyer since I was a child and so I set out to do just that. After a year and a half of college I lost interest. I felt like I no longer had any desire to make that happen. I switched gears and got my associates degree and a paralegal certificate. I met Ben at the Denver District Attorney's office where I was working as a receptionist making way less than I could stand. He was waiting in my lobby for a friend of his who was an assistant DA and when he introduced himself and I told him my name, he threw back his head in laughter. "Cherry Thomas", he kept saying, "What an amazing name." He gave me his card and said, "Give me a call if you ever want a real job." I called him the next day. He doubled my pay, introduced me to his wife, Margo who I instantly liked, and we have all been friends ever since. They live in Highlands Ranch, which is where people live who drive BMWs and have impressive bank accounts. Ben and Margo are cool and only about ten years older than me. Sometimes when they invite me over for dinner, I stop on the way and pick up a bottle of wine and a pack of American Spirits so we can sit outside after dinner on their enormous patio and laugh at the cookie cutter, rich suburban life while we secretly smoke cigarettes and drink wine.

I am lucky because I am one of those people who loves my job. It was one of those Celestine Prophecy moments, meeting Ben you know, because I like to believe that everything happens for a reason. Any interaction with any one could be life altering so you should pay close attention to the signs. I meet men every single day at work. Most of them are old Suite-C types and I am their daughter's age. As appealing as some women might think that is, I could never date a guy just because of his money, especially if he was old enough to be my dad. I never talked about being on a manhunt with Ben and Margo. They just figured I wasn't actively perusing a relationship or that I was just a free spirit. I am 100% professional at work anyway; there is no time for flirting. Even if sometimes those Suite-C types are in my age bracket.

So, where does a single girl find a man? My parents, who almost never went, always told me that Church was a great place to meet people. Church? The only time I go to church is if a Catholic friend of mine gets married or sometimes when I'm feeling crazy I will go to midnight mass on Christmas Eve. I'm not Catholic but it's the only kind of church I have really ever been in so it just feels right. I am definitely a Christian but I don't know much about the organization of religion. Weddings, on the other hand, are definitely a great place to meet men. I remember the year I happened to have a wedding invitation under a magnet on my refrigerator. Shaun and Johnny were finally getting married after over ten years of courting. That was really when this whole journey started for me.

The wedding was expected, but still very exciting because they waited so long to get married and we all loved Johnny as much as Shaun did. They decided to get married at the Hotel Boulderado in his home town of Boulder and my brother and mom were coming out for the wedding. I made sure that Shaun told Johnny that I would be "single and looking" because I knew that he had tons of good looking friends that would be at the wedding. I booked a room for that weekend to share with my mom, and my brother was bringing his girlfriend, you guessed it, Brittany, so he also booked a room. I was, of course, Shaun's maid of honor but the wedding party was small. It was just me, the maid of honor, and Johnny's slightly younger brother Chris, the best man. Chris is gay and fabulous and loves when I call him Chrissy affectionately. He is a perfect gay version of Johnny. Its like God said, "Let me make this great man, Johnny, for the ladies, and let his brother be just as great and for the men." He is a thoughtful God.

Shaun went to NYU with me and studied business. She left early too, when she moved to Colorado, and started her own Event Planning business. She had planned her own wedding and based on what she shared with me, it sounded like it was going to be amazing. The Hotel Boulderado is a historic, Victorian style, very romantic place full of dark wood and jewel tones. September in Colorado is arguably the most perfect time and place for a wedding. Shaun and I picked out my dress together and I just knew I was going to look gorgeous in it. It was chiffon in a shade of wine, just above the knee, and sleeveless. We would be carrying Victorian roses in shades of cream and soft pink. I had been looking forward to it for months and when my mom, Blayne, and Brittany arrived at my apartment on Friday afternoon, I was bouncing off the wall, excited that the wedding weekend was finally there. If I was lucky, it would be full of single men.

We arrived at the Hotel on Friday evening along with Shaun and Johnny and their other close family and friends who wanted to stay for the weekend like us. The wedding was Saturday afternoon and we were all checking out on Sunday morning. Everyone had planned to meet at The Catacombs, which was a bar in the basement under the Boulderado. It's called License No. 1 or something now and I have never been back, so I don't know what it's like anymore but it used to be such a cool place. It was always Shaun and Johnny's favorite and part of the reason why they wanted to get married in the Hotel. She said it was a

19

big part of their story. So, we checked into our rooms, freshened up and trickled slowly into the bar.

The Combs was full of college kids and locals when we showed up, and it felt like a full on party. Shaun ran in, smiling ear to ear. "Meet my friend, Cherry, we have been friends since kindergarten." She told everyone, it was her quote of the night. She kept saying, "We know all of each other's skeletons." It's true for sure, having a best friend who knows everything about you, and still thinks you rule, is a priceless gift that should not be taken for granted. I appreciated her really putting effort into making sure I met every man who walked through the door. We had a great time but other than the college guys, who had nothing to do with the wedding, I didn't meet a single guy who wasn't with his wife or girlfriend. Shaun kept telling me, "Don't worry, more people will be here tomorrow." I was counting on it.

Have you ever been excited to wear an outfit? I couldn't wait to see Shaun in her wedding dress, which she kept a secret from everyone, even her mother, but I was seriously excited about my dress. I had been a bridesmaid a few times and never had I liked the dress. Then again, Shaun has outstanding taste and I had some say in the dress style this time.

Chris finally showed up and I was thrilled as always to see him. "Chrissy! Please tell me there will be single guys at the wedding tomorrow, I'm finally looking for a husband." He laughed hysterically and said, "Girl, I was starting to think you were a lesbian.

Haven't you always been single?" Yes, I had always been single. I just smiled and said, "You're so funny." It was at that time that he started going through the list of the people he knew who were coming. Naming names of men I didn't know, some of which were his relatives and almost all of them were followed by "has a wife" or "has a girlfriend". He started laughing again and said, "There will be a couple. Oh! Our Uncle Barry is single." Hilarious. I couldn't even believe my ears. A couple? We were in our early 30s! You're going to tell me that everyone that Shaun and Johnny knew, important enough to be invited to their wedding, were spoken for? So, for the night, I gave it up and proceeded to drink like I was 21. It was amazing. After mom went to bed around 11, Shaun, Blayne, and I must have done eight shots a piece toasting Shaun and Johnny and their continued happiness. Some might say that's a lot, some might not. We sang Sweet Caroline and laughed so hard at times we couldn't breath. When the bar closed down we toasted with the last shot of the night, "To me", I slurred, "and my hunt for a husband." Everyone laughed, slamming their glasses together, and Chris yells, "I can't wait to introduce you to Uncle Barry!" Hilarious.

The wedding was perfect and Shaun's dress was like a dream. It was a big group of people and all of them stayed through dinner for the reception. I recognized a guy I had met before a few months earlier, very briefly and from a distance. His name was Mark. Whenever I meet guys named Mark, Rick, or Steve I think of Clairee Belcher, played by Olympia Dukakis in "Steel Magnolias". She said, "All gay men are named Mark, Rick, or Steve and all gay men have track lighting." This Mark was definitely not gay, though Chris was definitely hitting on him. I saw my chance to join the conversation. I reached out to shake his hand and said, "Hi, I think we have met before." He said, "Yeah, Cherry, right?" He shook my hand back and we continued with small talk. Chris told me that Mark was his favorite friend of his brother's growing up and that he was friend's with Mark's younger brother who is the same age as he. Mark had recently moved back to Colorado from LA and was working with his father. The conversation picked up momentum and I thought to myself, "see", this is how you do it. The old fashioned way. Meeting men socially is still the best way to find potential relationship material. I don't need Internet dating. That is for the next generation.

Mark and I ended up talking well into the night. As the party got smaller and smaller we remained sitting at a table talking and laughing at the post wedding shenanigans. He told me, "You're one of the coolest girls I have ever met. I would love to get your number." Jackpot. "Thank you. You are pretty great yourself." I handed him my card. Ben had cards made for me. He said it was worth it to him for free advertising and networking because women my age are always handing out their card. I had probably handed out ten cards in the almost seven years I had them. Turns out he didn't know what he was talking about, but tonight I was glad he gave me cards. Mark took the card and said, "Impressive." I smiled at him and, of course, said, "You're so funny."

I spent the end of the reception with Mark, Shaun and Johnny, my brother and Brittany, Chris, and a few other friends of Johnny's who were also staying at the Hotel. I saw my mom dancing with a guy and my jaw dropped. I gasped and said, "Who is mom dancing with?" In unison Chris and Johnny yelled, "That's Uncle Barry!" I was embarrassed as Chris caught everyone up on the Uncle Barry joke and how I was single and looking for a husband. Everyone roared with laughter and my brother hugged my neck playfully. I wanted to crawl under the table. I kept telling myself, "Don't look at Mark", "Don't look at Mark". But, of course, I did, I looked right at him and he winked at me. What a charming thing to do, wink. I already couldn't wait for him to call me in 5 days or whatever his waiting period rule turned out to be. As we laughed and drank the night away I was optimistic. I was totally open for whatever was going to come my way. The next phase of my life had really just begun like a chapter in my book. The next chapter was going to be called "Mark" and it was going to be epic! Or, so I thought.

Chapter 4 The Mark Situation

Mark definitely called me. He actually texted me within hours of when we all checked out and went our separate ways. He told me he was so glad he got to know me and he couldn't wait for us to hang out soon. I was psyched. He was a total catch and Shaun, even though she and Johnny were on their way to Curacao, texted me constantly about him. I told her about everything we talked about at the reception and asked her second level questions for her to ask Johnny. That's what girls do. Shaun kept telling me that she was so excited because she really liked Mark and never pictured me liking him but that it made sense. Then I asked her, "What does Johnny think?" It took her twenty minutes to answer. I figured she was on a flight or just busy honeymooning but then she answered with kind of a red flag. It was a red flag that I ignored. She said, "He thinks it's cool but wants to warn you that he doesn't think Mark is your type." I texted back, "What does that mean?" and she replied with, "Johnny thinks he is weird when it comes to dating. Girls always break up with him. Johnny said he is pushy. I don't know what that means. Maybe he just hasn't found the right one. He seems so perfect." I agreed with her and carried on. Our first date was set for the next Friday night.

Mark and I met at a restaurant in Uptown Denver called Il Posto. We had a conversation just as great as at the wedding reception. He was so easy to talk to and someone I actually liked. He was my speed.

Intelligent, funny, old fashioned, he loved movies, and he loved his mother. There were many things we had in common like art, music, and politics. I enjoyed myself so much that I didn't even think twice about blurting out, "Do you want to come to my place?" He smiled, said yes, and got the check. I had no intention of sleeping with him; I just didn't want the night to end yet. I got us a cab back to my place. As soon as we got home he went to use the bathroom and that's when things got interesting. I opened a bottle of wine and poured us both a glass. I was breathing in the aroma of this delicious Argentinean Malbec when he came out of the bathroom, bare chested, with his shirt in his hand. "Sorry, Cherry, I got my shirt all wet, do you have a dryer?" I just stood there with my mouth open and thought of that scene in the movie "Ghost". Remember when Carl, played by Tony Goldwyn, fake spills a drink on his shirt just so he can take it off? Secondarily I was distracted by Marks physique. It had been a while since I stood in front of a man with no shirt on and I liked what I saw. I finally grabbed the shirt and said, "Yes, of course" and threw it in the dryer to fluff. I told him I had a couple men's sized t-shirts that I wear when I paint that he could wear and he says, "No, I'm fine." Huh? I thought, "You're fine?" You're fine sitting in my living room with no shirt on drinking a glass of wine on the night of our first date?

"So, you paint. Are all of these paintings yours?" He looked around my living room at the paintings as I slowly move into the same area and said, "Yes, do you like them?" He said he did and that he is a fan of abstract art. I decided to relax. He isn't some random guy; he is a life long friend of a person I trust very much. So, we sat on the couch. We sat on the couch and talked long enough for us to finish those glasses of wine and I guess the "Carl trick" worked because I didn't stop him when he moved in for the kill.

Just so you can really picture the moment, I hadn't had sex in a while and Mark was the kind of guy who talks dirty. Have you ever dated one of those? He was a passionate kisser and kept saying things like, "You're so sexy." and, "Do you like that?" It was a real turn on. We sort of started off real slow like he was taking my virginity and had to make sure I was ok and then after we moved past a certain point, we were banging my headboard against the wall and he was almost as loud as me. I really felt like I hit the jackpot with this guy. He was totally and 100% good in bed. The next morning I woke up and he was nowhere to be found.

Oh, could it have been true? Could I have been a victim of a player so soon in the game? Could I have been an easy target as a girl who puts out on informally the second date and formally the first date? Either way, here I was and when I looked at my phone the twenty-seven texts were not from Mark but from Shaun who only had two more days left of her honeymoon. When I told her what happened she said, "Johnny told me he is weird with women." I promptly told her and Johnny not to worry about me. It's a lesson learned, no big deal. It was fun while it lasted.

———

I clean for a few different reasons. Because it's Saturday, which it was, when I have a lot on my mind, which I did, or when I have my period. So, for two out of three of those reasons I started cleaning my apartment ferociously. I like to start in the kitchen and end in the bathroom then take a shower when I'm done. It's a perfect routine in my opinion. I admit that while I was cleaning for the next few hours, I checked my phone several times. Nothing. So, after I polished up the toilet, I got into the shower and I started crying. Have you ever cried in the shower? I think maybe people cry in the shower sometimes because it's a very private place and because you can become deep in thought. I remember Sarah Cooper, played by Glenn Close in "The Big Chill", had a hard cry in the shower when she found out her friend died. Maybe that is where I got the idea. I saw that movie the first time when I was pretty young. Anyway, I don't think I was sad. I think that I was disappointed. When you allow yourself to get intimate with someone, it doesn't mean you are going to be committed forever, but you do expect a certain level of respect from the person you shared yourself with and waking up alone is a pretty blatant metaphoric slap in the face. I was just disappointed.

It was close to 2 PM when I got out of the shower and I had snuggled up on the couch to watch movies for the rest of the night. I thought maybe I would order Chinese food. Movies and Chinese is a great way to spend a Saturday night alone. I never really feel alone, though. I am my true best friend. I entertain and comfort myself. I have been bored before which really means I wanted to do something but didn't know what…I can't actually ever say, "I'm bored" or I will hear my mother's voice in my head. I should explain that to me she always sounds like a New York Jew. Imagine the accent as she says, "I never understood boredom." Then she makes a disappointed face and continues: "There is always something to do, something to read, somewhere to go, or something to create." As a child this annoyed me because she was right and I wanted to be the one who was always right. However, as an adult, I couldn't agree with her more. It's true, I am my very best friend and at the risk of sounding like Sybil, you can never be alone when you have yourself.

Just when I got really cozy, the doorbell rang. At first I didn't care, I just laid there. I hate when my doorbell rings when I'm not expecting someone. Seriously, it's like I figure it's either someone I don't know at the wrong door, some weirdo selling meat out of the back of a truck, or the FBI with a warrant for my arrest. It is an irrational reaction to a doorbell ring, but a reaction nonetheless. Ding Dong. The bell rang again and then there was a knock. So, I got up and snuck up to the door to look through the peephole. It was Mark. What? I ran to the bathroom and said, "Just a minute!" I had to make sure I looked somewhat acceptable having not done anything with myself after I got out of the shower. I looked pretty good, maybe a little puffy. As I opened the door I imagined myself expressionless. He holds out a bouquet of flowers and leans in to hug me. I didn't understand what was happening but I was pleasant and said thank you. He said, as he walked by me and headed to my bedroom, "You must think I'm such an asshole. Come here and look." I followed him into the bedroom. "I left my phone here I think." He kneels me down with him to look under the bed and there was his phone on the floor on the other side where he slept. He tells me he had to help his dad that day and he didn't realize he didn't have his phone until he was already where he was headed. He didn't want to wake me up because I looked so peaceful but he regretted that decision when he wasn't able to text me all day. I felt relieved. I mean, his phone was here the whole time and his story was actually legit. I did end up ordering Chinese food that night but not for a Saturday night alone. As it turned out it was for a third date, more sex than I had had in ages, and Mark didn't go home until late Sunday night. I officially was in serious like.

We spent most of the next few weeks hanging out together and having lots of sex. It was as if both of us were trying to catch up to something. We were making up for lost time in the bedroom. We were sort of like teenagers who couldn't keep their hands off of each other when we were alone. I dig that feeling. He was reserved when we were in public or with friends but at home he was very affectionate and loving. We had several double dates with Shaun and Johnny and even spent a long weekend in Estes Park at the end of October. I remember it snowed while we were there and the trip turned out to be a surprisingly romantic experience.

By November I was starting to get pretty excited for the holiday season. I go home every single year for Christmas and New Years Eve and Shaun and Johnny go to New York every other year to be with her parents. This year was a New York year and we were flying out and back together. I felt like inviting Mark was a little too serious so I talked about it very casually and asked him what he had planned for Thanksgiving and Christmas. He told me he had been meaning to ask me if I was going to be having Thanksgiving at Shaun's because Johnny invited him since his parent's were going to his sister's house in California that year. I was excited. It meant that we would be able to spend a holiday together without meeting either person's family and thus relieving us of all the pressures that come along with that. November flew by pretty fast that year.

On Thanksgiving it was the first time that Mark was affectionate in front of anyone. Shaun kept whispering that it was because I cooked for him. She might have been right, I'm just as good in the kitchen as I am, well, you know where. Shaun and I shared Thanksgiving dinner duties so it was a huge spread. That night, I stayed with Mark just because he lives closer to Shaun's than my place and when we had sex it was different than ever before. This was new territory for me. He was acting like he was very close to me. I always made fun of that term "making love" and figured it was an old fashioned way of describing sex. It honestly made me feel uncomfortable. Mark wouldn't let me go and he was doing a lot of staring into my eyes. There was a real connection happening.

—

30

When I turned off the light and we started drifting to sleep he whispered, "I think I love you." I thought, wow, I really got my Thanksgiving turkey that year, didn't I? I loved him too. I wasn't sure I felt like I was in love but I definitely loved him so, I told him the same, "I think I love you too."

I felt weird the next day. He was on cloud nine and I was a nervous wreck. It's an interesting thing to be with someone and never quite feel like you are experiencing the same thing at the same time. I didn't feel synched up. I was happy though. What did I know about navigating this kind of situation? Nothing. We had lunch with Shaun and Johnny on that Sunday and at one point both Shaun and Mark were in the bathroom. Johnny tells me he has never seen Mark this way and he has had a lot of girlfriends, they never seem to last long, he reminds him of Blayne that way. Blayne? Good Lord. Blayne doesn't really have the best track record for commitment, but please understand, he isn't really a player. He tries everything and it just never works out. When he is in a relationship he gives his all. He's a good guy, but I knew what it looked like to the outside world, that he goes through so many girlfriends. I honestly always thought that he never got over his high school love. I always thought they would end up together but she married someone else right out of college. Blayne broke her heart but he thought he was doing the right thing at the time. So, maybe that was Mark's story too. Maybe he just spent his twenties going through women who weren't the one. Maybe he thought I was the one. Was I the one? I suddenly realized when I was processing what Johnny was telling me, that I was supposed to be looking for a husband. I think I had forgotten about that for the last three months. Mark knew what my goal was on the first night we hung out, thanks to Chris, and he still pursued me. Usually men who are actually players run toward the hills at the first hint that a woman is looking to settle down. Or so I had been told. The whole experience was so interesting to me.

Winter that year started off great and as I was busy preparing for my trip back home, Mark wanted to spend as much time with me as he could. He told me everyday how much he was going to miss me and he couldn't believe that I was going to be gone for so many days. I am lucky because Ben takes off the last two weeks plus of the year because he can do whatever he wants so I also get that time off. I always fly out on about the 15th and come home on the 2nd. Shaun is self-employed so she plans her own schedule and Johnny just has a good job with a lot of vacation time. I was going to miss Mark too. I guess I was probably a little more excited to see my mom and brother and New York at Christmas than I was worried about missing Mark. I almost asked him if he wanted to go a couple times but something kept stopping me.

On the night before I left, Mark spent the night at my place. He was taking us all to the airport the next morning. We had some wine and good conversation and joked around about seeing each other "next year". At the end of the night when we were getting ready for bed and I was mostly packed and checking my travel list, he sat down on the bed and watched me for a few minutes. He reached out his arms and told me to sit down next to him. I made a dumb joke about us needing to talk and he didn't laugh. He just looked at me and said, "I really love you, Cherry. I love you so much. Are you committed to me?" I said, "Yes! Of course I am." It just came out. It was the most intense I had ever seen him and so I asked, "Are you ok?" He said, "Yes, I'm fine. I'm fine. I'm just really going to miss you." So, I took and deep breath and I said, "I love you, Mark. I will miss you too. It's only a couple weeks." He seemed to feel better, I could tell, and that night, after we went to bed, we consummated our pledge of commitment to the relationship.

Chapter 5 Amnesia for Christmas

Christmas in New York is absolutely the most magical experience. I spent Christmas in Denver the first year I moved there, because financially it just made sense, and I regretted it. It wasn't Denver's fault, Denver is lovely in the winter, but I need New York at Christmas like I need an old friend. We generally do everything the same every year too, and I like it that way. We skate at Rockefeller, we get a coffee or cocoa and wander up 5th Avenue looking at the window displays, and sometimes we go see The Rockettes at Radio City. Blayne spends a few nights at mom's in Roslyn and at some point we always meet up with old friends who are also home for the holidays at night at the "pond". "Roslyn Pond" is downtown in the Village. When we were kids we would go sledding around there and when we were teenagers that's where we would sneak smokes and swigs of cheap wine. It was a pretty cool place to grow up. I never really had anything to complain about.

The holiday festivities were as convivial as always that year and I was enjoying spending time with my mom and Blayne when he could be there for dinner. I texted back and forth with Mark and he told me he loved me and that he missed me every morning and every night. We even talked on the phone a few times. On Christmas Eve, Blayne was finally home for a few days with Brittany in tow, and Shaun and Johnny came over for dinner. We had a great time reminiscing and looking at old, funny pictures from our childhood. My mother loves getting the pictures out. Somehow, I often ended up looking like the Irish mafia in my baby pictures. I liked to dress up and wear hats. My mom gets mad at me when I say that and tells me, "You look like your English grandfather, Cherry." She doesn't find humor in mafia jokes. Since dad died we spend a lot of time telling our favorite stories about him. It makes us feel like he is with us. I was completely caught up in the moment and didn't even think about my phone, when, after mom went to bed, we decided to go down to the pond with a bottle of wine to see if anyone was there. It was so cold and had snowed that day so the ground crunched under our feet as we walked and laughed and sang songs from the 80's that reminded us of being young.

We saw a few random people from high school and were talking to an old friend of Blayne's, when the very guy I lost my virginity to, appeared down the path. You guessed it, Fred O'Bannion. I'm kidding, but he was close. He was a cooler version of Fred that was the kind of guy who *will* sing the "boy part" in Leather and Lace by Stevie Nicks and Don Henley. As he realized who we were and called out, "Well, well, well, look who it is." Shaun whispers, "Oh, look, the only guy in high school worthy of Cherry's cherry." I tried to drown out everyone's laughter by loudly saying, "Hey, Jimmy!" and ran over to hug him. Jimmy was my favorite. Of course, he liked me much more than I liked him back in the day so we never made it anywhere beyond "friends with benefits". There was not really too much wrong with him, we just weren't on the same plane. I was so excited to see him.

It's amazing being in your early 30s. There is more than a decade that had gone by since being a teenager and for most of us so many life-altering things happen in that time. For example, Jimmy had already been married and divorced, had become a father of two boys, and had been in the army for over twelve years. It seemed like he accomplished so much more than I had already and we were the very same age. We all spent what seemed like an eternity down by the pond that night. It was such an amazing Christmas Eve back in Roslyn.

Later, Blayne and I said goodbye to Shaun and Johnny and assisted Brittany to bed. She wasn't qualified in any way to drink as much as she did that night. I appreciated her effort. I laughed to myself that after New Year's I would never see her again anyway. Blayne and I sat down at the kitchen table. The kitchen is always where the best conversations happen at mom's house. The living room is absolutely the most comfortable but there is something about sitting around the kitchen table that kind of draws something out of us. Blayne said to me, "So, how are things going with Mark?" Mark! I had completely forgotten to even look at my phone since before dinner. I scrambled to find it and Blayne laughed at my near panicked behavior. Five text messages and two missed calls. One missed call was from Shaun and a text from just a few minutes after she left which said, "Mark is trying to reach you."

___

36

The other missed call and four text messages were from Mark spread out over the last five hours. 1. I miss you. 2. What are you doing? 3. Cherry, should I be worried? 4. I just tried to call you. I'm going to call Johnny. It's really messed up to not answer me for this many hours. Where are you??????" I immediately sent him a text back that said how sorry I was, that I had forgotten my phone, that I had been out, and for him to call me if he was still awake. Blayne laughed and said, "What? Is he mad that you didn't text him back? It's Christmas Eve, dude. You're busy. He better not want me to ring his bell." I laughed. Oh, Blayne, my big brother, he's always so protective and funny. I was sure it would be fine when the phone rang and it was Mark.

He was so upset and went on and on about how worried he was and wanted to know specifically what happened and what I did. He was mad but never yelled or really said anything too crazy; it's just that in my opinion his reaction was pretty extreme for not hearing from me for a few hours, while I'm on vacation on Christmas Eve with my family, and, by the way, one of his best friends. I didn't really say much because Blayne was right. It was stupid for him to be upset. I definitely did apologize by telling him I was sorry that I worried him so much, and assured him that he really never had anything to worry about. This was clearly a red flag, jealousy, or a control freak moment, and I didn't know what else to say to him.

The conversation ended calmly and I figured it was, for the most part, water under the bridge, but the next morning the first text I got from Mark was, "Who is Jimmy?" Sweet Jesus, here we go. I decided not to answer it until I had the coffee brewing. Blayne and my mom, who don't drink coffee, were already awake. I figured Johnny must have talked to Mark this morning and given him a synopsis of last night's events. I answered him, "A friend of mine from high school, we saw him last night in town."

"Hmmm."

"Why do you ask?"

He went on to tell me that I should tell him when I am hanging out with old boyfriends, blah, blah, blah. I couldn't even stomach having that conversation on Christmas morning and even though seeing Jimmy was great, it mattered not one bit in reference to my relationship with Mark. It was a platonic encounter between two old friends. The fact that we used to have sex didn't matter either. What would Mark suggest I do when I saw him? Run away screaming? I told Mark I would call him later.

I wouldn't say that this ruined my Christmas because we still had an amazing time, but it made me very emotional. I might have portrayed myself as a stonehearted bitch so far, but the reality is that I am very sensitive to other people's feelings and emotions and I don't like when anyone is upset or sad or hurt. I am an unyielding sugar coater and a person who always tries to keep the peace. I behave like a middle child even though I am younger than my only sibling. My mom says I am a natural "care taker". So, I did the very best I could to calm, comfort, and reassure Mark that I actually did love him and he still had nothing to worry about. I would be home soon and we could pick up right where we left off. He seemed ok for the rest of my trip and even gave me a little more space between our talks. That didn't stop me from having more anxiety than I had had in a while.

Back in Denver, we shared a cab back to my house and I drove Shaun and Johnny home. I texted Mark when we landed but hadn't heard from him yet. About an hour later he replied, "Glad you're back. I had a long day. Talk to you tomorrow." I was glad I was back too, I always feel so happy flying into DIA. I love living in Denver. It's a great feeling to be happy to go home from vacation. I don't take that for granted.

The next night Mark came over and nothing was the same. I was so excited to see him and was showing it but he remained standoffish and quiet. We exchanged our Christmas gifts. I gave him a sweater that I had picked up for him in New York at Calvin Klein and he handed me a box. It was a bracelet that I had seen when we were in Estes Park in October. He went back and got it for me. I was so moved by that. I was genuinely happy to be with him and even though I was all over him, he kept telling me he was tired. It was as if I had to make him want to have sex with me. That was new. I had never experienced that before. The worst part was that when we finally did have sex he kept telling me to keep it down. He told me I was being too loud, there are neighbors. This was, of course, a red flag because I very clearly remembered all of the sex we had already had in my apartment and the near damage that had been done to my headboard the first time. It was hard for me to continue after being shushed during sex but I did. Later on that night, when he fell asleep, I cried.

I had cried three times in the course of our four-month romance. The first time was when I thought he booty called me in the beginning, the second was out of frustration on Christmas Day, and the third time was when I came home and realized that it seemed as though Mark had forgotten that he loved me. Though the relationship ended I wouldn't say that it crashed and burned. It was more like someone turned it into dust in their hand and stood on a cliff edge and slowly let it blow into the wind. There was no definitive break up. He started talking to me like we were friends and we never had sex again. I didn't try to figure it out. Instead I was mad that he ended up wasting my precious time. I was mad that he made me feel even a little bit of love for him and then bailed out over what seemed like the slightest thing.

I was really upset through January and we talked less and less until we didn't talk at all anymore. Then one day I just decided that I did my best and that was all I could do. Did I learn any lessons? Maybe to take it slower, though I didn't really think Mark and I moved too fast. I mean, maybe he did, but I felt like I behaved and reacted appropriately. Shaun and Blayne agreed and they were really the only people my age whose opinions, supplementary to my own, mattered to me.

As January came to an end and Blayne said goodbye to his most recent Brittany, I had a great idea.

Chapter 6 Online Dating

February felt like a good month to create an online profile for Internet dating. It is the month of love after all, right? It was time for me to get back into the game. I invited Shaun over on a Friday to help. When the two of us are alone together we are not exactly the same as when we are out in the world. We are a little bit weirder and a lot sillier. But, no matter where we are, we are so close that it is as if we share a brain. I knew that she would be the perfect person to help me with this and she was 100% on board with the idea. Blayne, on the other hand, was so annoyed. He was worried about something bad happening to me. I was aware of the risks but, as far as I was concerned, this was the new way to date and I was a modern girl. I didn't want have to go to bars to meet people and no other normal part of my regular routine was leading me to single men. eHarmony was supposed to be the most legitimate site for "serious people" but there was no way I was going to pay to do this. So, I chose one that was free and seemed the most straight forward and went with it.

For my profile, I chose pictures that I felt showed my true self; a picture of me with and without glasses, a full body shot, a picture of me at a party, and a picture of me at work. When you set up an online dating profile there is no reason to post pictures that don't look like your true self. First of all, how will they know it's you when you meet? Second, why would you want to set yourself up for them seeing the real you and not liking it? These online dating sites are like a catalogue. The first thing you see is the picture and from there you read the profile. Imagine if you ordered an orange size extra large t-shirt and you get a size small purple tank. You'd return it and be unpleased with the time you wasted. Looks do matter; you just have to be honest with yourself. Luckily for all of us, everyone is attractive to someone.

Then I filled out the entire profile complete with a biography and matching questions like; "Do you smoke?" "Do you want to have kids?", and "What are you looking for?" I don't know why I remember those questions as opposed to the other ones but my answers to them were, "No", "Undecided", and "Long Term Commitment". A guy can look at those three answers alone and already know if he should be interested in continuing to look at the entire profile. One of the answer options for the "What are you looking for" question was "Sex", so, for a guy who chose "Sex" as his answer, right out of the barrel my answer of "Long Term Commitment" would make me a no go. It wasn't very scientific, which is why it was free, but I felt confident with my profile, and once I had chosen my handle OTA23 which stood for "Out There Again", part of my favorite quote from "When Harry Met Sally", and my favorite number, I went live.

Shaun was spending the night and we were already on our second bottle of cabernet by the time I submitted my profile. We were laughing so hard not having a single clue what was about to happen. We had absolutely no idea what to expect. Even though we both knew people who did online dating, and even a couple who met that way and got married, we had never gotten any details from any of them. We quickly realized that a person knows when you have looked at their profile so I completely stopped doing that and never did it again unless a person messaged me first. That's right, I completely relied on men to inquire about me or send me messages. I never proactively looked for men or reached out first. Call me old fashioned or weird but, I just couldn't bring myself to do it. I waited for the single men of "Denver and surrounding area" to come to me.

It was 2 AM and the second bottle was empty when Shaun and I passed out before there was any activity on my new account. Saturday morning was a different story. I woke up to Shaun laughing and yelling my name in a high-pitched squeal. "Cherry! Oh my GOD! Look at this!" She was holding my laptop and sitting on end of the bed. I had over ninety messages and almost three hundred profile views. Ninety messages? It took us the entire morning to get through them all and I only answered a fraction of them based on what they said and if they were even remotely my type. The large majority of the messages were charming and friendly, but some of them would haunt my dreams forever more.

Up until this point I have been very polite. I haven't said any bad words and I haven't talked about sex in a graphic way. That is all about to change and I'm ready if you are. I'm no prude and neither is Shaun. We have been known to be just as perverted as the next guy but we are still ladies at the end of the day. There is a time and place for everything and what we learned was that the free Internet dating sites are definitely a place to go for easy hook-ups, random sex, and…well…other stuff.

I wish I could remember how many messages contained these ever-popular two words, "Wanna Fuck?" Of the messages we put in the rejected pile, the majority of them were just that. It's a simple question, but not for the faint of heart. Ironically, on paper or otherwise, I had never been asked in that way. I've been asked by guys I knew for days, weeks, and sometimes years things more like, "Let's have sex", or, "I want you." or even a comedic Barry White imitation, "Let's get it on." No one had ever only known me by my picture and said, "Wanna fuck?" to me before. So, the first thing I thought was what kind of guy messages a girl something like that; someone who is not looking for "Long-term Commitment", so I deleted all of the messages with that question or similar first to get them out of the way.

Shaun and I definitely got a serious laugh out of the clever yet still totally unacceptable messages like, "Your eyes are beautiful what do your tits look like?" and, "I'm half Korean and half White-lucky for you I'm white from the waist down." and, "I'm touching myself to your glasses pic. I bet that was your plan." and my favorite; "Is your mom as hot as you? Three-Way?" There were more than one Three-Way invites. They wanted Three-Ways with wives, Three-Ways with current girlfriends, and BYOG Three-Way which means, "Let's have a Three-Way but you have to bring your own girl". Shaun and I were on the verge of hysteria and peeing our pants as we read through the messages and so far, though some of them may have really surprised us, the remaining messages in the rejected pile were just enough to assault our delicate sensibilities.

When you're afraid to Google something you don't know the meaning of for fear that the FBI will suddenly land on your roof and call you out of your house with your hands up, you know you're in over your head, however, I was determined to learn about what I didn't know. There is another subcategory in the rejected pile and I lovingly refer to it as the "Are You Intos". Are you into butt stuff? Are you into phone sex? Are you into S&M? All of those I was completely familiar with and the answer is none of your business, but it was the following three that I just didn't understand. Are you into Waterworks, are you into Vampire Sex, and are you into Furry Play? Shaun and I didn't know. We had no idea. She immediately texted Johnny and asked him if he knew what any of them meant. He answered and said, "I think the furry thing is when people dress up like mascots or someone and dry hump each other." What! What. That's a thing? I am borderline afraid of people in suits like mascots and completely afraid of clowns so I am going to say NO to "Furry Play". Shaun said she was sure that Vampire Sex was like sort of violent sex with biting or drawing blood. I agreed and decided to skip looking that one up but what did waterworks mean? I felt like it was safe enough to look up. If the FBI did stop by that day I would have just told them I was looking for a plumber. So, we did.

WaterWorks: *A nickname for urinating on someone or being urinated on during a sexual encounter.* Shaun and I laughed harder that we had all weekend. We were both aware of the secret desire that some people had to be peed on but we had never heard it be called that before. I mean, it sounds like the name of a water fun park. Someone actually asked me that as an introduction? Hi, I'm Harold, are you into WaterWorks? Sure, Harold, but you must take me to Applebee's first.

As Shaun and I recovered from our hysterical laughter, we realized it was already time for her to leave. She and Johnny were going house hunting that afternoon and other than going grocery shopping, I had nothing to do for the rest of the weekend. She couldn't wait to tell Johnny all about everything we had learned. How embarrassing. For about an hour I continued to weed out the rejects so I could get to the good part, which was finding potential dates. There were a few that I liked so I sent them all messages back letting them know that I might be interested and got ready to go shopping.

While I was out I got a call from Blayne. He asked me if I had made a dating profile yet and then proceeded to bust my chops about how stupid it was and that he was going to tell mom. We always say that to each other as a joke and never meant it. It was just a hollow threat that was carried over from our childhood. I didn't care if he told her anyway; I was planning on talking to her about it. She is very liberal and open-minded. She might be concerned for my safety a little but I always got the impression that she thought I could take care of myself. Blayne said, "What are you doing anyway?"

"I'm in the meat section at the grocery store."

"See, that's where you find a man like a normal person."

"In the meat section?"

"Yes! He'll be looking at steaks and you walk up to him with two different pieces of meat and say, "What's your favorite cut?" That's how you do it, Cherry."

I laughed and thought that was a good idea, but there were two people with me in the meat section at that time. An old lady and a mom with two punk kinds and a grocery cart full of what you shouldn't feed children. Better luck next time.

Blayne had a new girlfriend already. He told me all about her during that conversation. Her name was Peony. She's in retail. She likes the Giants. He was over the moon. We all agreed long ago that we would never make fun of him for his eleven month long relationships because we knew that he was a hopeless romantic and we found that to be something we love about him. Dad was a romantic, too, like I said, and it rubbed off on Blayne. I had a different idea of what romantic meant than your typical candlelight and roses type. My very favorite movie of all time is "True Romance" by Quentin Tarantino. Another time that I fell in love with a character played by the illustrious Christian Slater. I admit that he has always been one of my favorites but it wasn't just about him when it came to True Romance. The movie is star studded and action packed but the most beautiful thing about it is that Tarantino wrote the most intense and poetic love story that takes place amidst the worst conditions. Rescuing your girlfriend from her pimp, getting married in city hall, getting matching tattoos, having sex in a phone booth on the highway, writing love notes during a drug deal. That's my kind of romance. Needless to say, I would never find myself in most of those situations but it sure is fun to watch.

When I got home that night I had more messages and some replies to my replies. For the rest of the weekend all I did was talk to boys and I would be lying to you if I said I didn't love it.

Chapter 7 Rubber Boyfriend and a Movie

I had never been promiscuous but that doesn't mean I didn't have an appetite for sex. On the contrary, I think about sex a lot. More than some girls, less than others, I assume. I thank sex toys for helping women like me to *not* sleep around. Shaun always joked around that I went there so much that I had a punch card at the XXX store. When I walked in they yelled, "Norm!" These are lies, of course, as I was just a healthy young woman who wanted to keep her sexual partner "number" down to a minimum and who happened to have an impressive assortment of vibrators. I liked to refer to them as "Rubber Boyfriends" because since I had really always been single, they were the things I had sex with the most.

I've never been too much into porn. The whole objectification of women and potentially contributing to that turns me off. Besides that, guys in porn are just not attractive to me at all. I've seen porn and I am always distracted by the facial expressions that they make and get too creeped out to keep watching. I have a good imagination and was fine with just laying down on the couch at home to watch a movie, closing my eyes, and imagining something that turned me on. Some movies even help to be honest.

You know people who watch movies and get so enthralled that they compare their lives to the characters and start relating in one way or another to what is happening? Well, I'm one of those. I might cry a lot when I watch romantic comedies, and I might want to go out and drag race my car when I watch movies like Fast and Furious or Smokey and the Bandit. I might not have anything in common with the boys in Brokeback Mountain but love is love and it was all tears in my popcorn the first time I watched that movie. Watching movies is one of my favorite hobbies but I only buy the ones I really like or the ones that have good sex scenes in them like "Basic Instinct", "Boogie Nights", "Wild Things", "Blue Valentine", "The Notebook", "Chloe", "Unfaithful", and "Roadhouse" just to name a few. Patrick Swayze made some of the sexiest scenes in movie history.

I talked to the coolest guy on Sunday night. He was my age and worked in sales. He was clean cut and looked like a cop or like he was in the Army or Marines. I was usually attracted to those types. He was a movie buff and when we were going back and forth messaging each other about the classics, he asked if he could call me. I hadn't thought much yet about my rule for giving out my phone number, so when he asked I paused for a few minutes. Then I thought, of course I will give it out. I like this guy so far, we will probably meet, and if he turns into a weirdo I will just block him. Three minutes later my phone rang.

We talked for almost two hours. He had the sexiest voice. There was something intense about talking on the phone with a stranger like that. Sharing a little bit of your life story. Listening to each other breathing. I couldn't help it; it was a bit of a turn on. His favorite movie was Pulp Fiction, he said, or anything by Quentin Tarantino. That peaked my interest so I said, "Do you like True Romance? I'm watching it now." "You just said you love me, now if I say I love you back and just throw caution to the wind and let the chips fall where they may and you're lying to me, I'm gonna fucken die." My jaw dropped because this was a direct quote from the mouth of Clarence Worley played by Christian Slater in the cult classic, "True Romance". If he had asked I would have let him come over that night. But, he didn't and that was a good thing. Instead, after we made plans for dinner on Tuesday and hung up, I rewound True Romance to the first sex scene and had a little alone time on the couch.

The first thing I thought about when I woke up on Monday was him. His name was Mike, by the way. I texted Shaun first thing and told her good news, the search is over and it only took two days. She said. "Let's do lunch." Good idea. I was kidding about the search being over but I could picture Mike being a successful prospect. We had so much in common and I was excited about it all morning. He texted me around 10:00 AM and said that he was so excited to meet me on Tuesday. I thought that was a nice follow up. I was looking forward to talking to Shaun about my first semi-blind date.

We often meet at a sushi place very close to my office. Sushi is our favorite and since I get an hour for lunch and her schedule is a little more open, she comes to me when we do lunch on the weekdays. "Let me see what he looks like!" is the first thing that came out of her mouth when she sat down at our table. "Ooooh, he's good looking." she whispered. I told her about the Clarence quote and how he was probably the one because that had never happened to me before and she knows how I am about paying attention to the signs and how much that movie means to me. She laughed at me because I was maybe a little too optimistic and even though everything seemed really good, this was the first guy I talked to since creating my profile and we hadn't even met in person yet. I needed to relax a little. Of course, that was true, but I couldn't help being really excited.

We were almost done with lunch when Shaun said, "I have something to tell you." Oh God. I hate when people say that to me. Well, really it depends on their tone and hers wasn't good. "What?" I stared at her face and she said, "Mark came over after dinner last night to hang out with Johnny and you know, he just asked about you and talked about you the entire time he was there. He said he misses you and he knows he messed up." I didn't know what to say. He was so cold to me in the end. Technically if you really dissect our relationship, we never officially broke up. There was no communication. It was just obviously over. She continued, "He told me to tell you that he would love to get dinner with you some time and maybe you two can be friends."

"I could probably do that. Maybe I will text him. No big deal right?" I looked at her needing her approval and she said, "Yeah, I think it would be cool if you could still be friends. That way we can all hang out again some day and it won't be weird."

I agreed with that completely. I mean I was still friends with every guy I had ever "dated" or had sex with up until Mark and though our relationship was short lived, it was the longest one I had ever had and was definitely the only time I had ever "loved" someone I was sleeping with. I missed him, I couldn't deny it, but I didn't miss him like it sounded like he was missing me. I thought about it for the rest of the day and by that night I still didn't know what I would say to him yet. So, I held off on that text.

Tuesday night was here and I was so nervous! I was looking good but feeling crazy. I felt like canceling eight different times and was obviously psyching myself out. I had actually been on a blind date once before when I was about 21. My friend wanted me to go out with her brother; she just knew we would hit it off. We didn't…at all. I was not even remotely nervous before I met that guy but I think it was because there was no pressure, I wasn't looking for anything. There was no lead up to the moment. It was much more casual. I don't know. This time, however, I had intense butterflies so I decided to have a glass of wine before I left to calm my nerves. I took a cab so I could drink at dinner. Just in case. Alcohol can stand in as a wingman when your best friend can't be with you. It can comfort you in times of need. Or it can get you into trouble. You should have a wingman when you have alcohol, but you don't need alcohol to have a wingman, or something like that. I was willing to risk it so I made that glass of wine a double.

Mike met me at the door and was gorgeous. We nervously fidgeted our way through the first several minutes of the date but eventually things got smoother. We did a lot of flirting and recapping on our two hour phone call on Sunday night and then moved right onto continuing to get to know each other. He was great. He was a fan of micro brews and tried two different flavors while I drank red zinfandel and confessed that I had a glass before I left to calm my nerves. He said things to me like, "You're such a hottie", and "You are seriously so cute." He took my hand and caressed my fingers. It was really sweet and a little romantic but I couldn't help but be suspicious about how well this date was going. I didn't want to be negative but it couldn't possibly be this easy, could it? If it were then I could not wait to tell my brother that my first date was such a success.

After just sitting there for a minute enjoying him holding my hand like that I said, "Oh, I meant to ask you, your profile says you have kids. Just one or…" He looked down, let go of my hand, and cleared his throat. I thought, man, what did all that mean? I'm not Columbo but I was pretty sure I wasn't going to like what he was about to say. "I have a daughter who is 5. She lives primarily with her mother, my ex-wife in Aurora, and…" he paused. I thought to myself, what's the big deal, I like five year olds. Why is he acting so nervous? He continued, "and my ex is pregnant with my son and is due in April."

"Your ex wife?" I said and I tried to do the math in my head.

"No, my ex-girlfriend."

He took my hand in his again. It was like I didn't comprehend what was happening. I thought, so, he has an ex-wife and a daughter, fine, that's not weird at all, but, he also has an ex-girlfriend who is 7 months pregnant with his baby and he is out on a date with me? "You know, I knew there was something rotten in Denmark." (Another quote from Clarence Worley, and Shakespeare, of course.) I didn't really say it, but I wanted to so bad.

Mike went on and on for the rest of the date about how it was cool, they are great friends, she will like me. They are going to co-parent. It just didn't work out between them. He hoped I was ok with it, because he really wanted to keep seeing me. I was listening to him and I'm sure he meant everything he said, but honestly, I just couldn't handle it. He was going to have a baby. The kid wasn't even here yet and he already has a 5-year-old daughter. It was just too much.

I faked my level of happiness for the rest of the date and later while we waited for my cab. We hugged goodbye and I thanked him for dinner and he said, "Bye, Cherry. I really like you. Let's get together this weekend." He shut the door and I waved as my cab drove away. I rummaged through my purse to find my phone. One text from Shaun, "Text me when you're done and let me know how it went." And, one text from Blayne, "Tell me when you're home safe, I wish you were a lesbian, men are gross and hairy." I answered them both with the same message, "I'm fine, it didn't work out, talk to you tomorrow." I was feeling really defeated and had no energy to talk about what a shit show that date turned out to be. I was also a little bit drunk. I just stared out the window, ignoring the buzzing of my phone and suddenly started thinking about Mark and that first cab ride from Il Posto when he came over to my place. I thought about the message he had asked Shaun to give me and as I looked back down at my phone to answer their replies, "I'm totally fine, going to bed-talk tomorrow." sadness came over me. I pulled up Mark's name in my messages and texted him, " Hi Mark, I hope you're doing well. Shaun told me what you said. I want to be friends with you too. We can hang out whenever you would like. Take care. -Cherry." By the time I got into my apartment I got a reply from Mark and it said, "How about tonight." Without even a split second of hesitation, I replied, "Sure, the door is open."

Thirty minutes later a sad faced Mark showed up at my door, looked me right in the eye and said, "I'm so sorry." He reached out to hug me and I let him. It felt good. He felt good. Instead of a rubber boyfriend and a movie it was an EX- boyfriend and something that felt a lot like make-up sex. What was I getting myself into?

Chapter 8 Valentine's Day

Shaun freaked out when I told her about my over night guest. "You're kidding! And on a school night?" she yelled in my ear. I had been at a court hearing with Ben that morning so I didn't really have time to adequately text her until my lunch break so I just gave her a call. We talked about Mike telling me that he was pregnant first. He had texted me too that morning and I just told him, "I had a good time last night but I need time to think about this." He sent back a sad face that I never replied to. I was hoping he would just give up and spare me the trouble. Then Shaun wanted to know about what happened after the date. I told her that I just felt so sad or maybe not really sad but "overwhelmed by disappointment" and that I ended up texting Mark. I told her that after we both left my apartment to go to work he had been texting me things like, "I love you." and "Last night was so cool." and, "I can smell your perfume on me." We were giggling and doing the classic girlfriends Q&A for details that you do after an event like this and then she said, "Are you so happy?" Um, was I happy? I told her, "I feel a little weird actually. I'm not sure I can honestly say that after what happened between Mark and I that I would want to just jump right back in as if all was well. There are several red flags here, I can't just ignore them." Shaun said, "I know. You're right. Well, don't feel weird, though, just go with the flow and see what happens. Right?" I agreed. I was just going to see what happened.

Mark was seriously cute, by the way. He was tall and had brown hair and blue eyes and was built like an athlete. He was well dressed, generally laid back, and funny. He and I always quoted Joe Dirt to each other. When we used to kiss he would always say, "You keep that SKOAL, baby." Other than his paranoid, controlling, jealous, and non-communicative behavior he was a real catch. I was honest with myself about the whole thing. Mark was sweet; he wasn't a jerk. The pros outweighed the cons. The bottom line was, could I live with the cons? More importantly, I might not have been the one in charge of whether or not this relationship was going to work the second time around anyway. I definitely had no say the last time, but I wanted to try.

I was surprised when I got home that night that he was standing by my parking spot talking on his cell phone. He waved at me and smiled as I parked. I was excited to see him and that was a good sign. I got out of the car and he met me as he was ending his call. "Perfect, boss. All right, man, see you in the morning. Yup. See ya." He put his phone in his pocket and kissed me so hard. He pushed me against my car and pulled up my right leg. He held the back of my head with his left hand. It was so sexy. What was he doing? Besides driving me wild. I almost dropped my gorgeous Prada purse, a Christmas present from Blayne, and I would *never* let anything happen to that thing. Mark was fired up and all over me. "I missed you today." he said as he let me up for air, "Do you want to get dinner with me?"

"Are you going to take me on a date?" I fixed my skirt and hair and started walking toward my apartment.

"Yes, I am, I made us a reservation at Linger. I remembered you telling me you wanted to try it. Have you gone there yet?" Linger, which was relatively new back then is a seriously cool and delicious popular restaurant inside the old Olinger Mortuary on 30th Avenue in Denver. I hadn't been there yet. It was incredibly thoughtful of him. I always appreciated a man who listened and paid attention to the ramblings of a female, first the bracelet from Estes, and now this. I was impressed. We had such an amazing time that night. Quite possibly the best night we had ever spent with each other.

The next day Blayne demanded that I call him as soon as I could. I had been so busy that I never updated him on the current events in the life of Cherry Thomas. He was apparently on the edge of his seat. Blayne is a perfect brother because he is one of my best friends and since he is so genuinely interested in what I'm up to, he is like a girlfriend. I used to introduce him as my gay brother when we were teenagers, because even though he is, in fact, straight, he was with Shaun and me a lot and was definitely "one of the girls" at times. Shaun's boyfriends were always jealous, however, but we never cared. Johnny, who actually does have a gay brother, was the first guy that Shaun ever loved that didn't feel threatened by Blayne. It was destiny.

I called Blayne right after work. He answered, "What's going on?"

"Well, I have some news."

He laughed and said, "Please tell me it's that you are now a lesbian and no longer are doing on line dating." He has been saying that he wanted me to be a lesbian since we were teenagers too. He always said guys are gross and are only after one thing, he knew, because he was one. Shaun would always tell him to give it up, that I was just as straight as he was. Then she would say that I was only after one thing too so it worked out.

Blayne was horrified about the Mike story and laughed harder than I had heard him laugh in years. He also shared his opinion about the Mark situation with me; "I haven't liked that dude since the way he acted on Christmas Eve. I don't know why you would give him a second chance. He seems like he has issues." I know, I know. He was right, but maybe Mark just got scared or something. Maybe he really loved me and it freaked him out. The last couple of days had been amazing. I was still willing to give it a try. I tried to change the subject and ask him how everything was going with Peony and if he had seen mom lately but he kept going on and on about red flags. Then he started laughing and said, "You really lucked out by getting back with him this week. Valentine's Day is next Tuesday. Peony and I are going to the Poconos for a long weekend and guess what; she is originally from Scranton, PA so her parents are going to meet us one day for lunch. Did he make Valentine's Day plans with you yet?" I wanted to make fun of him for already having to meet the parents but all I could say was, "Valentine's Day?" I hadn't even thought about it. You know the old story, break up before Valentine's Day or wait until after Valentine's Day to ask someone out so you can avoid having to spend money. I never knew anyone who ever did that but I was sure it happened to someone out there. I decided right then and there that I would not mention Valentine's Day at all and see if Mark did. I just didn't want to be the one who brought it up.

The week flew by and I had been ignoring my online dating account. You can suspend them while you're dating someone but I never got around to doing that. I just didn't look at it. Mark and I had plans for dinner at Shaun and Johnny's on Friday night and I was looking forward to it. Shaun said she had a surprise for Mark and I, and Johnny had a surprise for all of us. I had no idea what that meant and neither did Mark. When we arrived we saw a car parked outside that we didn't recognize. As soon as we walked in there was Johnny's younger brother, Chris to meet us, "Hey bitches!" he yelled and hugged us both at the same time. I didn't know he was going to be there and I was very happy to see him. "Hey man", said Mark, "I haven't seen you since the wedding." He brought us into the kitchen and sitting around the table talking were Shaun, Johnny, and Chris's ex-boyfriend, Felipe. I hadn't seen him for over a year. Chris sat on Felipe's lap and told us to make ourselves comfortable. I loved Felipe and I was so sad when they broke up. "Hey Felipe!" I kissed his cheek as I sat down next to him and said, "What exactly is going on here?" Johnny, who was leaning his chair back, so that it was on two legs was smiling ear to ear and said, "Chris has some news to share with us." We were all looking around at each other and then back at Chris and finally he said, "Felipe and I ran into each other after the wedding and we realized that we had just been dying without each other and were still madly in love. We have been back together ever since and last weekend, Felipe asked me to marry him! We are doing it in California and you're all invited!" We all screamed and jumped up to hug them, well, Shaun and I did anyway; Mark and Johnny just laughed at the four of us squealing with happiness and said congratulations. Johnny knew but managed to keep it a secret all week. We talked about it for a while. What kind of wedding they wanted to have, what part of California, how frustrating it was that gay marriage wasn't legal in Colorado yet. Then I remembered that Shaun told me there were two surprises.

"What is the other surprise, Shaun? Didn't you say there were two surprises?"
She smiled and said, "Yes, Johnny and I have exciting news!" Chris screamed, "OH MY GOD YOUR'E PREGNANT!" and made us all jump and start laughing.
"Honey no, kid's are a bad plan." Shaun said with a serious face and continued, "We found a house last weekend and yesterday we made an offer and they accepted! We're moving to Boulder!" This was good news. Shaun and Johnny had been trying to figure

out where they wanted to live for five years and had been renting an overpriced, but nice, large apartment in Denver for just as long. They kept going back and forth, Denver, Golden, Littleton, Boulder, should they build, should they buy. We celebrated late into the night and crashed at their place.

That night, as Mark and I got ready for bed in the guest room that I always stayed in and called the "third wheel room", he was being so sweet and affectionate. He said, "What do you want to do for Valentine's Day, Cherry?" I immediately thought of Blayne laughing at this very subject a couple of days earlier. "Oh, Valentine's Day, I don't know, did you have something in mind?" I tried to sound like that was the first time I had thought about it. He asked, "Do you think you can get Tuesday or Wednesday off. It's on Tuesday."
"Yeah, I'm sure I can, I can text Ben in the morning. Why? What do you have in mind?"
"I was thinking we could stay at The Brown Palace and get dinner and then do a couple's massage thing before we check out."
"Really?" My eyes widened. I was surprised- I mean this was a seriously romantic and very generous offer. The Brown Palace is amazing and definitely not cheap. I had been to a couple private parties there, but I had never stayed and I had definitely never gone to their spa. We lay in bed and he was wrapped up against me and he said, "Yeah, think about it, we can decide tomorrow." Sure, I would think about it, but the answer was going to be yes.

—

64

In the morning we decided on staying Tuesday night and taking off Wednesday. I texted Ben and got approval and Mark called to make a reservation. I was worried that maybe it would be booked since it was Valentine's Day and we were calling just four days prior, but he was able to get a room and an appointment in the morning for a couple's massage. We got lucky, in that they said there was only one spot open. I was so excited! We planned to go to lunch with Shaun and Johnny that day and then go check out their new house, so I jumped in the shower to get ready. When I got out of the shower I went back to the guest room and Mark was standing there with my cell phone in his hand. He shut the door behind me and said, "Who is Mike?" I had a flashback of the time when he asked me a similar question. That time it was who is Jimmy? I gently took my phone out of his hand, put in down on the bed and started brushing my hair, "Mike is a guy that I met and went on a date with last week before I saw you again." "Why is he texting you today telling you that he is thinking about you?" Mark was visibly upset. I didn't want to be defensive about it and though it annoyed me that he looked at my phone, I didn't blame him for being freaked about a guy texting me that he was thinking about me so I said, "Look, Mark, I don't blame you for asking, he didn't get the hint when I never texted him again but I should have texted him to tell him that I was back with my ex-boyfriend so that he knew that he should lose my number." It was at that moment that I realized that I said I was back with my ex out loud. "We are back together aren't we? I mean we never talk about our relationship it just either is or isn't happening." I looked right at his eyes. He sat next to me on the bed and said, "Yes, we are together. We should have always been together. Please text him and tell him to lose your number." So, I did, "Mike, after I met you I ran into my ex and we are happily back together. Thank you for your understanding. I hope you find what you are looking for. Take care." I showed Mark and he said, "Ok." as if I was looking for his approval but instead of being annoyed all day, I decided to move forward and be cool and so I said, "Now, let me see YOUR cell phone." and then winked at him. He kissed me playfully, pushed me back on the bed and said, "You keep that SKOAL, baby."

I told Shaun about our little incident as soon as we could speak privately. She said Mark and I were evolving. I wanted to agree but why was he looking at my cell phone. It's a common cause of fights, isn't it, privacy? What kind of privacy is deserved and what kind of privacy is sneaky and secretive. In reality he could look through my phone any time he wanted and it wouldn't matter, but isn't that kind of weird? Shouldn't there just be enough trust between two people in a relationship to the point where neither one of you ever feels the need to look at the other one's phone? I didn't think I could give myself a definitive answer.

Valentine's Day had finally arrived and I was excited. Mark had roses delivered to me at the office and since that had never happened to me before, Ben started questioning me, "Who is this guy, what are his intentions, does he have a real job, is he Jewish?" Ben is like a brother to me and I love that about him. He has always joked that I need to find myself a good Jewish guy and that they are the best. Then he always points at himself and says, "Goldwitz! I know what's up." I always reply with, "Give your dad my number." and we laugh. I would have loved to date a Jewish guy. There are so many more Jews in New York. My brother has like three Jewish ex-girlfriends. My mother always says, "The Jews are the most beautiful people." They very well could be. The situation was, however, that my current boyfriend was a basic white dude and as far as I knew, Irish. He did have a good job but I really still wasn't sure what his "intentions" were.

Mark was going to pick me up at my apartment right after work so we could check in and go to dinner. I packed an overnight bag, freshened up and waited for Mark to text me. I was excited so I kept looking out the window. Eventually a black limousine pulled up and I thought, awe, my neighbor is going out in a limo. Mark texted, "I'm here." I looked at my phone and then looked back outside and saw Mark getting out of the back of the limo. I couldn't believe it. He was so crazy! I ran outside and over to him and hugged him, "I can't believe you did this! You're so funny!" He squeezed me tight and said, "You deserve it."

We crossed town in style and I was beaming as we arrived at the Palace. We were a handsome couple for sure. The room was gorgeous just as I expected it to be, and we definitely could not help but try out that king size bed before dinner. There is something really fun about having sex in a Hotel room, don't you think? I'm not sure I can even put a finger on why, but everyone loves it. That is just a known fact. I looked exceptionally sexy that night, which was cause for talking a bunch of pictures together, boyfriend selfies at their very best. A "Happy Valentine's Day" post on Facebook was necessary that year for sure. I was already having such a great time before we even got to dinner. We went to dinner at Palace Arms, which was the white tablecloth fine dining spot inside the Hotel. I had never eaten there before, but always wanted to. It is romantically lit and has an outstanding menu. I didn't want to order wine because it was so expensive but Mark insisted and said, "We can share a bottle of Malbec." That sounded perfect. I always loved that he liked wine, too. So many men don't do wine. They get beer or liquor. I like beer and liquor, too, but I am definitely more of a wine drinker. I most often drink red wine and my favorites are Zinfandel, Cabernet, and Argentinian Malbec. I don't drink Merlot. Did you ever see "Sideways"? I laughed so hard when Miles, played by Paul Giamatti, says, "If anyone orders Merlot, I'm leaving. I am *not* drinking any fucking Merlot!" God, I love that movie and Paul Giamatti.

Mark was making a lot of eye contact and flirting with me incessantly and I was enjoying it. What an amazing boyfriend he was turning out to be. I couldn't believe it to be honest with you. It was a far

cry from the middle of January when I was crying in my eight-dollar bottle of red blend. After we finished our meal, the waiter came over with the desert choices and Mark asked him to give us a while to think about it. He took my hand, which reminded me of Mike, which reminded me of how awkward the "I'm expecting", conversation was. Mark said, "What's wrong?"
I must have been grimacing at the memory. I said, "Nothing, I'm great." and gave him a big smile.
" I have something to give you."
"What? Haven't you done enough? I didn't think we were going to exchange gifts, though I did get a little something." I got him a new bottle of cologne, nothing fancy. He takes a little velvet black box out of his pocket. I thought, "Oooooh, jewelry!" my favorite. Then he said to me, "Cherry, I love you so much. Thank you for your understanding and for your patience with me. I want to give this to you so that you understand my level of commitment to this relationship." I was shocked at his choice of words. Was he proposing to me? He couldn't be. He opens the box and it was a sterling silver band with six little channel set diamonds. "For the six months of our relationship", he said. Six months. That's right. Six months, one of which was spent broken up and he was giving me a promise ring? This move totally freaked me out.

I was flattered and appreciative of the time, and effort, and *money* that had gone into this whole night but he was moving a little fast wasn't he? We had only been back together for 1 week. I wondered if he got this idea from Chris and Felipe. They had been together for three years before they broke up and then got back together. It was not the same thing. I didn't know what to do but I took the box and looked at the ring. It was lovely. Classic. I must have looked shocked because he said, "Are you ok, Cherry? I thought this was what you wanted. Commitment."

I gave him a confused look and said, "Is this a promise ring? Or, are you just giving me a ring to sort of symbolize a new start and a six month anniversary?"

He sat back in his chair and said, "It's a promise ring, but yeah it means all of those things." I remember that there was a long silence as I just held it in my hand staring at it. I never even knew anyone who gave someone a promise ring. Then, even though I really just wanted to hide under the table, I took the ring out of the box and said, "Which finger does it go on?" He smiled and leaned back toward me, "On your ring finger, I traced this ring for the size." He pointed at a sterling silver dome ring that I always wore on my right ring finger. Shaun had given it to me when we were 17. That was a smart move. I never saw him do it. So, I slid my new ring onto my left ring finger, a finger that had never worn any jewelry before. It felt like I was losing my mind. "Thank you, Mark. I don't know what to say." I showed him my newly jeweled hand and he said, "Happy Valentine's Day."

Chapter 9 Not So Fast

When I got home after our stay at the Palace, I texted my mom, "Call me as soon as you aren't busy." She replied, "Ok, sweetie, I'll be home in an hour." I was in serious need of her wisdom. I just didn't feel right. I had thought it before, it seemed like Mark and I were never on the same page. I was sitting on my couch twirling the ring around and just staring at it. I was trying to figure out how I truly felt about it. My phone rang. It was Shaun. I answered it fast, "Hey, girl." "Hey!"

"Did Mark give you a fucking promise ring, Dude?"
"Yeah, I mean, I can't believe it, but he did."
"What? That's insane! What did he say?" she was almost yelling. I told her the whole story and she told me that Johnny had just texted her and said, "Mark just told me he gave Cherry a ring. Have you talked to her?" So, she immediately dialed me. She asked me how it made me feel. I said, "I feel crazy. I don't want to be dramatic but I think, though it is just a symbolic piece of jewelry, it is still a ring and it feels like Mark is moving really fast. Don't you think?" She yelled, "Uh, Yeah!" This was the first time that Shaun had been concerned since Mark and I got back together. She had been very excited and optimistic up until then. I thought it was ironic that I felt just as freaked out about his extreme commitment as his disappearing act earlier that year. Why couldn't he just be a normal guy somewhere in the middle? I told her that my mom was calling me soon and she said, "Oh, good, let me know what she says."

After Shaun and I hung up I texted, Johnny and said, "What is your opinion of this? Do you think it's cool?" He answered me saying, "I think it's weird. I'm not sure what he is thinking." I just left it at that and didn't say anything else to him. Then I sent a text to my brother. He called me instead of texting me a reply and started talking as soon as I picked up, "Cherry, you're messing with me right? Who gives promise rings? Who gives any ring for that matter to their girlfriend unless they are proposing? Do you know that I have never given a single girl a ring in my entire life? What did he say that he wants to marry you?" These are the times that I wish Shaun, Blayne, and my mom were all in the same room at the same time so I could tell my story once and then take any questions. I told him the whole story and his answer to everything was, "You have to give that thing back."

The third and final time I had to tell the whole story was when my mom finally called me. She was mostly interested in what I was thinking and feeling first and then gave me a large dose of the wisdom I was looking for and can only get from her. This is basically what she said; "There are only three reasons why men move too fast in relationships. One of them is to get in your pants." She assumed Mark and I had already crossed that bridge, "Another is because of the need to be in control of the other person or to be the metaphorical "driver of the car" i.e. controller of the relationship. When the reason is control, one must step back and look at the relationship. Really look at it. What will the future bring? Do I know this person truly? Am I in charge of my own emotions? Am I watching the road? The third reason is something that was said best by Harry Burns, played by" in my mother's opinion, "the most adorable Jew, Billy Crystal, in "When Harry Met Sally"." (I told you I got it from her.) "Harry said, after he told Sally that he loved her, and I quote, "It's not because I'm lonely, and it's not because it's New Year's Eve. I came here tonight because when you realize you want to spend the rest of your life with somebody, you want the rest of your life to start as soon as possible."" Then she told me her and my dad were like that. They moved *way* fast. They were like magnets, inseparable. They knew right away like you know about a good melon. Another "When Harry Met Sally" quote. So, which one was it? Was it situation Two, or situation Three?

When we got off the phone I was really upset. I knew it could definitely be the second choice that he was controlling, though what he had done in the past was pretty minor when I really thought about it. I also knew that it could be the third choice. He seemed so in love and so excited for our future together. I knew I didn't feel like I was experiencing that. Wasn't I supposed to feel something great? Something that made me want to climb Pikes Peak and shout, "I love Mark!" from the top of the mountain? I obviously needed to have a real conversation with him to get this all out and off my chest. I just had to build up enough courage first.

That night at about 8:00 PM, someone knocked on my door. It was Mark. I opened it for him and said, "Hi, I wasn't expecting you!" and I gave him a hug. He said, "I wanted to surprise you. What are you doing?" I thought it might have been nice if he had texted first, but it was no big deal. He had his backpack with him and as he walked into the bathroom he said, "I just brought a few things over with me." "Oh, ok." I said. I figured you know, maybe a toothbrush. We lay down on the bed and turned on the TV to watch a movie or something. He turned something on the History Channel and about thirty minutes later I was asleep. I must have been beat because I slept through the night in my clothes on top of the blankets with my makeup on.

The next morning, I woke up to the sound of Mark getting ready for work and realized that I hadn't set my alarm either. Luckily for me he goes to work a lot earlier than I do so I got up and started the coffee while he was in the shower. All I could think about was how I needed to have a real conversation with him. That I needed to figure out how I actually felt about us. I went to my closet to get my work clothes out and noticed that Mark had hung a couple shirts and pairs of pants. That was a funny thing to see. I guessed he had brought them in his backpack. When Mark got out of the shower I was drinking my coffee and he talked to me about what he wanted to do this weekend. His parents wanted to get together with us. I had met them at the wedding briefly so at least it wasn't a "What are they going to think of me" kind of anxiety that I was feeling but I did feel nervous because I wondered what he had been telling them about me.

Mark sort of got ready in a hurry and gave me a quick kiss before rushing out the door to get to work on time. I was glad I still had an hour before I even needed to start getting ready. When I finally went into the bathroom I was surprised at what I saw. Remember the movie "How to Lose a Guy in 10 Days"? Andie Anderson, played by Kate Hudson fills her boyfriend's bathroom full of pink towels and feminine hygiene products. Well, there weren't any pink towels, but it was like Mark brought everything he keeps in his bathroom at home and put it in my bathroom. I texted him later and said, "You movin' in?" and he replied, "lol."

"LOL"? What kind of response is that? I was praying that Shaun could meet me for lunch that day, I needed her to get me amped up enough to initiate this air clearing talk that I needed to have with Mark. She texted me and said that she was going to invite me to go Steuben's with her and Chris. She said, "Chris is dying to talk to you about the Mark situation." "Perfect", I said, "that is exactly what I need to talk about anyway." Steuben's is one of my favorite places in uptown and is modeled after a New England mid-century hot spot that was owned by the Denver owner's family back in the day. The menu is great and the ambiance is right up my alley. As soon as I saw them, Chris demanded that I show him the ring and said, "Girl, what *is* that thing?" I always laugh at everything Chris says but this time I kind of laughed a little too hard, instead of crying. I told them about my his and hers bathroom and the plan to get together with his parents and then I asked them if they thought I was crazy, "Isn't this what I wanted, to find someone who could commit to me and then plan a future with me? They both said the same thing, "Yes, you do want that but do you want it in a couple months from a guy who you barely know if you like?" That was exactly what I needed to ask myself. Did I like him? I mean I knew I liked many things about him but did I like him enough to be with him forever? I told them both that I wished I had asked Johnny more about his advice or reasons for his opinion of Mark that he shared with me in the beginning that I basically ignored. Then Chris gave me a piece of information. He said, " When we were seniors Mark's younger brother Travis and I were friends, remember? And, we were hanging out one night at his house. Mark came over and asked Travis if he could borrow his car. Travis got mad and was questioning him about it because Mark obviously had his own car and I overheard Mark telling him that he thought his girlfriend was cheating on him and wanted to drive by her apartment incognito. She ended up breaking up with him eventually because she felt like he was a stalker. Then a couple years later he had another girlfriend who I kind of knew and she broke up with him because he was "controlling" and ended up moving to California. That's why he went there. To be with her, but it still didn't work out so he moved back here." Shaun and I just stared at him. It was anticlimactic but it sounded just like him unfortunately. Chris continued, "I have always really

---

liked Mark, but he has had a lot of failed relationships and I think what you are dealing with is a guy with some old wounds who is trying to hold on to his woman and who's behavior is just barely on the verge of being a red flag."

We ended the lunch with the understanding that I would make sure I talked to him before this got any deeper and definitely before we hung out with his parents. He was already "home" when I got there and was sitting on the couch watching TV. He got up to kiss me and told me how much he missed me that day. He continued with the basic end of the day questions like, what should we do for dinner, how was your day. I told him I would make something at home and opened a bottle of wine. I was going to need it. I took a nice big gulp of whatever $9.00 "you can get it at Costco" I happened to have that week and said, "Mark, what do you love about me?" Women are so annoying to men when they ask questions like that, but honestly, its because we genuinely want or need to know and they usually struggle with the verbalization of their attraction to us or of their feelings in general. Is it looks, personality, or both? Is it something next level that can't even completely be explained? I sat down right next to him and noticed him fidgeting and looking around the room. Then I said, "Like, how do you tell someone about me?" He said, "You're so weird, why are you asking me this stuff?" I said, "Because we never talk about anything. I don't know why you fell in love with me or what made you want to give me this ring for example." He looked mad and he said, "I already told you, it's a token of commitment and to let you know that we have a future together." I said, "Yes, but what made you feel like you needed to do that?" He said, "Because I don't want to lose you."

This conversation went back and forth for a while until I finally asked him questions like, what is your favorite color, and where are your ancestors from, and what are your dreams? He had a hard time with my third degree as he called it but did answer all of my "tell me about yourself" questions. After a while I went back to something similar to my original question and asked, "Why do you love me?" He said, "I don't know, you're sexy, you're smart, you're funny." Then I said, "Tell me how I make you feel." He said, "Nervous." Wow, nervous? So I asked him what he meant. He started laughing, stood up and went to the kitchen to poor a glass of wine, and said, "You're so independent. You don't need me ,it's obvious. I see the way other men look at you and it makes me crazy because I wonder what they are like when I'm not with you." He was out of breath a little and I thought, "Other men? What is he talking about?" He continued, "Honestly Cherry, I'm glad you brought this up because everyone has been razzing me since I told them I gave you that ring and I guess they are probably right when they say I move way too fast. I have done that with girls since I was a kid. I think I fall in love too easy. Then I am constantly worried that the bottom is going to fall out of the relationship, or that they are going to cheat or find someone better." Man, was this an amazing break through? I was like Dr. Phil and Mark was "today's guest".

We ended up talking until after midnight. One delivered pizza and two bottles of wine later; we decided that this relationship was never meant to be. We would be friends forever, though, because what ended up happening is, instead of a fight or two broken hearts, we were finally honest with ourselves. Both of us had realizations that night and we had each other to thank for it. His was primarily that he doesn't need to have a girlfriend to feel whole and when he finds someone worth his time he needs to take it slow and communicate with her about how she feels and what she wants and if it truly matches up to him, then together they will move forward. He decided he needed time for himself to figure out what he actually wanted in life. He needed to work on his jealousy and insecurities. He said he wanted to be a man that a girl like me could fall in love with. I was confident that one day he would. Just hearing a man talk like that and really be honest with himself, was one of the sexiest things I had ever heard.

What I learned about myself over the few days, before that night, was that even though I am in control of myself in so many ways and always talk about how confident I am and how tough, the truth was, that I was allowing Mark to control the direction of our relationship or "metaphorical car" completely and I just sat there in the passenger seat letting him take me wherever he wanted us to go. He didn't really know he was doing anything wrong by me because I never said anything to him. I needed to allow myself to have a real voice. The reality was that I was just as guilty of not communicating as he was. Eventually, we talked so much that night that our tongues were numb. We spent a little time laughing. We spent a little time crying. Just before we both passed out from exhaustion, we had sex one last time. It was the greatest "goodbye sex" I had ever had. People call it different things, but it is the sex you have when you are mutually breaking up. It can be emotional or not, it just depends on the relationship that is ending. Sometimes you cry, it's true, but sometimes you don't feel anything. Remember the goodbye sex in "How Stella Got Her Groove Back"? It was amazing. It was arguably the best goodbye sex scene in the 90s.

I felt so much better the next morning. It was very pleasant between us and we were both so obviously relieved. It was finally Friday and what a long week it had been. Mark packed up his backpack and got ready for work as I drank my cup of coffee. When he was ready to go he hugged me and whispered in my ear, "Thank you, Cherry." It was a long and emotional hug and the kind that seems like it will last forever. He kissed me goodbye, and I handed him his ring. We smiled at each other as he walked out my door for the last time.

Chapter 10 Never Say Never

I stayed in that Friday night. As a matter of fact I stayed in all weekend. It snowed anyway and I felt like I needed to do some reflecting. I spent most of Friday evening on the phone explaining the end of my short-lived relationship and what I had learned to Shaun and Blayne in two different hour-long phone calls. Shaun texted me around 9 PM and said, "Get back online and see what's new. I bet you have a million messages!" I had completely forgotten about my profile. I had thought about it a few times since "Mark round two" but hadn't ever looked or logged on to suspend it or anything, so when she reminded me, I admit I was excited to check it out.

When I logged on, there were so many messages, I couldn't believe my eyes. I did the same thing I did the first time, which was weed out all the obvious weirdos first and then narrow down the good messages to the guys I could be interested in meeting. One specific guy caught my eye because of his sweet and persistent messages. It was clear that he had noticed that I wasn't checking them so he sent funny notes about being excited for when I finally logged on and that he hoped he would finally hear from me. I looked at his profile and he was handsome, he had no kids, he was looking for long-term commitment and his bio was well written. He was into art, cinema, and road trips, which are three of my favorite things. He was a little older than me and said he was "undecided but open to kids". His name was Dan.

There was another guy named Matt with the best profile I had seen so far. Hilarious pictures and a bit of humor in his bio about being a guy who knows what he wants and that he will expect to exchange phone numbers and pictures from any female he plans to meet. He said that if they plan to show up in yoga pants, they need not apply and if they try to pay for their meal, he will make them pay the whole meal and never speak to them again. He was obviously old fashioned and making jokes to say that chivalry was not dead. I was interested in his candor.

As I looked and looked and deleted the majority of my messages, I received a chat from Dan. "Hey there! You finally made it to the party."
"Yes, I am finally free enough to check my mail."
"How did you fair over Valentine's Day"
"Oh, it was one for the books, you?"
"Me? I waited until Wednesday and went out and bought a bunch of 75% off boxes of candy." "Great idea." I actually giggled. This whole thing was so funny. Going on line and being messaged by strange men in my age bracket and general geographic location. I talked to Dan for hours that night and Saturday, and as it turned out, Sunday as well. We made plans to meet on Monday night. The roads would be clear by then. I decided I would drive to my dates from then on because there was no reason to drink so much that I can't drive and I needed to be able to leave if I needed to after what happened with my first blind date. I mean I would never just skip out on anyone but having my own car to leave in when the time came was just smart.

Dan asked me if I wore heels or flats. I told him usually heels. Then he asked me if I wore boots with heels. I said of course, that is one good thing about living in a place with all four seasons, you get to wear boots in the fall and winter and then trade them in for strappy sandals and flip-flops in the spring and summer. I am a shoe girl. Not all of us have shoe obsessions but I most definitely do. I was glad when he said, "I'm just asking because if you wear some black heeled boots to meet me, I will know it's you when I see you." because I was starting to worry that he had some kind of weird foot or women's shoe fetish, which guys, I am sorry but I just can't handle foot stuff. I had yet to meet a guy who had a foot obsession and I was good with that.

He asked me to meet him at a place called Kitty's, which was an old bar and grill that I had never even heard of until then. He said, "It's good, a cool edgy dive, you'll like it." I was down to try anywhere new and was just glad he didn't want to go to a chain restaurant. I would definitely not call myself a food snob or a foodie per se, I just get a lot more out of trying the food crafted by a person who only owns one or two restaurants and genuinely cares if you not only love the food, but enjoy yourself while you eat. It's much more intimate that way. At a chain I just feel like a number, get them in and get them out to seat the next guy. Maybe I'm the old fashioned one.

Kitty's had it's own parking lot which is a nice thing to find in Denver, the closer to downtown you are. I may be from just outside the boroughs of New York but I enjoy not parallel parking. I walked to the door and saw a guy walking from the other side of the building toward me, "Cherry?" he yelled. "Hey." I said and smiled. "I would recognize those black boots anywhere." he said and gave me a nice to meet you in person hug. It's so bizarre to meet someone you have only seen in pictures. They never look the same. He was cute but just different than what I was expecting. You have to be careful to not get too wrapped up in those kinds of thoughts because you will start to wonder if they think you look different or if they like the pictures of you more than the real you. They only sometimes say something like, "You look better that your pictures!"

As soon as we walked in I felt uncomfortable. The place smelled a little like, how do I describe this, like broken dreams. It was a punch in face kind of smell like cigarettes, coconut lotion, and unforgivable mistakes. It was darkly lit and had a jukebox full of 80s hits. I love 80s hits so I just decided to focus on the music. As we sat down he said, "Those are great boots, you are really very attractive and well dressed."
I laughed and said, "Why thank you! It's refreshing to be complimented like that."
"Oh yeah, no problem, I know nice clothes when I see them."

The waitress reminded me of Lydia Deetz, played by Winona Rider in "Beetlejuice". She was sweet but would much rather have been at home smoking clove cigarettes and listening to Ministry or The Cure. We ordered our food and continued with small talk. Things were going well and I felt like I was experiencing something new and different. I was having a great time.

We were about halfway through our meal when Dan said, "I really love when women wear heels. I think they are so sexy."
"Oh, they are, you mean the way they make a woman's legs look, or whatever people always say, that they accentuate their leg muscles?"
"Yes, but the actual shoe itself it so sexy. Men just wear blocks on their feet, you know," he laughed, "women get to wear these pieces of art." I just looked at him, smiled and nodded and took a bite of my burger. He has to be one of those shoe fetish guys, oh God, I thought. Then he said, "You know what my fantasy is?" I wanted to shove my whole burger in my mouth so I didn't have to speak but instead I said, "What?" He smiled from ear to ear and said, "Now, don't think I'm weird, but I would love it if a girl would let me wear her high heel boots and she would wear a strap on, bend me over a couch and do me from behind." We just stared at each other. He was smiling so big he looked like a golden retriever waiting for you to throw his ball. He was so happy to have shared this information with me and I was actually, for the first time probably in my life, completely without words. *What* did he just say to me? I had to answer him, I couldn't just stare at him forever, so I said, "Wow. That's quite a fantasy." He was obviously excited like he had finally just told a

secret he had been holding in for years and said, "I just think it would be so exhilarating, you know, like a roll reversal. I know a lot of women feel like the man is always in control of them and I like to think that I am a little more progressive in my thought processes." Was this guy for real? I just smiled and said, "Oh", and "Right", nodding and thinking to myself, "Cherry, you have to leave." I looked around and found the bathroom sign and said, "Dan, would you excuse me for a second, I have to use the ladies room." He said, "Of course! It's right over there past the kitchen." "Perfect." I said and thought, "Hopefully by the back door too."

I went into the bathroom and paced back and forth, intermittently looking at myself in the mirror and had one of those silent conversations that you have with yourself. I said, "This guy is a four alarm fire of crazy and you have to go. You have to leave out the back door or through the kitchen or call 911 or something but you aren't finishing this date. He wants you to bend him over a couch, Cherry. No, you're leaving." I looked in my purse to see if I had any cash so I could pay the bill and bail on this date. I did! So, I thought I could just pay the waitress secretly and then leave out the back door. I knew I could do it based on the positioning of everything without him seeing me. I guess I was wrong when I thought I would *never* skip out on someone and was thankful that I had made the decision to drive my car to dates. I peaked out the door and saw the waitress standing in the kitchen doorway. I said in a loud whisper, "Hey!" she turned around and looked at me. I motioned with me hand and said, "Can you please come here?" She slowly walked toward me. The cook that she was talking to just stood there starring at me. I whispered, "I have to leave ok? He can't know. I will give you money for the bill. Everything is ok but I have to leave now. Where is the back door?" she seemed worried for me and brought me into the kitchen. I said, "Look, I'm fine, I don't want to seem dramatic but this is a blind date and I just have to go." She had a beautifully monotone voice and without any expression she said, "I understand. I went out with this guy last year who told me he listened to NickelBack and I was just like, no dude. No." I laughed and said, "I agree with your taste and let me just tell you, I *wish* that *that* was what was wrong with this guy. If only he could *just* be a NickelBack fan, I could at least finish the date and then never speak to him again." The cook pipes in and said, "That bad huh?"

I paid the bill and they let me leave out of the back of the kitchen, which led to the alley. The cook actually walked me to my car. Now, that was good customer service. I pulled out of there like I was running from zombies. The entire way back to my neighborhood I was laughing hysterically. I was cry laughing as I drove down the road. I was thinking I couldn't believe these are the guys I am choosing. There was nothing wrong with either of them when it came to their profile but then why would they divulge those kinds of secrets online? They would never get dates. Hi, I'm Dan and wait until you hear my fantasy. Hi,

I'm Mike; I am having a new baby in a month. What a complete nightmare.

It was only 7:00 PM and Shaun was at a dinner party with Johnny. I just couldn't imagine going home. I felt too weird and creeped out so I decided to go to the movie theatre. There were two movies playing that I wanted to see that night, "The Vow" and "This Means War". I went with "This Means War" because I heard "The Vow" was kind of sad and I was in no mood to cry. Have you ever seen a movie by yourself? I find it to be very therapeutic. I usually have a friend with me but sometimes when the mood strikes or there is something I can't wait to see I just go in early, sit in the middle of the very back row, and enjoy popcorn and a movie all by myself. One of the funniest times for me in a movie all by myself was when I saw Bridesmaids. I went alone and laughed so hard at the Jewelry Store scene that I couldn't stop laughing. No one else was still laughing and I was inconsolable like when you're in class and you're not allowed to laugh so you laugh harder. I liked The Vow, too, when I eventually saw it but I was glad I chose Reese Witherspoon dating two men for my movie that night. It inspired me to keep on trucking on the dating front. I laughed so hard when Reese's character, Lauren is in the bathroom mirror at the restaurant giving herself a pep talk because I had literally just done the same thing. Actually, though adorable as always, it wasn't really Reese's character who inspired me in that movie, it was her best friend in the movie, Trish played by Chelsea Handler. My favorite quote is when Lauren thinks she needs to stop dating both guys after sleeping with one of them and Trish says, "You think Gloria Steinem got arrested and sat in a jail cell so you could act like a little bitch? You get out there! You be flexible." These are words of pure genius. I was going to date my way to a husband, no two subpar dates were going to discourage me. No man in black leather high heel boots with his ass in the air was going to squash my dreams. Tomorrow would be a new day.

Chapter 11 What About Matt?

For the next two months I went on more dates than I can even remember. Their names are a blur to this day; even their faces, and I can barely remember where I went with all of them. Not one single one of them was good enough to see a second time. I felt like the Red Socks and the curse of the Bambino, because this losing streak went on until about July when I started talking to this nice guy named Dominick. He was a very handsome, Hispanic guy and was originally from Las Vegas, but had just relocated to be closer to his sister and her family who had moved to Denver. We had our first date at a sandwich shop for lunch. I had recently discovered the appeal of lunch time dates. Not only are they much more laid back, there is a certain amount of safety, whether it's a false security or not, that comes from meeting strangers during the day. It is also much less expensive, so if the date isn't going well, you can always decide to make it Dutch treat and pay your own way. I was starting to feel guilty about all of these men I wasn't interested in buying me my dinners. That is a perk about being a woman in the dating game, but being a man must be horribly cost consuming. A girl can literally say to herself, "I'm broke and I feel like pizza and beer," make a date with some random guy, make him think she's cool for wanting to get pizza and beer, go out with him, eat pizza, drink beer, and then never speak to him again. Dating doesn't have to be all about food anyway. I would have loved it if someone took me to Denver

Museum of Modern Art, or to the Zoo. As of yet, I hadn't met a guy with much creativity when it came to where we met for our date, but I wasn't giving up on the possibility.

Dominick and I had a great time. He was very suave. He was very funny. He kept saying, "How many dates until you let me kiss you? I just love those lips!" I would just laugh and tell him he was funny. What was my rule for kissing? I think you should only hug on the first date, maybe a kiss hello, goodbye on date two, and then if things go well, try to wait as long as you can stand it before having sex. It is such a lame thing that we make rules for ourselves but, like I told you before, I had no intention of becoming a promiscuous girl now and I just had to make sure that any guy I was thinking about it with was on the same page as me.

Dominick told me he had a 6 year old daughter with whom he shared custody with his ex for summers and every other Christmas vacation. He was a Pharmacy technician and was considering going to school to be a Pharmacist. He had only been to California, Nevada, Utah, and Colorado and really wanted to travel. He said his sister was his very best friend and that she was visiting their parents in Vegas that weekend and had his daughter with her. Dominick had just started his job and couldn't get time off yet. They weren't coming home until Tuesday. We told each other a bunch of life stories during that date and Dominick told me he felt like he had known me forever. It was like catching up with an old friend and I really liked the way that felt. He told me he wanted to hang out on Sunday too so I asked him if he wanted to meet me at my place and then go to this cool gourmet taco shop that I had been wanting to try for lunch. He said, "Oooo gourmet tacos? Check this white girl out. Me encantaria. Amo los tacos." I had no idea what he said but I liked hearing him say it. I tried to be cool and pretend I knew what he said so when we said goodbye I kept repeating, "Me encantaria. Amo los tacos." over and over in my head until I got to my car and could Google it. "I would love to. I love tacos." It sounds so much sexier in Spanish. I have always been a fan of the language.

The next day, the lunch hour came and went and Dominick was a no show. Around 1:30 PM I got a text from him saying, "I'm so sorry I'm late, I got called in to cover the morning shift. Do you want me to bring food to your place? I can get tacos?" I was starving and my house was clean so I said, "Sure, see you soon." As soon as he arrived I realized that he was the first guy since Mark that had been in my apartment and I was a little nervous about it. I wasn't nervous about who he was, or safety, I was nervous because I actually liked him, and being in my apartment is much more intimate than a restaurant. I didn't want things to go too fast. I also realized that the tacos he decided to bring were from Taco Bell. I wanted to laugh so badly, but I held it in because I didn't want to hurt his feelings. I had been known to slam a couple Taco Bell tacos down before, who was I to judge. So, I said, "Amo los tacos!" He smiled ear to ear and said, "Oh, nice, you have been practicing." I laughed and said, "Yes, now I can say I love tacos, where is the bathroom, and where are my pants in Spanish."

Dominick and I had a great time. We ate our tacos and then decided to put in a movie. His favorite genre is Horror and I have many to choose from so I let him pick. We didn't pay much attention to the movie because he just couldn't help but kiss me, and I let him. He was a great kisser. It was surreal, making out while watching a horror movie, I felt a little like a teenager. It wasn't a bad thing to me. Feeling like a teenager sometimes can be very refreshing. We were watching the end of "The Others" with Nicole Kidman when his sister called. He had to answer it so I paused the movie. Have you ever been in close quarters with a person whose cell phone is so loud that you can hear what the person on the other end of the call is saying? Add a completely silent room to the mix and you could find yourself in an awkward situation. After he answered, his sister said, "Hey Nicky, I just wanted to check in with you." He replied with, "Hey thanks, how's everything going, how's my angel?" I thought it was so cute that he called his daughter angel. She was six. Sister said, "She's great, the kids are in the pool, it's like 110 degrees today." "Ha ha, yep, I don't miss that!" "What are you doing today?"

"Oh I'm hanging out with a friend."

"A date?"

"Yes."

"With who, Crystal?"

"No."

"Rachel?"

"No, just…"

She cut him off and said, "Monique?"

He laughed and said, "No. No one you know." I
pretended I didn't hear any of this.

"Is it that new girl, Kristie?" Silence. "Jen?...Nikole?"
He laughed and said, "Ok I'll talk to you later,
Manita." I looked that up too, it means "little sister".
"Why won't you tell me?" and as he hung up she was
laughing and said, "Is it Blanca?"

I actually couldn't believe my ears. This dude was
either the biggest whore in four counties or his sister
was out of her mind. Either way, the flame between
us fizzled out like the end of the movie. I was very
sweet to him regardless and pretended I didn't hear
his list of girlfriends but let him leave without making
plans for a third date. It was another Sunday night at
home alone with my laptop and countless messages
from "Sleepless in Denver" for me. It was beginning
to be like hanging out with a friend, logging onto the
website. It was amusing and a little like shopping. As
soon as I went into my pending messages I saw that I
had a message from that guy Matt who I hadn't heard
from since the Dan at Kitty's fiasco.

I was excited to read the message. It was a long one. He was telling me that he was a photographer, did mostly weddings but had finally made a dream of his happen. He had just returned from Iceland on a personal trip but where he got some of the best pictures he had ever taken in his life. How exciting, I thought. Iceland is on my bucket list and I am an amateur photographer in my own right. I always thought that being a photographer for National Geographic would be the greatest job ever, either a photographer or a legitimate artist who actually makes money for their work. It was so nice to read something on the site with a little substance. No matter where we are or what we are doing at any given time, there is a girl somewhere who is sick to death of guys asking them to send them "boob pics". If I had a dollar for every time I had been asked I could save Detroit. So, I replied. "What an amazing adventure. I would love to talk to you more about it over coffee sometime. Let me know if you're interested. Have a great night!" Then I continued to peruse.

I did something I had never done the next morning and checked my messages before I went to work. He had answered which was exactly what I wanted to know before I left. "I would love to! Text me today and we can set it up." He signed with his name and his phone number. I quickly added it to my phone and headed to work. I waited until the afternoon just so I didn't appear desperate to speak to him and texted,

"Hey Matt, this is Cherry. Now you have my phone number too. I am at work until 5:00 PM." Smiley face.

He texted me back at about 4:30 and said he was off for the week with no planned jobs. He said he would love to speak with me on the phone tonight if I was up to it. I thought that sounded great. It was a nice natural progression to email or message first, then move on to phone calls, and then eventually meet. I just had to remember to keep it reigned in, because as I had learned, phone calls aren't the same as meeting in person and leave a lot up to imagination. I wasn't in the mood to be let down, but who is? That night I ordered Chinese food delivery and put in "Joe Vs. The Volcano".

I like to watch Joe when I need to feel inspired. If you haven't seen it I highly recommend picking it up. It's about love, it's about adventure, and it's a story about setting out in search of the meaning of life. Tom Hanks plays Joe and Meg Ryan plays three different women who make their way in and out of his life. At one point Patricia, played by Meg Ryan says, "My father says that almost the whole world is asleep. Everybody you know. Everybody you see. Everybody you talk to. He says that only a few people are awake and they live in a state of constant total amazement." That one line means so much to me now and has since the first time I watched the movie. It is my mantra.

I was so excited to get on the phone with Matt. I was surprised that he was a little bit soft spoken. Not to say that he wasn't confident, just that I pictured a booming voice based on the humor in his writing and by what he looked like. He had a kind voice. We talked and talked for hours. He told me a lot about his trip to Iceland and that he had also been to Australia, because a friend of his got married there. He mostly does photography for weddings in Colorado but has traveled to quite a few places for jobs. I thought it was so cool-freelance photographer. What an outstanding job. He was pretty conservative in his thinking, but seemed very open minded, played football in High School, had never been married, no kids, and was originally from Kansas City. I couldn't wait to meet him. He seemed like a real catch.

We talked on the phone every single day that week and finally agreed to meet for dinner on Thursday. We went to an Irish Pub. I am probably most comfortable in pubs, or wine or martini bars vs. clubs where you can't talk to the people you are with because it is so loud. I enjoy deep and meaningful conversations. Sometimes when Shaun and I get together we just drink wine and talk until three in the morning and those are some of the best times we have ever had. Matt was very attractive. He looked like a football player and had a little bit of a beer gut. I think I was into that type, strong, but not with a perfectly athletic physique. There is something hot about a guy who lets his figure go a little but still looks good naked. Men have it so much easier than women when it comes to physical appearance. I think a lot of women would agree that most men still look sexy when they are a little over weight, and women get grief for it. Men look sexy with crow's feet and grey hair around the temples, and women get Botox, surgery, and hair dye. Matt was my age and it seemed like we had a lot in common.

We had an amazing time that night and he was very transparent about the way he felt about our date. He said, " I really like you. We should hang out more this weekend. How do you feel about our date?"
" Well. I think you're really very cool and I would love to hang out with you this weekend. What would you like to do?"
"Well, since you're an artist I thought maybe we could go to one of the museums. Would you like that? Which one is your favorite?" I was thrilled. I mean I had just been thinking about how cool it would be if a guy brought me to a gallery or museum on a date. I answered, "Yes! MCA!" I love The Denver Art Museum too but had been there last, so I chose the Museum of Contemporary Art Denver.
"Great!" he said laughing at my obvious excitement, "Saturday afternoon?"
"Perfect."

When we said goodbye in the parking lot he kissed my cheek and I thought it was so sweet even though it was a clear violation of my previously stated rules on date etiquette. It was becoming quite obvious that I had no idea what I was talking about when it came to dating. I was right in the middle of it and was not a veteran on the subject. I had no skill set and I had no idea how to make it work. I was like a passenger on a plane, completely out of any control and at the mercy of the pilot and the weather. There was nothing I actually knew at that point. I needed to stop being so hard on myself and start going with the flow.

I texted Blayne and my mom and told them, "I think I met a good one." My mom said she was excited to hear all about it and Blayne said, "LOL, I'll believe it when I see it." I wasn't mad at him for being such a hater. I thought it was funny. He was right to be so pessimistic but I had a good feeling about this guy. Shaun was coming over on Friday night and I was so excited. It seemed like forever since we had had a "girls night". Those times had become few and far between since she and Johnny had moved into their new house. There was a lot to change, all cosmetic, but still very time consuming. I stopped at Costco, got some wine to try and some meat and cheeses. I have been calling appetizers "meat and cheeses" since I saw Melissa McCarthy and her husband playing Megan and Air Marshal Jon in the awkward yet visually appealing "foreplay scene" with the giant sub in "Bridesmaids". She says, "Is there a hungry bear anywhere? I just happen to have this bear sandwich, is there a hungry bear? Do you want a bite of that sandwich? Its meat and cheeses." I become hysterical when I see that scene. The "first sexual encounter" is what she calls it. If only we could all have "Megan's" confidence and charisma in the beginning of our relationships.

Shaun came over at 6:00 PM and the first thing we talked about was what Chris was planning for his wedding. She said they would be sending out invites that next week for September in Santa Barbara and had everything planned, except for who was going to perform the actual marriage. Chris wanted a Justice of the Peace wearing a rainbow tuxedo and Felipe was saying hell no to that. We were laughing as Shaun poured us our first glasses of wine, handed me mine and said, "So. What about Matt?" I was very excited to tell her about him and was swooning a little. There were so many cool things about him and I just didn't have one negative concern. She said she hoped we didn't find out later that he was a convict or really bad in bed. I was thinking that I might find out soon. Not if he was a convict but if he was good in bed, though, I would rather he not be a convict.

I remember that night was so beautiful. We sat on my balcony and drank our wine and reminisced our childhood. Shaun and I wanted to open a store together when we were little. We were going to own a store that sold only socks. Not just any old socks, designer socks. In the 80s socks were much more fun and important to your outfit. Even though we have noticed them coming back lately, in general, they lost their importance in style over the years and the business would have suffered. Of course, that is what we say to make ourselves feel better. At least she has started her own business. I had still not actually figured out what I wanted to do. Luckily I genuinely loved my job and my boss so I didn't really have anything to complain about. I just wanted something more and I wasn't sure what it was.

We spotted some young men walking around wearing dress shirts and ties carrying backpacks and pleasant smiles on their faces. You know the ones- they are recruiters for some organized religion who go door to door handing out pamphlets and asking if they can have just a minute of your time. They are always very sweet and probably exceptional at taking rejection. They should give classes on that. They could call it, "How to Handle Rejection". They could make millions. Shaun started laughing and said, "Do you remember that guy in Roslyn who used to go to everyone's house and tell them they were going to hell if they didn't go to his church?'

"Yes! I was just telling that story to Ben the other day."

"Which part?"

"Your dad, Shaun! I will literally never forget it. Remember we thought it was so funny and it sounded like something my dad would say too. When that guy went to your house he was yelling in the front and your dad went outside and shut him down. He said, "Look! I'm not going to hell, I don't want you to go to hell, but I *do* want you to get the hell off my property."

We laughed hard remembering her father's perfect response. Shaun said, "Oh, man. Leave it to my dad."

"He's a genius."

I got a text around 10:00 from Matt that said he was excited for MCA tomorrow, which reminded Shaun to have me show her what he looked like.

"Girl, he is so gorgeous. Nice work!" She commented on how every guy I had gone out with was really hot but none of them were what she truly thought was my type. I wasn't sure I really had a type and she wasn't sure what she thought my type was either. Like I said before, I usually dated clean-cut, athletic types, conservatively dressed, and taller than me. I had dated white, black, and Hispanic guys. I went out with a Korean guy when I was about 25 years old. I had never really been attracted to guys with long hair unless their name was Eddie Vedder or Johnny Depp. I had never really dated a blonde guy and I had never dated anyone shorter than me before. I thought I was pretty open when it came to looks. I was interested in their personality and what we had in common. I thought it would be nice to find an engineer like Shaun did. When you're looking for love you can't be worried about things like that. It needs to be more about your spiritual connection. Financial stability is a plus but not a mandatory requirement. I wanted a man who made me feel "awake and in constant total amazement".

Saturday with Matt turned out to be one of the greatest dates I had ever had in my life. He was a gentleman, he was fun, and he was playful. He really seemed to enjoy the museum and paid for everything we did that day including lunch and dinner. We ended up going back to my place after we ate for a cocktail. He was a beer drinker and luckily I had a six-pack of a beer I had just bought earlier that week. He was lucky Shaun and I didn't drink it all the night before and stuck to wine. It's called Pinstripe and is a red ale made by Ska Brewing Company out of Durango, Colorado. It's absolutely delicious if you like reds. He was transparent and very direct again that night and said to me, "I actually really like you and am going to suspend my dating profile pending the potential relationship that is forming between us." I laughed out loud and told him, "I have never heard anyone talk like you before. There is no bullshit. You make your feelings and intentions known all of the time." He smiled and said, "It's so much easier that way." I agreed and told him I could learn a lot from him. He left that night but came right back on Sunday just to hang out and talk. No alcohol, no food, just the two of us talking and telling stories. I was completely smitten. On Monday I made an appointment for a bikini wax.

Chapter 12 True Colors

Matt and I had been seeing each other for just over two weeks and he was occupying most of my time. We had the "let's be exclusive" conversation and were finding it impossible to keep our hands off of each other. Sex was inevitable and I was honestly very nervous about it. He was so sexy and was a great kisser, I was sure he and I would make fireworks happen in the bedroom. The next weekend we decided he would spend the night at my place. I also finally got an invite for Chris and Felipe's wedding. It was a contemporary card with navy blue, gold, and a blush pink shade. I thought those colors were gorgeous. The card announced that they would be married at Butterfly Beach in Santa Barbara and guests could stay wherever they wanted but that they would be staying at the Franciscan Inn. I was seriously excited for this wedding and a reason to go to California. I had only been to LA and Santa Monica and hadn't gone to any other cool parts of California like San Diego, San Francisco, and Santa Barbara. I wanted to go to Santa Monica since I was little and my favorite TV show was "Three's Company". Shaun and I went together in our 20s just so we could say we did. The invitation said, "To Cherry Thomas and Guest." I wondered if in two months Matt and I would still be dating and close enough to travel together. It was possible.

On Saturday afternoon Matt showed up and was holding a bottle of cabernet. "I brought you some vino." He said as he walked in the door. What a charmer. "Why thank you, sir, I would love to open that." We hung out all day and into the night and I was getting antsy. All I was thinking was, "Let's have sex. I just have to know! Is this going to happen?" He was trying to take it slow and I could appreciate that but I had needs and it had been months for me. I am a little old fashioned and never initiate sex for the first time with a man. After the first time is over I might initiate every single other time we have sex but never the first time. I was so turned on just by the thought of us finally having sex and that we had waited an appropriate amount of time to do it. I went into the kitchen and poured another glass of wine. I said, "Do you want another beer?" and suddenly he was behind me. He wrapped his arms around me and kissed me on my neck. Now, that is my spot and I melted right into his arms. I put down the glass and turned around to face him. We kissed and kissed and it felt so good. He lifted me up on the counter and kissed me everywhere as he removed my top and then my bra. I leaned my head against the cabinet door and thought to myself, "This is exactly what I was hoping for."

Matt grabbed me and pulled me down off of the counter and led me into my bedroom. He pushed me down on the bed and pulled down my shorts and panties and just stood there looking at me while he took off his clothes. "You're beautiful." he whispered. I don't think I had ever been lying on a bed naked while a man stared at me before and like always when I feel vulnerable or even mildly uncomfortable, I deflected my feelings with humor, so I said, "Paint me, like one of your French girls." Then laughed hard at my own joke. He laughed and said, "Did you just quote Titanic?" Yup, sure did. I just laughed and reached out my hand for him to join me. What was great about Matt was that he was very much into foreplay and made the sex seem like it lasted forever which was a good thing because the actual old in and out was over in a hot minute. I mean, don't get me wrong, it was pleasurable and considerably good sex but I was hoping for a round two that lasted longer. Well, maybe in the morning.

I was right about round two lasting longer, it did, but it wasn't in the morning. He said he was never in the mood in the morning. That was disappointing to me because I love being woken up by my man caressing me and kissing me. It's the best way to start the day. I never met a single guy who didn't love it except Matt. This was not a deal breaker for me, however, because Matt had turned out to be amazing in so many ways and I was thrilled about him. He stayed all weekend and told me, "Next weekend you can come to my house. I want you to feel as comfortable there as I feel here." What a sweet thing to say. I was looking forward to it.

That week was a busy one for both of us and we talked every day but didn't see each other at all until Friday. Ben had a big case and we were at court almost the entire week and Matt had two photo shoots in Colorado Springs. Family pictures. Garden of the

Gods and Pikes Peak are understandably very popular backdrops for professional pictures no matter what the occasion. I was really looking forward to Friday night because I was taking my weekender bag, lovingly referred to by Shaun and I as "the whore bag", to my new beau's house for the first time. He periodically texted me throughout the week with, "I can't wait to get you naked." and counting down the days. This part of a relationship is so fun. It has the new car smell and is so hyper focused on sex for both people. "Send me pics." he texted, "I miss you." I took a sexy selfie and a cleavage picture in the bathroom. I *was* naughty. Friday couldn't come fast enough.

Matt had a much nicer apartment than mine but he also made much more money than I did. That was a perk of being a successful freelance photographer. One thing I was looking forward to other than spending the weekend naked was looking at his portfolio. He had been telling me about his favorite shots in the Rocky Mountains and on his trip to Australia and Iceland. I was even excited to see what he had been doing all week in Colorado Springs. He had a website that I had looked at but it mostly just had wedding and family picture examples. Those were the moneymakers. When I arrived on Friday evening he was making us dinner. I was impressed and felt bad at the same time because I had definitely not cooked for him yet. I have always been a good cook but didn't do a lot of cooking at home unless I was having a dinner party or something.

Matt handed me a glass of Pinot Grigio and told me to make myself comfortable. I smelled it and he watched me and said, "It will taste good with the chicken." I'm sure it would I thought, but I never drink white wine. I don't care what I'm eating. When I was in my 20s and switched from drinking beer and martinis all the time to primarily wine I got into pairing and understanding what kinds of wines taste best with what kinds of food but after a while I just really developed a taste for reds and now no matter what I am eating, I'm a red wine girl. But, the Pinot was delicious and I definitely appreciated his gesture. I started looking around at his photography that he had framed and hung on the walls. I laughed and said, "Do you remember "Check Your Head" by the Beastie Boys? You just reminded me of "Blue Nun"." I laughed and he just looked at me so I quoted, "Our evening began at Peter Sichel's comfortable study in his New York townhouse, where the candlelight was just right, the hi-fi was in the background, and the wine was delicious." He had no idea what I was talking about but I continued, "What's the secret Peter? Naturally, I'll say it's the wine. Mmmm it does go well with the chicken. Delicious again, Peter." I was laughing as he said, "I never really listened to the Beastie Boys." The horror! I moved on to the next subject.

"So, do you have a favorite picture of all time?"

"Yes! I think it's one I just got in New Zealand. I'm excited to show you those pictures after dinner. I know you'll like them."

"I like to say I am an amateur photographer."

"Really? Cool! I'm looking forward to fall this year, have you ever been to Steamboat Springs? Maybe we could take a little road trip and find some aspens and fall colors to shoot."

He was excited. That sounded like the greatest time ever. I was so happy. I was really just in heaven. There was nothing wrong with this guy, other than the Beastie Boy's thing so far, and I really liked him. I felt like I was at home and it was an amazing feeling. I got a text message from Shaun that said. "How's it going? Did you bring your whore bag? LOL."

"Yes, I sure did. Going good what's up?"

"If Matt is up for it, I can't wait to meet him; we could all four go to lunch on Saturday."

"Great idea, I will ask him at dinner."

Matt motioned to the dining room. "Dinner is served." He placed the last dish on the dining room table. "Yaye!" I walked over to him and said, "I always kiss the cook." I wrapped my lovin' arms around him and kissed him like he was the love of my life. Like he was the last man on earth! I was feeling so lucky. Dinner was so delicious. I was impressed. How nice to think of having a boyfriend who would be cooking sometimes. The presentation was gorgeous but I wasn't surprised as he was the artistic type. I could probably learn to look past the fact that he didn't listen to the Beastie Boys, though it would take time. At dinner I asked him what kind of music he listened to. Music is pretty important to me and I have a wide range of favorites. He said he mostly liked classic rock like Led Zeppelin and The Who and The Doors, which are all on my list of favorites. I said what about Pink Floyd? He said, "Yeah, they're cool for sure." I thought, oh thank God, I can't handle someone not liking Pink Floyd. Then he told me, "I just never got into rap."

"Not even old school, good rap, or funk?"

"No, I guess I'm a rock n roller."

"Well, there is nothing wrong with that."

Matt picked up his beer, held it out toward me to toast and said, "I have to talk to you about something important." I picked up my glass and said, "You do?" At this point hearing words like that gave me anxiety; nothing could scare me more. I was sure he wasn't expecting a baby so I got ready for whatever he was about to say. "This last month has been amazing with you and I hope that you feel the same way." He stopped and I said, "I do! It has been so great." He continued, " And, I would like to know if I can start officially referring to you as my girlfriend." I didn't even think twice and said, "I accept your offer and would love to start referring to you as my boyfriend." I was giggling and fidgeting as he clinked his beer against my glass and then leaned in for a kiss. It seemed like a done deal and I was psyched.

Once August was nearing an end, I felt like I might be in love and we were even talking about the fact that after my lease was up the next year that I should move in with him, just because his apartment was cooler and bigger. By the time my lease was up we would have been dating for almost a year. We were making plans for the future but everything was moving at a nice and normal pace. We were inseparable and Shaun and Johnny totally loved him when they met him. I had become so caught up in my new romance that I hadn't even looked into planning my trip to Santa Barbara for Chris's wedding. It was only about four weeks away. I was hoping to be able to still get a room at the Franciscan because Shaun and Johnny were of course also staying there. Shaun texted me and said, "Have you asked Matt if he wants to go with you to the wedding yet?"
"No, he is in Jackson Hole, Wyoming doing a wedding shoot, I will ask him tonight when he calls."
"Good"
"It is going to be so fun!"

I really could not wait for that trip; they always say in a new relationship, you really learn a lot about each other when you travel together. We hadn't even gone on a road trip yet, but were still planning on Steamboat in the fall.

That night when he called me, I asked him, "I keep forgetting to ask you. My friend Chris, who is actually Johnny's younger brother, is getting married in Santa Barbara at the end of September. I have to book my trip pretty soon and I wanted to know if you wanted to go with me."

"Oh man, I would love to. I love Santa Barbara."

I squealed, "Oh cool! I am looking up flights and rooms now just to see what there is but when you get home we can book the tickets together. I will make the room reservation tonight though. We are staying at the Franciscan. Have you heard of it?"

"No, but I'm sure it's really great, Santa Barbara is a really nice area, have you been there?"

"No, I haven't. I have only been to Santa Monica and LA."

"Oh, cool. Well, this should be really fun, thank you for including me, Cherry."

We spent the rest of the call flirting and talking dirty to each other and I ended up on the couch with an old rubber boyfriend that had probably been feeling very neglected lately. Having phone sex with your boyfriend is one of the hottest things ever. When you have to be apart there is no reason not to keep the lust alive with a little talking dirty over the phone. The imagination is an amazing thing and I am a firm believer that when we can enjoy our own bodies alone we become better lovers to our partners.

I really wished I could have gone to Jackson with him, he went on a Thursday to get a bunch of pre wedding and family shots and the wedding itself was on Saturday. He told me he was coming home on Sunday and it was about an eight-hour drive. He said he wanted to see me before the work week and was leaving really early in the morning so I could meet him in the afternoon at his place. We had exchanged keys about a week ago so I spent the night at his place that Saturday. I wanted to be there when he got back. I loved staying at his place.

I woke up Sunday morning and cleaned his whole apartment, did his laundry, and organized his cabinets. He was going to love me for it too. August was a busy wedding month that year and he had spent a lot of time away from home. He got home around noon and had flowers for me when he walked in. What a romantic. They were small hot pink roses, which are probably my favorite. We spent most of the afternoon having sex and then finally before I had to go home and do my own laundry for the week we sat down to book a flight together. Matt asked me, "So does Chris live in Santa Barbara?" I said, "No, he actually lives here in Denver. He and his fiancé, Felipe had been there before on a vacation and loved it so since they had to go to California anyway to get married legally they naturally chose a place that already meant something to them. Lucky for us it is a great destination."
Matt looked at me blankly and said, "Chris and Felipe? Two dudes?"

"Oh, yes, I thought I told you Chris is gay." I laughed and said, "Have you been to a same sex wedding? I haven't but I've heard the only real difference is that they are often much more stylish than a straight wedding." It made me think of Sex in the City, the movie, when Big kept calling it a "Gay Wedding", and Carrie kept saying it's not a "Gay Wedding", just a wedding that happens to have two grooms and then there were swans and Liza Minnelli. I was sure that Liza wouldn't be at Chris's wedding but one could dream.

Matt said, "No, you didn't tell me that." He wasn't smiling or making any expression for that matter which led me to ask, "Is that a problem for you?" He stood up and went to get water and said, "Well, it's none of my business what people do but I don't personally believe in same sex marriage. I'm glad it isn't legal here." I was shocked. How do people describe it usually; my jaw hit the floor? It was my mistake really, because we hadn't ever talked politics or religion. I figured that he might be a republican and knew that he believed in God but we had never officially gone over our beliefs with each other yet. He seemed so kind, and accepting, and artistic, people like that never turn out to be people who "don't believe" in same sex marriage. I honestly didn't know what to say.

We ended up talking a lot about it and put a pause on the ticket buying to hash out our stand on gay rights and same sex marriage, a conversation I never expected to be having at that length with him. It wasn't just that he believed in the old school sanctity of marriage, he actually had a little bit of a problem with gay people in general, lesbians, gay men, all of them. He said it wasn't about religion, he had been to church like three times in his life, it was that he thought being gay was a choice and that a lot of times it was because they were mentally ill or had been abused. I was so mad, but really the emotion I was feeling was sadness. This wasn't going to be something I could overlook. I hadn't known a homophobe probably ever in my life. It was completely un-evolved and taboo to be anti-gay in this day and age. What would Johnny say? What would Chris say! I would be so mortified.

He said to me, "I can tell you're upset. I'm sorry. It's just the way I feel. I can skip the wedding if it makes you feel uncomfortable." Skip the wedding? I was thinking I don't even know this guy anymore. It felt so uncomfortable just listening to him talk about it. He was an intelligent man. How could this be what he believed? Then he said, "I also don't agree with interracial relationships, meaning black and white people. I've gotten grief for that before but I just can't help it. I feel like it's wrong." What the fuck did he just say to me? I seriously wanted to crawl out of my skin. I said, "Are you trying to break up with me? I feel like any second you are going to start laughing and yell, "Psych!"" He laughed and put his arm around me and said, "I'm sorry. I guess I'm really old fashioned."

"Old fashioned? I think you might be racist, Matt." He became visibly defensive and argued, "I am not racist. I have black friends, I just don't believe in interracial relationships, I don't have a problem with black people." I didn't know what to say. I was sick to my stomach.

I let the conversation fade out and eventually found an organic moment to pack up and head home and we parted peacefully. I cried all the way back to my apartment. I loved a racist bigot homophobe. As soon as I got home I called Blayne. I told him everything that had just happened between Matt and I. He said, "You're shitting me!" Then he laughed for what seemed like five minutes. "Where did you say this guy is from?"

"Kansas City originally."

"Well, it's not Kansas City's fault but this clown has problems. What are you going to do?"

"I mean, I have to dump him. I have no choice. I'm really upset because I fell for him. I would have never guessed that he would be so ignorant. He seemed like the coolest guy ever. I couldn't wait for you to meet him. I knew mom would love him." I started crying again.

Blayne got serious and said, "Cherry, you will be ok. This guy is not good enough for you. This isn't your fault. There was no way you could have known that he had these archaic beliefs." He consoled me and made me feel better and eventually I calmed down. I fell asleep so early that night, around 8:00 PM. I felt so drained. I was already asleep when Matt texted me "Goodnight, love you."

The next morning I woke up and remembered how sad I was. You know how that happens? You open your eyes and immediately remember the subject of your sadness and feel like you can't even get out of bed. But, I had to get out of bed. It was Monday and I had to get to work. All through my shower I thought about how I was going to handle this. I started to feel angry. I was sad at first because this realization was heart breaking and then I was mad because he was such an ass. He wasted my time! I knew from then on I was going to ask anyone I date from the get go if they are racist, homophobic, sexist, a sex offender, had fifteen girlfriends, had violent tendencies, had a baby on the way, or liked to be bent over couches by anyone. I texted Shaun and told her as much as I could. She was appalled of course and asked me if I could get lunch later. I said, "Yes please." It was a date.

I ignored Matt's texts even though they were sweet and totally normal. He either was pretending that nothing was wrong or seriously didn't know anything was wrong. I waited until I was with Shaun at lunch to deal with it. Sometimes you just need your best friend. I told her the story in detail and she basically had the same response as Blayne accept she didn't laugh. She could see how upset and angry I was. I actually loved him. I showed her the text messages and she asked me, "What are you going to tell him?" I said, "I don't think I can ever face him. What if I just sort of broke up with him over text message? Would that be the lamest thing on earth?" She answered, "Maybe, but not as lame as thinking that black and white people shouldn't have interracial relationships." So, I texted him and said, "I'm sorry I haven't answered you I figured you would sleep in today." He texted me back and said, "No, why did you think that?"

"I figured you would be tired from staying up late burning crosses or like rainbow flags in people's yards." I showed Shaun and she gasped, covered her mouth with her hands and started laughing hysterically, "You didn't!" She said it a little loud and looked around embarrassed. I couldn't help myself. Matt answered me right away with, "LOL, I'm not racist, Cherry."

"Sure you aren't."

He told me to call him that night and I figured I would. That would be when I would officially break up with him.

That night when we got on the phone I tried to be very kind and diplomatic about the whole thing. I explained to him that I would never be able to look past the way he felt about gay people or interracial relationships and that he was entitled to his opinion but that I couldn't respect his opinion and therefore I knew that this was never going to work. I told him I take some blame because I should have talked to him about subjects that were important to me earlier on before we got to deep into a relationship. I explained that at first I felt tricked by him but that I know now that I was naïve to assume that based on everything I knew about him so far, he probably shared my ideals or beliefs. I also told him that I wished him the very best and that I hoped that someday he would become enlightened on these important subjects. He stumbled over his words a lot and apologized and got really upset. Eventually I cried and could no longer speak and he told me he loved me and that he hoped I would change my mind and I told him I hoped *he* would change *his* mind. We finally said goodbye. I bought my ticket to LAX and then I cried myself to sleep.

Chapter 13 Sad September

There are a few songs and albums I like to listen to when I'm sad about love. When I'm at home I watch movies more than I listen to music but it depends on my mood. I also have a record player and enjoy the crackle of classics on vinyl from time to time. I'm the kind of person who needs music when I am out and about. I listen to Pandora at my desk all day at work and I listen in my car, of course. One of my favorite things to do is drive, listen to good music, and sing my heart out. I do some of my best thinking when I'm driving. September was here and I decided to take that day trip to Steamboat in search of the golden Aspens anyway even if it meant going alone.

It was the weekend of September 15th, I remember only because of the fact that Chris's wedding was only two weeks away. I was incredibly depressed and I really needed a change of scenery. September was always my least favorite month. It had always meant summer was over, summer love was ending, school was starting, or winter was coming. So many people love it but to me it had always been so ominous. I figured I needed to live somewhere with no seasons to avoid "Sad September" as I always called it. Somewhere like the desert of Arizona where September means it's only 90 and not 120 degrees anymore or where there are palm trees and cactuses and no changing of the leaves. Although, the leaves are quite a site, and I meant to appreciate them that year.

On Friday night I checked the route to Steamboat and picked out my favorite albums for times like these, to listen to on the way there and back. My first pick was Prince, "Purple Rain". Prince is one of my all time favorites. Then I grabbed Pearl Jam, "Ten". It was a pretty big part of my teen years. Next is Sade, "The Best of Sade". Do you remember when Marcus, played by Eddie Murphy in "Boomerang", said he wanted to just "go home, stare at the wall, and listen to Sade"? I knew the feeling completely and I say that joke all the time. Then I chose Fiona Apple, "Tidal". I went through a pretty intense Fiona phase when that album came out. I remember it came out in 1996 and I bought it in '97. I listened to it relentlessly. Next on the list is Temple of the Dog- the one and only. God, I love that album so much. It might be my favorite album of all time. Then Lynyrd Skynyrd, "Second Helping". My favorite song on that album is "I Need You". I love that song so much, but Second Helping also has "Call Me The Breeze" on it. That album came out in the early 70s, back when songs were over 6 minutes long. Next pick was Led Zeppelin, I bought a re-mastered "best of " album called "Mothership" because it has some of my favorite LedZep songs on it like, "Ramble On", "Babe I'm Gonna Leave You", and probably my very favorite, "Since I've Been Loving You". Finally, I chose probably one of the most intense, romantic, poignant, and soulfully poetic albums of all time, Jeff Buckley, "Grace". That album is so special to me that before iTunes I bought the CD three different times and played it until it was destroyed. There is not one single song on that album that doesn't move me to the core.

I left on Saturday morning at 7:00 AM with my music, my camera, and some snacks for the road. The drive to Steamboat is so beautiful. Northern Colorado is absolutely breathtaking. One thing I always loved about the West are the wide-open spaces. You can see a storm coming from miles and miles away. I stopped several times and took pictures. In between stops I listened to my music and sang and cried a few times but it was therapeutic. I had to get it all off my chest. I had to move on. I had to move forward.

When I got to Steamboat it was about 11:00 AM. I had taken my time getting there because it's really not even a three-hour drive up from the city. I drove into downtown and just loved it. I thought it looked exactly how I pictured it would. Shops everywhere and a western, mountain town kind of feel. There weren't many people around and it seemed pretty slow paced. I was hungry so I decided to look for a place to eat and turned down 12th Street. There was a little park and a river ahead. I could smell sulfur, which isn't the most pleasant smell but I thought it was cool anyway. There was a place on the corner called Double Z Bar & BBQ. I thought that sounded like the perfect place to eat. It was open so I found a parking spot and went to check it out. I asked the girl, "Tell me what the locals order? I'm thinking about a sandwich or a burger." She smiled at me funny but was cute; maybe since I admitted I wasn't from around there and said, "You have to get the Z-Burger." I looked at the menu and it said it was a burger with hot links. "Yes, please." I smiled at her and handed her back the menu. I ordered the food to go and about ten minutes later when she handed me the bag she said, "I put some ranch in there. We always eat the fries with ranch. We have the best ranch in Colorado." I thanked her and when I went back outside I decided I would sit by the river if I could.

I walked over to my car and found a place to sit down and eat with a view of the Yampa River. That burger was so amazing that I still think about it to this day and she was right; it might have been the best ranch I have ever had in my life. I just stared at my surroundings and did some reflecting. I wasn't actually depressed. I was just "situationally depressed". I was sad about another disappointment but I was not discouraged and I was going to be fine. It was hard to admit that I fell for someone who turned out to not be who I thought he was. I started counting my blessings and being thankful for the person I was. I was thankful that I was good, and tolerant, and loving. I was thankful that I was hopeful, and optimistic. I was thankful that I had so many beautiful people in my life, people who genuinely loved me and cared about me as much as I cared about them. I was thankful for my life, and my health, and my mind. There was so much to be thankful for.

I decided I would drive over to ski mountain to see if I could navigate my way up the winding roads to some views and some yellow leaved aspens. Mt. Werner is its name. I drove past some resorts and golf courses and the places where people stay in the winter. It was totally dead up there. I just followed the road whichever way looked the best until I was on Fish Creek Falls Road. It just kind of ended eventually and there were many people hiking the area. It was so amazingly beautiful. I took pictures and breathed in the clean air. I didn't hike anywhere but I got to the river, or stream and enjoyed the sound of the water flowing, the changing leaves, and the incredible views of Mt. Werner. I must have stayed there for an hour. I almost didn't want to leave.

I decided I didn't want to get back home later that dusk so I started making my way back to Denver. This time I stopped at a gas station in a little town called Kremling about an hour southeast of Steamboat. It was like the Wild West for sure. Everyone I saw while I was there looked right into my eyes, smiled, and said hello. I think it might be the exact opposite of New York. It was in every way, the exact opposite. The ride home was much happier for me. I was really proud of myself for going on that little adventure and I had a new attitude. I considered the idea of waiting a little while before I looked into dating again. My account was still suspended from when I got serious with Matt and I figured I would just let it sit there until I got back from the wedding. So, that was exactly what I did. I took a month off. I will always think of Steamboat Springs with love and fondness. It cured me in a way.

The wedding weekend was drawing near, so Shaun and I went shopping together. We wanted to find the perfect outfits for everything on the agenda including the wedding itself. September in Santa Barbara has an average temperature of about 74 degrees and most of what we were doing included a dressed up, but casual beach type attire except for Friday night when we were planning on going out for cocktails. I wanted to find something really hot to wear that night. We went to the mall and shopped for hours until we found the perfect things. Shaun and I happen to love shopping and enjoy shopping with each other. I have other friends who are miserable to shop with and either hate everything or want to spend a million hours in the dressing room using me as their personal critic. Shaun and I are somewhere in the middle of those two extremes. My favorite find of the day were some purple two-inch heels with a pointed toe. They were so fly. I had literally never owned purple shoes, not even in the 80s.

Since I had totally slacked on getting my ticket, I didn't have the same flight as Shaun and Johnny but we were departing and arriving at almost the same times so we shared a taxi to the airport and met up at LAX when we arrived. We took a Santa Barbara airbus to the Hotel from the airport. It was so much cheaper to fly into LAX so it was worth the drive. It was fun being on a charter bus anyway. We were just ready to spend some time on the Pacific coast so everything was fun. Shaun and I definitely miss the ocean, being so landlocked in Colorado. Since we only ever go to back home in December we don't get a lot of beach time. We always went to Jones or Long Beach growing up and in the summer going to the

Jersey Shore is just what you do. I think the water is a little warmer there than the Pacific in the Santa Barbara area. The Pacific Ocean is darker too. It freaks me out a little to be honest with you, but I was still overjoyed to be there and couldn't wait to lie in the sun surrounded by sand at some point, even though it was September.

We met up at the Inn and when I saw Chris and Felipe I got pretty emotional. They were so happy and so madly in love. They were genuinely grateful for every single guest and family member who was there and they let them know it. Chris came up to me, squeezed me hard and whispered in my ear, "Shaun told me what happed with your last boy. I want you to know that I love you. You are a dear and cherished friend. Both of us love you. Ok? Thank you for being here." Then he leaned back and looked me in my teary eyes still squeezing my shoulders with his hands and I looked back at him and my voice cracked as I whispered, "Thank you, I love you both too and I am so very happy to be here with you." It was basically at that moment that I realized I had no reason to be sad. I was truly happy and we were going to have a fantastic weekend.

The wedding was just as perfect as I imagined it would be. Chris and Felipe wore cream colored linen pants with bare feet and Chris wore a blush pink un-tucked button up shirt. Felipe wore a navy un-tucked button up shirt and the two of them wore flowers pinned to their shirts that were the opposite color. There was a white trellis on the beach draped in a flowing off white colored cloth and paper lanterns on long white poles stuck into the sand that were gold, navy, and blush pink. We all took off our shoes and stood around them as they said their vows and I-dos. It was so beautiful and incredibly romantic. We stayed right there at the beach for dinner and the reception. It was catered with seafood and a tip only bar, and there was a little three-person cover band with a female lead singer who had long dreadlocks. She turned every song into reggae, soul, and funk. It was without question one of the best weddings I had ever been to.

Shaun and I were dancing at one point to one of the best covers of "Sugaree" by the Grateful Dead that had ever blessed my ears, when Chris and Johnny's parents, whom I love, came over to dance with us. Johnny's father said, "This is our kind of music!" I said, "Mine too, trust me!" Then Johnny's mom put her arm around me and said, "Your wedding is next, Miss Cherry. I just know it." I laughed and kept dancing with her. "One can only hope, sister", I thought, "One can hope." I looked over and saw Chris and Felipe dancing with each other, staring into each other's eyes, and periodically looking out at all of their loved ones around them. I wouldn't have missed that beautiful union for anyone or anything. That was real. That was what it was all about. As the band played Bob Marley and my toes sank in the sand, I felt better than I had felt in years.

When we got home to Denver it was October and I had officially survived the emotional rollercoaster that September always seemed to be. On the contrary, it had turned out to be a wonderfully eventful September full of happy moments and therapeutic self-realization. I was happy with all of it and looked back on it thinking that I might remember it forever. That turned out to be true, of course. I sat in my apartment on Monday night after I got home, put on "Lost Boys" to remind me of the Pacific coast that I already missed, and re-activated my dating profile. I was watching the scene when Michael, played by Jason Patric (swoon) first lays eyes on Star played by Jami Gertz and I thought, you know, I really need to find someone who looks at me like that. Or the way Tim Cappello looks at his saxophone. Or the way I look at Tim Cappello's muscles. Either way, I needed to be looked at. I also needed to download "Still Believe".

Chapter 14 People Are Strange

I had to get my nails done; they were looking a little messy, so I made an appointment for Shaun, my friend Sarah, and I to get them done together. I needed a "girls day". My girlfriends are one of my favorite things about me. Women need time with their girlfriends no matter if they are single or not at least once or twice a month. We need to be able to act a fool and laugh until we pee our pants sometimes. We need to talk about boys and world news and eat sushi and groom ourselves. That's just what we do. We always went to the same place to get our nails done. My favorite artist's name was Christine and she was from the Philippines. I think she just liked me because I tipped her well but she was exceptionally talented and funny so I loved her. Shaun never cared who did her nails but I always asked for Christine. Sarah is the funny and sarcastic type. We call her Rocky because she is the token over protective friend who always threatens to fight anyone when we are out in public who wrongs us in any way, like a bodyguard. We always told her that she was more east coast than we are. On this day Christine asked me if I was seeing anyone yet and asked me how on-line dating was going. The last time I saw her she had started a profile but was worried about "all the freaks" as she put it. This time she told me she had been on a couple dates.

This topic had Shaun, Sarah, and every other woman within earshot of us completely interested in what we had to say. It was like being at a barbershop. It could have been because it was just an interesting subject, or maybe it was because they were either dating on line too, or knew someone who was. I told Christine I had taken September off and since the last time I saw her nothing new had happened. I asked her how it was going for her. She told us something I hadn't really thought of much before that day. You know when some people who are rich or famous have a hard time meeting people that they trust truly like them for who they are and not just for the money or association? It reminds me of "Coming to America" with Eddie Murphy. He pretended he had nothing and she liked him anyway. Then when he turned out to be a king she was shocked at first and then basically just accepted that she lucked out and he knew she was genuine. Christine compared her situation to that and said, "I honestly don't know if when a guy starts talking to me or wants to go out that he is really interested in me or just has an Asian girl fetish." We all gasped and laughed but unfortunately totally understood what she was saying. We had probably all known at least one guy who wasn't Asian and had some kind of weird Asian girl "thing". Blayne dated an Asian girl named Lee and she actually said something like that to him about it as a joke. He just blew it off and said he had never thought about it. But, after hearing Christine talking about it I totally didn't blame Lee for bringing it up. It is totally a thing. There are all of these weird dating fetishes and stereotypical cliché's that we women have to avoid somehow. "Black guys like thick white girls." The lady next to me piped in. "You see my ass?" She sort of looked behind herself and directed us to look, "It's a hot commodity to black guys." We all laughed. Shaun said, "That's why black guys don't like you, Cherry, your ass is flatter than a day old soda pop!" Everyone laughed but me and I said, "What are you a West Texas Rancher now? Who talks like that?" It was true and I am sensitive about my white girl booty but it still looks good in jeans and that is all that matters.

Sarah is Hispanic and she added, "Guys are afraid of me. They always say Latina girls are intimidating." I knew that was a true story and had heard it a million times. Then as she laughed at herself she said in a fake Cuban Scar Face accent, "Guys don't know what they are talking, mang, but I *will* cut them." We were all laughing so hard as Christine said, "The only way we know that a guy isn't after us because we are Asian is when he is also Asian but I don't like Asian guys as much as I like blonde white guys." Sarah jumped in and said, "Ooooh me too! Because they look nothing like my brothers." Shaun, laughing, said, "You are all totally insane." There was one black woman in there and luckily for us she joined the conversation too. She said, "I'm partial to black guys myself, but they always want to date white girls and I'll tell you why." I swear I was on the edge of my seat to finally hear the answer to this question that white people can't ask because they are afraid of sounding racist. She laughed at our silence and complete devoted attention to what she was about to say and continued, "You bitches let them touch your hair." I seriously laughed so hard I almost peed my pants. We all called bullshit and she laughed and laughed and then told us, "Let me get my brother on speaker phone, he is dating a white girl now, he will tell you." We were covering our mouths with our hands trying to muffle our laughter like we were at a slumber party prank calling boys and she put her phone on speaker. A low and sexy baritone male voice answered and said, "Hey."

"Hey, tell me again why brothers always wanna date white girls."

"What? Am I on speaker?"

"Yes, I'm getting a pedicure, tell us, why do brothers always date white girls?"

He laughed and then said, "Because they let us touch their hair."

Everyone in the room erupted with laughter.

It took us a while to recover from our laughter and tears but then finally Christine said, "What is your type, Cherry?" I said, "I'm not sure I really have one. I was just thinking about this recently I have dated every race; I usually like sort of straight, clean-cut guys. My last two "boyfriends" were white, but I am attracted to Hispanic, and black guys too. I dated a half Korean, half white guy once. I really don't know. You can have the blonde white guys though, I like dark hair." The lady next to me says, "Have you ever noticed that black guys will tell you everything they think about you in three minutes and white guys will tell you one thing a month for like a year before they get to the good stuff? That's why I like black guys, they know what they want and they tell you." The black woman responded and said, "Mmhmm, that's how black girls are too. No nonsense. We just don't have the time. That's why I have no interest in white guys. They are still on the appetizer when I'm fixin' to get my dessert. You know?" The two of them gave each other a high five and we were hysterically laughing again.

I definitely had never had so much fun getting a manicure before and wanted to keep hanging out with all of them all day but eventually we were done and Shaun, Sarah, and I went to lunch. Sarah was seeing a new guy named Corey that we hadn't met yet and was on her cell phone a lot while we sat in the restaurant. "Are you sprung, Sarah?" I joked.
"I am dating one of those visually needy types. He likes a lot of pictures and descriptions of what I am doing throughout the day. Have you ever dated a guy like that?"
"I mean most guys ask for pictures. I probably haven't dated anyone I would call visually needy but I totally know what you mean. I think all men are visual creatures. That's one reason that they all watch porn isn't it?" In unison Shaun and Sarah both said, "Yes!" Then Sarah said, "I don't have even remotely enough time for all of the pictures this fool wants in a 24 hour span so I spend like twenty minutes a night taking a bunch so I can send them to him throughout the next day when he asks. He has no idea that I didn't "just then" take them, you know?" I totally knew and I thought that was a genius idea. Shaun asked, "So, what is your opinion on what pictures are ok and at what point in a relationship? You know, I was wondering that. Since Johnny and I have been together since before everyone had cameras on their

cell phones we missed this whole sending naughty pictures to each other obsession. I still send him stuff just because I think it's fun, but he is my husband. How do you two who are dating and not married yet know you can trust a guy with your pictures?" I said, "I have only sent naughty pictures to Mark and Matt and they were both technically my boyfriend at the time so I guess I felt like I could trust them, as short lived as those relationships turned out to be, I assume they would never betray me. I also never show my face in pictures that are risqué'. The pictures with my face are just naughty, but if my mom saw them or my boss for example, it wouldn't matter. They wouldn't know they were of me. Those are sort of my guidelines. The whole thing is so stupid." Sarah added, "It is stupid, and I agree with you. I have the same guidelines. Corey sends me pictures too and I always tell him I will betray him with them if he betrays me. If you are going to exchange sexy pics it should never only be you taking the risk." Shaun raised her glass to toast us and we looked at her, smiled and raised our glasses too. When we clinked them all together she said, "To my favorite sluts. I love you both." Sarah fake threatened to throw her drink in Shaun's face and we were laughing again.

That night when I was at home I was still laughing at the memories all of the amusing things that we talked about earlier that day and I thought a lot about what my type might be. I couldn't imagine myself saying that I was into a certain race or not. I think that I have always found Hispanic guys the most visually appealing. I definitely like tall, dark and handsome white guys and muscular black guys. It was true what those two girls at the nail salon said about black guys. In general, of course, they are so expressive. I had gone on a date with a black guy at the beginning of the summer and through the whole meal he looked at me like he was Sylvester and I was Tweety Bird and talked to me like he was Pepe Le Pew and I was that painted cat. It made me laugh to think back on it. He was seriously attractive and I just could not handle his directness.

I think I had changed a lot since my teenage days when I thought every guy was a moron and when I was so picky that my friends just knew I would die old and alone. My "turn offs" list had gotten a lot smaller. It was obvious at that point that I had no time for even the slightest amount of racism, sexism, or homophobia. I wasn't sure how I could look past a guy who listened to NickelBack or wore affliction gear unless they were legitimate fighters, I guess. I had always thought that guys who don't use correct English were a turn off, unless English was not their first language, of course. It isn't just guys anyway. When people say "suposably", or "I seen", or "Expresso", I lose my mind. I'm totally a person who corrects them, if I really know them that is. It's annoying to be a grammar policeman, I know, but saying "I seen you at the mall" is cringe-worthy and I will take the risk of you hating me to correct you and save you from future embarrassment because, I am not alone on this.

I can't handle secretive types either. Those are the guys who literally never tell you anything but want to know all about your life and business. There is a difference between secretive and mysterious, I like mysterious. When it comes to the subject of sex I might actually be pickier than you think. I can't handle guys who are hyper sexual and want to hump like rabbits and I also can't handle guys who are unassertive and never initiate sex. I like a guy to be *very into sex*. I think that is somewhere around an 8 on the scale of 10 is the hyper sexual guy. I like a guy who is adventurous in bed but I am not into anything too kinky. I bet you're wondering what my idea of kinky actually is. I'll tell you this; I think I got through all "Fifty Shades" when I was in my 20s. I was sleeping with this guy when I still lived in New York, you know, the college years. He didn't last and neither did college, as you know. He was completely and 100% into S&M. It's the only way he wanted to do it. He would tie me up, make me beg, and definitely left a few bruises on me. My mother would be horrified if she knew. We would laugh so hard after we had sex and there would be a bruise. I would always tell him, "I'll see you at the Police Station." Rough sex is fun. For me it was a phase. I think I mostly just wanted to feel something new or different; something that had nothing to do with love in any way. He gave that to me. During that kind of sex you go into a state of euphoria, I would tell Shaun that he could have invited two guys dressed up as clowns to join in and I would have been ok with it as long as he didn't stop pleasuring me the way he did. I think of him fondly when he crosses my mind.

I knew I really wanted to avoid guys with too serious of a fetish or who were too focused on what they wanted, because I would be annoyed to have to try to measure up. I was never going to be into the large majority of things guys get weird about like too much anal sex, or foot stuff, or having three-ways. I wasn't looking for vanilla; I was looking for something I hadn't found before something I considered to be healthy. Something that was so good you gotta tell somebody. I knew I would know when I found it.

Jim Morrison was right, People *Are* Strange but we are all people aren't we? We are all a little strange or at least we are all probably strange to someone. It turned out that I was going to go looking again and this time with fewer rules of engagement.

Chapter 15 Let's Be Friends

I felt like I was back to dating for free meals again because I had been on another streak of "One Date Wonders" and then I started talking to a guy named Evan. He was adorable and an introvert but the fact that he was such a great conversationalist really helped me to look past how shy he seemed to be. We talked on the phone for almost two weeks before we finally met and he talked to me about everything but his kids. He said that was a part of step two and that we were currently involved in step one. He was so cute. I knew that this guy was never going to be someone I would end up with but I liked him anyway.

When he finally asked me out he wanted to go Dutch treat to see a movie. There are two things that are something to take note of when it comes to a first date offer like that. Number 1 is the fact that he wants to go Dutch. It's fine with me; if I were a guy I wouldn't want to waste a movie ticket and popcorn on a girl I might not end up liking either, but unfortunately it is an undeniable fact that when a guy doesn't want to pay for you, a flag is thrown on your metaphoric playing field and a little metaphoric coach in your head yells, " Foul! Player could have financial problems!" This could potentially be a big problem, depending on what *kind* of financial problems. Number 2 is the fact that he wants to see a movie on a first date. Two important things that people do on first dates is look at each other and talk to each other, neither of which you can do while you're in a movie theatre. The thing was, though, that we had talked so much over the phone already, maybe it would be nice to just be in the same room, not saying anything. I accepted and on a Friday night we met at the theatre.

I can't remember what movie we went there for but we were very excited to finally see each other, so, as soon as we met we hugged like we missed each other. I bought my ticket and he bought us popcorn to share and drinks. I thought it was a pretty smooth move for a guy who was potentially on a budget. Another thing I always remember is that when a guy has kids and no wife, he is probably paying child support of some kind and that is definitely not cheap. But, like I said, we hadn't gotten to that part of the story yet.

After the movie we went to Tom's Diner to talk. When I imagine going to a diner after a movie with a guy I just met I am back to daydreaming, thinking about "True Romance". The diner scene in the beginning of the film when they sit and eat pie together and talk about their favorites. Clarence asks Alabama, played by Patricia Arquette, "Tell me about yourself, for starters what do you do, where are you from, what's your favorite color, who's your favorite movie star, what kind of music do you like, what are your turn ons, turn offs?" There is something amazing about being in a diner. It isn't the same as any other kind of restaurant. You can glance around and write a story in your head about who everyone is and why they are in there. Evan answered all of Clarence's questions. I already knew what he did and where he was from; Manager at a Costco gas station, and he was from Thornton, Colorado. Then he told me his favorite color was green, he likes action movies, Bruce Willis, movies about cars like Fast & Furious and Vin Diesel; his favorite music is rock, mostly alternative rock from the 90s like Nirvana and Stone Temple Pilots. His turn offs he said first; he hated liars and then he paused before answering the "turn ons" question. I said, "You don't have to answer that if it makes you feel uncomfortable." He smiled at me and said, "You know, what really turns me on is a good woman, a woman who can be a good mother and a good wife. She has to be kind. I have never had a relationship with a woman like that." I remember looking at his face and noticing his eyes for the first time since I had been looking at him. They were so sad. On some people's faces you can really tell a lot about them by their eyes. Most women love a man's eyes but it is more than just the length of their lashes and the color of their iris. It's almost more about what is behind them. It's about the way they look at you and other people.

I was scared to ask but I went ahead and said, "Your ex wasn't a good wife, but is she a good mother?" He looked down and said, "No." I leaned forward and sort of put my head down enough to see his eyes and guided him back up to look at me. He smiled at me and said, "I have the kids most of the time, she has them every other weekend. She has them now. The problem is that I still pay her child support."
"What?"
"Yeah, most of my check goes to her and she is always threatening me and holding them over my head. She uses the money for herself. I pay for

everything. It's a nightmare and that is why I never wanted to talk about it with you."

"I am so sorry, do you have a lawyer?"

"I had one for the custody arrangement when we got divorced but not anymore, I can't afford it." "Do you feel like you can't stand up to her?"

"It's embarrassing, I never have been able to. She's crazy. I feel bad saying that about the mother of my kids but she is the woman that every man dreads meeting. She is the woman who gives exes a bad name."

I sat there for a few seconds just thinking about what a mess it sounded like. I could only assume he was telling me the truth. He was such a sweet guy, but there are always two sides to every story.

It was a sad end to the date but it was almost midnight and we were both yawning. We knew we had to call it a night. When we got out to the parking lot we hugged and said goodbye, I told him I would talk to him on Saturday. When I got home I kept thinking about how frustrating it would be to be at the mercy of an ex-spouse who was threatening, deceitful, and manipulative. I have known both men and women with Evan's story. I considered myself to be lucky to have never had to deal with that. I had no crazy exes, I had never been divorced, and since I had no children, I had never had to go through a custody battle. I knew that he really needed a lawyer and I felt so bad for him because it was understandable that he couldn't afford it. I could barely afford a lawyer if I ever needed one. But, I knew a bunch of lawyers and

I decided that I would call Ben in the morning and ask him if he had any ideas.

Ben gave me the number of one of his friends who does family law and said if I call him myself and tell him who I am he might give Evan some free up front counsel at least. It drives me crazy that we have to know someone to get what we need in life but that is just how it goes. No matter how big the town is that we live in we all "know a guy". We know a guy who will fix our car, we know a guy who will hook us up with a good attorney, and we know a guy who can get us out of a jam, depending on what the jam is. I texted Evan right away and asked him if he could meet me for lunch on Sunday. He said yes and I called Ben's friend.

On Sunday I was so excited to talk to Evan about the good news I had. Ben's friend was more than willing to help and told me a story about himself. He had gone through this very same situation when he was in law school and it was what made him choose Family Law eventually. He had no money after the divorce and said that being down and out like that and being desperate to be able to be with his kids as much as he and they deserved gave him a certain amount of compassion to the people who had struggled before him and after him with the same thing. He said a lawyer gave him a break once and he has spent his career paying it forward to the men and women who remind him of his situation. "There are plenty of people who can pay me, it's only right to give it away once in a while." he said, "Give your friend my number."

I was nervous to bring it up to Evan, however, I didn't want to freak him out or offend him. At this point I figured we would be friends, I really liked him and there wasn't any sort of spark between us; I assumed he felt the same way and I hoped he would be receptive of this offer. We met at a café near is house and I just went ahead and didn't put off the subject. I said, "Evan, I have something to give you and I want you to know that it is with my respect that I offer you this. I mean no offense and I don't want to overstep my boundaries with you. I think we are going to be friends and I want to help you." He just looked at me with a slight smile and a furrowed brow. I handed him a my business card with Ben's friend's name and number written on the back and said, "This is a colleague of mine. He can help you with your child support and custody situation." He just stared at the card. I said, "I didn't tell him anything that wasn't his business, that's up to you. It's also 100 percent up to you if you call him or not. You don't have to tell me anything; it's none of my business either. I just had to give you this after what you told me on Friday night." What he did next was something I will never ever forget. He reached out and took my hand in his and squeezed really hard and with his other hand he put his sunglasses back on. Tears streamed down his face immediately and he whispered with a cracking voice, "Thank you so much, Cherry. Thank You." He kept squeezing and again said, "Thank you so much." I felt so moved. I said, "Thank me if he helps you." I giggled but then I got choked up and teary with him. "You're welcome, Evan. I hope he can help you." "I'm so glad I met you, you are a great person." I took his other hand in mine, squeezed it and said, "Yaye! Let's be friends!" We laughed, wiped our tears and enjoyed the rest of our lunch date.

I realized that Evan wasn't the only guy I had cried with that year. Luckily both times the tears came from being overwhelmed in the moment and not really from pain or heartbreak. When I got home I put my favorite Rolling Stones album in, "Tattoo You", so I could listen to "Start Me Up"- you make a grown man cry, but I always listen to that entire album. I love it. My favorite track, "No Use in Crying", might be the greatest "we are done, I'm gone, and I'm never coming back song" ever. I felt really good that night. I felt like that day was an important moment in my life and that there had been a real reason for meeting Evan. I don't want to get too deep but this is what I meant when I talked about the importance of the interactions we have with people we meet and how imperative it is to really listen and pay attention. The slightest moments can change our lives forever. I was optimistic about Evan's situation then and I was right to be. Ben's friend was able to help him and we are still friends to this very day.

Chapter 15 Those Purple Heels

It was almost Halloween and I was getting excited because Shaun was having a house warming/Halloween party at her house. They were finally done with all of their cosmetic updates and ready to invite all of their friends over to celebrate, and what better way to do it than during a Halloween costume party. Shaun and I had lunch the week after I met up with Evan and after I told her the story we laughed about how much I had been dealing with since I started this whole dating on line thing. I told her that though it had definitely been entertaining and a learning experience, I felt a little like Sarah, played by Jennifer Connelly in one of my favorite movies of all time, "Labyrinth". Sarah was trying to get to her little brother, Toby, who was being held captive by Jareth, played by my dear love, David Bowie, at his castle. Instead of Toby, I was trying to find a husband and instead of Jareth interfering, tricking me, and distracting me from making my ultimate goal, it was all these crazy boys. It gave me a great idea and I decided that I would dress up like Sarah when she was at the ball for Halloween. It would be perfect! All I needed to find was some kind of poofy 80s wedding dress and I could make it happen. We laughed so hard when I told her she should dress up as David Bowie and wear a jock strap and tights but she had already promised Johnny that they would be Claire and Mike Wellington in "The Stepford Wives". He thought it was funny because they were in their new home and she was the hostess, but we both knew it was mostly because he wanted to be Christopher Walken, so he could do his imitations all night. We are all huge Walken fans.

I was talking to a guy named Zack, who was very funny and very flirtatious. He was a travel agent. I thought that was cool. He did a lot of trip planning for corporations. He was also so well groomed that I felt like he might be prettier than me. I never dated a guy who was so perfectly manscaped. He clearly got his eyebrows done and had one of those tidy facial hair situations. It sort of reminded me of Prince and I love me some Prince. We tried to make plans for a week and things kept coming up for him. I wasn't exactly sure if he was truly that busy or if he was having cold feet about meeting me. The weekend before Halloween I asked him if he wanted to meet me for coffee. I was going to go shopping at several of the thrift stores around Denver that Saturday to look for a wedding dress for my costume, Shaun couldn't help me because she was too busy with an event she was working on.

Zack and I met up on Saturday morning and pulled into the parking lot at the same time. He drove a black mustang. I saw him get out of the car and watched him walk to the door. He was really good looking and like I said, almost pretty. He was over dressed for coffee and had perfect hair, perfect clothes, was tall, and small framed but very muscular. He said he was black and Asian which meant that he had the most beautiful skin color. He really was a picture. I finally got out of my car and went to the door to meet him. He squealed when I walked in and said, "Cherry!

Girl, you are so pretty!" I laughed as he squeezed me tight and looked around as people stared at us smiling. He had more energy than anyone I had met in a while. We ordered coffee and sat down. He said, "I love your hair!" and then he started playing with it. I didn't mind. I am one of those girls who love having their hair played with.

We spent about an hour talking and laughing and telling each other our favorites and he asked me what I was doing for Halloween. When I told him my plan and what I was doing that day he became so excited and said, "Oooooo! I want to go with you! I need to find a costume too. It will be fun!" I thought it was funny how enthusiastic he was about everything and was happy to have him come with me. We decided that he would ride with me in my jeep and just leave his car in the parking lot. "I never went on a date with a girl who drove a jeep before." He laughed and said, "It's pretty badass." I basically laughed at everything he said and when I turned on my car I asked, "Do you like Prince? That's what's in the CD player right now." He said, "Girl, Prince completes me!" As we drove toward the first stop and were singing along to the Purple rain album, I asked him, "Do you have any idea what you want to be for Halloween?"
"I was thinking about being a super hero, or a Troll Doll, or maybe a gladiator." He started laughing and then said, "I will know when I see it. But I think Troll Doll would be so funny right? I could just find underwear or shorts that are the same color as my skin and a big ass florescent Troll Doll hair wig."

"Oh my God! That would be so funny. I don't think I have ever seen anyone be a Troll Doll. It would be cool to be a gladiator too." There was something about him that reminded me of someone I knew and I couldn't put my finger on it.

"Yeah, I would look sexy as a gladiator but I usually always do funny costumes. I always show off my abs though." He laughed at himself.

"I'm sure it makes for a good time on Halloween night."

We found nothing at the first three thrift stores we stopped at then on our fourth stop we sort of hit the jack pot. There is an ARC at Iliff and Quebec that always has good stuff. There were so many wedding dresses there that I literally had the pick of three poofy 80s style gowns and Zack and I had so much fun as I tried each one on and modeled it for him. We ended up choosing one that was striking and absolutely a match to the original Labyrinth ball gown because of its poofy sleeves, rhinestones and length. I wanted to see if there were white shoes of any kind that might work so I went to the shoe section and Zack went to look in the men's clothing. I didn't luck out in the shoe department, so I made my way to the home décor section just because I can't help myself. I love it there. I rounded a corner and something caught my eye. It was a huge white fluffy long faux fur pillow and it had a blue stain on it. I started laughing because I thought maybe Zack could somehow make a wig out of it. The blue part could be discarded. I picked it up to go show him and noticed that he wasn't in the men's section; he was in the women's section. I walked over to him and said, "Zack! I think I found something!" He turned around to look at me and in his hand was a light brown sleeveless women's leotard. We both started laughing hysterically. I had to bend over so I didn't pee my pants. "Oh my God!" he squealed, "I can make the troll hair out of that!"

"Yes! And I guess you found your body suit."

He laughed and held it up to himself, "Do you think it will work?" We couldn't stop laughing and again people were staring at us. He said, "Girl, I have to try this on, let's go." When he came out I almost passed out from laughter. You know the laugh when only air comes out and you can't catch your breath? That's what I was doing. I took a picture of him and sent it to his phone but secretly I also sent it to Shaun and I texted, "Can I please bring a date to your party?"

We made our purchases and went to the craft store so I could get ribbons for my hair and see if there was anything else that either one of us could use. He needed a crystal or something for is belly button like the Troll Dolls have. We found everything we needed including glitter lotion, which was for me and while we were there, Shaun texted back and said, "UHM Yes! He looks like a riot!" So, I asked if he wanted to be my date to a Halloween house party and he joyfully accepted the invitation.

The party was actually on November 2nd, because no one wanted to party on a Wednesday night when the majority of us have day jobs but we didn't care. It was almost the same. On Sunday Zack came to my house so we could work on our costumes together. He was so fun to hang out with. I just loved him. He went on and on about my paintings and said he wanted me to paint something for his living room. "Something really big." he said. We talked and laughed for hours as well as designed and put our costumes together. I still didn't know what shoes I was going to wear with my costume so when I told Zack he said, "Let's take a look in your closet." He went in and said, "Hello, Sarah Jessica Parker, do you have enough shoes?" Suddenly a light bulb went off in my head and I felt this wave of realization come over me. He reminded me of Chis, as in *my* Chrissy, Johnny's brother. Right after that I asked myself in my own head, "Oh my God, is he gay?" He turned around with my purple heels in his hands and said, "These are perfect and by the way, I love you. I don't know anyone who has purple heels. These are so hot!" Silently, to myself, I said, "Yuh, he is definitely gay."

As much as I knew he was gay, I knew he was right about those purple heels. They *were* perfect for this costume. When he left that night I called Shaun. She said, "Are you sure? Maybe he is just really cool. Maybe he just has really good taste."
We laughed and I said, "I mean, I could be wrong but let me recap this for you. I knew he reminded me of

someone and I finally figured out that he reminds me
of Chris. Also, he gets his eyebrows done."
"That doesn't mean anything, Blayne gets his
eyebrows done."
"I know but his whole face is done I think. He is
perfect, like a ken doll. Also, he calls me girl and
plays with my hair."
"So does every black guy either one of us have ever
dated."
"I know you're right, none of this is coming out right,
you just have to see it, it's different. He sang Prince
with me!"
"Bitch, the other day Johnny was singing "When
Doves Cry" in the shower."
After I finished laughing again, "I said, "You will
meet him on Friday and you will decide for yourself,
Chris and Felipe will be there, right?"
"Yes!" she yelled, "They will know."
"Oh, they will know. Don't say anything to them
about it, let's just see what they say when they meet
him"
"Ok, deal."

I got a call from Blayne that night right before I went
to bed. He said, "What are you doing for
Thanksgiving this year?" "Nothing." I said, "Shaun
and Johnny have plans with his family this year." He
said, "Good, I think Peony and I are going to go there.
Is that cool? Mom is going to Cape May with a
couple of her girlfriends and Peony said she would
rather go to Colorado than go to Scranton."
I screamed! "Yes!" I was jumping up and down.
"Yes, yes, yes! I'm so excited! Maybe we can go

somewhere cool for the weekend, or at least for Thanksgiving itself."

"Yeah! That's what I was thinking, a cool restaurant or Hotel or something. Think about it and I will let you know as soon as I know if it's happening." He asked me how everything was going and I made myself laugh because I told him, "I'm fine, doing well, I am currently dating a gay man. How is everything going for you?"

"What? A gay man?"

"Yes, I'm pretty sure he is gay." I told him the whole story and he agreed with me.

"That dude is definitely gay. Well, good, I would rather you date a gay guy than a straight guy." We laughed and then he said, "He sounds perfect, loves to shop, loves shoes, isn't going to have sex with you and then never call you back."

I laughed, "He's the man of my dreams."

I was so excited for the party. My costume was amazing and Zack spent the whole week texting me and telling me how much he was looking forward to it. The night of the party he met me at my apartment and said he would be the designated driver because he rarely drank. We got ready together and his costume was one of the funniest things I had ever seen. He was prancing around my apartment in it flexing in the mirror and asking me if I could tell that he wasn't wearing any underwear. He said, "I don't want there to be a line." By the time we headed out to Shaun's my sides hurt from laughing so hard. We made a grand entrance and probably about half of the guests were already there, including Chris and Felipe. I introduced Zack to Shaun and Johnny first. They both hugged him and laughed hard at his costume, and Chris and Felipe came over and I introduced them all. Chris was doting over my costume and telling me how much I looked like Sarah and how much he loves David Bowie's package in Labyrinth. Then Zack said, "Doesn't she look hot? She was having a hard time figuring out which shoes to wear and when I saw those purple heels I was like, hello, these are perfect!" We all laughed and as Shaun took Zack into the kitchen to meet some other friends, Chris whispered in my ear, "Cherry, your boyfriend is gayer than a unicorn in a gay pride parade on the way to Cher's house for the after party."

I had to put that conversation on hold so I could say hi to everyone there, like Sarah and her boyfriend Corey. I knew Chris would catch it fast and confirm everything I had suspected. I couldn't help but wonder if Zach was in denial about being gay, or if he was really not gay just really well rounded, or is he just oblivious? Maybe he is bisexual? I grabbed Chris again and said, "Help me out with this. We just met, he isn't my boyfriend, I was pretty sure he was gay. I wonder if he needs help or is in the closet or what. Maybe you can figure this out. You will like him, he is basically you." Chris replied with, "Girl, I'm on it! Lets get this gay to come out and play!" I just laughed and shook my head. I cannot imagine a world without gay men.

I was talking to Sarah and Johnny came up to us and said, "Cherry, you got the wrong tone, it's all wrong.

Let me ask you a question. Does your mother sew? Get her to sew this!" in his best Christopher Walken voice. It's never not funny. He was wearing a yellow suit and had a grey wig styled like Walken's hair. I was actually pretty impressed with his work. Shaun looked great as a Stepford wife and Sarah and Corey were a lady cop and an inmate wearing a black and white striped jumpsuit. Other than Zack, the funniest and most creative costume was Chris and Felipe who were both dressed as bumble bees. They came with their friend, Ryan who was dressed as a King. Get it? Bee Bee King. I never saw bees so cute in my life.

We were all having a great time and Zack was a social butterfly making friends with everyone. He was spending a lot of time with Chris, Felipe, and Ryan and I was glad about that. I felt like he was the best date I could have ever had for a Halloween party at my best friend's house. About an hour after we arrived Mark showed up. I hadn't seen him since the beginning of summer but had texted with him a bunch of times since we officially broke up. We were absolutely still friends and he seemed to be doing well. He was still single. When he saw me he came over and hugged me. "Wow, Labyrinth? You look great."

"Thank you, yes! It's good to see you, how are you?"

"I'm doing really well. Yeah. Nothing new to tell you."

He was dressed as a doctor wearing scrubs covered in fake blood and a stethoscope. I pointed at it and he said, "I borrowed it from my mom. This isn't the first time I have worn this for Halloween. I have been so busy lately with work. I had no time to plan for this party."

"Well, who cares, you look great."

"Thanks," he smiled, "So do you. Are you seeing anyone?"

"Not really, my date is the Troll Doll." I pointed to him, "I think he is gay though. Doesn't matter, I adore him." As we laughed I added, "Well, you need someone who you can be your true self in front of."

As we laughed I looked at him and he said, "I'm so happy to see you, Cherry, and I am still so glad we are friends."

"I am too. I really am." I hugged him again.

I can honestly say that though it was great to see Mark, there wasn't a single bit of old feelings popping up for me. It was undeniably a closed book. It had always been easy for me to stay friends with someone I dated as long as they weren't a complete asshole. It is rare that they don't try to come back, even if only for sex. I wasn't going to do that with Mark. Not after what happened the last time. I didn't avoid him at all but I completely ignored his flirting and just acted oblivious to it. He was just as charming as the first night we hung out and wasn't easy to resist. But, I did it.

Shaun put on "As the World Falls Down" by David Bowie from the Labyrinth soundtrack for me so I could wander around the party, doe eyed with my mouth open like Sarah did during the ball scene. We laughed so hard. We also had real entertainment when Chris, Felipe, and Ryan did a lip-syncing act to BB King, "Everyday I Have the Blues". Ryan did the fake singing with a cucumber as a microphone and Chris and Felipe were back up dancers. It was hysterical. I think that is probably my favorite BB King song. The cover that John Mayer did on his "Where the Light Is: Live in Los Angeles" album is amazing and the sole reason I decided I liked him. I was fortunate to have seen him in concert and he slayed live.

The party was a great success and there was no doubt to anyone that Zack had a good time. He exchanged numbers with Ryan because he said he was going to "play tennis" with him. Chris assured me at the end of the night that he was 100% certain that Zack was gay and he bet me that by Thanksgiving he would admit it to himself and tell me all about it. He said, "Ryan wants to play with more than just his tennis balls." "Oh my God, Chris." I laughed as we hugged goodbye. He's so crazy and amazing.

Zack hugged every single person at the party and kissed Shaun on the cheek. He said, "Shaun, you're the hostess with the mostess, thank you for having me and thank you all for making me feel like an old friend. I haven't had this much fun in forever." The whole way back to my apartment he went on and on about how great the party was and how lucky I was to have such an amazing circle of friends. He was right. Shaun and I were so lucky. We were Colorado transplants, hated by some and loved by everyone else and we had a circle like we had lived there our entire lives. I wouldn't want it any other way.

Zack was leaving on that Monday for a trip that he had earned at work and was going to be gone for two weeks on vacation. I was excited for him. He was going to Saint Thomas, where I have always wanted to go, and said he got an amazing deal because it is just after hurricane season and just before prices start going up. Shaun and I had been to the Keys when we graduated high school and I loved it more than anywhere I have been. The islands anywhere are my kind of vacation. When we got back to my apartment he hugged me really hard and kissed me on the cheek just like he did Shaun and said, "I just love you, Cherry. We are going to be friends forever. I am so glad I met you!"

"Awe, I am so glad I met you too, Zack, you make sure and send me a post card from the Virgin Islands, I am so jealous."

He got back in his car and said, "I promise I will, I'll see you soon!" I waved goodbye and took a deep breath and exhaled. What a night.

Chapter 16 Coffee Talk

As appealing as it almost is to date a gay man, I was back on line looking for some new prospects. I never thought of it as prospecting while I was doing it, but it seems fitting to call it that now since that is exactly what it was. I was interested in a guy named Erik who had messaged me a couple times. I actually thought he might be a little mysterious. He would ask me a lot but tell me very little, and take forever to answer back. I wasn't getting anywhere with him at all and I figured I would probably just give up.

On Sunday morning I was craving espresso so I walked to the Starbucks in my neighborhood. It was a cold day. I remember realizing winter was finally here and that it was really windy because when I walked in, I made a little bit of a scene when the door flew open and my hair flew over my face. Shaun and I always fake having the wind blow our hair all sexy when we walk into a room like a model in a music video, or something that makes everyone turn their heads to look at us. That was what happened except it wasn't sexy, it was a mess, but everyone looked at me anyway and one guy came over to help me pick up a bunch of napkins that blew off the table closest to the door. I said thank you five different times and fixed my hair as he did most of the picking up. He was gorgeous. He was really tall, had blue eyes, a shaved head, he was wearing gym clothes, and was extremely muscular. I couldn't help but stare.

The line was long and he was right in front of me. He said, "It's cold today, huh. Seems like it hasn't really been cold yet until today."

I looked at him and smiled, "Yeah, I was just thinking that. I can't believe how windy it is. I walked over from my place and misjudged the weather."

"Oh yeah? I live right over there." He pointed at the apartment complex next to mine. "I go to the gym next door."

I knew the gym. I had a membership there too and probably went like five times total since I got it.
"I have a membership there. I haven't been able to go there lately, been so busy with work." I didn't know why I was lying to this guy but I laughed to myself and decided I was going to go ahead and flirt with him.
"I'm a gym nut, can't help it. I work the night shift so I always go in the morning after work. I have Sunday and Monday off. I come here for a coffee on Sunday before I go to the gym. It's my Friday, you know? I'm usually totally beat on Sundays."

"What do you do for work?"

"Oh, DPD." He answered confidently, and was obviously proud.

"Oh, really? Denver PD, that's awesome. I used to work at the DA's office but now I work for a private attorney who does corporate law."

"Sweet. Lawyers drive me nuts." He joked. I just smiled at him. We stood there silently for a couple minutes as we continued to wait in line and then he said, "Where are you from, Jersey? You have an accent."

"Yeah, I'm from Long Island. Born and raised."

"Cool, cool." He looked away and then looked back at me and said, "I'm from Rifle. You know where that is? The Western Slope?"

"I think I do, west of Vail and everything? Toward Grand Junction right? I haven't been out there before. I really want to go to Ouray. I heard it was beautiful. Is it near Ouray?"

"Ouray is like three hours south of Rifle, near Telluride."

"Yeah! Telluride, I want to go there. I went to Steamboat in September, it was pretty cool." I had been to the mountain towns so far but hadn't done much more exploration of the Western Slope as he called it. He said excuse me as he ordered his coffee and then after I ordered mine he continued talking to me. "My name is Trent by the way." He reached out and shook my hand.
"Nice to meet you, Trent, I'm Cherry."
I shook back and he looked side to side and then back at me and said, "You serious?"

I laughed and said, "Yep, that's my name." He threw his head back in laughter and said, "Well, Cherry, that is a sexy name and a first for me." He already had his coffee and stood with me as I waited for mine. When it came he grabbed it and handed it to me. As he did he noticed and pointed at "Cherry" written in sharpie on the side of the cup and I laughed and winked at him. He flirtatiously smiled at me and watched me laugh for a second and then said, "You wanna sit down with me?"

"Sure." I said and followed him. This was so New York. Sitting down at a coffee shop after meeting a guy seven minutes earlier. I loved it.

"I've seen a lot of weird or uncommon names in my line of work."

"Oh, I bet!"

"A couple weeks ago I ran a guy whose last name was Assman."

I laughed, "Man, I love that name, is it English?" We both laughed and I said, "How do you say that on the radio?"

"I just spell it phonetically, Adam, Sam, Sam, Mary, Adam, Nora."

"Oh, right! I bet everyone got a good laugh out of it. I have always been interested in Law Enforcement and Dispatch. They are honorable professions. And, you know, my boss, the Lawyer, he is 100% pro-law enforcement. He said he doesn't trust criminal defense attorneys."

Trent laughed kind of loud that time and said, "Then I have something in common with your boss."

I had such a fantastic time talking with him; I was completely attracted. He was like a cliché. He was gorgeous, first of all, but aside from all that cookie-cutter-ness, I have to admit, what I really liked about him most was how inquisitive he was. He asked me so many questions. I loved answering them. He was easy to talk to and I bet I would have told him anything he wanted to know. My father used to always say the same thing to people who asked a lot of questions, he said it to me when I was little too during my "why?" to everything stage. He would say, "What are you writing a book?" and "What are you a cop?" When I was little I didn't get it and only figured it was funny because he would always laugh at himself after he said it and my mom would say, "William!" But, she would always laugh when he said it to their friends or to random people we didn't know. Blayne, Shaun and I love saying it to people to honor my father's amazing sense of humor. So, Trent was a cop and he was naturally inquisitive. He was an observer too. He sat in the corner of the room and every time the door opened he looked closely at the person or people coming or going. He was a multi-tasker. He never skipped a beat during his conversation with me. I got the feeling that he was in complete control in some way and I found it exceptionally sexy.

"Let's exchange numbers." He said and he picked up his cell phone, "Give me yours and I will text you so you have mine."

"Sure." I liked his confidence. He was more confident than me. He didn't ask me, he told me to give him my number, and I did it.

"I like your style, Cherry, we should get together soon. I gotta hit the gym," he said, getting up and picking up his sling bag, "Cherry Pie. Does anyone ever call you that?" he laughed as if he had just come up with something I had never heard before.

"Never." I replied and winked at him again. He laughed again and as he walked toward the door, he sang, "She's my Cherry Pie!" under his breath. Hated to see him go but I loved watching him leave. Him *and* his perfect Adam Sam Sam.

Later that night I got a text from Trent that said, "Hey, Cherry Pie."

I filled up with butterflies and texted back, "Hey there."

"Let's hang out tomorrow, want to?"

"Sure! What do you want to do?"

"Ever been to the Snug? Let's split a cab so we can get some beers. You do drink beer don't you?"

I thought, for him, I would drink Colt 45. I answered, "Love the Snug. Meet me any time after 5:30 PM, apartment 2180."

"Sweet." I'll be there at 6. Goodnight."

"Night." I answered and kept myself from sending smiley face emojis, though I wanted to.

The Snug is actually called "The Irish Snug" and is off of Colfax near the cool old neon signs like at the Bluebird Theatre. I love it over there. I had been to the Snug probably twice before and liked it a lot. I have always felt comfortable in Irish Pubs. Shaun is completely Irish and I always told her that I identify as Irish". I think a lot of us do. Everyone wishes they were at least a little bit Irish, especially on St. Patrick's Day. Maybe Trent was. Imagine going all the way to Denver, Colorado to meet an Irish cop when they are around every corner in all of New York. Either way, I was excited to pieces about my Monday night date with a cop I met in a coffee shop.

Finally I heard from Blayne about Thanksgiving. He said he and Peony were definitely coming out. I was so psyched. Right away I started searching for ideas on what to do while they were here. I was focused on going to Aspen. I had wanted to stay there for a while and thought if I could find a good deal and a cool restaurant that was serving Thanksgiving dinner then Blayne might agree to pay for most of it. Who doesn't want to be able to take their east coast girlfriend to a Hotel in Aspen, Colorado for the Holidays? I found a place called "The Gant". It had great reviews, good prices, and two bedroom suites, which would be perfect to fit the three of us and still have privacy. I also found a website that listed restaurants that were serving Thanksgiving diner. After I looked them all up I chose a place called Ajax

Tavern, which is located at the "Little Nell Hotel".
The Little Nell is where I would stay if I were rich.
It's amazing. Ajax was serving a three-course meal
for $45 a person. That was also one of the best prices
I found. I was so excited I called Blayne and pitched
my idea to him. He was relaying the information to
Peony in the background and she was squealing "Oh
my God, oh my God!" Blayne laughed at her and
said, "I guess that's a yes."
"Yaye!" I cheered in his ear.
"Ok, the two of you need to calm down. Yeah, this is
a great idea, nice work, Cherry."

After we hung up, I made all of the required
reservations with Blayne's name and credit card and
went to bed in a blissful mood.

On Monday I told Ben that I was going out with a
DPD cop and he said, "Oh, Cherry, tell me Denver's
finest don't have to go on line to meet women! What
is the world coming to?" He was always so dramatic.
I laughed and said, "No, I met him the old fashioned
way, by chance in a coffee shop." He said, "Well,
imagine that. Coffee talk. I didn't even think that
happened anymore, I'm proud of you." Well, thank
you, bossy" I said. I could not wait to get out of work
that day. It was dragging on and on. Trent texted me
a couple times to say hi and confirm our plans and I
also heard from Zack who was on his way to Saint
Thomas. He sent me a couple selfies with his friends
and told me he was going to wear the leotard he wore
for Halloween to the beach. Man, I love that guy.

At 5:00 PM sharp I sped home to get ready. I was thinking I shouldn't dress up too much. We were going to a Pub and this was never officially labeled a date. He might just want to be beer drinking buddies with me. That would be fine, I had been adding a lot of good looking men to my friends list lately. No matter what I wore, I had to look good. Better than I looked when he met me. I went with a form fitting black top, dark jeans and black leather riding boots. I wore dark eye make-up and clear lip gloss. I looked good and I felt good. Trent showed up at 5:55 and I invited him in so we could call a cab. He looked good in real clothes, you know, as apposed to gym clothes. He smelled good too.

I said, "Welcome to my flat, please make yourself at home." He laughed, "You are so polite, Cherry Pie." He gave me a big hug and said, "Damn, you look great!" I thanked him and kind of fell limp in his arms for a split second and focused on the muscles wrapped around me. As I called the cab company he went over to my fridge and asked if I had any bottled water. He went ahead and grabbed one as I talked to the dispatcher and, I nodded my head. I watched him wander around, he looked at my paintings and at a couple pictures I have of Blayne and me and my mom, and from Shaun's wedding. As I hung up I said, "They are ten minutes away."
"Who's this?" and pointed at Blayne.
"That's my brother." I walked over to him and said, "This is my mom, this is my best friend, Shaun, this is us when we graduated, and when we were little."

He looked at me and said, "This red-headed chick is named Shaun?"

"Yes."

He laughed and said, "That's pretty hot, imagine two chicks with totally unusual chick names being best friends."

Like I always do, I laughed and said, "You're so funny." We went outside to wait for the cab after a few minutes and he said, "I'll pay for everything tonight if you get the cabby."

"Deal."

I really liked how easy he made everything. He was a natural leader. When we got to our table at the Pub I asked him, "What's your birthday, if you don't mind me asking, are you an Aries?"

"Holy shit, weirdo, how did you know that? March 20th."

I laughed at him calling me a weirdo and explained, "My birthday is March 23rd and I just know Aries. It was obvious to me. I dig astrology."

"That's pretty cool, I don't think I could ever guess someone's sign but I definitely have read about my sign and the descriptions are pretty accurate. So, we were born 3 days apart, what year?"

"1977, best year ever."

He held out his fist to bump and said, "Yeah, me too, isn't that funny. Everyone I have ever known who was born in '77 says the same thing. You think people born in other years think they are as cool as we think we are?"

"I don't know, that's funny, they couldn't be right? '77 *is* actually the best."

We had a great time. We tried several different beers; he goes there often, so he recommended a couple. We shared two different dishes, both of which were delicious. I realized I really liked the Snug and that I should go there much more than I did. Snug actually means a private room in a Pub where a patron (usually women) could go to privately drink and not be seen in the bar. It's where a cop would go for a few sips, or maybe a priest back in the day. I'm also sure couples could be found "snuggling" and necking in between their drinks in there. It's a romantic idea. I was thinking about it when suddenly Trent said. "So, Cherry pie, I'm just going to come right out and say this." I looked up at him and gave him every bit of my attention. He continued, "You're fine as hell and I would love to have sex with you. I am not looking for a committed relationship I just broke up with my ex of three years and I have a busted heart over it. I'm certain that I like you and that we are going to be friends and I think it would be cool if we also had sex sometimes. I work constantly and when I'm not working or sleeping I am at the gym. I can't offer you any more than that." He took a big drink of his beer and said, "That's what up." I know I stared at him wide eyed at first and this is exactly what I thought in that very moment; YES, PLEASE.

I wasn't offended, I wasn't shocked, I thought it was cool that he was so direct, especially for a white guy, and I thought that that was exactly what I needed, a new friend…with whom I have sex sometimes. It reminded me of "The Witches of Eastwick" when

Alexandra, played by Cher meets Daryl Van Horne, played by Jack Nicholson for the first time and after lunch he "seduces" her by just coming right out and saying in so many words, "Hey let's have sex, I like sex after lunch." At first she is disgusted but then he puts a little spell on her and she jumps into bed with him. I love that movie, and I love Cher and Jack Nicholson. So, I looked at Trent and thought, "I am going to Daryl Van Horne the hell out of you." But what I really did was put my napkin on the table and said, "When can we start?"

Chapter 17 Check Please

We didn't wait until we got home to be all over each other, we waited until we got into the back seat of the cab. He pulled me over so I was sitting right next to him and he started squeezing my thigh. He reached around me and turned me toward him so he could kiss me and I put my hand on his leg and brushed softly against his obvious erection. He was so sexy. He kissed me hard like he had been waiting to do it forever. He squeezed me and pulled me right against him so close I could feel his heart pounding in his chest. What a complete turn on. I was on the edge. I said, "Who's apartment are we going to?" he said, "Doesn't matter, we can go to mine, I have a king size bed." He talked into my mouth and never stopped kissing me as we made our plans. He stopped and said, "I have to calm down or I'm going to get us arrested in this cabby. You're so sexy." I giggled and wiped his kisses off of my mouth.
"You're sexy."
"You shut your mouth and stay over there. " We laughed. It was so fun being so sexually tuned up and trying to keep our hands to ourselves when all the while we knew we were on our way to have sex for the first time with each other. It was invigorating.

We pulled up and he took my hand to help me out of the cab. I was walking, weak in the knees like a baby deer, so I laughed as I let him pull me up the stairs to his apartment. He unlocked the door and as he led me in he whispered, "You get in there." I scanned the apartment quickly since I hadn't been there before, and noticed that it looked just like mine. It was almost the same but it smelled like cologne and was a lot more contemporary. He pushed me against the door, pulled my shirt off over my head and pulled my bra down and started kissing my stomach and my breasts. God, it felt so good. He picked me up and threw me over his shoulder and took me to his bedroom. I laughed and pretended to try to fight him off. He threw me down on the bed and jumped on me. I started undoing his jeans and pulled up his shirt as he kissed me and kept saying, "Mmmm, so sexy." I was so turned on by him and from the anticipation of this moment that I just wanted it to happen. I took off all of my clothes myself and just looked at him. I wanted him so bad. "Get a condom." I whispered. "You ready?" he asked playfully and reached into his nightstand. He flipped me over on my stomach. "You want this?" he said. "Yes, yes…I want you." I looked back at him and he grabbed my hair and pulled me up against him by my waist. Oh, God. He felt so good. He was so strong and put me wherever he wanted me. He was amazing. I hadn't had sex that good in a long time.

I fell asleep for a couple hours. Eventually he woke me up and said, "Do you want to sleep here or go home, we probably should have gone to your apartment since you have to work in the morning." "Oh, yeah, I should probably go home." "I'll take you because I'm gonna go to the gym. "Oh, thank you, perfect." I gathered my clothes from all over the bedroom. He just sat on the bed and laughed at me. "You are so fine, Cherry Pie." He smacked my naked butt as I pulled my jeans on.

"You are the sexiest neighbor I have ever had."

He laughed and said, "Convenient isn't it?"

I was so tired at work the next day, of course, and Ben made fun of me all day. He kept saying, "Someone stayed out too late on a school night." I made coffee three times. I thought about Trent all day and hadn't heard from him, but I knew that he was sleeping. I wondered how often we would see each other at this point. I couldn't imagine minding if he wanted to stop by every single night before work but he was just another "Jareth" trying to distract me and I knew I had to keep him out of my mind as much as I could.

When I got home that night I fell asleep right away and didn't even care about eating dinner. Trent texted me before he went to work and said, "Cherry Pie, you sexy thing, I'm on my way to work. Keep in touch, looking forward to our next rendezvous." I answered him right away and said, "I will, be safe. I'm going to sleep, someone kept me up too late last night XXX." He answered with a winky face.

As I fell asleep I imagined him all over me in the cab and how sexy it was. I was always good at having a friend with benefits, or as I like to call it, a "Special Friend". I felt bad for him that he was recovering from a broken heart. I also found it extremely attractive that he was so honest with me about what he wanted. I wondered what he saw in me that made him think I was a safe bet, that I was a girl without any crazy. I decided that eventually, when we were closer, I would ask him. Just so I could start putting it on my resume.

For the next several days Trent and I saw each other almost every single night. As I was enjoying my unattached sexual trysts, Shaun was growing increasingly concerned. I hadn't spoken about Trent to Blayne because I didn't feel like getting my chops busted. All he was interested in talking about anyway was the Thanksgiving trip so I never brought it up. Shaun was worried that I would get attached or that I wasn't focused, or that I was adding to my "number" recklessly. She kept telling me, "You're one guy away from having sex with more guys this year than I have had sex with since I was 16."
"I know, I know." I kept telling her, "Everything is cool, I'm still single and looking, Trent is just filling a void."
"That's not the only thing he is filling."
"Jealous!"
"As if, "Cherry Pie"." She made fun of Trent's nickname for me, and continued, " Just tell me you'll go on line and check, please, to see if there is anyone you might be interested in meeting." "Ok, I promise."

Before Thanksgiving week, I went on a couple dates with guys I met on line for Shaun's sake. Just so she didn't think I was settling to be a booty call. To this day I don't even remember their names. They were forgettable. I remember that one date took me out the Saturday night before Thanksgiving and Trent texted me that he wanted to hang out before he went to work. I told him I had plans and that I wouldn't be home until after he left. He said, "Oh man! What are you, on a date?"

"Yes, as a matter of fact."

"Ok, let's hang out tomorrow night?"

As I texted him back, "Yes." I thought about how much fun it was to be able to tell the guy with whom I had an intimate thing going that I was out on a date; he didn't get weird, just remained cool about the agreement that we had. It let me know that he really had no feelings and wasn't actually trying to stop me from dating other people. He was truly a FWB and I didn't have a single negative thing to say about him. I was still hoping that I wouldn't end up "catching feelings" as people love to say about situations like mine.

On Sunday morning when Trent got home from the gym, he texted me and asked me to come over at 5 PM, wake him up, and we could order food and hang out. He left a key for me under his doormat. I felt like he might want me to "wake him up" wake him up. So, at just before five, I went into his apartment, snuck across the living room floor and into his bedroom to find him sleeping. I took off all of my clothes and got into his bed. He had those really thick black-out curtains in his bedroom so that he could sleep during the day easier so it was very dark in there. When he realized I was there at first he jumped.

I felt bad just because I was sure he wasn't recently used to anyone waking him up that way but I just whispered, "Trent." He put his arm around me and mumbled, "Mmmm, Cherry Pie." Even though Shaun thought it was lame that he called me Cherry Pie, I happened to like it. I hadn't liked it before from other guys but when he said it I knew he was being funny and to me that was sexy. Then he said, "Let's have morning sex." Well, at least it was morning for one of us.

We ordered dinner and he told me about the crazy calls he went to the night before. I could listen to him talk about work for days; it was so crazy. Sometimes what he told me sounded so incredibly dangerous and intense, sometimes so stupid, and sometimes the saddest things I had ever heard. It is an emotional roller coaster, being a Police Officer. I was sure it is also like that for Dispatchers, and Firefighters, and Medics. Sarah is a nurse and works at St. Joseph's emergency room. The stories she tells are crazy, too. I have so much respect for people who do jobs like all those and serve the public no matter how physically dangerous or detrimental to their mental health it may be.

As we were eating our food Trent said, "You know, Cherry, I was so jealous last night when you told me you were on a date." I was surprised and just laughed and pushed him in his shoulder. He laughed back at me and playfully pushed my shoulder too and said, "I was. I know you're looking for a serious thing. When you find it we won't be able to hang out like this anymore and we definitely won't get to have sex and I really like you."

"I know. I like you too. We will always be friends though. Don't be so dramatic."

He laughed at me again and sang, "She's my Cherry Pie, cool drink of water such a sweet surprise. Tastes so good makes a grown man cry. Sweet Cherry Pieeeee-yeah." I could never help but laugh when people sang that to me and I said, "Mm, the lyrical wizardry of "Warrant" just cannot be beat."

Chapter 18 What Happens in Aspen

I was beyond excited to pick Blayne and Peony up at the airport on Wednesday. I got lucky because Ben wanted to close his office up at lunch that day and start the holiday weekend early. That made it possible for me to pick them up instead of them having to get a cab. I packed the night before and brought my bag with me making it easy for us to just head up to Aspen early and maybe beat traffic on I-70. This would be my first time meeting Peony, as you know, and I was looking forward to it. Maybe she was the one.

As soon as I saw the two of them in the airport they weren't smiling. Ever since we were little, my brother and I knew what the other one was feeling based on certain looks we make. We are like fraternal twins. When Blayne saw me he looked at me in a way that I knew. He was annoyed. They were standing by the belt waiting for their luggage. I ran up to them, hugged Blayne and hung on his shoulders like I do when I haven't seen him in a while. He's about 6'2" and I'm 5'8" so next to him I feel short. He whispered in my ear, "We're on each other's nerves." I let go of his shoulders and played it off like I didn't hear anything and hugged Peony. "So good to finally meet you!" I said and squeezed her, whether she wanted me to or not. She was very pretty. Very put together. Judging by her purse, and carryon bag she was a "logo-pattern girl". This is what Shaun and I lovingly refer to the girls whose expensive purse is covered with the designer logo over and over all over

it. A coach bag covered in C's. You know what I
mean. You could never look at these types of pieces
and *not* know what it was. You become a walking
advertisement, a human billboard. Forgive us, but it
just isn't our style. One logo is enough in my very
humble opinion. There were two checked suitcases
and my brother's was black and Peony's was a Louis
Vuitton that matched her carry on. I remember my
mother telling Shaun and I when we were teenagers
and she overheard us saying we didn't like LV gear
because of the "repeat logo pattern" that our
"husband's will appreciate that when you don't want
to spend four grand on a suitcase". I could see Blayne
seeing me see, if you know what I mean. But, to each
their very own and I am not altogether too
judgmental.

I think it's funny picking people up at DIA who have
never been to Colorado before and are picturing the
great Rocky Mountains. You have to explain to them
why it looks like Kansas. I told Peony, "Just wait,
you're in for a mind blowing drive right through the
heart of the Rockies." Blayne added, "Yeah, babe,
it's insane." It was only about 2 PM when we got
back into Denver and onto I70 headed west. I filled
Blayne in on current events in my life and he sat in
the back seat so Peony would have a front row view.
I admit that I am always so excited when I bring a
friend over the first entrance into the Rockies near the
Buffalo Herd Overlook, Genesee Park, and the
Sleeper House on Genesee Mountain, which could
very well be the coolest house I have ever seen in my
life. People always gasp and I am like a tour guide

pointing out everything I love. I expect they will it love too. Peony said, "I thought they would be bigger." I looked at her; she was looking out the window. Then I looked at Blayne in the rear view and he was rolling his eyes. Red flag on the play, coach. I couldn't believe my ears. Well, maybe she wasn't the one.

After that I really sort of stopped being a tour guide unless Peony asked me a question. She was nice to me, not rude, just a little bit unappreciative and negative. Two very attractive qualities in a woman, I'm sure, for some men, but not for Blayne and I was beginning to think that this one might not even make it to Christmas. Blayne and I continued to talk and laugh and I tried to involve Peony by asking her questions about herself. She was pleasant but I still hadn't heard her laugh nor did I witness even a shred of a personality. I was dying to get Blayne alone so I could ask him what the hell was happening. Finally she needed to go to the bathroom so I pulled into a McDonalds. When you're on the road and you don't need gas remember that a fast food restaurant bathroom is potentially much cleaner and safer than a gas station bathroom. I don't know why, but those are the rules. They get robbed far less than convenience stores. I like the odds. She wouldn't go in without Blayne, so while he was in there, waiting for her, I texted him. "What's up with your girlfriend?"

"She's being a bitch, I don't know what her problem is, she has been like this all week."

"So this isn't her normal personality?"
"Actually it is. She is being quieter than usual probably because she is out of her element."

"Does she know I will destroy her if she keeps it up?"

"Lol."

It was just before 5 PM, and the sun was setting as we pulled into Aspen. It looked a little like Steamboat, but what I noticed then was that it seemed a little less populated with locals and ranchers and a little more commercial and celebrity friendly. I'm sure the people of Steamboat think they lucked out on that note. We were all feeling sleepy and ready to get settled in for the night, so we made our way to the Hotel. It was a cool place. Blayne was proud of my choice and kept saying, "Everyone is so nice here, how do you handle it? It's amazing." Our room was beautiful. I, of course, chose the second bedroom and gave them the suite. I liked where my room was, right off the kitchen and front door. I opened one of the three bottles of wine that I brought with me from home and changed into comfy clothes. It was very cold outside and I loved having a snuggly room in the mountains that was basically like a condo. I called the front desk and asked them if they needed to turn on the fireplace or if I could do it myself. In a thick Texas accent the lady said, "Honey, we'll send someone up, you just sit tight." I love that accent. She could have told me to do anything and I would have done it as long as she said, "Bless your heart"

after. I yelled in to Blayne, "They are coming up to start the fire place. I have wine, Peony."
"Ok, be out in a minute."

I checked my phone and had a whole bunch of messages. Chris, Shaun, Mom, and Trent. I texted Mom first and told her we were safe and sound in Aspen. Then I texted Trent who said, "I miss you, have fun, see you Monday." Then I looked at Shaun's message, "OMG, Cherry, Chris is trying to get in touch with you- your aren't going to believe it!!!" So, I texted, "Ok." And then looked at Chris's message. She was right. He had actually sent me about five texts. I called him right back and when he answered I said, "Hey Chrissy, sorry, I'm with Blayne, we were driving to Aspen, what's up?"
"Oh my God, I forgot. Do you remember Ryan that wanted to teach your friend Zack how to play tennis?"
"Yes, I do."
"You are never going to believe this. Zack got him some kind of discount on a flight and flew him down to wherever he was on vacation, The Virgin Islands or whatever, and they *hooked up*! I can't even believe it!" He laughed hard and said, "Can you believe it? He says they're dating!"
"What? You're kidding me!"

The maintenance man came to turn on the fireplace so I quickly got off the phone and told Chris I would follow up with him about it later. I was still laughing as I opened the door, the guy must have thought I was insane. Finally, Blayne came out and he showed him how to do it so we didn't have to call him again for help. Meanwhile, I was texting Chris and we went back and forth about how we knew it and I called it and "Inter-gay-tion". When the guy left, Blayne whispered to me, "Peony is going to take a nap." I decided not to say anything snarky about it and just spend time with him. It was my ultimate goal anyway. I told Blayne the whole story about Zack and Ryan. We laughed and laughed. I was so happy about it. I could not wait to see Zack and wondered when he would tell me. Blayne and I shared that bottle of wine and talked about all of my stories of dating and caught up on what we hadn't talked about over the last couple of months until about 9 PM when Peony came out.

"Can we go to the hot tub?' She interrupted us. "Sure. I would love to do that." I stopped talking and answered her. Blayne looked at her and was obviously appalled at how rude she was, but like I said before, my main focus was to have fun and hang out with my brother, so I chose to ignore her sour attitude and make the best of it. Blayne looked at me and said, "Can we drink down there?"
"Yes, but let's use travelors instead of glasses." We popped open another bottle filled up our cups and headed down to the pools. What a cool place it was. There was a couple just leaving and they said, "If you're quiet you can usually stay out past the curfew time, this place is pretty lax." We thanked them for letting us know but figured 10 o'clock would be late enough. Both Peony and I were wearing UGGS. In times like that, UGGS really meant something to me.

Surfers back in the day would wear them to keep their feet warm when they got out of the ocean. They weren't even really meant for harsh winter boots. It was cold and we were getting into a hot tub and when we got out I was going to happy to put my feet in my warm cushy boots.

I had so much fun. Blayne and I told old stories to Peony that I thought might make her laugh and understand Blayne through my eyes. I tried to get to know her but she just wouldn't really speak. I reminded her that every sip of wine was like five sips because she had just gone from sea level to 7900 feet. She didn't understand, so Blayne had to explain it to her again. He had a different way of speaking to her than I had ever heard him speak to a woman before. It is hard to explain, but it almost reminded me of the way my father would speak to me when I was a teenager. Picture dad walking on eggshells a little, because of the possibility of a pubescent hormonal outburst, but also being a person who was responsible for me and who was older and wiser and had only the intention of trying to help me navigate through life. It had become increasingly obvious that I had to speak with Blayne privately to get a clearer picture of what was going on because I couldn't imagine him enjoying himself over the last several months spent with Peony.

On Thursday, Thanksgiving Day, we went to downtown Aspen and walked around looking for brunch or lunch. Peony seemed to lighten up a little and seemed to really like it. We spent a couple hours going to shops and exploring everything that we could. Blayne bought her some earrings by Harmony Scott at her old shop. I got some postcards and some little turquoise stud earrings. Blayne tried to buy them for me but I wouldn't allow it. I told him he had done enough. Peony chimed in and said, "You can buy me something else if you're feeling generous." He just laughed her off and reminded us of the time.

Once we got back to the condo to get ready to go out for our feast, I could see that Peony was back to her "self" that she had been when I met her and I came to the conclusion that maybe she was only happy when Blayne was buying her presents. I was actually starting to get annoyed and found it less and less easy to remain cool about it. I could hear her raising her voice while they were in their room getting ready and Blayne kept saying, "Baby, relax."
She started yelling, "I forgot my shoes that go with what I am wearing tonight, Blayne. Don't tell me to relax."
"Hey, you have two other pairs of black heels, both of which will look good with that dress. If my sister can hear you yelling at me I'm going to be pissed, you're embarrassing yourself."
"I really don't care if your sister can hear me, Blayne."
"Well, I do. You've been rude as hell since we got off the plane and haven't shown a single bit of appreciation for this entire trip that she planned, so she could hang out with me and meet you. Don't make me regret bringing you out here."

After that was silence. I was ready so I grabbed my laptop and went down to the lobby for some coffee and maybe they would hash it all out and get over it while I was gone.

While my brother spent his afternoon being treated like a chump by his girlfriend, I at least tried to enjoy myself a little by logging on and seeing what I had been missing from my Denver dating scene. I had a message from a guy named Dean. It said, "Your eyes are incredible. Dean." I decided to look at his profile. He was very handsome, dark hair, light eyes. He had a certain style, like rockabilly or a modern day greaser. It was sexy, whatever it was. He talked a lot about music and didn't have a single picture of himself smiling. "I did it for Johnny!" was what came to my mind; one of the greatest movies of all time, "The Outsiders". Dean was the kind of guy who wore black t-shirts, jeans and chucks all the time. I found it 100% attractive.

I realized Dean was on line so I opened a "chat" with him so I could thank him for his compliment and see if he would answer. "Hey, Dean, thank you for the message, how are you?"
"Well, hello. I'm just relaxing at home."
"No Thanksgiving plans?"
"The kids are with their mom this year so I am staying in, listening to music, enjoying my weekend off what about you?"
"I'm in Aspen with my brother visiting from the east coast. Just for the weekend."
"Aspen huh? That's not even real Colorado."

I laughed. He was right. Aspen is gorgeous but a little too touristy and not much for the locals, but I was still enjoying it. So far, what I learned about Dean was that he had kids, he was into music, he has a negative outlook but it might be sexy and he probably did it for Johnny. Blayne texted me, "We're ready." I sent Dean another message telling him that I thought he was probably right about Aspen and that I would love to talk with him more if he was interested. He said, "Sure, I'll be around here and there." Perfect.

When I walked into the room with my laptop in hand Blayne said, "Oh my God, Cherry, were you talking to boys?"
"Sure was", I fake yelled, "just because I'm on vacation doesn't mean I'm not looking for a husband." Peony laughed. Blayne and I both looked at her with our eyes wide because it was the first thing I said that she laughed at and that made Blayne and I laugh too.
"Peony, you look hot. Everybody ready?"
Blayne opened the door and said, "Yup, let's go get our Thanksgiving Turkey." We all laughed so hard because of how it sounded, maybe we were getting somewhere with Peony. We could only hope.

As we arrived at Ajax Tavern, Peony began to complain about a nail she had chipped. I handed her a file that I had in my purse and I told her, "I'm sure we can go get a manicure somewhere tomorrow. Until then, file it a little so you don't think about it." She took the file and didn't say anything. Blayne just looked at me and shook his head. We had a reservation that I put in Blayne's name. The host said, "You sure are a lucky man on this Thanksgiving Day." We had a perfect table so we could look out and see the whole restaurant. Those are my favorite. It was pretty casual, but everyone was dressed up festively. I remember what I ordered to this day. Part of the reason is because Peony complained, when she saw her choices that she didn't like anything, and secondly because it was so delicious that I remember it and recommend Ajax to anyone who tells me they are going to Aspen. It was a special menu. Blayne and I both ordered the same course choices. "Rainbow Beet Salad" was first with pistachio, citrus, and fennel pollen. Second we chose their most classic Thanksgiving collection, even though they had other options, for example Peony ordered the lamb and ate every bite. Ours was turkey, stuffing, veggies, cranberry, mashed potatoes, and gravy. I have a rule that I always say at Thanksgiving and that is: "Can't nobody never have enough GRAVY." I say it in my very best Barry White voice. Finally for desert we had apple crisp and vanilla ice-cream. It was classically delicious.

Blayne went to the bathroom and I decided I would try to level with Peony and see what I could find out about her (in reference to why she was acting the way she had been since I picked them up at the airport). I took a big sip of my wine and said, "Peony are you enjoying yourself?"
"Yes. I like it here."
"You seem upset a lot. Is there anything I can do to help with anything?"

She just looked at me and then her cheeks filled with color. She said, "I think it's my birth control, Cherry. I just changed to a different kind two weeks ago and I am realizing that maybe it is affecting me." Wow. That was not what I was expecting.

"Oh, my God. I'm so sorry. You know, I have never taken birth control. I just use condoms." We both started laughing and that was when Blayne got back to the table. He said, "This is nice to see. My two best girls, laughing together." He sat down and picked up his glass to toast us both, "To us."

I felt a lot better about Peony, now that I knew she wasn't just a snotty bitch, but she was a sister in the middle of a hormonal hurricane. I had heard legends of these things from other girlfriends, and when we were teenagers Shaun used to be out of her complete mind every month right before she got her period. I have absolutely had my moments, believe me, but for the most part my P.M.S. struggles are more about, acne, cramps, and bloat. I started calling it "Bloat" after I saw Slums of Beverly Hills. I love that movie so much, for a million reasons. Every single one of the cast members are amazing, first of all, and because of the fact that Vivian and Rita, played by Natasha Lyonne and Marisa Tomei, speak "gibberish" to each other. Shaun and I were determined to learn it one day. More importantly, however, because of a true story about my father that reminds me of the movie. Remember Elliot, played by Kevin Corrigan is wearing that Charles Manson shirt? That shirt got kind of popular as disgusting as it, is but Murray, the father, played by Alan Arkin

asks him, "Who the hell is on your shirt?" and Eliot answers, "Charles Manson, sir." This part reminds me of my father because my mother, who has never seen this movie told me a story about my father, who definitely never saw this movie, that was even more entertaining than Murray in a similar situation. There was a work crew at their agency, Thomas Real Estate in the late 90's working on the landscaping and one of the guys went into the office to have my father sign some paperwork. The guy was a young, white kid wearing that very shirt as seen on Eliot. My father said, "What the hell is that?" and points at the kid's shirt. The kid just looked at him and my father continued, "Do you know who that is?"
"Yes."
"Do you know what he did?"
"Yeah?"
As described by my mother, my father, sounding a little like Robert De Niro said, "Get the fuck out of here and don't come back until you take that piece of shit shirt off. Have a little respect." The kid stared at him shocked. So, my father said again, "Get out, you moron, get some better roll models."

My mother, who was sitting at her desk in the same room, watched the interaction from above her glasses slipped down the bridge of her nose without saying a word. When the kid left and the door closed behind him my father looked at her and said, "Can you believe that shit?" and she answered, "You sure are sexy, Will." This immediately calmed him down and they erupted in laughter at how mad he had gotten. The kid never came back in and the owner apologized and gave my parents a discount for their "trouble". I love telling that story.

The three of us drank the night away and ended up having a great time. Peony loosened up a little and began speaking to me more like I was her friend than a stranger and I could tell that it made Blayne very happy. Unfortunately that happiness and festivity all but completely disappeared the next day. Friday was our last day and night left in Aspen and it consisted of Peony fighting with Blayne and Blayne trying to calm her down. I did what I had done before Thanksgiving dinner and left them alone in the room so I could go down, drink coffee and get on my laptop.

I wanted to talk to that guy Dean some more anyway. That is exactly what I did. He was on line when I logged in so I started chatting with him again. We talked for about an hour and decided to make plans to see each other that next weekend. Blayne ended up joining me and grabbed a cup of coffee for himself. I ended my conversation with Dean so I could focus on my brother. "So, what's going on, Blayne?" I asked him and I know I looked at him like I felt bad that he was miserable.

"We're breaking up. I'm done." I was a little surprised at his abruptness and I said, "Are you sure? I mean, she said she realized that her birth control might me affecting her moods or emotions." I could tell he was surprised that she shared that with me and said, "If that were really the problem, I would be a lot more patient about this and see her through getting it straightened out. I'm not an asshole. But, Cherry, I swear this is just her and she keeps saying that when people call her out on her bullshit."

"Are you sure?"

"Yes, dude! She has always been like this. She just changed her pill like two weeks ago and there has been no difference. I am just over it. In the beginning when the relationship had the new car smell she was different, but it didn't take long for her true self to show up and I don't happen to like that person. I have put up with it for as long as I can. I honestly thought maybe this trip would help in some way, but I was wrong."

I didn't know what to say at first. It had been a long time since I actually was with him when he was breaking up with someone. For the last several years I was in Denver, and he would just tell me over the phone something like, "We broke up. I have a new girlfriend now." Blayne looked at me just looking at him and said, "I think I am going to stop dating for a while. I need to spend some time alone. I have never been single."

"If that is what you think you truly need, then I think that is a great idea." As we sat and drank our coffee I looked at him and said, "What happens in Aspen stays in Aspen. Here's to your happiness." I raised my coffee and he did the same.

"To *our* happiness, and to enjoying being single." I just winked at him because as you know, I had no intention of staying single.

Chapter 19 A Soundtrack Worth 1000 Words

The ride back to Denver was brutal. I couldn't imagine that they would still be here another night in my apartment not speaking to each other. Since everyone was mostly radio silence while we drove, I did a lot of thinking. I was sad that the good moments while Blayne was here were so few, I missed him so much all the time since I move out west, but I remembered that I would be seeing him again soon when I got back to New York in December. It would just be mom, Blayne and I and it was going to be really good for us. I made it a point to remember to remind him of that before he left to go home on Sunday. Peony took a Valium and slept in the back seat most of the way, which allowed Blayne and I to do a little bit of conversing and listening to music. I felt bad for him. This was the first girl that didn't even make it until Christmas. In my opinion, being single for a while was really a good plan for him. I hoped he would stick to it just to see what happened.

It was awkward to say the very least, but I had prepared the guestroom earlier that week and continued to be very sweet to Peony of course. She went to bed early and Blayne said he was sleeping on my couch. I was glad we got to hang out alone, anyway, and we didn't talk about anything that Peony couldn't hear if she was standing in the room with us, just in case she was listening (to see if we would talk about her). Instead, we looked at all of my old pictures and reminisced. Shaun came over and we shared a couple bottles of wine and told Glory Day stories. It was just what I needed. The old crew together again. Shaun and Johnny weren't going to New York that Christmas so I was glad that she got to see Blayne while he was in town.

I read a few pages of an old diary in my picture box and we laughed so hard at my childish opinions about what is important when you're young. When I was little I thought I knew everything. Turns out I was just a punk with an impressive self-esteem. Tucked inside one of the pages, we found magazine page cut outs of River Phoenix, Wil Wheaton, Corey Feldman, and Jerry O'Connell. Shaun was so excited. I'm sure at least some of you know that what the four of those guys have in common is "Stand By Me", which is one of our favorite movies of all time. We can basically speak to each other in quotes forever. Not just from Chris, Gordie, Teddy, and Vern, but also from Eyeball, played by Bradley Gregg, Ace, played by Kiefer Sutherland, and Billy, played by Casey Siemaszko. I said to them, "So what's with you and this Connie Palermo chick?" Shaun answered, "I've been seeing her for over a month now and all she'll let me do is feel her tits." Then Blayne said, "She's a Catholic, Man. They're all like that. If you wanna get laid, you gotta get yourself a Protestant. Jew's good." Ah, the classics. We went on and on all night.

Shaun went home just before the sun was about to come up and Blayne and I went to bed. Their flight left at 11:00 AM so we only had a few hours to sleep.

On the way to the airport I reminded Blayne that I would see him in a couple weeks. I didn't hug Peony goodbye when I dropped them off in front of the Delta door but I told her that it was very nice to meet her and I hope that she enjoyed Colorado and wished her a safe flight. She was cool to me in the moment but went inside without Blayne while he and I hugged goodbye. I told him, "Try to be sweet to her even though this is happening. Be cool."

"Always. See you soon. Thanks for everything."

"You're welcome, favorite brother."

I drove straight home, went to sleep, and stayed asleep until I had to get up for work the next day.

I was excited to see Trent Monday night, I kind of missed him but all this talk about hormones and PMS was ironic, because my monthly visitor came that day. I was off limits for the week and that was a good thing because I was excited to meet Dean and wanted to chill out a little with the Trent situation. I hoped we could still hang out at least a little without the expectation of sex. We would see, because he was coming over when I got home. I started dinner and was having a bottle of 2010 Santa Julia Argentinian Malbec, when Trent showed up. He came into the door singing, "She's my Cherry Pie!" I laughed, hugged him and went back into the kitchen. "What are you making, sweets?" he followed me and looked over the stove. "Fajitas!" I answered and gave him a high five.

"You're crazy." He laughed at me and then said, "Did you have fun with your brother?"

I spent the next hour telling Trent about everything that went on over the weekend and that for the first time since my High School years, I had a front row seat to witness another one of Blayne's relationships crashing and burning. Trent asked me, "The last time he broke up with someone was in High School?' I answered, "Oh, no, the last time I was *there* for one of his break-ups was when I was in High School. He has had a million girlfriends since then."

"Oh! I was confused. What went wrong that time?"

"Blayne broke up with his High School sweetheart, Amanda. I believe she is the one who got away. Too bad for Blayne, he thought he was doing the right thing because they were both going to different colleges. He didn't want to mess with her life plans, or something. I think he was just scared. He loved her. He has been trying to fill the Amanda void ever since."

Trent looked sad and said, "How could he break up with a girl named Amanda? Amanda's are always hot. What happened to her?"

"She got married after college. I don't know anything more than that but her parents still live where we grew up, near my mom, so she hears things about her once in a while. Blayne pretends he doesn't care."

Trent stared at me for a minute and eventually I said, "You ok?"

"Yes, Amanda is my ex's name. The one I told you broke my heart. It was a mutual break up but not really, you know? I didn't really want it to happen." He got up to take our dishes to the sink. "Do you want to talk about it?"

"Honestly, it's cliché. She couldn't handle me being a cop. I'm sure you've heard about the epidemic of police-wives or girlfriends who crack eventually under the pressure of fear and the unknown. It's always in the movies."

I knew exactly what he was talking about. Several movies came to mind as soon as he said it. First of all, how about "Die Hard" which happened to be one of my father's favorite Christmas movies. Holly, played by Bonnie Bedelia could never handle it but she sure was grateful of it when John McClane, played by Bruce Willis kept saving her. Then what about Justine and Vincent Hanna, played by Diane Venora and (one of my top five I wish I could meet him celebrities) Al Pacino in "Heat"? Their love was true but he was more married to his job than he was to her. It was heart wrenching. I always figured that any job that requires long and unpredictable hours could potentially cause problems in a person's marriage. If you add an element of fear because of the unquestionable danger that comes with being a cop, then I guess only the strong survive.

Trent told me the whole story and you won't be surprised when I tell you that he cried. It was a turning point for us because like I have said, when a man can cry on your shoulder about lost love, he is most likely your true friend. I thought it was very moving and realized just how sweet he really was under his tough exterior and frat boy sense of humor. I was, however, really starting to feel like Barbara Walters, you know, because she made everyone she interviewed cry. I gave him a shoulder rub and told him to stay and have a platonic sleep over with me. It was nice. He definitely made me feel safe, which I imagine is one of the many perks of being with a cop.

By the time 5:00 PM on Friday came I was growing increasingly excited because on Saturday afternoon Dean and I had plans to meet at a new coffee shop in Capitol Hill called RoosterCat. He said he had never been there before and that it had just opened. He also said he was on a quest to try, at least once, every coffee shop in Denver. He had a thing about coffee and, compared to me, he was much more educated on the topic. Dean let me know that Denver was making its way to catching up with the coffee shop capital of the country, Seattle, Washington. Seattle is one place I haven't been and have it penciled in on my "Travel USA" bucket list. I happened to be impressed with his appreciation of indie coffee shops. I was guilty of going to fast and easy chain coffee shops and hadn't really enjoyed lounging in a café since I was a teenager. "Singles" the movie, came out in 1992 just when Shaun and I were at our most impressionable age (almost 16) and sent us right over the edge. I think we saw it when we were 16 actually. We started wearing dark lipstick, ripped jeans, and hanging out in coffee chops. We lost our minds over the Seattle music scene. It was just what we had been missing. Eddie Vedder, Chris Cornell, Matt Damon, just to name three, were so hot we could barely stand it. That soundtrack! It was basically the beginning of the creation of Pearl Jam, the first time we heard Alice in Chains, arguably one of my top ten favorite bands of

all time, and "I Nearly Lost You" by Screaming
Trees, it made us cry and pine away for love, as we
believed and agreed with Bridget Fonda, that a man
who says, "Bless you" is absolutely worthy of our
attention. The mid-90s was our romance-period.
Nothing since then has ever felt like it did when we
wore Doc Martins and crushed on longhaired boys in
the Pacific Northwest.

Dean was about 6-feet tall, dark hair, blue eyes. He
was thin and handsome and wore a black t-shirt,
jeans, and black boots. He wore a thick gunmetal
silver chain bracelet, which I thought was sexy. We
ordered our coffees and found a seat by a fire pit
outside. It was cold but tolerable that day at about 50
degrees so we felt daring. It's nice to be able to sit
outside in Denver, even into the cold winter months.
He had a hard time making real eye contact with me
and was looking around a lot, taking in the café's
ambiance. I didn't blame him, but I was more
interested in looking at his eyes. They were intense.
I said, "Do you get compliments on your eyes a lot?"
He let out a quick, one syllable laugh and said, "Do
you?" I smiled at him as he sat back in his chair and
crossed his right foot over his left leg like men do.
What an interesting compliment. Then I said, "I never
asked you what you do for a living." He answered
with a disinterested tone, "It's probably the least
interesting thing about me. I work for an Insurance
Company pushing papers. What about you?"
"I am a paralegal or legal assistant to a corporate
lawyer."

He looked at his coffee, took a sip and said, "*That's* probably the least interesting thing about you."

This guy was a hard shell to crack, as my mother would say, so I decided to ask him about something I knew he was interested in and that was music. I said, "Do you like to go to concerts, I saw that you were really into music?"
"Yeah, music is a pretty big deal to me. I actually haven't been to a show in a while; they are so expensive these days. The last one I saw was Gwar in Boulder at the Fox Theatre. Have you seen Gwar? They are total freaks."
"I haven't, my best friend and I almost went to that show, in March?" He nodded and I continued, "We read that they spray fake blood all over the audience."
"Yeah, they are total fucking weirdos. It was just funny to say that I did it, the tickets were cheap."

We spent the next couple hours talking about music and telling each other who we were, like you do on a first date. He became more inquisitive as time went on but remained a little mysterious by answering questions with questions and did a lot more listening that talking. I kept making sure I wasn't talking too much. Eventually when it was time to move along he asked me if I wanted to go to his place to continue hanging out. He lived nearby in an apartment complex. I thought, why not, and accepted the invitation. His apartment was like a dorm room that is not subject to inspections. He had mismatch furniture, posters for art, and macaroni and cheese in a bowl in the sink. He had black curtains and an entire wall of

CDs. It was like stepping back in time to when I was a teenager visiting my friend at their very first apartment. I found it charming.

He immediately walked over to his CDs, chose something and as he put it in his dusty CD player he said, "Do you like Belly?"
I thought to myself, "No man has ever spoken such beautiful words to me." But what I said was, "Oh my God, Dean, I love Belly, so much, well actually specifically I love Belly "Star"." That was my favorite album for a while when it came out. I continued, "I'm a Tanya Donelly fan, also loved The Breeders back in the day." He looked at me and smiled as "Someone to Die For" started playing, the first track on "Star" and said, "Yeah, I had a crush on Kim Deal from the Pixies." I said, ""Where is My Mind", best Pixies song. Or "Wave of Mutilation". That song reminds me of "Pump Up the Volume", remember?"
He laughed again and said, "Oh, man, yeah, that movie had a great soundtrack. I love "Everybody Knows" by Leonard Cohen." I agreed and at the same time we both said, "And Concrete Blonde" and then we laughed at each other for saying the same thing.

After about an hour "Star" was over and we had spent the entire time talking about good music from the 90s and found we had many favorites in common. He found a new CD, put it in and I watched him switch to track 11 and he said, "Do you know "She Wants Revenge"?" I said, "No, I don't think so." The song started playing; I recognized it right away and said,

"Oh! Is this the song that is playing during that sex scene in "The Number 23" with Jim Carey and uhm…" I couldn't remember her name. I continued, "She's really hot, she was in "Sideways", you know?"
He sat down next to me on his couch and said, "Virginia Madsen."
"Yes! That was going to drive me nuts. I love this song. I meant to look it up. It's pretty hot."
"Yeah. I think its pretty wild."

Suddenly I was aware of how close he was to me. I got tingly and a little nervous. I looked at him and I whispered, "Oh, hello." The song in the background sang the words, "I want to fucking tear you apart." He smiled at me, acknowledging that I was flirting with him and he said, "Hey." He got right next to my face, closed his eyes, brushed his fingers across my cheek, and just breathed a little against my lips. I closed my eyes and could feel his heart beating like it was coming closer to me. Boom. Boom. Boom. Boom. Then he said, "Do you smoke? Let's have a cigarette." I exhaled. I hadn't even realized that I was holding my breath.

Who was this guy? He was so intense. I could not believe how cool he was. I joined him for that cigarette because sometimes a girl just needs a smoke. It was almost the same as taking a cold shower. We went out to his patio and by then it was almost 8:00 PM. He said, "My ex is going to drop off my kids soon. It would be weird for them if you were here."
"Oh, yeah, I completely agree. I'll take off then."

He stared at me as I took a drag off of the cigarette he gave me then finally said, "I want to see you again."

"I want to see you again too."

"I know you do. It's written all over your face."

"Really."

"Oh, yeah. I can see it. You can come over any time you want next weekend. It's my off weekend with the kids. I have them all week and every other weekend. Today they had special plans with their mom. That's why she has them on my weekend."

"Wow, she only has them every other weekend?"

"Yeah, it's just temporary. Usually it's 50/50."

I decided not to keep asking questions about it. This was the most personal information I had gotten out of him so far. I put out my cigarette and said, "Well, Dean. It was an absolute pleasure. I haven't enjoyed a conversation with a man this much in a while."

"I feel the same. I'm glad we met."

I picked up my purse, reached out to hug him goodbye and he kissed me. Hard. He kissed me aggressively on my lips and then moved his kisses to my neck, which made me weak in my knees. He whispered, "I want to tear you apart." He let me go, looked at me one last time. With the softest voice I have ever heard myself speak, I said, "I'll see you." He smiled a crooked smile at me and walked into his house. That night I fell asleep on my couch watching a movie, if you know what I mean.

I remember what it felt like when I was very young and first liked a boy before I realized boys were gross. My parents took us to the Jersey Shore for a month one summer and while we were there I met a local boy my age and he the coolest kid ever. His name was Sam. He would come find me every day and hang out with me at the beach or on the boardwalk. He drove me crazy. I had butterflies constantly, I missed him when he went home at night and I would watch for him in the morning like I was waiting for my sailor to come in after months away at sea. He was my first kiss and we spent most of our time together practicing. I never knew his last name and I never saw him again but I think about him sometimes and I thought about him a lot that week because I felt like I did that summer at the shore. Except this time I was in my 30's and I undeniably had lust in my heart.

Shaun and I had lunch together that week and I filled her in on my new male interest. She was excited to hear the details but immediately started busting my chops about Trent. She said, "I hope you're not going to have sex with Trent and Dean at the same time."

"At the same time?" I looked at her like I was shocked at the suggestion.

She laughed and said, "You know what I mean. Cherry, do you want to end up on Maury?"

"Oh my God. First of all I haven't had sex with Trent in a couple weeks and I have no idea if Dean and I are going to hook up. It is still completely unknown."

"I know but if you do, you have to tell Trent that you aren't sleeping with him anymore."

"Shaun, I will! You're being dramatic. When have you ever known me to just sleep with guys all over the place?"

"Never. I'm sorry. I'm having anxiety about your dating life." We laughed at her and I lovingly told her to get a grip. Then she said, "Do you think this Dean guy is boyfriend or eventually husband material?" "Honestly, probably not, but he is so hot and so cool I don't even care. For example, I can't imagine him hanging out with Blayne or Johnny or really any of my friends, except you, I know you would like him."
"Yeah. That's what I was thinking."
"I'll just see what happens. I'll be going to Roslyn in two weeks anyway. Not much can happen in that time."
"Are you kidding? At the rate you have been going this year you could have a whirlwind romance, break up and meet a new guy in two weeks."
She was right. Time means nothing when you're doing online dating.

I had plans to bring Chinese food over to Dean's house on Friday night that week. He was dressed exactly the same in a black t-shirt, jeans, and black boots. I laid out the food on his coffee table in the living room and he said, "I was thinking about some other soundtracks that I really love this week since we were talking about "Pump Up the Volume" the other night. Do you like the "Pulp Fiction" Soundtrack?"
"Oh, totally! I love Urge Overkill's cover of "Girl, You'll be a Woman Soon" and my favorite is "If Love is a Red Dress" by Maria McKee. I love that song."
"Yeah, I think that one is my favorite. It's pretty great, she has a cool voice."

As we started eating he said, "I'm a huge fan of anything Tarantino and he does his own soundtracks. It's pretty amazing."

"Me too, huge fan, and I feel the same way about anything that Scorsese does. Soundtrack gold."

"Oh, man. Scorsese is the best."

"Exactly."

At my request, when we finished eating, Dean put in "Nothing Shocking" by Jane's Addiction. I clearly remember listening to it with him in his dimly lit living room. I will never forget the first time I heard that album. I don't think I actually listened to it until "Ritual De Lo Habitual" came out in the early 90s. It blew me away. I still feel the same way I felt as a teen when I listen to it now. Jane's Addiction is on of my all time favorites. Dean felt the same about them and had all of their albums. His house smelled like incense. I imagined that maybe once and a while, when his kids weren't home and it was very cold outside, that he snuck a smoke in his apartment. We went outside a couple times for a cigarette. He was a bad influence on me, but with him I felt something kind of deep. He talked to me like a friend and he looked at me like he wanted me but still, I wasn't sure.

He told me to choose some music when we came back inside. I looked at his wall of CDs and it reminded me of the summer after Shaun and I graduated High School. We wanted to take a road trip and bought tickets to see the Grateful Dead at Highgate in Vermont. Bob Dylan was headlining. We

figured we shouldn't miss it and we were right, as it
turned out, because Jerry died that year. My mother
still tells the story that when I came home I told her,
"I don't know mom, I don't think Jerry has much left
in him."
"What? He's my age, what do you mean?"
"I bet he drank a lot more whiskey and did a lot more
acid than you too, mom. He didn't look good."
When she tells the story she always says, "And then
two months later, he was dead. Cherry knew."

Anyway, Shaun and I decided to take the long way
home from Highgate and went to Maine. That drive is
gorgeous. New England is so beautiful in most places.
We stopped in Portland, Maine and got a hotel, but
the reason I bring up this story is because we also
each got a tattoo. I can't remember the name of the
shop but the guys name was "Captain" something.
He gave me a discount because he liked where I was
getting my tattoo. Shaun and I giggled the entire time
we were in there, but I will never forget that he
pointed us toward a wall of CD's and told us, "Pick
your soundtrack because I listen to music while I
work and you're not allowed to speak." I have no idea
what Shaun chose but I chose Depeche Mode,
"Violator". To this day when I hear that album I
remember, "Captain something" stabbing me in the
chest with a tattoo gun for an hour.

I looked through Dean's music and eventually chose
Deftones, "White Pony" because it has Passenger
featuring one of my favorite artists ever, Maynard
Keenan of Tool. I love that song. I switched the disc

to track ten and started swaying back and forth to the music, continuing to look at his CDs when Dean came up behind me. He wrapped his arms around me, kissed my neck and whispered, "I want you." I just stood there letting him do what he wanted. My breathing got heavier and I felt awakened by him, and the song, and the musky smell of incense. He turned me around and kissed me as he gently pushed me against his wall of music and pinned my hands against the plastic edges. He whispered, "Do you want me?" I kissed him back and whispered, "Yes." Our tongues danced to the beat of the drum and when the chorus began Dean became more aggressive. He led me to his bedroom and pushed me back on the bed and pulled off my jeans. I pulled back my shirt and he pulled his off. I grabbed his belt and pulled down his pants. When the piano and keyboard notes nearly distracted me, I continued to stare at him and he ran his fingers through my hair. He was so sexy standing there as Passenger ended and Change began. I got up on my knees and kissed him digging my nails into his back. He moaned. I said, "Do you have a condom." He said, "Yes." He backed away from me slowly; not taking his eyes off me and went into the living. When he came back I lay back on his bed and watched him as he pulled down his boxers and opened the condom wrapper. He had a Prince Albert piercing. He slipped the condom on and crawled over me kissing me from my knees up my leg to my stomach to my breasts. He reached under me and unsnapped my bra. I was in this intense state of ecstasy as the song ended and I felt strange about the silence, but then the song started again. He had

207

switched it to repeat when he was in there getting the condom. The light was off in his room and the only illumination was from the dim light in the living room. Sometimes he whispered the words, "I watched a change…" I just moaned quietly as he ran his tongue all over me until he was face to face looking at me. He stopped moving and just stared at me his lips slightly against my lips. He moved slowly into me. I cried out. He whispered the lyrics, "You feel alive." He started off very slow and he ran his fingers up and down my neck and breasts until he started thrusting harder and faster but still to the beat of the music.

It felt like forever until we climaxed together and I trembled under him. He lay down next to me until I caught my breath. I stared into the black listening to our breathing in my mind I repeated it over and over and continued to tremble. He rolled over toward me and started blowing on my wet skin. He whispered, "Let me cool you down." I lay there with my eyes closed and enjoyed every second of it. Never in my life had a man blown air on my skin like that. It was the sexiest thing I had experienced.

For a little while we were silent. Then he got up and handed me my t-shirt. He said, "Let's go smoke." I sat up and put on my clothes. He went to the bathroom and I followed after him. When I came out he was in the living room changing the music to A Perfect Circle, "Thirteenth Step". I met him in there and slipped on my boots to go outside with him. When we got outside and lit our cigarettes he said, "How do you feel?"

"I feel…I feel so good. That was so good, Dean."
He took a drag and said, "Good. It was pretty
incredible."

I stayed for about an hour longer and when I left he
said, "I want to see you again before you go to New
York. We will figure something out. I'll let you know
when I get home tomorrow night." He had plans with
friends and I told him I understood and that I hoped
we could make it happen if not tomorrow sometime
before the 20th. He kissed me hard again when he said
goodbye. It completely overwhelmed me every time
he did that. I was sure that he could tell and that was
why he did it. I walked backwards away from him
biting my lip and smiling a coy smile. He called out,
"You stop flirting with me." I laughed and got in my
Jeep.

Chapter 20 Eastbound and Down

I slept in the next morning. I slept for as long as I could stand to. My mind was completely focused on Dean. I thought about the men I have had sex with starting back at Jimmy in the 90s. He was the first and last guy since Dean that played music in his room when we had sex. We were always listening to the Beastie Boys together. "Check Your Head". The best songs for sexin' on that album are "Namaste" and "Something's Got to Give". I used to call him "Jimmy James" which is another track on the album. "Oh, Jimmy James." I would always say, "Take me to bed or lose me forever." You have to know that movie quote- Meg Ryan, "Top Gun". You know what it's like when you have sex for the fist time; you want to do it all the time. His parents were never at home, until a few hours after we got out of school, so we were always hanging out in his room.

I wouldn't say that Dean was the best sex I had ever had, but it was intense and unlike anything I had experienced in bed somehow. It was exceptionally passionate. I could still feel his breath on my skin. It drove me crazy all day. I told Shaun everything that happened and she said, "Oh, God, Cherry, that sounds so hot! He has a Prince Albert piercing? I've never even seen one in real life before." I thought it was interesting that Dean never told me he had it. I found out when I saw it. I've known a few guys who had piercings and I feel like they couldn't wait to tell everyone about it. Dean was different. He knew exactly who he was and it was obvious that he wasn't looking to impress anyone with anything.

I didn't reach out to him at all that day. I wanted to just wait and see if he was going to invite me over that night. I got ready just in case, which just means I shaved my legs again. If he didn't get home at a good time I was going to go to Shaun's for dinner instead and if I never heard from him, I would probably just spend the night over there. I promise you I don't like having my world revolve around a man but it was more of an insatiable desire to be with him in his dark bedroom again that was keeping me on the edge of my seat. It was 90% lust and 10% the fact that I enjoyed hanging out with him and listening to music. By the time evening came I hadn't heard from him so I headed to Shaun's house.

Shaun made margaritas, which she calls her spirit animal. My mother and Shaun are both lovers of tequila. I can have one, if I keep going I get heartburn. So, I had just one. I was glad I only had one because at about 9:00 PM I got a text from Dean, "I just got home. You can stop by if you want." I read it to Shaun and she said, "You can stop by if you want? What does that mean? He sounds like he can't be bothered."
"I can see why you would say that but what it really means is, "Please come over quick so I can make passionate love to your body." Johnny burst out laughing and said, "That is what it means, she's right." I smiled at Shaun and she said, "I guess I'm

lucky I'm married because this shit would drive me nuts."

I texted Dean back and said, "I would love to come over. I will be there in about 30 minutes?" He replied, "OK." I showed Shaun and said, "See, look how excited he is."
We laughed and she said, "I like Trent better, are you sure he doesn't want to date you?"
"Trent is amazing but no, he is on a different path. It's ok. December doesn't count. It's the last month of the year and there is a lot of time to play. January is a clean slate and everything matters in January. December is my freebie month."
"Freebie for what?" Shaun looked at me confused.
"Free to do whatever I want!" I laughed at myself.
"Bitch, you mean *whomever* you want. Maybe tonight he'll play some Enigma while you have sex."
I spit my drink out laughing so hard. She could make fun of me all she wanted, I would laugh, but at the end of day there is nothing funny about having multiple orgasms.

I drove across town and when I arrived at Dean's he was smoking on his patio. I walked up to him and said, "Look I bought you a new pack since you have been sharing them with me. He said, "You bought me dinner last night." I said, "Oh well, still, I think I will have one with you." I asked him if he had a good night and he mostly just shrugged and told me that he went with his friends to see one of them do stand up. Dean's voice was sexy. It was baritone and soft spoken. He never had a shred of excitement in his tone, but he did laugh often. His laugh was quiet too. He laughed when he was mildly amused rather than because he thought something was funny. He is the kind of person who honors you by laughing at something that you say. As we talked on the patio, I went outside of myself metaphorically speaking, and watched myself interact with him. I was doe-eyed. He was in charge of our interactions. I found it quite interesting that I had found another man who takes the lead when we are together.

I wondered if it was obvious to him that I hoped that we had sex. I wondered if he could feel the tension that I felt. He was doing nothing to turn me on, yet I was *so* turned on. I wanted to tell him how sexy he was and how I hadn't been able to get him out of my mind all day. I wanted to tell him that the thought of him kissing me, running his tongue across my skin, and blowing the sweat from my body had me on fire all day. I just stared at him as he spoke and he said, "What?" It jolted me back into the moment and I said, "Nothing, I am just so attracted to you." He smiled a crooked smile again that also drove me wild. You know like Leonardo Dicaprio, Tom Sizemore, Corey Haim, and Gerard Butler to name a few. Crooked smiles have always been a thing for me.

He said, "What do you want to listen to?" Knowing what happens when he plays sexy music, I thought to myself, 'How about "Erotica" by Madonna or "How Does it Feel" by D'Angelo" speaking of sexy crooked smiles, but I knew he would never have those artists on file so I said, "Do you have any Type O

Negative?" He stood up and said, "Of course." I said, "October Rust?" He said, "Yeah, that's a good one." I watched him as he put the CD in and I took off my boots. As the intro started he said, "I saw them in concert in 2003 at the Ogden." I was jealous, "I never got to see them." I made a sad face and continued, "I've never been too much into the allure of vampires but I had a serious crush on Peter Steele. He was Goth-Metal sexy and I was devastated when he died so young." Dean came over and sat next to me on the couch and looked at me looking at him for a minute then he said, "Yeah, man that was harsh. I felt so lucky that I got to see him live." He ran his fingers through his hair a couple times kind of fixing it. He had that long on top short on the sides' kind of men's haircut. The kind that can be styled professionally while you're at work, but when you're at home you can still be yourself and have long hair.

He was looking at me differently. I had no idea what it meant but it made me lose my breath. As "Love You to Death", which happens to be my favorite Type-O song, kicked in he moved toward me and that time pushed me back on the couch and started kissing me. He felt so good. I closed my eyes and focused on the music and his lips. "Let me love you..." He sang along quietly and kissed and licked my neck. "To death..." he whispered and then he hovered over me and stared at my eyes. He had gold flecks in *his* blue eyes. He stood up and put the song on repeat and grabbed a condom and then my hand and led me to his bedroom just as the song was ending and starting again.

We stood there and kissed in the dark next to his bed. We took off each other's clothes and he pressed his body against mine, wrapped his arms around me and squeezed me tight. He put his fingers around my neck and squeezed a little pushing back my head then he nibbled and licked my neck and shoulders. I couldn't feel my legs and felt weak; him holding me was the only reason I was still standing. He turned me back to him and grabbed my hair to wrap around his wrist, so he could kiss the back of my neck. With his right hand he held me by my breasts and then suddenly, like he had had enough, he pushed me back on the bed. I was never so quiet during foreplay. It was like I couldn't wait to see what was going to happen next.

Once he was hovering over me and pushing into me I couldn't be quiet anymore. He kept saying, "Yeah." in a deep breathy voice. I opened my eyes and looked at his face. His eyes were closed tight and his lips were pressed hard together. He went harder and harder until I realized how loud I was. Eventually, he said, "Tell me when, Cherry." I opened my eyes and said, "Now." He squeezed my neck and kissed me hard as we both climaxed together. I tore into his back with my nails and he arched up with his mouth open. We were both moaning and trying to catch our breath as he flopped down half on me half on the bed, his face in his pillow. I lay there listening to Peter Steele's dark words until Dean sat up and asked me, "Do you feel good now?" I said, "Yes, I feel good. Do you?" He stood up and as he walked toward his bathroom he said, "I feel as good as you feel."

We hung out for another hour, just like the night before, until I was so tired I had to go home. We left it the same way too; maybe we'll see each other before my Christmas break, maybe we won't. When a guy has primary custody of his kids and they don't know you, you end up being the one on an every other weekend schedule. I was hoping for a special circumstance to come up but either way I was just glad I got to see him again.

I was meeting Trent for coffee in the morning and I promised him I would go to the gym with him. I hadn't been in over a year, but I still paid for the membership. I told Trent I was supporting the organization of health by doing that. I texted Dean when I woke up and said, "I had an incredible time with you the last two nights. You are beyond, beyond sexy." He answered about an hour later and said, "It's intense when we claim each other." I had never met a man who talked like that. It drove me wild. Trent was already there when I got to Starbucks and as we talked and drank our coffee, I thought about what I was going to say to him to let him know that I couldn't have sex with him anymore. Or, at least as long as I am sleeping with Dean because who knew how long that was going to last. I didn't want to tell Trent anything though. I wasn't sure what the future held for Dean so I felt like I was trading one friend with benefits for another and I still really liked sleeping with Trent. The real difference was that Trent was not an option and Dean was a guy I met on a dating site who was supposedly looking for a relationship. As it turned out, however Trent and I hung out all day and on Monday and the subject never came up.

Ben and I were so busy that week getting everything done for the end of the year. Every night I was going to bed close to 8:00 PM. I texted with Dean a few times over the week and had random meaningless conversation with him. On Sunday I finally heard from Zack. He said, "OMG, Cherry, can you get lunch this week, I have so much to tell you!"
I was excited to hear from him and texted, "Yes! I would love that! I'm free for lunch Monday, Tuesday or Wednesday."
"Great! Let's do it tomorrow! Steubens 11:30 AM?"
"Perfect, I'll see you there." I didn't see Trent that Sunday because he had special duty, which made me sad because I was really enjoying our Sundays together and because I would be gone for two weeks after Thursday, but we planned to go to dinner on Monday night.

I wore my purple heels for old time's sake on Monday because I was meeting up with Zack. Ben said, "You might think I don't approve of your shoes but I do. I was a teenager in the 80's."
"You want to borrow them for roll playing with Margo?"
"I don't think you and I have the same size feet."
I laughed so hard and said, "See, I set it up, you knocked it down."

The last week of work in December was always my favorite. Even though Ben is always fun and we work so well together, he is in an exceptionally good mood right before being off of work for 14+ days and of course, so am I. I asked him, "How did Hanukkah go last week?"

"It was great, thanks for asking. Yesterday we sang "Dreidel, Dreidel, Dreidel" and had potato pancakes."

"That sounds like a nice little Sunday."

"It was. It really was."

"You know, the Jews are the most beautiful people."

"I know. It's always them."

I was ecstatic to hear what Zack had to say to me. When I got to Steubens, he wasn't there yet so I grabbed a table and ordered a salad and Steuben's Fries. When he finally walked in, he squealed when he saw my heels and when he bent down to hug me he said, Oh, Cherry, you fine, purple heel wearing thing! I missed you!"

"I missed you too! What has been going on? How was your trip?"

"Let me just start by saying that I am sorry I have been MIA but I had a life-changing event and I have just been so busy re-adjusting that I didn't have time for anything."

"I forgive you. What life-changing event?"

He motioned toward the door and I saw Ryan standing there, smiling from ear to ear. When he saw Zack motion to him, he walked, almost skipped over to our table. He looked at me and said, "May I join you?"

"Yes! Of course!" Then I reached out to give him a hug. The waiter came over and they both ordered salads as well. "Zack reached over and took my hand and said, "I invited Ryan to fly down to St. Thomas to meet me while I was on vacation because we just hit it off so well at the Halloween party and while he was there something amazing happened." I was smiling and trying to figure out if I was supposed to be shocked or what I was supposed to do. He continued, "Now, since then Ry has advised me that you, Chris, Felipe, and he *knew* I was gay and were determined to help me figure it out." I could feel my face turning red and hot. I was embarrassed that Ryan told him that. I tried to speak and he stopped me and continued, "No, don't say anything. I have struggled with these feelings since I was 11 years old and just never had anyone to talk to about it. My parents are very straight Christians and I have lived in denial all this time. I have always been attracted to beautiful women and that has concealed the truth in me for years. I am lucky I met you, because you brought me to that wonderful and tolerant party and it was there that I met Ry." He took Ryan's hand and was now holding both of our hands. He said, "I am so in love with Ry and he loves me and I am a gay man and I am proud of that. I will always love you, Cherry, for your part in this and for leading me to Ry and ultimately, Ryan, you have lead me to be the happiest I have ever been in my life." I looked at Ryan and he was tearing up. I was glad because I didn't want to be the only one crying. Through my choking voice I said, "I am so happy to hear this and I am so happy for you both. This is amazing!" Zack stood up and hugged me and then hugged Ryan before sitting back down. We spent our lunch talking about their beautiful tropical rendezvous and immense happiness.

I was in the greatest mood ever after that lunch and was looking forward to seeing Trent and telling him all about it. Trent picked me up in a taxi at 5:30 and we went to Fogo de Chao Brazilian Steakhouse on Wynkoop. It is one of my very favorite places in Denver when I am in the mood for red meat, an impressive salad bar, and incredible Brazilian Martinis. We had a fantastic time and both got a little loaded. Trent said, "Cherry Pie?" I said, "Yes, Trent Reznor?" We both laughed so hard that I said that. It just came to me and was so dumb but we were intoxicated so everything was funny to us. He continued and raised his glass, "You have become one of my very best friends. I love you." I clinked my glass against his and said, "Awww, I love you too."

He had turned out to be one of my favorite people of all time. He had the taxi drop me off before him because it was a work night after all, and we had enough fun for one night while we were still at Fogo. When I got out of the car he said, "I can take you to the airport on Thursday after I get off work. It's no big deal."
"Oh, cool, ok. I'll see you at 7:00 AM then?"
"Ok, sounds good."

As I got ready for bed I thought about "When Harry Met Sally" again. Harry knows how long Sally has been dating her boyfriend because he gave her a ride to the airport. He says "You take someone to the airport, it's clearly the beginning of the relationship. That's why I have never taken anyone to the airport at the beginning of a relationship." Sally says, "Why?" Then Harry answers, "Because eventually things move on and you don't take someone to the airport and I never wanted anyone to say to me, How come you never take me to the airport anymore?" I texted Shaun who is fully aware of my love of this movie and said, "Trent said he would take me to the airport on Thursday."

"You never take someone to the airport in the beginning of a relationship."

"Lol."

Then I immediately fell asleep.

I had hoped to be able to see Dean before Thursday somehow but he texted me on Tuesday and said, "Have fun in NY. Let's hang out when you get back." I was disappointed but I would get over it because he had a good excuse: Kids. Kids should always be top priority. I was going to have to suppress the desires he had awakened in me while I was away for two weeks. I still felt a little insatiable. Then again, I might not be able to give Dean all the credit for that. I was in my early 30s and the word on the street is that those years are a woman's sexual prime. However, I along with many people who have done studies to argue that idea, would tend to disagree. I'm sure it has more to do with life, hormones, the fact that you have a good sex partner or not, and general availability. For example, when I was 18 I was up to my ears in sexual desire, when I was 25, I was still up to my ears in sexual desire, when I was 28 I was busy and uninterested, and once I turned thirty I went back to feeling like I did when I was 18. Some women my age are having babies. I'm sure they are too tired to have as much sex as they were having before they got pregnant. I imagine some guys at a party talking about their hot 33-year-old neighbor who they wanted to sleep with made it up, "Dude, she's like 30 something and she's in her prime, man!" Then it just spread like wildfire. You never know.

Trent picked me up at 7:00 AM on the dot on Thursday morning and was visibly either tired or sad. I asked him, "Rough night?" He said, "Long night, I'm cool though. You excited?"

"Yeah I always am. Christmas in New York is the best and I miss my family."

"I bet."

After a few minutes of silence and yawning I said, "Do you have plans for Christmas by the way?"

"Yeah, I'm going to my parent's house on Sunday and staying until Christmas morning."

"Oh, cool, how long is the drive?"

"Only about three hours."

"Ok, don't drive sleepy! I don't want to have to worry about you."

He laughed and said, "Don't worry about me."

It was silent for a few more minutes and then he said, "Cherry, do we tell each other if we start sleeping with someone else?"

I was surprised to hear him bring that up and said, "Is it bothering you? I could tell something was wrong."

"I was just thinking that we should just have a plan for how to talk to each other about it." I said, "You're right. We should. Are you sleeping with someone else?"

"No, you are."

I looked at him surprised, he didn't look at me because he was driving, but he knew I was looking at him, because he was biting down on his molars which is what he always does when he is stressed out about something or talking about something serious. He had a sexy jaw line. His face was a little stubbly that morning like he might have skipped his shave the night before. I said, "How did you know that?"

"Because, we haven't been sleeping together. I figured you aren't the kind of girl who sleeps with multiple men in the same time frame."

"You're right, I'm not. I met a guy and we have been seeing each other for a couple weeks and the weekend before last we hooked up."

He was silent again and then he said, "I'm so jealous! Who knew I was going to be the jealous one when I asked you to be my "no strings attached FWB"?"

I laughed and said, "Why are you jealous though?"

"I don't know, it's probably more about possession. We hang out the same amount of time as ever, so it's not like I miss you, but I was hoping we would be able to sleep with each other for a longer period of time."

I laughed and put my hand on his shoulder, "I adore you, Trent Reznor. You mean a lot to me. I just happen to be looking for a husband. It probably won't work out with this guy anyway.

"Really? What's his story?"

"I don't know. He is a little bit closed off and mysterious. I like him but I can't see a future I just see right now."

"Man, this sucks."

"Trent don't you want to start dating and see if you can find someone to love again? It's been almost a year."

"I do. You were making me happy until I was ready though, that's probably why I'm so bummed."

"I am flattered by everything you say to me and the feelings are mutual trust me. I will never be anything but honest with you."

"I know. I trust you, Cherry Pie."

"You're the sweetest thing ever."

"Don't tell anyone, you will ruin my reputation."

He helped me with my suitcase and gave me a big hug when we got to the airport. He said, "Text me when you land every time just so I know you're ok. Even if I'm asleep I will get the message when I wake up." I said, "Ok, I promise." We waved goodbye as I went inside. I felt sad after that conversation. It was great that we got it all out, but Shaun was right when she said that seeing Trent the way I had been was complicating things. I was so glad that I had him though. We would probably be friends forever. I thought when I got back I should probably start helping him move forward and start dating too. I'm sure I had filled a void but that wasn't good enough. He filled a void for me, too, and it wasn't good enough for me either. Then I thought neither is Dean. I felt depressed as I buckled my seatbelt and looked out the window over the wing. Usually I was so happy on this day but I'm afraid this time I was Eastbound and Down.

Chapter 21 Fairytale of New York

By the time I landed in New York I had forgotten
about the trouble of my sex life and was anticipating
getting home to my mom's. Once I got off the plane
and through the airport, I was surprised and so thrilled
to see that both Blayne and my mother were there to
pick me up this time and were waiting for me at
baggage claim. They hadn't done that in years.
Blayne was holding up a sign however that said,
Welcome Home from Shady Acres Mental Hospital.
All of the people around him were laughing at him
and the sign, to see whom he was waiting for. I
thought about just walking outside, but then I decided
that it was funny and I could handle the
embarrassment. I would get him back one day,
though…just wait. I walked up to my mother, hugged
her and then Blayne hugged us both aggressively,
putting on a show for his fans. Everyone cheered and
clapped so I waved to them and mouthed the words,
"Thank You, Thank You."
We laughed about it all the way home from the
airport.

Let me explain my childhood home so you can
picture it. It is a three bedroom, three bathroom,
center hall colonial, built in the 40s. You know the
kind of house that you always draw when you're a kid
with four windows and a door on the front, shaped
like a rectangle with a chimney on one side. When
Blayne and I were growing up there were only two
bathrooms, but my parents added another one. The
bottom half of the house is brick and top half is siding

with one of those octagon windows above the front door. In the 90s, when they were empty nesters, my mother painted the front door red and I always thought that was a good idea. Inside it has hardwood floors, with mostly updated interior. There is still wallpaper in a couple areas. My mother told me that if she wanted to sell it now she could list it at a million, which blows my mind and honestly, if that house hadn't been handed down to my father from his parents forty years ago they never could have been able to afford it now. It's expensive. The school district is phenomenal so Blayne and I got lucky. Shaun's parents are both Doctors and have a lot more money. They moved to Roslyn from the city in the late 70s to raise Shaun. Our house is in great shape and the property is nice with a big back yard but if you put it in Denver, which has become a pretty expensive city itself, it wouldn't sell for more than maybe $400,000. Real Estate has always driven me insane, Blayne too. That is why we didn't follow our parent's footsteps. Blayne does, however like money, which is why he got into investment banking. He learned a little of that from our dad. My mother always pretends she has it better than her best friends who are mostly millionaires and tells them, "I've never had a mortgage my entire life." Blayne and I love our childhood home and would only sell it if we had to, even though neither one of us have any intention of living there down the road. We avoid the topic completely.

When I walked into the house it smelled like pumpkin pie and I immediately noticed that there was no

Christmas tree in the living room. I gasped and said, "Mom! Why don't you have a tree?" She said, "Because you and Blayne and I are going to pick one out and decorate it together this year. I looked at Blayne and he smiled like he was actually excited. "Ok" I said, "I approve of that plan. Can we get it in Hollis?" My brother laughed because he knew I liked to go to Hollis, Queens and listen to Run DMC when I was home for Christmas. Specifically I liked to drive down Hollis Avenue and blast "Christmas in Hollis". There was a Walgreens on the corner of Hollis Ave. and Francis Lewis Blvd. where a guy sold live Christmas trees in the parking lot. She said, "Yeah sure, I haven't been over there in years." It was only about a twenty minute drive from mom's house, depending on traffic.

I have my specific favorites when it comes to Christmas music. I love "A Jolly Christmas from Frank Sinatra" from the 50s, on vinyl, and "Elvis' Christmas Album" from the 70s on vinyl. My mom has both and we play them every single year. My favorite Christmas songs are before mentioned "Christmas in Hollis" by Run DMC and "Fairytale of New York" by The Pogues featuring Kirsty MacColl. I have to admit though that I listen to Fairytale of New York all year long. It moves me. The song paints such an amazing picture of Christmas time in New York and a strange love between two regretful and sad would be Broadway stars. I always imagined that the very same conversation was happening in real life all over New York when there has been too much booze and too much "I could have been someone" and "You took my dreams from me". It's a romantic tragedy and a fairytale indeed. I love The Pogues and may Miss Kirsty MacColl rest in peace forever on "an empty bench in Soho Square".

Since it was Thursday when I got in, Blayne took Friday off so he could stay at mom's all weekend and through Christmas. He didn't have to go to work until the 26th. Mom was so happy to have us both "under one roof" as she always said. We got the tree on Friday morning and spent the rest of the day and night decorating it. My mother has such an amazing collection of ornaments. She prides herself on them and remembers just where every single one of them came from. I really enjoyed hearing the stories because it had been so long since I was there to help decorate.

Mom started cooking dinner and Blayne and I continued working on the tree. From the kitchen she said, "Oh, Blayne. I ran into Amanda Beth's mom, Jo-Anne, at the salon the other day." I looked at Blayne and he took a deep breath and said "Oh yeah?"
"Yeah, she said she was teaching elementary. She's in PA, you know."
"Yup."
"Still married but when I asked about it Jo-Anne rolled her eyes. I don't know what that means but it was interesting."
"Don't know." He looked at me with an annoyed expression so I changed the subject for him and said,

"Mom will you make homemade hot chocolate sometime this week?" Blayne smiled.

"I guess. You can make it too you know."

"No, I can't. Only yours is good."

On Saturday we went to Blayne's place in Manhattan so we could enjoy all of our traditional festivities. We skipped Radio City that year and went to the Manhattan Museum of Modern Art and that is when I got to see "The Scream" by Edward Munch. It was unforgettable. Then we had an early dinner at Patsy's Italian Restaurant on 56th street, which is our favorite Italian in Manhattan. We walked down 5th Avenue and stared starry eyed at the famous window displays. The next morning we finished off our time in Midtown with some ice-skating at Rockefeller Center. Through it all I sent Shaun pictures of what I was doing. She was jealous, but she wanted to see everything so she could be there in spirit. I thought about her having to miss this every other year out of respect for her husband wanting to spend time with his family for the holidays. I realized that someday it might be something I would have to compromise on. Trent texted me often that weekend, but I didn't hear from Dean at all, so I sent him a picture of the three of us in front of the tree that we took after we went skating. He answered, "Cool." When I sent the picture to Trent he answered, "Oh man! Awesome! I have always wanted to go there. Tell your fam I said hi." They were such different people, the two of them. Dean saying "cool" was actually a great response for him, but if you didn't understand that you would be disappointed from his seemingly constant lack of interest.

We got back to Roslyn late in the afternoon on Sunday and I was looking forward to spending some time talking to my mom. Conversations with my mom, especially over wine was one of my very favorite things to do. Shaun always loved it, too. She calls my mom "mom" and says that some of the best times in her life were spent sitting in the kitchen at my house talking to my mom and me about life. Blayne had plans with his best friend, Brett, from High School, who lived in LA and was home for the holidays, too. They were meeting at Chalet and invited me but I felt like staying in and being cozy. So, he went out and left my mom and me at home.

Mom poured us a glass of red zinfandel and said, "So, Cher-bear, tell me what's new." I always liked being called "Cher-bear" but probably never told her. "Well, you know, I'm just living the dream, doing what I do, looking for a husband." She laughed and said, "You don't tell the guys you meet that you are looking for a husband do you?" I answered her with a sarcastic tone and said, "Yeah, you think that's a bad idea?" She laughed, "Blayne said you were seeing a Police Officer, that sounds promising." "Actually, I'm not seeing him. We are just friends. I'm "seeing" a guy who has two kids and hates his job and doesn't talk about anything personal and who is incredibly passionate but I can't imagine him hanging out with or even meeting anyone that I care about, including you, because he is a little dark and very mysterious."

"Wow. Is that true?"

"Yeah. I know it won't go anywhere but he is Mr. Right Now and I happen to like him."

"I had a couple of those before I met your father." I leaned in to listen. She continued, "One of them was named Rex and he was a wild man. I dated him after High School when I was rebounding from my first love. I knew I could never introduce him to my parents. He worked as an attendant at Brackin's Gas Station. He would roll his cigarettes up in the sleeve."

"I always thought that was sexy."

She laughed and continued, "I hated that he smoked, but he did have nice arms. It was brief but intense. I knew something sweet in him that other people didn't see. Eventually I broke up with him because I just knew it wouldn't work out. He was very upset and said something I vaguely remember, but that reminds me of that scene in "Moonstruck". Do you remember? When Nicholas Cage talks Cher into admitting how much she loves him by saying something like "love isn't always nice and sometimes it ruins things". Do you remember? Something like "the stars are perfect, but we aren't perfect, and sometimes we love the wrong people"."

"I remember the quote but not verbatim." I thought that was the coolest thing I had heard in a while. The actual quote she was referring to was Ronny, played by Cage talking to Loretta played by Cher and he said, "Love don't make things nice! It ruins everything. It breaks your heart. It makes things a mess. We aren't here to make things perfect. The snowflakes are perfect. The stars are perfect. Not us. We are here to ruin ourselves and to break our hearts and love the wrong people and die. The storybooks are bullshit! Now, I want you to come upstairs with me and get in my bed!" As utterly moving as that scene was and though it worked for Loretta, my mother and I agreed that we had a different opinion. True love is nice, and I wanted it badly.

Chapter 22 Left to Interpretation

The rest of my trip home turned out to be just perfect. The three of us spent tons of quality time together and even ended up going through all of our old stuff. We took a bunch to Goodwill and organized the rest. My mother had hope chests for us, both full of our most prized possessions from childhood. You can tell a lot about a girl by looking at what is in her hope chest. It is nostalgia at its very best. I think it's harder to look back on old memories than it is to look forward to new ones. Being sentimental can be a real heart breaker, but I have no plans to change that about myself. Spending that much time with my mom and Blayne was just as therapeutic as I had hoped it would be. When I got back to Denver I felt rejuvenated. I also had an overwhelming desire to see Dean. I texted him as soon as I got home and since I knew that the next weekend was his "no kids" weekend, I asked him if he wanted to hang out. He answered me after about three hours that time and said, "Sure."

It was January, and January was always my clean slate month. I had to figure out what was really happening with Dean other than obviously incredible sex. It was nice to see that on Friday he invited me to go with him to see a local band play at Streets of London Pub. Streets of London is a great British bar to see locals bands and metal, drink beer, and be rowdy. It's on Colfax near the Snug, where I went with Trent. I had only ever been there once because my friends never wanted to go there. It reminded me a little of a place that Shaun and I used to go to back in New York that didn't card us. Those were definitely the days.

Dean met me there and I felt uncomfortable at first, because he knew a bunch of people there and they kept pulling him away. It wasn't that they were pulling him away that bothered me, it was that they didn't even know I was with him, and he wasn't introducing me to anyone. I decided that was unacceptable so I started introducing myself. I would reach out my hand and say, "Hey, I'm Cherry." They'd looked me up and down, smile at me, like I was hitting on them, and then I would say, "I'm here with Dean." Then they would look at him surprised and say, "Oh, hey, nice to meet you." I wasn't annoyed with him for it, because it just seemed as though he didn't know how to handle this kind of situation. I think he appreciated that I was an extrovert. I also realized that we had never discussed how long he had been single or if he had dated since his divorce. His friends were genuinely elated to meet me and so cool, but obviously very surprised that he had a girl with him.

I got a seat at the bar, which is always my favorite and I admired that they had the Pabst Blue Ribbon Unicorn Tap. I don't actually drink Pabst, but if I had to, I would drink it out of a unicorn. The band was great and I was having a lot of fun, but all I was thinking about was whether or not we were going to go back to his place when Dean came up to me and whispered in my ear, "You ready?" I wasn't exactly sure what that meant but I said, "Yes." So, he started

saying his goodbyes and telling everyone that we were calling it a night. When we got outside he said, "Follow me home?"
"Sure."

When we got to his place he didn't go right in but instead stopped at the patio and handed me a cigarette. I laughed and said, "You know I don't smoke at all unless I'm with you?"
"I like being a bad influence on you." We sat there quietly and it was so cold outside that night. January is always the worst. He said, "My friends really like you."
"That's cool, I liked them too. I like to hear that."
"Yeah, you fit right in there, "Cherry Thomas"."
I laughed and said, "The Brits are my people."
He laughed, "I thought so."

When we got inside he put in The Cure, "Wish" and put track number three on repeat. As he took my hand and led me into his bedroom, "Apart" started to play. It's a song I know well and that I played a lot when I was a teenager. For the next several minutes I focused on the lyrics as hard as I could as Dean ravaged me slowly and meticulously like the instruments in the song are played. I heard his message loud and clear. "He waits for her to understand but she won't understand at all. She waits all night for him to call but he won't call anymore. He waits to hear her say, "Forgive", but she just drops her pearl black eyes and prays to hear him say, "I love you", but he tells no more lies. He waits for her to sympathize but she won't sympathize at all. She waits all night to feel his kiss but always wakes alone. He waits to hear her say, "Forget" but she just hangs her head in pain and prays to hear him say, "No more, I'll never leave again". How did we get this far apart? We use to be so close together. How did we get this far apart? I thought this love would last forever."

I imagined that to him this song represented two parts of his current "love" life. It was clear that I had charmed him, but someone else had already bewitched him. Based on what I had seen and what I knew about him, which was very little, I would say that it was possibly his ex-wife. I felt like he was telling me that though he liked me, he could never love me and maybe he was confessing about a little bit of baggage that he was still carrying from his previous relationship. The song itself is clearly about one relationship but in his heart Dean was having two and what I knew for sure, was that he communicated best through music. His world, much like mine but even more intensely, had a soundtrack and that was part of what attracted me so deeply to him. I had to let him know somehow that I understood and that it was ok.

That night I stayed at his place. It was so late by the time we fell asleep that it just happened organically. When I woke up the next morning he was outside on his patio smoking. I went to the bathroom quickly and washed my face and used his comb to brush my hair. I got dressed and went outside to join him. He didn't look at me but he said, "Want one?" and handed me his pack of cigarettes.

I took it from him and lit a cigarette. I said, "How did you sleep?"

"Pretty good."

"So, how long ago did you get a divorce?"

"A year ago."

I was nervous but I asked him anyway, "What happened between the two of you?"

He lit a new cigarette and finally looked at me and said, "She cheated on me." That surprised me completely. I absolutely did *not* expect that to be his answer and it left me struggling to find words. He noticed the look on my face and continued, "I wasn't very appreciative of her. I took her for granted. She turned into the mother of my sons and I neglected her as my wife." This was the most profound thing I had heard him say.

"Do you still love her?"

He looked down at the ground and said, "No."

I didn't know whether to believe him or not. I said, "Have you forgiven her?"

"Yeah. I guess. I just want to be able to co-parent and be myself. We have the same friends. She wants to move back to Denver and I don't know how this will go."

"Oh, where is she now?"

"She's in Ft. Collins. It was temporary. I'm not sure what will happen."

I smoked more of my cigarette and thought about what he had just told me and then I said, "Do you feel single?"

He looked at me again like he was relieved. Maybe I had figured something out. He answered, "No. I don't."

"Do you want to be?"

He paused for an uncomfortable amount of time and finally said, "Yes."

He was so interesting to me. I said I had charmed him, well, he had captivated me. This situation had red flags being thrown all over the field but I still wanted to stay to hear the judges ruling. I should have run for the hills but I didn't want to leave his side. It was like summer vacation. Soon it would be over so I wanted to make the most out of the time I had. He asked me, "Do you want to go get breakfast?"

"Yes! I would love to." We went to Tom's diner and talked about how I got to Denver. When he asked me if I drove out when I moved I got excited because I always love talking about that road trip. Shaun flew to New York and rode with me. We stopped a lot and tried to do as much sight-seeing as we could. When we got to St. Louis we got off the highway to stay the night and looked for a place to eat. We ate at the White Castle at South Broadway and Gratiot. I can't forget that because when we were finishing up some cute guys came in. They had no interest in us and only cared about getting their burgers, but when Shaun and I went back outside to our car we noticed that the SUV they came in had a "For Sale By Owner" sign in the window with a phone number. We laughed hysterically at each other because we were both thinking the same thing. Let's call the number and mess with them. We could see them inside eating and I told Shaun to record me with her phone as I dialed the number with mine. We tried to muffle our laughter as we watched one of the guys scramble for his phone. He said, "Hello?"

In the best southern accent I could muster I said, "Hey! I'm callin' about your truck for sale?"

"Oh yeah, hey!" We watched as he stood up and Shaun kept recording.

"How much is it?"

"Uhm, I'm asking 2500 for it?"

"Oh, can you meet me somewhere so I can take you for a test drive?"

He started walking toward the door like he was going to go outside so we panicked and burst into laughter and he looked at his phone, looked at his friends and said, "It's those girls that were just in here!" They all turned and looked toward us. I hung up the phone and hauled ass through the parking lot as fast as I could with a U-Haul trailer attached to my car. We laughed so hard we actually *did* pee our pants a little. All night we were paranoid that they would find us and get us back somehow.

Dean was entertained by my story and said, "I bet you and Shaun are fun to hang out with when you're together."

"Oh, yeah, it's the most glorious thing on earth."

He laughed and looked away from me. The times that he looked me in my eyes were few and far between so when I was able to get him to do it I held the gaze as long as I could. To me it was like a game. I said, "I have such a good time with you when we are together."

He looked at my eyes and said, "Oh yeah?"

I just smiled at him forcing him to smile and again he looked away. There was just something about him that drove me crazy.

We went our separate ways after breakfast and I went home to shower. I was feeling very emotional and like I needed to do some thinking. I decided to have some wine and listen to my vinyl collection. I opened a bottle of 2011 "Earthquake" Cabernet Sauvignon. It was a New Year's gift from Ben and Margo when we got back to work, and I thought I would save it for a while but a while turned into three days. It was so delicious I was glad I didn't have to share it. I sat down on the floor in front of my turn table like I did when I was little, and put on Aretha Franklin "I never Loved A Man the Way that I Love You" just because I wanted to sing. I always skip "Respect", not because I don't like it, but because it's played out and the best songs are the rest of the tracks on that album. My girl, Aretha, makes you feel like the most painfully blissful love is out there waiting for you, but you might never ever find it because everyone is doing each other wrong. After Aretha, I put in Rickie Lee Jones' self-titled album that came out in 1979. This was one of the first albums I claimed as mine that actually came from my parent's collection. I listened to this album relentlessly when I was little. My favorite ever song sung and written by Rickie Lee is "Last Chance Texaco" which is a metaphorical story about bad timing in love and heartbreak. She sends shivers up my spine as she sings the sound a truck makes passing by on the highway. I always imagine myself as Rickie's biggest fan on earth.

Then I listened to Stevie Nicks, "Bella Donna". That is another one of my favorite records of all time. When I was little I couldn't wait to be 17 and I played "Edge of Seventeen" over and over trying desperately to interpret the lyrics in my young mind. I thought it had to be about love but as it turned out it was partially about the death of John Lennon. Her songs are so symbolic you can get lost in what you *want* to get out of them. That's what happens with art. Some songwriters don't even want to tell you what their songs mean.

I was in deep thought when I had a knock on my door. Like always, my first instinct was to turn off the lights and hide like I had warrants but instead I tiptoed to the peephole and saw that it was Trent. I was so excited to see him! I opened the door, "Trent! What are you doing here!" and gave him a hug.
"I took a personal day! Do you want to hang out? I have a pizza…"
"Of course! Come in."
It's such a great feeling when a friend shows up at the perfect time and I am always available for pizza.

Trent went to my fridge and said, "Oh, I knew you would have beer in here!"
I laughed and said, "Great, you make me sound like an alcoholic."
"No, you're just a good hostess."

I flipped through the movie channels to see if something good was on for background noise and found "Beautiful Girls". I love that movie. It's set in Massachusetts and because of that, it is how I picture every town north east of Connecticut charming and New Englandy and full of people like the cast of Beautiful Girls falling in love at old bars, singing "Sweet Caroline" by Neil Diamond. It reminded me of Roslyn. Trent said, "I love this movie."

I smiled at him and said, "So, how was your week?"

"I was crazy!"

I laughed at him being so dramatic and said, "I'm sure it was."

"I actually delivered a baby. For real. In the lady's living room. When I walked in the baby was on his way out. I only beat the ambulance by about two minutes, but two minutes is a lifetime when you have a baby coming out of your vagina, right?"

I almost choked and he started laughing at my reaction. I said, "That's amazing! You must feel so good after calls like that."

"Yeah man, I love my job."

We talked and laughed all through the evening and then he said, "Ok, I want to tell you something. I thought a lot about the conversation we had when I took you to the airport." I got nervous because there were a couple parts to that conversation, and I wasn't sure what he was about to tell me.

"Which part?"

"About me dating again."

"Oh, good! Do you want to try it?"

He took a deep breath and said, "Yes. I'm ready to stop being a heartbroken lump who thinks having unattached sex is the answer."

"This is very exciting news, Trent Reznor. You are healing!"

"Yes! I'm going to be ok."

"Are you going to try online dating?"

"Oh noooooo. I don't think so. I'm just going to become available and women will just flock to me. Just like you did. All I had to do is say hi to you at a coffee shop and you were putty in my hands."

I hit him with a couch pillow and said, "You must have lost your mind saying that to me. You couldn't resist my sweet ass."

He laughed and said, "I can't resist your sweet Cherry Pie."

I picked up my phone and pretending to make a call and he said, "Who are you calling?"

"My mom, I'm going to tell her what you just said." Then he hit *me* with the couch pillow. After we got done laughing I said, "I feel so much better, I needed some Trent in my life.

"That's what I'm here for."

We had another "platonic sleepover" that night after a little too much alcohol and he made me go get coffee and go to the gym in the morning again. The amount of energy he always had was inspiring. Later on that day, as I was doing laundry and hanging out with Trent, I sent Dean a text message that said, "I had a great time with you this weekend. I hope you have a great week." He replied, "Me too." Trent said, "So, how is it going with the guy you're seeing?"

"Every time I see him might be the last. It is a real nail biter."

He looked at me with a scrunched brow and said like he was asking a question, "That sounds awesome?" I laughed and said, "He is a fascinating man and like my mother always says, this relationship will be "brief but intense", and for some reason that I can't explain, I am ok with that."

"Ok, you know what you're doing."

"Do I?"

Chapter 23 Closer

Almost two weeks had gone by and again I was
wondering if I was going to get a kids-free weekend
invite from Dean. When I didn't hear from him I
decided to change things up and invite him over to
my house for dinner. To my actual surprise he
accepted. I told him I was making steak and
asparagus to make sure he liked it and asked him
what he wanted to drink. He said, "I'll bring
something." 7:00 PM on Friday night it was a date.

I was working on dinner and listening to The Doors,
"Waiting for the Sun" album when Dean got to my
place just before 7. He had a six-pack of "True
Blonde Ale" from Ska Brewing. I said, "Oh, I love
Ska, my favorite is PinStripe, the red. You like
blondes?"
He laughed and said, "No, I like brunettes."
I just smiled at him, gave him a hug and asked, "How
was your week?"
"Can't complain."
Back in the day people could put a grill on the patio
in apartment complexes like mine. I brought the
steaks out to the already hot grill and said, "I could
use a cigarette. I bought us a pack to share."
"You're a great hostess."
"I've been told that."

We smoked and talked as the steaks slowly cooked
and I noticed that he seemed a little shy. He was out
of his element and it was the first time he had been to
my place. When we went inside I said, "Make

yourself comfortable, we can sit at the coffee table if you want. Feel free to put on another album. I'll bring dinner over in a second." I watched him looking through my records as I prepared the plates. I wondered what he was thinking about my collection compared to his. He picked up my Jackson Browne, "Running on Empty" record.

"Oh, man. This reminds me of my childhood; it's cool that you have it on vinyl."

"Oh, yeah, I love that album so much. It reminds me of my childhood too."

"My parents had this record I think." He put it on and dropped the needle still staring at the track list on the back of the record case and said, "Rosie. That song is pretty rad."

"Totally, Rosie, Cocaine, and Love Needs a Heart are probably my favorites but I love every single song. I saw Jackson Browne in concert when I was like 19. In Jersey."

"Cool. Yeah, I bet that was a good show to see live."

I brought the plates over, handed him a new beer and sat down on the floor at the coffee table across from him. I said, "When I was little, like 4, my cousin was getting married in Jersey and my mom had to stay home with my older brother because he was sick. My parents decided that I could still go with dad and they told me, "Daddy's going to wake you up in the middle of the night and you're going to drive to Jersey with him to see cousin Sadie get married, ok?" I asked them, "In the dark?" Dean laughed and I continued, "Anyway, my father listened to this album all the way there and I have this vivid memory of him singing and me waking up with the sunrise illuminating the New Jersey turnpike." I pointed at my album and said, "The cover, with the purple drum set in the middle of the road and the light on the horizon, just accentuates my memory, as if that was what it really looked like to me as a child. You know?"

He hadn't taken a bite yet and was just staring at my face, like he was hanging on to ever word I said. I smiled at him and he said, "I like the way you tell stories."

I held my smile and said, "Thank you."

He started cutting his steak and said, "You're a pretty cool girl, Cherry Thomas."

I winked at him and said, "Back atcha."

By midnight the alcohol was all gone and my records were all over the floor. I asked him to stay and he accepted. We got into bed and laid there together, just staring at the ceiling until he said, "I'm not sure what is going to happen." I didn't say anything at first because I had a flash of our conversation a couple weeks ago on his patio when I asked him about his ex and he talked about her moving back to Denver from Ft. Collins when he said, "I'm not sure how this will go." and "I'm not sure what will happen." Finally I said to him, "You said that before, what do you mean exactly?"

"She wants to move in with me. She wants to get back together."

I wasn't surprised so I just stayed very, very calm and said, "Is that what you want?"

"I want it because we are both struggling as single parents and together we would be back to the way we were, you know, financially and with working and taking care of the kids."

"Those are good reasons."

"Yeah."

Then there was a long silence and it was deafening. I said, "Tell me how you feel."

"I'm not exactly good at that."

I turned toward him and I cleared the hair from his forehead with my fingertips and said very softly, "Dean, how do you feel?"

"I feel close to you."

"Literally?"

He laughed and said, "Yes, literally, physically, mentally."

"Really?" He didn't answer so I said, "I mean how do you feel about her?"

He paused for just a few seconds and then said, "I feel unfulfilled. That is what she said to me when I found out she cheated on me."

"I don't think you should take the blame for her cheating. It's cool that you had the self-realization that you did about taking her for granted but she could have handled it differently. Right?"

"Yes, that's why I divorced her. She doesn't actually want to be happy I don't think."

That reminded me of something. I couldn't put my finger on it then.

"What about you?"

"I want to be happy."

"I hope you will be."

He kissed me in that moment and as his hands searched every square inch of my skin I knew I was once again having temporarily satisfying goodbye sex. We spent the night falling in and out of sleep and he would wake me up kissing me and we would have sex again and again until finally we were so exhausted that the sun shining into my bedroom put us to sleep.

We woke up at about 11 AM and I said, "Do you want me to make us breakfast?"
"No, let's go get coffee somewhere, I don't have to be anywhere until 4."
I felt that summer vacation almost being over thing again. I was excited for the time I had and nervous because it was almost over. We took quick showers and went to Black Eye Coffee in LOHI. It wasn't packed, which made me happy. We grabbed a seat and just sat there for a few minutes in silence. I was staring at him when he looked at me, laughed and said, "See something you like?"
"You're easy on the eyes."
"Back atcha."

I remember what I had been reminded of the night before when he said that his ex-wife didn't actually want to be happy. It was the movie "Closer". Larry, played by Clive Owen tells Dan, played by Jude Law that Anna, played by Julia Roberts doesn't want to be happy. Dan says, "Everybody wants to be happy." Larry says, "Depressives don't. They want to be unhappy to confirm they're depressed. If they were happy they couldn't be depressed anymore. They'd have to go out into the world and live. Which can be depressing." Eventually I said, "I know what's coming, Dean."

"Me too."

"I'm glad for the time I have spent with you."

"You make it sound like I'm dying." He laughed and then he got a very serious look on his face and said, "You are a cool girl, Cherry. This has nothing to do with you."

Very confidently agreeing with him, I said, "I know." I reached for his hand and he took my hand instead and said, "That is why you're so cool."

Goodbyes are crazy, aren't they? They are always emotional no matter what kind they are. Sometimes they feel as though they will rip your heart right out of your chest. Sometimes they lift an immeasurable weight from your shoulders. Dean and I weren't breaking up because we were never together. We were acknowledging that what we had was done and then we were moving forward in two different directions. It wasn't my fault and it wasn't his fault. I still didn't want to say goodbye and struggled with the emotions that were coming up for me. So, when the time came that we had to part ways we hugged and I squeezed him for an extra long amount of time. I whispered in his ear, "I will never forget you and *you* will never forget me."

Chapter 24 The Trouble with Andre

I was never more grateful that I had Trent than ever before when Sunday afternoon came and Shaun was out of town with Johnny. I admit that though I didn't love Dean, he tapped into something up deep inside me and emotional doesn't even begin to describe how I felt. Trent came over and helped me keep my mind right, as I like to say. He asked me if I was going to get back on my profile and look for someone to go out with. I asked him if he was curious about it and he admitted that he was so I got my laptop and showed him what it was all about. We laughed just as Shaun and I had when I first signed up at all of the shocking and ridiculous messages from the men of online dating in the greater Denver area.

Eventually we found a message from a guy named Andre that caught my eye. It said, "OTA23, You are very beautiful. I would love it if you would message me back so that I can introduce myself to you. Have a great day, Andre." I told Trent, "This message is what I expected to see when I was new to this. I expected to see polite messages from men who were interested in meeting me."

"As cops we always have to remind ourselves that the bad people and the scumbags that we run into every day and night are the bottom 2% of society. There is still a whole world out there full of good humans. Once you forget that, you are doomed."

I laughed and said, "Are you sure it's only 2%?"

"Absolutely not."

I returned Andre's compliment and message and wrote back, "Andre, My name is Cherry. I would love to talk to you. Thank you for the compliment, you are handsome as well. I hope you had a great weekend."

Trent laughed and said, "You forgot to add, "Would you like to go square dancing?"

"Whatever, he was polite to me and I am always polite."

Trent scanned his pictures again and said, "He has some kind of uniform shirt on in this picture. It's cropped out but I can see that it is a uniform."

"Maybe he's a police officer!"

He looked at me with a furrowed brow and said, "You want a police officer? You can just date me. I'm much better looking that this dude."

"It's not all about looks. It's about their heart, mind, and soul."

"Yes, I know, Cherry Pie, that's why *I* don't date *you*, you're not very smart."

I gasped and hit him with my couch pillow. I said, "Why do you make me beat you every time you're here?"

"Beat me? I thought you were just flirting with me."

"You're probably right. I have really bad taste in men."

After Trent went home and I was straightening up getting ready for bed, I looked and saw that Andre had messaged me back. He said, "Here is my cell. Text me anytime. Hope to hear from you soon." I put his number in my phone and went to sleep.

For the rest of January, Andre and I texted back and forth every single day. He seemed very sweet and very busy. He had an ex-wife and two teenagers as well as a full time, plus overtime job as a security guard. Trent was right about the uniform shirt. Andre worked the evening swing shift and had Saturday and Sunday nights off. We made plans for the first time the first Saturday in February. I was looking forward to it but I wasn't exactly excited. What was making me excited, for lack of a better word, was remembering having sex with Dean. I admit that I would fantasize about it a lot alone, on my couch, with an old trusty rubber boyfriend, and my memories of Dean whispering song lyrics in my ear. Shaun said I needed an exorcism. She said, "We have to start making more plans together mostly because I miss you and you have been so busy every weekend hanging out with boys, but also because now I just picture you masturbating all the time in your apartment with the curtains drawn."

I laughed and said, "Well, you're not far off but, I don't draw my curtains."

"You're a sex crazed exhibitionist!"

I just laughed and made fun of her for "picturing me masturbating" as she said.

Andre asked me to meet him on Saturday at 1:00 PM in a pay lot at 13th and Logan. He said, "As far as what we are doing, it's a surprise, but you will like it." 13th and Logan is right in the middle of Capital Hill so I wasn't too worried about meeting a stranger for a "surprise" first date. I actually thought it was pretty charming that he seemed to be putting a little effort into it. He knew what kind of car I was driving so when I pulled up I saw him standing on the sidewalk waving at me. He didn't look like his pictures. There was nothing wrong with him, but let's just say he was very photogenic.

He met me at my Jeep and was all smiles but a little shy. He said, "Hi. It's good to meet you." I replied, "Hi!" and gave him a big hug. He smelled like old school Old Spice. I said, "Are you taking me to Pub on Penn?" I knew it was a couple blocks away; otherwise I hadn't been to any of the businesses in this specific area.

"No, I have a cool surprise for you."

"Ok, lead the way." He seemed really sweet but I couldn't help but feel a little nervous about his secretive plan. I mean this is a first "blind date". Surprises are for relationships. He was a little too "ask me to help him put his couch into his van, throw me in and kidnap me" like in "Silence of the Lambs". Shaun and I use a color chart like the Government does. White for zero threat, could be asleep. Yellow for, be aware of your surroundings, anything can happen. Orange for alert, something isn't right, be prepared to run. And, red for ABORT, arm yourself, and fight. I was comfortably at Yellow.

I was glad I wore flat heel riding boots because he took me for a walk down 13th Avenue to Pennsylvania Street. We walked by Subculture and Pablo's Coffee, which were two places I had never been and I thought of Dean. I wondered if he had been to Pablo's yet. Then Andre said, "It's just right up here." He hadn't spoken much since we left the parking lot but I was enjoying the walk with him anyway. Eventually he said, "Here it is." And he raised his arm for me to go ahead of him. Depending on who you are, you may know about this treasure in the Capital Hill area of Denver. It happens to be the Colorado Home of the one and only Unsinkable Molly Brown. Some part of the Denver Historical Society had preserved it and opened it as a museum. I had never been there, but I knew about it. I also knew Molly Brown, or rather, Margaret Brown because my mother is a fan of old musicals and Blayne and I endured, and sometimes admittedly enjoyed various musicals on VHS during our childhood. Some of her favorites being "Seven Brides for Seven Brothers", "Camelot", and "The Sound of Music" but in relation to this story, "The Unsinkable Molly Brown" with the beautiful and amazing Debbie Reynolds, mother of my favorite, Carrie Fisher, was luckily on her list.

I looked at Andre with a smile and said, "What a creative idea." As we walked to the entrance of the house I saw a lady who looked at us and smiled. Andre said, "Hey Carla!" "Andre!" she exclaimed, "It's weird to see you in your real clothes." I looked at him confused and he introduced me, "This is Carla, this is Cherry. I work security here so I get tickets for free to the museum. I know Carla from my shift rounds." I said, "Oh, cool, hi Carla, nice to meet you." I reached out and shook her hand. She was a very sweet middle aged women. She escorted us into the first area of the house and I actually felt excited to see it. I knew that Shaun was going to make fun of me and this was absolutely the most random date idea ever, but when I heard that he got in for free, it made sense. I appreciated his craftiness. I thought he was lucky that I happened to be a modern woman who appreciated that kind of history. He said, "Have you seen "The Unsinkable Molly Brown"?"

"Yes, my mom loves musicals. It's one of my favorites. I am actually excited. I like this kind of thing."

"Oh, cool. I had never heard of her until I got this job. My son also likes musicals and we watched it together for the first time about a year ago."

"Oh, really? How old is your son?"

"He is 15 and he is gay. We don't have anything in common, but I love him." I smiled at him. He continued, "I want to take him hunting and he's like, Dad, let's watch Glee." He laughed.

"He sounds adorable."

He smiled at me and said, "He is pretty cool."

We walked through the whole house, being educated on the life and times of Miss Margaret Brown and I learned a few things I didn't know. For example, she died at the Barbizon Hotel in Manhattan. I had been by that place a million times. My favorite parts were the old pictures and historical references. The rugs were incredible and I knew my mother would love them. The staircase is lined with a gorgeous, colorful, decadent rug. Molly Brown was a very cool woman, feminist, and philanthropist. It was an interesting experience to be inside her Denver home. I bought a postcard to send my mom and we headed outside.

Andre asked me, "Do you want to go to Subculture?"
"Sure! I have never been there." We headed down the sidewalk and he was quiet again. I said. "Do you like your job?"
"Yeah, it's pretty cool. I used to want to be a cop but I'm too old for that now. I have a pretty good thing going with this security company. I'm a trainer too so that's cool."
"Oh, that's good." Again there was silence. As we neared the parking lot of Subculture I said, "Have you been to this place?"
"Yes, I like it because it's cheap and it's in my shift area." We got inside and I liked the place. There was artwork by local artists on the walls and Colorado beers. It was my style. I ordered first and paid for my food just because I got the impression that he was on a low budget. I chose the Manhattan sandwich, which is pastrami, turkey, and provolone with Thousand Island dressing and, because I was feeling crazy, I also ordered a Subculture cocktail called "Jim Jones Rum Punch".

I was glad that the food was delicious and the people-watching was prime because Andre wasn't much of a conversationalist. I kept asking him questions and he kept giving me basic short answers. Then he would smile at me awkwardly like he was shy or maybe he just didn't like me. He was being pleasant and was very sweet but he was much more talkative via text message as opposed to when we were sitting face to face. I said, "How is your sandwich?"
"Oh, it's really good."

"Mine is too, it's delicious. I will totally come back here."

"Yeah, I was glad when they opened up."

I just looked at him and smiled and he smiled back at me.

By the time we got back to my car I felt relieved. I didn't know what else I could do to make him talk and he was very sweet, but it was just going nowhere. I said, "Thank you, Andre, for the very creative and original date. I had fun. I will have to bring my mom to Molly's house next time she comes to visit."

"Oh yeah. Me too. I'm glad we got to meet."

We hugged and I got in my jeep and drove away. I thought about how hard it must be in general for people to date when they are shy. There was really nothing wrong with him he just didn't have a lot to say, which is fine but maybe not when you are in the "let's get to know each other" phase of a friendship or dating relationship. But, then I thought, like I said, maybe he just didn't like me. Either way, it was a Saturday night and I found myself with no plans. All of my favorite people in Denver were busy with their mates and the only single friend I had was Trent who happened to be working that night. It would just have to be a wine and movie night at home alone for me.

I chose Zach and Miri Make a Porno, Heathers, and Hysterical Blindness and sat down to enjoy my evening. At about 9:00 PM I got a text from Andre that said, "I had fun with you today, sorry I am so shy. I really like you."

How cute, I thought, what should I say to this? I wrote back, "I had fun too. You're a sweetheart."

"I have to go to a birthday party next Saturday for a friend of mine, I would love to bring you as my date if you're not busy."

I figured why not, I'm not busy and said, "Sure, I would love to."

"Cool, it starts at 4 PM and should last just into the evening, not too late."

"Ok, see you then!"

I thought, "Cherry, what are you doing? You don't even like this guy." But maybe we would be friends. I didn't have plans so who cares. The problem is when you go out with a sensitive guy who likes you more than you like him you will have to eventually tell him that you aren't interested and the further you go the harder it is to break it to them. I just didn't have anything better to do so I talked myself out of feeling weird and into feeling like he is a sweet guy and if I want to hang out with him I can. Then Shaun texted and said, "Ok, we need to make plans. Next Saturday I am coming over to spend the night and I am going to buy like 20 tallboys to share and smoke cigarettes and be weird. It has been too long since we hung out."

"Oh man! I want that so bad! I literally just made plans for 4PM until sometime in the evening with a guy I just met."

"So I can't come over until 7ish, so that will probably be fine."

"Ok, cool. Yaye!" Then I told her, "He took me to the Molly Brown house today for our first date."

"What!? Hahaha! That's amazing! That reminds me of your mom!"

"Haha."

"I'm gonna learn to read and write!"

I laughed and remembered that line from the musical and replied, "French!" Never in my wildest dreams did I imagine that in our thirties Shaun and I would be texting quotes from "The Unsinkable Molly Brown" musical. But, we did, and it was definitely funny.

On Friday I got a text from Andre that said that he had to work for a co-worker during the day on Saturday which was normally his day off so he asked if he could just meet me at my house and change into his clothes to go to the party. I didn't mind and told him I would see him tomorrow. On Saturday I texted Shaun and told her to just let herself in if I wasn't home when she got there and that I would be home as soon as I could. She said, "You better hurry up. I'll bring the beers and the American Spirits." Andre showed up in his little security guard uniform and admittedly, I didn't find it as attractive as I did Trent's uniform. I am definitely a girl who likes uniforms but I have my limits I guess. He said, "I will just leave this all here and worry about it when we get back, ok?"

"Sure, you ready then?"

"Yes, I don't want to be too late."

The party was at an apartment clubhouse. He introduced me to everyone and they were all very nice. I hung out with Andre the whole time and no one talked to me unless he was standing next to me.

Andre was much more comfortable in that setting than he was on our first date but he was still a little shy with me. He said, "Are you having fun?"

"Oh yeah! Thank you." I wasn't having any fun, bless his heart. I couldn't wait to leave. At 7 PM Shaun texted me and said, "I'm at your place; what the hell is this uniform hanging in the bathroom, you better be on your way home soon."

"That's Andre's! Don't mess with it. Leaving soon!" I kept my phone in my pocket on vibrate so I would know if she messaged me, but I didn't want to be rude and text too much. About twenty minutes later, she texted a picture of herself drinking out of a bottle of Arrogant Bastard Ale. I replied, "You better wait for me!" Arrogant Bastard tastes like poison but we love it. It's like an accomplishment to get through a glass of it.

By 7:45 I was starting to get impatient and though everyone else was leaving, Andre was still mingling with all of his buddies. I got another text and when I looked I saw that it was Shaun again. This time it was a picture of her standing in front of the bathroom mirror with Andre's uniform shirt on! I almost peed my pants trying to keep from bursting out into laughter in front of all of these strangers and I replied, "Shaun! HAHAHAHAHHA! Take it off!" She sent another "selfie" picture of herself in his shirt lying on my bed with a fake sexy look on her face and said, "This thing smells like Old Spice." I replied, "Shaun!" I told Andre, "I have to go soon, my best friend is already at my place we have plans tonight, I should have told you but I thought we would be back by now." He said, "Oh, that's cool. I'm ready to take off." I thought oh, thank God and we started saying our goodbyes.

I wanted to laugh all the way home but I held it in and texted Shaun, "Take that shit off, we are on our way." We walked into the apartment and I was a little nervous like she was going to be standing in the living room already drunk, wearing only the shirt or something just to be funny but instead she was sitting on the couch fake reading and the shirt was hanging exactly as he left it. She jumped up, "Hi, I'm Shaun, Cherry's best friend." He smiled nervously and said, "Hi, I'm Andre." She said, "Nice to meet you, Andre." He went into the bathroom to get his stuff and Shaun and I covered our mouths to keep from laughing. I wanted to punch her for making this moment so awkward. Andre came out of the bathroom and said, "Thank you so much for being my date, I had fun." I said, "Me too! Thank you for inviting me to meet your friends." He looked at Shaun and said, "It was nice to meet you." She smiled at him and said, "You too!" He gave me a hug and left.

Shaun handed me a full glass of beer and a cigarette and said, 'Let's smoke, that guy isn't even your type."
"I know. He is sweet though."
"Mmhmm, sweet and shy and wears Old Spice. Not the good Old Spice the old 80s Old Spice."
"I know, I hate it."
"I had a dream that you got married. I never saw the guys face though."
"Oh, that helps."

"Maybe you should give it up. Then suddenly a man will fall into your lap."

"Sometimes that happens, but not usually. I don't feel like giving it up."

Shaun spit out her drink laughing on my patio floor and said, "That's not what I've heard."

We laughed and I said, "You shut your mouth! And, I'm gonna beat you for putting on his uniform shirt, you bitch!" We laughed all night about it and finished every drop of 7.5% or more alcohol content beer. It was a perfect and much needed slumber party.

In reality there was no argument from me about what Shaun was saying. I knew that Andre wasn't for me. I was also starting to feel like I was getting absolutely nowhere with dating and I definitely was over figuring out different ways to tell someone I didn't want to keep seeing them as much as I was over being told that they didn't want to keep seeing me.

On Sunday after Shaun left, I cleaned my apartment all day and listened to music. I put in my girl, Shelby Lynn. I have two of her albums, "Love, Shelby" and "I Am Shelby Lynn". My favorites on Love Shelby are "Killin' Kind" and "Wall In Your Heart" but my favorite album is "I Am Shelby Lynn" My favorite songs on that album are "Leavin'", "Gotta Get Back", and "I Thought It Would Be Easier" which I play over and over. I remember either seeing her in an interview or reading it in a magazine a long time ago and she said something like, "I sing songs that move me." I have never forgotten it and I relate to that sentiment. I was thrilled to see that she was cast in the role of Carrie Cash, Johnny's mother in "Walk The Line". I happen to be a Johnny Cash fan.

At about 5 PM I got a text from Andre that said, "I am going to be near your neighborhood tonight and don't have to work. I was wondering if I could stop by." My stomach sank and I felt guilty because I was about to lie. I answered, "Oh, I'm sorry, Andre! I'm at Shaun's. I won't be home until late." He answered. "It's ok. I thought I would check. Have fun!" I said, "Have a good night!" About an hour later I got a text from Trent. "Cherry Pie! I'm coming over." "Yaye!" I answered. That was exactly what I needed. Ten minutes after Trent texted I heard a noise outside my door that sounded like paper crinkling. I looked out the peephole and there was nothing there. Then I got a text. I looked at my phone; it was from Andre and it said, "You'll have a surprise waiting for you when you get home." I just stared at my phone not understanding what that meant and then I looked out my window and saw Trent walking by Andre in the parking lot. I ran to the door, opened it and there was a bouquet of flowers wedged in the doorknob. I quickly grabbed them and put them in a vase just as Trent knocked on my door. I felt so embarrassed that that had just happened! I let him in and he said, "Hey Cherry Pie!" and gave me a hug. He leaned back and looked at me and said, "Why are you out of breath?" "Am I? I don't know. I've been cleaning."
He looked at the flowers and said, "Who are those from?"

"What are you? A cop?" He laughed and sat down on the couch. "They are from Shaun. How was your week?"

"Oh, you know, fighting crime, saving lives."

"Same here." I laughed at my self then asked, "Do you want some Iced Tea?"

"Yeah! Sweet Tea?"

"Yeah I just made it."

We continued to chat as I poured us two glasses. I walked over to the couch and handed Trent his. I was distracted because I felt so weird about what had just happened. I couldn't believe they passed each other in the parking lot. I was thinking, "My neighbor's probably think I am a prostitute. Wait until I tell Shaun. She is going to make so much fun of me." I sat down on the couch and Trent smiled at me. He said, "You ok? You seem out of it." I turned to face him and bent my left knee to put my leg up on the couch and as I opened my mouth to speak I felt something vibrating. Trent's eyebrows raised and I looked down and around trying to figure out what it was. Trent said, "What the hell is that?" I moved my butt over and realized it was coming from in the cushion. I reached in and pulled out a florescent pink vibrator shaped like a wand that also rotates and just held it in front of my face staring at it with my mouth wide open in complete and total embarrassment. Trent started laughing hysterically. Finally I turned it off and jumped up to put it in my bedroom. I said, "Oh my God!" He started laughing again. I came back to the couch and looked at him smirking at me and said, "I am so embarrassed." He said, "Come here." And reached out his hand. I put my hand in his and sat down next to him and he said, "I think it's sexy." I looked up at him and smiled my best crooked smile and said, "Oh yeah?" Then, much to my surprise, but not really because honestly we had been fighting the sexual tension for weeks, Trent and I had some intense and memorable sex just the way we used to; hot and with no strings attached. Oh, man was Shaun going to bust my chops about this story.

Before I went to sleep later that night I texted her and said, "Can you do lunch tomorrow?"
"Yeah! Let's do it!"
"Good, I have a story to tell you."
"Oh God! What about???"
I thought of Shakespears Sister's cassette single "Stay" that I had in the 90s. The "B" side had a bonus song that didn't even get played on the radio and, I answered, "The Trouble With Andre."

Chapter 25 Rein It In, Cherry

Lunch with Shaun the next day was a "laugh riot" as my mother would say. We laughed so hard that we caused a scene, but it was ok, because the people were entertained. After discussing my current situation in great detail, to the point that I was a couple minutes late to get back to work, I decided that I was going to delete my dating profile and focus on meeting men the old fashioned way; through mutual friends and in coffee shops or meat sections at the grocery store like Blayne always said. After all, I did meet Trent that way and he turned out to be really cool, though only as friends and the occasional romp. I thought it was good timing, too, since another Valentine's Day was about to come and go.

At work Ben was having a slow day and took two hours for lunch so he didn't even know that I was late. I told on myself anyway when he got back and he pulled up a chair near my desk. He said, "How are you doing lately, Miss Cherry? Are you seeing anyone?"
"It's funny you should ask that today, because no, I am not seeing anyone and I went to lunch with Shaun today and decided after some recent events that I am going to close the online dating account and go ahead and start meeting men the old fashioned way."
"I think that is wise. Do you know that I don't know a single person who is married to someone they met on line? I do, however, know one who has a restraining order."

I laughed and said, "I have just decided that I will meet the right guy by chance or by mutual friends." He smiled at me and then I said, "Don't you and Margo know everyone in Denver? You have to know at least one single guy who I would find attractive." "Hmm. Let me think about that." "Good. You should. I'm sure one of these days I will start hearing my biological clock and I don't think you want that kind of drama in your office." "I will consider this a priority."

That night I got a text from Ben that said, "I told Margo what you said today and she said she has someone in mind that she had been meaning to tell you about. Come over for dinner on Friday night and we will tell you all about him." I quickly answered, "What? Awesome! Can't wait!" I went on my profile and began the process of deleting my account. It's funny, they want to know if I am deleting because I met someone and if I met someone they want to know if it was on their site and if it was on their site they want to know who it was. I wished they had a choice that read "none of your business" but they didn't so I chose "other" and called it a day. Later I would learn that they do in fact pull statistics from these online dating sites for age, sex, and race and who dates whom. It's a little weird if you spend any amount of time thinking about it. I chose not to, closed my laptop and put in a movie.

"Overboard", with Goldie and Kurt. I love that movie so much. The fact that Kurt's name is Dean in the flick meant nothing to me. I was over that too. I had a clean slate, ready for love and kindness. That is what I was looking for all along; Love and Kindness. Overboard is a good movie to watch when you need to feel inspired about falling in love when you least expect it. Plus, it's good for a few laughs. Furthermore, who doesn't love Goldie and Kurt's love story in real life? They are one of the only celebrity couples that would actually mess me up a little if they broke up.

On Thursday, which was Valentine's Day, Trent stopped by on his way to work looking all sexy in his uniform and had a single rose in his hand. He said, "I wanted to give this to you because you deserve a Valentine. From the bottom of my heart, I am glad we are friends. You are a down chick, Cherry Pie." I was so touched by that. I hugged him tight and thanked him for being my friend too. He said, "I gotta go in, you sleep well." I knocked on his bullet proof vest with my knuckles and said, be careful out there Trent Reznor." He laughed and ran down the stairs to his car. What a sweetheart, I thought, as I put my rose in with the flowers from Andre. So many men so little time.

Once Friday came I was excited to see Margo and to learn about the guy she had in mind for me. I brought wine and got to their house at about 7:00 PM. Ben greeted me at the door with a glass of cabernet already poured. He said, "Cabernet Sauvignon pour vous." I answered, "Merci." I can say "thank you" in French, that's about it. I hugged Margo and said in my best fake southern accent, "If I knew y'all were gonna be all fancy shmancy I would have brought some Arbor Mist instead of Boone's Farm." Margo threw her head back in laughter and said, "I have missed you! What the hell have you been doing? Benny says you've been dating up a storm." We went into the kitchen and sat down as Margo continued cooking.

"I have been busy looking for a husband. I couldn't be bothered."

"No luck though?"

"No and I'm two clicks away from being a promiscuous girl so I decided to rein it in." Ben laughed hard and held up his glass to toast us. He said, "Rein it in, Cherry." We clinked our glasses and laughed.

I looked at Margo and said, "So, what's this I hear about a single guy you know?"

"I want to tell you all about him and you tell me if you think you might be interested. We are friends on Facebook too so I can show you pictures."

"Oh, cool."

"I was thinking about inviting him over when we had you over for a bar-b-q or something this summer but Benny said you are worried about your eggs dying by then." She laughed and Ben said, "I said you were talking about your biological clock." We all laughed and I said, "I know I sound like I'm in a hurry but it's really not about kids. I just want to find the one. Everyone can't be as lucky as people like you guys. In love for fifty years."

Ben yelled, "Hey-O! We are only like 10 years older than you, fool."

"Whoah! Did you just quote Ed McMahan and Mr. T in one sentence?"

Over our laughter, Ben said, "I believe I did."

We sat down to eat and Margo said, "So, his name is Felix. Isn't that a cool name?" It's a very cool name. Over dinner they told me about their friend, Felix who is a couple years older than me, single, no ex-wife, no kids, hard working, owns a small specialty concrete company. He is from Denver mostly but was an army brat, owns his own house in Golden, is Hispanic, is muscular, has a bunch of tattoos. They said they met him years ago when they hired him for a job and the work was great so they hired him again and then started recommending him and eventually became friends. Margo said, "He is one of the sweetest men I have ever met in my life. I can't imagine why he has been single for so long." Eventually she showed me his Facebook page and when she handed me her phone to look the first think, I noticed was his full name; Felix Santoro. That might be the sexiest name on the planet and from the looks of his pictures he might be the sexiest guy ever. He was burley and obviously spent time at the gym and he had kind eyes which is what really did it for me. I handed her back her phone and said, "Yuh. I want to meet him. Show him my pictures and if he is interested give him my number." Ben laughed and said, "Yes ma'am." Margo said, "I wasn't sure if you cared about tattoos Ben said you had been dating really straight guys." I said, "I have dated every guy. I don't have a type. I don't care about tattoos either, usually I like them. I care about personality, humor, kindness, no felonies, you know, shit like that." They laughed and Ben said, "Yeah, he is legit and in case you were wondering his company is pretty successful. It's small but that just means he doesn't have a lot of overhead. He said he gets the majority of his work just by word of mouth. He doesn't even use a website, just a Facebook business page." I said, "This is all very exciting. I hope he is interested in meeting me." Margo said, "I am sure he will be."

We spent the rest of the night laughing and talking and even had a few smokes with our wine on the patio. I love them and consider them like family. I could not be more grateful to Ben for being such an amazing boss and to both of them for being such great friends.

On Sunday Margo texted me and said, "I gave Felix your number and he said, "She can text me." So, here is his number too. You should reach out first." "Thanks! I will!" "This is exciting! If it works out I assume I will be your made of honor." "Haha, I think its matron of honor when you're already married." "Yeah! That's the thing!"

I stared at his number after I loaded it into my phone as I lay in bed that night. I decided I would wait until Monday night to text him. Felix Santoro, a cool name indeed.

Chapter 26 Mr. Santoro

Ben and I were so busy on Monday because of a case he was working on that we barely spoke about Felix or how much fun we had on Friday night. Still, I thought about it all day. Since I had been doing on line dating, the unknown easily excited me. It was like putting a quarter in one of those machines in the lobby of the grocery store as a kid. You saw what was possible but never knew which one you would end up with. Dating like that and setting myself up for blind dates had me on the edge of my seat. That was probably why I stuck with it for as long as I did. But, this wasn't a game to me. I had a goal. It was fun; I really wasn't in a hurry though it seemed that way. It was simply the fact that I had a goal. True love was that goal. I had every intention of finding it.

On Monday night I sent a text message to Felix much like I had sent to the guys who messaged me on line. I said, "Hi, Felix! This is Cherry, Ben and Margo's friend." Then I put my phone on the kitchen counter and started making my dinner. Eventually he texted back and said, "Hi. How are you?"
"I'm great. How was your day?"
"It was good. Busy."
"Is this weird for you? I thought it would be cool to meet you some time. Margo and Ben say great things about you."
"Lol, yeah they are great. I've never texted a girl I don't know but they said you were cool."
"I would love to talk sometime, when you're not busy or tired."

"Yeah. I would like that too. I'm always home on Sundays. That is the best day for me."
"Ok, I will reach out to you then."
"Cool. Have a good night."

Based on that short conversation I would say that he was either A. Very tired (understandably). B. Thinks this is the dumbest thing ever. Or C. Thinks I'm crazy. I thought, who cares, I have literally nothing to lose and like Sophia Petrillo on "The Golden Girls", I went back to my meatballs.

Once Sunday finally came around I thought of a nice and easy text message to send that didn't seem too desperate or like I had thought about it all week, but that also seemed like I was outgoing and interested. I simply texted him and said, "Hi there! I hope you had a great week." About 5 minutes later he texted back and said, "Thanks you too. ☺"
"I did. I'm really lucky to have a boss like Ben."
"Yeah, he's cool. I'm really lucky to have a boss like me lol."
"What is your company? Ben and Margo said it is specialty concrete and landscaping and that you are very good."
"Lol, yes, they are my best customers. It's called Santoro Landscape Design."
"By the way, Santoro is a pretty rad last name."
"Thank you, it's supposedly an Italian name but my father's family is originally from Mexico. My mother's too."
"That is really cool. I'm fascinated with people's family heritage; my father's family is originally from

the British Isles. Cherry farmers, which is where I got my name."

"Really? That's cool. I have never met anyone named Cherry."

"Well, I'm glad to hear that. I like to be original."

"You definitely are."

We went on small talking for a couple hours and in general I enjoyed his company. I thought he was humble, funny, and interesting. So, by Wednesday that next week we had been texting every day and I could tell that though he was stand offish in the beginning, he was starting to warm up to the idea of having a pen-pal via text. On Thursday morning which happened to be the last day of February he texted me first thing in the morning and said, "Good morning. ☺"

"Was I the first thing you thought of today?"

"Yes."

"Good. Same for me."

On Thursday night I told him, "I would love to see you this weekend, and officially meet."

"You would?"

"Yes, what about Saturday?"

"K."

I could tell he was nervous. I guess I was too because I liked him so far, but I was no rookie and texting is only a minor and often inaccurate form of communication for two people who don't really know each other. I just knew that I was done with texting only. I didn't care that I was about to make the first move. I said, "You let me know what you would like to do and when and I will be there."

"Rodizio's 7:00."

"I'm a vegetarian."

"There is a salad bar."

"Lol, I'm kidding, I love meat."

"Oh, thank GOD."

I hadn't been to Rodizio's since I went there with Trent. That was the best time I had ever had there too. On Saturday I was so psyched that I was beside myself. I got a text from Felix at about 4:00 PM that said, "I can pick you up, what's your address?" I gave him my address and told him, "I am looking forward to it!" Then someone knocked on my door. I figured it was Trent and I yelled, "Just a second!" When I opened the door it was Shaun! "Yaye! What are you doing here?"

"I literally was in the area and I thought I would surprise you and help you get ready for your date."

"Awesome! He is picking me up at 6:45."

"Perfect."

Shaun pulled a bottle of cab out of her purse, "Let's take the edge off." I laughed and told her I had a couple outfits picked out to choose from as she poured us a glass of wine.

"He is a sexy Latino, no?"

"Yes!"

"Then you must have at least a little bit of cleavage."

"Oh, you know I will."

It was finally March, my favorite month and when you live in a place that has seasons, a person can get excited in March, because March is the beginning of Spring and Spring signifies new beginnings, fresh starts, flowers, and cleansing rain. March is the month of my birth and when I feel the most confident. March is when people get "Twitterpated". I specifically remember watching "Bambi" when I was very young. I mostly understood what twitterpated meant but still asked my mom for further explanation. She said, "It's when you fall in love with your perfect mate. Spring is a good time for it because winter is over and summer is coming." Shaun reached up her glass for a toast and I picked up my glass of wine. She said, "Happy March." I nodded and said, "It will be a good one."

When 6:30 rolled around I was ready to go and I looked good. Shaun ducked out and went home as I patiently waited for Felix to show up. Felix. What a cool name. I got a text message, "I'm here, black pickup." I looked out my window and there he was parked behind my jeep. I texted back, "On my way." I grabbed my jacket and my purse and headed out the door. I waved at him and he got out of his truck and met me in the brightness of his headlights. I gave him a hug and said, "It's so good to meet you, Felix." He smiled at me and said, "You too." Then he followed me to the passenger door and opened it for me. I said, "Why thank you, sir." He just smiled and I jumped into his truck. I watched him walk around the front of the truck again and noticed how attractive he was. Picture him: Shaved head, kind dark brown eyes- the color of chocolate, a nice looking goatee, about 5 foot 9, seriously burley- huge arms. As he got into his truck and shifted into drive, I noticed how big his hands were. They were sexy man hands. He was strong. I felt extremely attracted to him as I sat next to him in the cab of his truck.

We made small talk as we drove toward Wyncoop. I said, "You're a very good driver. My father always said a real man is a great driver- the kind that makes you feel safe."

He laughed and said, "Thank you."

"Is Rodizio's your favorite?"

"One of them. I'm a meat eater and I figured it has a good atmosphere for a date. I have been craving it lately."

"What part of Denver do you live in?"

"Golden. I have a house there. It was my grandparent's house."

"Oh, that's right. The house I grew up in was my grandparent's house. That's part of the reason why we could afford to live in that area. Golden is similar, expensive housing, right?"

"Yes, actually, my neighbor's houses are going for more than I could afford if I was buying so I got lucky. People actually leave me notes on my door saying they want to buy my house."

"I have totally heard of that happening. My mother is a real estate agent, my father was too, and my grandparents."

"Family business?"

"Yeah, just wasn't my thing."

"I don't blame you."

We arrived and parked in the area and as we walked toward the restaurant he continued to be very chivalrous by walking on the street side of the sidewalk and guiding me without touching me in a safe fashion until we got to the door where he walked ahead of me, opened it and said, "After you." I find chivalry very attractive and took note of the fact that he must have been raised right.

He had made us reservations. The hostess said, "Right this way, Mr. Santoro." He looked at me and winked. What a name. He sounded like he was in Good Fellas with that name. I said, "Your name makes you sound like a big deal." He laughed and looked away kind of shy. He was just so adorable. When we got to the table he asked me where I would like to sit. We sat across from each other and put our coats on our chairs behind us. He was wearing a nice black t-shirt, black slacks, and boots. I admittedly stared at him when I realized that he was covered in tattoos. He had full sleeves and tattoos that spread to his neck and the backs of his hands. After the hostess left us I said with wide eyes, "Felix, you're a canvas." He laughed, looked at his arms and stretched them out which accentuated his triceps, which just so happens to be my favorite muscle and said, "This is what happens when you have more than one friend who is a budding tattoo artist and why I didn't become an executive." I laughed and said, "Why would you want to be an executive?"

As time went on I would catch myself staring at his face, and he reciprocated in a bashful way. He was funny. He was sweet. He said sir and ma'am to everyone who came to our table. He was gorgeous and he was kind. I thought about my parents who always talked about how they fell in love in an hour and even though I always lovingly made fun of them for it, I had to pay attention to the fact that it crossed my mind as I sat there in front of Felix. I had to pay attention to how I felt at that moment. I felt something I had never felt before. It wasn't because of any profound thing that happened. He was like no other guy I had ever met, but why? We were just talking, sharing, and eating, well, like I had done on countless other dates before. It was the way I felt with him. It was the way he made me feel. It was like peace. It was like comfort. There was a twinkle in his eyes. I was enamored of him.

We finished our meal finally and without hesitation I said, "I don't want to stop hanging out with you. Do you want to come back to my place?" He blushed and he said, "Yeah, sure, I can probably make it a couple more hours. I usually fall asleep at 9:00." We laughed and I said, "Well, you have already made it to 9." He looked at the time on his phone and said, "Wow. I'm impressed with myself." He paid the bill and though I offered to go Dutch, he insisted and took the check from my hand.

On the way back to my place I wasn't as talkative. My mind was racing. I felt a smile on my face as I looked out the window at the lights of Denver. I said, "I love this town."

"Me too."

"We you born here?"

"Yes, at St. Joseph's."

"My friend Sarah works there in the ER."

"It's not the same as it was in the 70s, I bet she has a lot of stories."

"She totally does."

"I meant to ask you where your parents live now."

"Colorado Springs. My sister too."

He had spoken to me about his sister at dinner. They were twins and were very close he said. Shaun always said, "Sisters are the worst. They don't like you before they even meet you and when they do meet you, good luck." I never had a problem with anyone's sister as far as I could recall but what did I know.

We got to my apartment and I let him in behind me. I said, "Make yourself cozy, I am going to have some wine, do you want anything?"

"Tea or water?"

"I have sweat tea!"

"Perfect."

Felix sat down on my couch. After I gave him his tea I took off my boots, sat down next to him, and turned on the TV. "Captain Ron" was in the DVD player. I laughed when it started playing and said, "Do you like this movie?"

"Yeah, I haven't seen it in years. Do you not have cable?"

"No. I am a movie watcher."

"You just watch movies all the time?"

"Yes. I'm an addict."

"I have like four hundred movies."

"Wow. I don't even have that many. What are you, blockbuster?"

We continued to talk and laugh as Captain Ron played in the background. Eventually I changed into comfortable sleepable clothes and we were both yawning so I said, "You can stay here if you feel too tired to drive." He just looked at me for a second and I thought, "Please stay. Nothing will happen but please stay with me." But I didn't say it out loud.

"Ok, sure."

"Slumber party!" He laughed and I went into the bedroom to turn down the bed. I said, "Do you need anything?"

"Do you have mouthwash? I will just use that instead of brushing my teeth."

"Sure." I put it on the counter and went and got into bed while he was using the bathroom. I was so happy to just have him there with me. It didn't feel weird at all it felt right. He came in eventually, looked at me and said, "You look cozy." I said, "I am! You will like my bed. It's a pillow top." He laughed, turned off the light and took off his pants in the dark. He crawled into bed and squirmed around until he was comfortable. I said, "I had fun with you tonight. I am so glad we met."

"Me too. I am so full."

"So am I."

I turned to my side and faced him and said, "I feel like I have always known you. You're a familiar face." He turned and looked at me. I could see him illuminated by the streetlights outside. He turned to lay on his side too and he kissed me. It was a passionate, slow, soft kiss. He didn't do anything else, just kissed me, and minutes later we were both asleep.

Chapter 26 Birthday Number 36

On Sunday morning I woke up to a big sexy man snuggling me in my bed at about 6 AM. I whispered in my sleepiest voice, "Good Morning." He said, "Sorry, I'm an early riser." I said, "I think you beat the rooster." He laughed and said, "Watch your mouth." This made me laugh because it was something I always said. He sat up and stretched and through my half closed eyes I studied what I could see of his tattoos. I said, "Does your mother like your tattoos?" He laughed and said, "She thinks I won't be able to find a good woman." I said, "Oh! Well, introduce her to me. I'm as good as it gets!" He laughed and said, "You do seem pretty good." I felt like he was mine. He got up and walked to the bathroom and I just lay in my bed staring at the ceiling. We had fallen asleep with our lips touching. It was the sweetest thing I had ever experienced in my life. I didn't even completely understand how I was feeling but I knew I didn't want him to leave.

He came out of the bathroom, put on his pants and said, "Do you want to go get breakfast?"
I sat up and said, "Yes!"
"Oh good." Then he slipped on his t-shirt.
"I'll just straighten up a little and put on something that makes it look like I just went to the gym or yoga class."
"Awesome, the low maintenance type."
I laughed and said, "Maybe I'm low maintenance or maybe I'm just really hungry."
"Either way, I like you."

I just smiled at him and walked backwards into the bathroom so I could look at him as long as possible.

We went to Snooze near the ballpark. It's literally the friendliest place I have ever been to. They must pay their staff well or threaten them or something. As we munched on food and sipped our coffee we had one of those True Romance, Clarence and Alabama conversations. Remember? The "favorites" talk? He said, "So, what is your all time favorite band?" Well, by now you know that I am a huge lover of music and have a very eclectic taste. You might imagine that it would be hard for someone like me to choose one favorite band. But, it isn't hard at all. Years ago I would often say my favorite was Alice In Chains but my real honest answer is, "Led Zeppelin." I will tell you like I told him why, "I have always said that Led Zeppelin is my "deserted island" band because if I could take the box set with me I might feel musically satisfied. With Led Zeppelin you experience so many things. There are songs for every mood, and every emotion. Led Zeppelin is transcendent. Even though they are primarily rock n roll, they are hard rock, they are soft rock, they are classic rock, and they are soul, blues, and jazz, even rockabilly. They can make you want to dance, they can make you cry, laugh, lust. They tell you stories, reality and fantasy. They talk sing about falling in love, breaking up, politics, religion, regret, hate, sadness, happiness, bliss, kindness, scandal, and most importantly sex. You can be from the country, the city, and everywhere in between, everyone can dig on Led Zeppelin. Everyone."

Felix just looked at me, right into my eyes and smiled. I assumed it was because he was amused by my long winded answer. When he didn't say anything in response I said, "What's yours?" He said, "I love Zeppelin too. You're right about them." I smiled at him, appreciating the validation and he continued, "I think my all time favorite might be Black Sabbath." I excitedly said, "Oh, yeah, another classic. Shaun and I saw Dio Era Sabbath, no Ozzy when they did the "Dehumanizer tour in 1992. They played at the Tower Theatre in West Philadelphia. When we bought the tickets we were under the impression that Danzig was opening and when the show started instead of Glenn and his muscles, out came Prong." Felix laughed and said, "Oh man, really? I vaguely remember Prong."

"They sucked, but Dio and Sabbath were Epic. We were so glad we saw them. Plus, Tower Theatre is an awesome venue."

"I really want to go to Philly some time. Mostly for the food."

"Philly is awesome. Shaun and I used to hang out on South Street when we were teenagers. Mostly to scam on Philly boys who were always cute and always crazy." He laughed and looked down. I said, "Not as cute as you though."

He blushed and said, "You're not so bad yourself."

I enjoyed making this burley man who looks so tough and intense blush and smile bashfully. I felt like I always either wanted to squeeze his cheeks or make out with him.

Felix pulled up in front of my apartment to drop me off after breakfast and we gave each other a quick peck on the lips before I got out of his truck. I waved goodbye again and headed up to my place. My head was metaphorically spinning as I walked in and put down my purse. I just stood there and smiled and became aware of how good I felt. About 3 minutes later there was a knock at the door. I looked out the peep hole and it was Felix. He was looking down at his feet. I opened the door and began to talk and he grabbed me and squeezed me in this amazing big bear hug. I fell limp and focused on his arms around me. I said, "Awe, you're so cute, what are you doing?"

"I really like you." Then he kissed me. He kissed me passionately. I had never ever before been kissed like that. His lips were so soft. I melted in his arms and just hung on to his shoulders because my legs were like jelly. I leaned my head back and looked at his face. He opened his eyes and focused on mine and I whispered, "I really like you too. I mean…I REALLY like you."

"You should be mine."

"Ok."

We giggled and held each other for a minute and he said, "I have to go. I'll see you soon."

How was I going to keep from sleeping with him? I laughed to myself. I have never wanted to rip someone's clothes off so badly but also I really loved that he hadn't tried that with me. He was trying to take it slow too, though, we had only spent not even 24 hours with each other and we had basically made it official already. I knew Shaun would tell me not to buy the cow before I tasted the milk but my first thought after he left was to text my mom. I said, "Wait till you meet this guy. I feel like I fell in love in an hour. Now I think I might know what you and Dad were always saying." She didn't answer me, but two minutes later my phone rang and it was Blayne. He said, "I'm at mom's. She said you're in love."

"Maybe I am. He could be the one." I proceeded to tell him all about Felix.

"So, what is it about this guy that makes him different?"

"It's more than just the fact that so far I like everything about him, it's the way I feel when I'm with him."

Blayne laughed and said, "You sound like Baby talking to Patrick Swayze in Dirty Dancing."

"Yeah! It is just like that. I bet Felix would dance with me on a log in the woods too!"

We laughed and he said, "Well, I'm excited to meet him, I'm coming out to Denver for a two day conference in May."

"What!" Yaye! How many days will you be here?"

"Saturday through Wednesday, May 1st through the 5th. I already have my ticket."

I could not *be* more excited. I really didn't think I would see him until my Christmas break that year. Don't worry, I hadn't forgotten about getting him back for what he did to me at the airport back home. He would soon find out how creative I can be. May was a long way away and I had something much more important to plan. It would soon be my birthday. Shawn hosted it at her house that year. I was very excited as always for my birthday because I considered it a national holiday and I liked being able to invite everyone I knew. Having a best friend with a house when you don't makes that possible. Shaun and I were having lunch that week to start planning and deciding on the invite list. Since she was a professional I expected the best.

On Monday morning and every morning after that, Felix texted me first thing and said, "Good morning, Sexy." I couldn't wait to see him over the weekend and I couldn't wait to talk Shaun's ear off about him at our lunch. We met on Thursday, spent the first half talking about Felix and then she said, "Will you still be inviting your boyfriends?"
"I am still going to invite Trent, if that's what you mean, and if you would please casually invite Mark for me? Let him know in some way that I will be bringing a date but that he is invited, you know, so it isn't weird. I'm sure by now he doesn't care anyway.

I will do the same thing I always do and tell Felix at some point that I am still friends with some guys I have slept with. Real men don't care."

"Yes. I agree with that. I will have Johnny invite him. Did you invite Felix yet?"

"Not yet. We are hanging out this weekend, I will invite him then."

"I seriously can't wait to meet him."

"You are going to want to squeeze him."

Felix was coming over to hang out after lunch and then was staying for dinner on Saturday so I cleaned my apartment in the morning and planned to make a chicken pasta dish with garlic bread. He said he was a garlic addict and I wanted to make sure he knew I was a good cook. I told him to bring a couple of movies from his library that as far as I was told, was much more impressive than my movie collection. He ended up bringing "The Immortals" and "Paul" about the alien with Seth Rogen's voice. I seriously love that movie and Simon Pegg and Nick Frost. In the movie they talk about Wyoming and actually go to "The Devil's Tower" which is a rock formation-tourist attraction in the North-Eastern part of the state. Felix said, "Oh, that reminds me. I am going to Laramie, Wyoming to do a property this week. I'll be gone from Tuesday until probably Sunday the 25th."

"What! I thought you just did Denver area."

"I do usually but this is a client who has a house both here and in Laramie and he's really cool and is paying for lodging so I accepted the offer."

"That's really cool, I'm only sad because my birthday party is Saturday the 24th and I was really hoping you would be there."

"Oh, man, that sucks. I planned on probably finishing that day and heading home on Sunday."

I sat down next to him and handed him some tea and said, "It's ok, I obviously understand." He put down our drinks, smiled at me and pulled me to him so that we were snuggled up on the couch and as I leaned against his chest I could hear his heart beating and felt the warmth of him. I forgot about anything that was on my mind. I felt so safe. I felt so comforted. I felt like I loved him. And then…we fell asleep.

I can't explain the way it feels to be so comfortable with someone you just met and just fall asleep in their arms. I didn't care if I snored and if I drooled on his shirt. I was completely free and I assumed that he related to the way I felt, because he was snoring away about two hours later when I woke up and realized that it was time to make dinner. I whispered, "Felix." He opened his eyes and closed his mouth and I giggled and said, "You're the cutest thing on earth." He smiled and sat up straight. I got up and he said, "We must have been tired. You put me to sleep."

"You are so snuggly, it was easy."

"You're snuggly too."

Over dinner we were a little quiet. He loved the food, I could tell he was happy, but we did a lot more looking at each other, smiling, and I think both of us were in deep thought. Whatever I was feeling for him I could tell he was feeling for me. I felt like we were on the same page and that we were connecting more and more every minute. It felt like being a kid again and having a crush and not knowing entirely how to act but just feeling really happy. When he left that night we kissed for a while and I said, "I'm going to miss you while you're up there. Hurry back to me, ok?"

"Trust me. I'll be back as soon as I can, sexy."

I stood in the door as he walked to his truck and watched him. As Uncle Angelo on The Golden Girls said it, Felix "had a behind so round, so firm, you've got to fall down on your knees and cry out at it's magnificent regal beauty". He seemed perfect. I could not wait to find out what he had to offer in the bedroom.

I gave Shaun's address and phone number to Felix just in case he was able to make it and made sure he knew that I understood that he couldn't. On the day of the party, as guests were arriving, he called me and told me he was so sorry he was away and that he hoped I had a great time. He wished me Happy Birthday and I went back to my celebration. It was a great party. All my favorite people in Colorado were there. Ben was there going on and on about how he better be the maid of honor if Felix and I end up getting married and Mark even showed up for an hour or two.

At about 10 PM I was on the back patio relaxing by Johnny's chiminea with some of my guests and about 2/3 of the way through a bottle of "Skinny Girl

Margarita" that my friend Kelly had given me, when Shaun walks out with a mischievous smile on her face. She says, "I have a present for you, Cherry." She was drunk and I started laughing at her adorable Irish sway as she stood over me and then she turned and pointed at the sliding glass door. Looking directly into my grey-blue eyes, as Felix says, was Felix himself. He walked toward me and my mouth opened. Someone yelled, "Is that Felix?" I jumped up and swung my arms around him. He squeezed me tight and whispered, "Are you surprised?" I said, "Yes! Totally."

Everyone swarmed him a little for the next hour and I was basically just staring at him, in awe really. He was so sexy, so kind, so charming, so thoughtful, and so cool. After a majority of the guest's left he whispered in my ear, "You wanna get out of here?" I said, "Absolutely." We said our goodbyes, which took another thirty minutes and Shaun gave her 100% approval of me leaving my own party saying, "Oh man, he probably IS the one" and Felix helped me into his truck. He said, "We're going to my house, it's closer." I looked at him as he got in and started up the rumble of his big pick up and said, "10-4." He looked at me and smiled and I said, "Take me to bed or lose me forever." Thank you for that line, "Top Gun".

Chapter 27 Regal Beauty? You can say that again.

It would be cliché of me to say things like, "It was the best sex I ever had" or "he had the body of a God" or you know, "we did things that night that are illegal in some states" so, I won't bore you with the details but what I will say is that the next morning, on the 25th of March, 2013, I was completely in love and so was Felix Santoro when he said, "Cherry?"

"Yes?"

"I love you."

Then I said, "Oh thank you, Jesus, I love you too. Let's tell our moms."

He laughed and took me to breakfast.

I told everyone who would listen how happy I was and how he was the hottest thing since sliced bread as it were and I was on a total cloud of pure bliss every single day. We spent as much time together as we could given our busy schedules and I was usually at his house because, well, it was a house; a beautifully landscaped house, too, with an impressive concrete driveway. Shaun and Johnny loved him, Sarah and Corey loved him, Chris and Felipe loved him, and Trent loved him. Speaking of Trent, I did tell Felix that I was still friends with a couple guys with whom I had been intimate and his exact words were, "Ok, it's not like I thought you were a virgin, but don't tell me which ones. We will just call the past the past."

I said, "You're the one." And laughed of course.

Felix talked to me like we were going to be together forever. He talked about the future. He talked about me being his wife and making babies and when I was completely honest with myself all alone, staring in the mirror, like women do but never admit it, I knew that I was at least right now, completely committed to him. I knew that if I got pregnant I would be thrilled. I did not have a single reservation about it. Felix was the kind of man you wanted to have a baby with. He was the kind of man who wanted to be a father. He was the kind of man who you wanted to introduce to your parents.

I emailed mom a few pictures of him on day while I was at work and she promptly said, "Cherry, does he have a tattoo on his neck!" I knew she would bust my chops about that. My mother is a kind and tolerant woman, a woman who loves all of mankind, but she abhors tattoos like she abhors camping. When Shaun and I got our precious Captain somebody tattoos in Maine and my mother saw mine, nicely placed on my chest she gasped and said, "How will you get married in a wedding dress?"
I said, "I'll wear a turtleneck, ma, who cares."
Though she didn't like tattoos, she still wasn't the kind of person who judges a book by its cover so I said, "You will love him. I know this with every fiber of my being."

I also could not wait for Blayne to arrive, so a couple of weeks before he got there, Shaun and I began planning a good revenge. We thought of asking Trent to fake arrest him but knew he would never agree to it. We also thought of going to the airport, hiding and pretending that we forgot he was coming or not showing up at the airport at all and even though that made us laugh until we peed our pants a little, we knew that was too much. So, after a week of brainstorming, Shaun texted me and said, "I have just been given a couple of comped limo rentals for referring the company to a couple of clients. What could we do to Blayne that included picking him up in a limo?" I got excited and thought for a few minutes and it came to me.

"Let's dress up as hookers and greet him holding a sign that says, "John".

"HAHA YES!" she answered.

Felix and Shaun and Johnny came over to my place the day that we were meeting Blayne at the airport. Shaun and I got ready there and the guys were going to stay and wait for us to get back with Blayne so we could change and all go to dinner with him. I couldn't wait for Blayne and Felix to meet and it was important to me to see if they ended up having a connection. Felix and Shaun and Johnny were already becoming good friends in just over a month of periodically hanging out. Shaun and I came out of the bedroom with our best "high dollar hooker" outfits and I said, "How do we look?"

"Like sluts." Johnny said.

Felix burst into his classic booming laugh. He has the kind of laugh that you can hear around the block, similar to mine but in a contest he would win. When people with laughs like Felix and I laugh it either makes people plug their ears or laugh with us.

Throughout my life I have always heard, "Your laugh is contagious." Felix shares that trait. You don't get to choose your laugh and you are stuck with it like you are stuck with a flat butt. The wisest thing to do is embrace it.

The limo arrived and we assured the driver that there was nothing for him to worry about, we were 100% straight laced and to just pretend it was Halloween. We were laughing basically the entire way to the airport, just anticipating Blayne's embarrassment. We made an arraignment with the driver that he was dropping us off and then we would text him to pick us up once we met Blayne. He was amused and said this would be an easy and entertaining night. Right before we got there Shaun said, "I really love Felix."

I smiled and then put my hands on the sides of my face like Kevin in Home Alone and said, "I know! Isn't he so great?"
"I mean he really is." She looked right at my eyes. "I think you are going to marry him."
"I know. I *feel* that I am going to marry him."
"He already talks about you like you have been together forever."
"He does! It's fascinating. You know, I will finally meet his parents and sister next weekend."
"Oh, man. That's going to tell you a lot. I remember when I first met Johnny's family. His mother was nervous with me but his father liked me right away and kept giving me beers."
We laughed and I said, "You were like another son."

"That is exactly what Chris said. He said, "Now dad has two straight sons."
Laughing I said, "I'm really excited to meet them, especially his sister."
"Oh! Didn't you say that she was his twin?"
"Yes! Isn't that fun? I hope we like each other and can be friends. It would be so great."
Shaun smiled and said, "I'm sure you will be."

The driver pulled up to the Delta arrivals and rolled down the divider window. He said, "We're here ladies, try not to get arrested." We giggled as he came around and opened the door for us and I said, "Shaun. Get into character. It's show time." We put on sunglasses, wiped the smiles off our face and stepped out of the limo. People stared at us. I just assumed that meant that we had done a good job with out outfits. Shaun whispered to me, "People always stare at people getting out of limos. They think it could be a celebrity."
I whispered back, "Also we look like prostitutes, Shaun."
"I know," she nodded at some boys in uniform and said, "let's avoid the heat."

Trying desperately not to laugh we made our way to where we could hold up the sign and meet Blayne. He didn't have a check bag this time and had just texted me to say, "I'm getting off the plane now." I told Shaun, "He's coming." She held up the sign. People stared, laughed, gave us dirty looks. It was glorious. Shaun said, "This is the greatest idea we have ever had."

___

"I'm glad you suggested that we keep our shades on, that way I don't have to look anyone in the eye."
"Yes, I'm Catholic, I wouldn't be able to handle the guilt."

A few minutes later we saw Blayne coming down the escalator toward us. We tried to remain cool like we didn't know it was him and Shaun subtlety texted the limo driver that we would be outside in 5 minutes. As Blayne got closer he obviously realized it was us and could probably see the sign enough to read it. I heard him say, "Are you kidding me?"

Shaun whispered to me, "Dude, don't laugh."

We continued to act and looked around at everyone until finally he walked up to us and snatched the sign out of Shaun's hand laughing in embarrassment he said, "I can't believe you did this."
We looked at him and I said, "Sir, are you our John?"
"Cherry! Are you trying to get arrested?" and was bending over laughing.

Shaun took his arm and said, "Sir, our Limo is waiting for us."
Blayne laughing continuously said, "Oh yeah, I'm so sure."

We escorted him to the curb and he continued to laugh saying, "You really got me back." And "Oh my God, we are getting so many dirty looks." And "Cherry, there better not be anyone here that recognizes me this week at the conference."

As we walked up to the Limo and the driver opened the door for us Blayne said, "Hell no you did not really get a limo." We turned to him and put out our hands out so that he could help us in. As he did he looked at the driver and said, "Dude, are you in on this or do you really think I just got picked up by two hookers?"

The driver said, "I believe they like to be called, "Ladies of the night", sir."

Shaun and I both burst into laughter and Blayne just stared at us with this big smile on his face. He finally got in the limo and then he said, "You win. This is an epic revenge."

On the way back to my place we explained to him why we had the limo and that Johnny and Felix would be joining us to go to dinner after we quickly changed into more appropriate clothing. He said, "I'm actually very impressed. I should always arrange for a limo. It's my style." We talked about Felix and how excited I was for Blayne to meet him and he said, "I'm really excited to meet him. He looks like a big dude. I'm not sure I could fight him so hopefully I like him." I assured him that he would.

Back at the apartment and after a quick change and introduction, the five of us piled back into the limo and headed to dinner at Root Down. "The root place" as he calls it is one of Blayne's favorite restaurants in Denver and a place that Felix had never been. Blayne put up his hands, made fake quotation marks with his fingers and said, "I'm all about the "farm fresh" scene. You look like you're probably a meat eater, man. I am, too, but I love this place."

Felix laughed and said, "Yeah, Cherry said there is meat there. I have been meaning to go to this place for a couple years now. I've heard good things about it. I could never be a vegetarian but I agree with you, if I could eat farm fresh veggies every day, I would be a happy man."

Blayne laughed and said, "On the side of a ribeye."

I just stared at them laughing and talking to each other and I could see Shaun smiling out of the corner of my eye. I knew they would like each other and hit it off. They have a lot in common actually. Very social, great sense of humor, into food, and they both think I'm awesome. My mind drifted as I watched until we were in front of the restaurant. Shaun says to the driver, "Ok, boss, we'll take it from here." We gave him a big tip and thanked him for being the greatest limo driver ever. He handed us his card and said, "It was a good gig."

Felix took my hand and walked in next to me holding the door for all of us. Blayne put his hand firmly on his shoulder and said, "Thank you, you're a gentleman." We had a reservation and were seated in one of their awesome green booths big enough for five. Blayne sat in the middle so he could talk to all of us as he put it and Felix and I faced the phone wall.

The phone wall is literally an entire wall decorated with hanging vintage rotary phones of many colors. The food at Root Down is great but I admit I am usually most satisfied with the restaurant's style when I go there. It is original and unique. Felix said, "This is right up your alley isn't it." I gave him a kiss and snuggled into the booth between he and my brother. I said, "You three are my favorite boys on earth."

Johnny laughed and said, "I am glad to be one of your favorite boys."
Shaun pinched his cheek and said in a baby voice, "You're a cute boy, Johnny."

Blayne pretended to throw his fork on the table and said, "Oh God, here we go, I'm the fifth wheel. Just what I always wanted."

I laughed and reminded him, "Blayne! You have literally always had a girlfriend. God forbid we should show our love and affection to our men folk in front of you."

Shaun laughed as Johnny and Felix pretended to be focused on their menus and said, "I'm sure there is a Brittany here somewhere." Then she looked up and out into the restaurant and pretended to call out, "Brittany?" After we were all done laughing I had to explain to Felix about Blayne's love of Brittany's and how he was single this year for the first time in a long time. Felix looked at him and said, "I was single for like five years before I met Cherry. Sometimes being single puts a lot in perspective."

Blayne smiled mischievously at him and said, "I assume you were going through a lot of Jergens." "Yup…sure did." Felix laughed and inadvertently looked at his hands.

Johnny erupted with laughter and Shaun and I pretended we were offended.

"Ok," I chimed in jokingly, "Everyone just calm down."

As we ate, we laughed continuously, and talked and enjoyed the incredible service and atmosphere at Root. I felt so complete being there with the four of them. I thought again about how excited I was to meet Felix's family the next weekend but I was most excited for him to meet my mother. I know she was looking forward to it, too, and I was sure that she would have a lot of questions for Blayne when he got back to New York.

We all went our separate ways after dinner and, understandably, Blayne passed out right away. It was too early for me so I hung out in my bedroom watching "Groundhog Day". Bill Murray is my spirit animal and though I love all of his movies, "Groundhog Day" is by far my favorite. Shaun and I always refer to anything that makes us have to repeat ourselves or have to deal with the same thing over and over again as "Groundhog Day". We also quote "What About Bob" and say we have "fingernail sensitivity" when we are sick and complaining about it. There is basically a reference to Bill Murray that can be made for every situation in life. Anyway, I started to organize my closet and refold my clothes because I was too wired to sleep. I was in deep thought about how great it was to see Blayne and Felix hit it off at dinner. I couldn't wait to hear what Blayne had to say about him. Felix sent me a text that said, "Goodnight, baby, I love you." As I continued to organize I began to fantasize about moving in with him and of course living happily ever after. I was in full on "doodle my first name next to his last name" mode, "Cherry Santoro". I'm sure my father would approve. I laughed at myself because never before had I ever done that. Never had I felt like I loved a man so much that I pictured marrying him. Is that what was happening to me really? Was this what the truest love would do to me? Honestly all I wanted to do was squeeze him and fantasize about my future with him.

I opened the bottom drawer of the dresser I keep in my closet and it is where I kept my small but nicely assorted collection of rubber boyfriends. I hadn't been paying much attention to it as of late because I had been spending my time in the throws of passion with my shiny new real boyfriend. I turned my nose up at them and thought, "I'm over you." I laughed at myself and grabbed an empty shoebox. This was a new day. Out with the old silicone memories, in with my new love. I put every colorful one of them in the box and took them to the kitchen trash and as I placed them in the bag, I said, "Thanks for the memories." Then I laughed at myself again because I had said it out loud. I thought, wait until I tell Shaun. Of all people *she* would know this meant I was completely sprung.

Blayne and I stayed home, talked, watched movies, and ate literally all day on Sunday. I made breakfast and we ordered out for lunch and dinner. That night as we ate dinner, he said, "I was seriously moved by seeing you and Felix together."
I smiled as big as I could and said, "I'm so happy to hear you say that, tell me exactly what you mean."
"It's like you have already been together for years. I never saw you look at anyone like that."
"Dad would like him, huh?"
"Yeah dude, Dad would like him and so do I."
"He likes you too, Blayne."
"I want to find that, Cherry. I want to have a family. Dating disposable girlfriends has me jaded. At this point in my life I don't see the point of being in a relationship unless she has the potential to be my wife and the mother of my children."
"I know what you mean. I know you will find it. I know you will." We clinked our glasses together.

Blayne didn't have to leave for the conference until about an hour after me on Monday, so when I left I said, "I'll see you tonight, please take all of our take out trash and everything to the dumpster?" He laughed at me juggling my purse, coffee mug, and briefcase as I ran out the door.
"Yes ma'am!"
"You're a good brother!"

I wasn't running late, but I was barely on time, so I didn't even check my phone until I was sitting at my desk. I was glad Ben wasn't there yet that morning and I was alone opening up shop, because when I finally did look at my phone I had five messages from Blayne and they went as follows:

"Cherry! I'm gonna beat you when I see you!"

"Leave you right where I find you!

I laughed at his Joe Peschi quote and continued to read.

"Hey pervert!"

"I took the trash out and when I threw in the bag the bottom ripped open and a rainbow of dicks fell out all over the ground!"

I erupted into laughter and continued to read his fifth and final text.

"Why do you have so many? Why are they all broken!!!!!???"

I couldn't even answer I was laughing so hard. I had to regain my composure. Ben walked in seconds later and said, "Good morning! What are you laughing at?"

"Something funny on Facebook."

Luckily he was in a hurry because he just smiled and went into his office without any more questions. I quickly texted Blayne, "I'm sorry that happened to you. They aren't broken I just don't need them anymore. HAHAHAHAHAHHA RAINBOW OF DICKS!"

"I'm telling mom, Cherry."

"Go ahead, punk."

He wouldn't dare tell her. She wouldn't believe him anyway.

Chapter 28 Welcome to the Family

Even though Blayne made fun of me continuously the rest of the time he was in Denver, we had a great time. By the time I got home to my empty apartment on Wednesday, all I could think about was the coming weekend and how ecstatic I was to meet Felix's family. Colorado Springs is only an hour away, depending on traffic, but I was still excited to have my first mini-road trip with him. We left early on Saturday morning and planned to spend the night and come home on Sunday. I was looking forward to his mother's cooking for sure, but that was the least of it. I really loved him and wanted to love them too.

We walked in at about 8:30 and were greeted by his Father first. He had kind eyes like Felix and a huge smile on his face. He grabbed Felix by the shoulders and hugged him tight saying, "Hey! Mijo. How are you?" Felix turned to me as we entered the front room and said, "Dad, this is Cherry." His father hugged me just as he had Felix and said, "Cereza." Now I know that means cherry in Spanish. "I'm Felix Sr. You can call me Sr. or him Little Felix." He laughed at his own joke as he led us toward the kitchen. Felix's sister was standing in the doorway smiling and holding out her arms toward me. She hugged me and said, "Hi, Cherry! I'm Felicity! I'm so happy to meet you!" Her son ran up from the lower level of the house and jumped on Felix's back. "Uncle Felix!" Felix pretended to do a wrestling move on him and yelled, "Get this monkey off of me!" Felicity looked at me and said, "This is my son, Alex." I said, "Hi,

Alex, it's nice to meet you." I held out my hand to shake his and he blushed as he put his hand in mine. He whispered, "Hi." Felicity smiled at me again and said, "He's five."

Felix Sr. pointed into the kitchen and said, "This is Jr.'s Mother, Maria." I looked over and she was smiling at me, looking me up and down. She quickly dried off her hands and came over to hug me. She put her hands on my shoulders, leaned back and looked right at my face. "Aww, Mijo. Ella es mui hermosa." Felix hugged her and laughed and I said, "Did you just say I am pretty?"
"Yes! Oh, I'm sorry! Do you speak Spanish?"
I looked down and said, "No. I just understand a tiny bit of it."
Felicity said, "Felix and I don't speak Spanish either. Mom didn't want us to have an accent." I said, "Oh, no, Espanol es bella."

Everyone sat around the table talking and laughing for hours in the kitchen just like at moms. At one point Maria said, "Are you Catholic, Cherry?" I felt my cheeks heat up and I said, "No ma'am, please forgive me. I am Protestant." She smiled at me as if she was ok with it and then said, "Oh, that's ok, honey, but do you want kids?" Felix started laughing and Felicity nearly shouted, "Mom! Don't be a cliché'. Cherry, you don't have to answer that!" I laughed at Felicity's reaction and said anyway, "It's ok. I totally do." Maria winked at me and handed me some strawberries in a bowl, "Have some, they are so fresh."

I noticed Felicity smiling at me sort of just observing me sitting there, so I smiled at her in return, which prompted her to say, "I prayed for you." I swallowed the strawberry I was eating and giggled, "What do you mean?"

"I prayed that my brother would find a girl like you." I looked at Felix and he was smiling a bashful smile. Then I looked back at Felicity and said, "I prayed for him too." Maria said, "I never thought my son would be able to find a good woman who deserved him because he let his friends cover him in tattoos." Felicity shouted, "Mom!" just like she had done before. I looked at Felix and he was affectionately rolling his eyes at his mother and then I got very serious and looked around at each of their faces staring back at me and I said, "What happened is that he was raised to be one of the most beautiful, kind, loving, smart, funny, charming, and respectful men I have ever had the privilege of knowing and I feel very lucky to have found him." Maria smiled at me and her eyes welled up with tears. She said in almost a whisper, "Thank you for saying that, Cereza, I am very happy he found you, too."

We spent the rest of the night laughing and telling stories. I felt the way I feel at home; I was exceptionally comfortable with them. Even Alex warmed up to me and started asking me questions like, "Do you love Uncle Felix?" and, "What kind of car do you have?" He kept talking about his father who couldn't make it that night because of work. Felicity said she married her High School sweetheart and in the beginning they weren't sure they would have kids then once they decided they wanted to try, it took them a few years. Then there was Alex, named after his father. I asked Maria, "What was it like having twins?" Her face lit up and she said, "Oh, it was wonderful! They were great babies and they have grown up as best friends. I was so lucky I got a baby girl and boy in one shot! All I ever wanted to be was a mother. I love my kids so much." Felix Sr. said, "It made my job easy, being a father to a daughter because Felicity had her brother to protect her when I wasn't around. Jr. was already bigger than me when he was 14." Everyone laughed and then Felicity said, "That's why I was always skinny, my brother ate all of my food."

They enchanted me. I couldn't wait to tell my mom that I already loved my prospective in laws. I knew what she would say when I called her that Sunday night, "It's only been three months, Cher-Bear, you sure you're that serious?"
"Mom, remember "Mermaids" with Cher and Wynona Ryder?"
"Yes."
"Remember Wynona was obsessed with Catholicism and being a nun and constantly prayed about love and boys?"
"Yes, and they were Jewish."
"Yeah, so when she prayed she said, "Please don't let me fall in love so easily and please let someone love me back."
"Ok?"

"Well, I was like 13 or something when that movie came out, and I probably related more to Christina Ricci's character honestly, but even when I saw it again later, I didn't relate to Wynona's boy crazy ways. I related more to Cher and her fear of commitment right?"

"Right, ok."

"So, since then I've kind of loved a couple guys, you know, I felt love for them. I felt love and lust." My mom giggled and I continued, "Not until I met Felix could I ever have comprehended that the way I feel was the way people feel when they fall in love. I imagine it's what you and dad felt like." I heard her sniffle. "Mom, I'm serious when I tell you, this is exceptional, it's sensational, the way I feel with Felix. I've been thanking God since my birthday. I'm like, dude, you really pulled through for me this time."

Laughing she said, "This makes me emotional."

"Me too!"

"Well, you really explained yourself well, Cherry, I could not be more excited to meet this Felix. Do you think you'll bring him with you for Christmas?"

"Yes! I will ask him soon and see what he says."

"By the way, Blayne told me about his little mishap at your dumpster. Why do you need so many, Cherry?"

"Oh my God! He's so dumb! They were all different kinds! It's not weird. I assume you have one, mom."

"Me? No way. Why would you say that? A vibrator?"

"Really? Because women have needs, that's why."

"Honey, no. Give me a glass of wine and a Colin Firth movie and I'm in ecstasy."

I always wonder if other mother daughter conversations are as entertaining as ours. Shawn always said, "I relate more to your mother, mine is such a stiff." I would always tell her, "Not a stiff, just a conservative."

Felix texted me before I went to bed that night and told me that his family loved me and his mom and Felicity wanted my phone number. Of course, I quickly answered him, and said, "Give it to them! Make sure you tell them how much I loved them too."
"I will. I guess I should marry you."
"Ever though I'm not Catholic?"
"Yes, still."
"What will they say if I get pregnant before we are married?"
"Probably welcome to the family."

Chapter 29 Love Was In The Air

By the time June came all Felix was talking about was going to New York in December. He had accepted my invitation to join us for Christmas and New Years. Winter was, of course, the very best time for a guy in the concrete and landscaping industry to take a vacation. I personally wanted to focus on summer in Colorado, however. Denver is throbbing with summer energy and the countryside has fully bloomed. We went on a couple of road trips that month to places I hadn't been before. Royal Gorge outside of Canyon City, and one weekend we drove all the way down to Ouray. I've been to amazing places, before and after Ouray, but I have to tell you few match its level of awesome beauty. My mother always complains that the word awesome has been diminished by the fact that it is a popular slang word for my generation, and she is right, so try to remember the true meaning of the word and believe me when I use it to describe Ouray. If you're the religious type, or even if you aren't and you find yourself in doubt that there is a God at all, or you need to reconnect with your long lost faith, go to Ouray, Colorado.

My favorite weekend that month was the end of June when Felix surprised me one Saturday by taking me to the Denver Art Museum. He said the last time he had been was when he was in High School and it was a school trip. I was excited but worried that Felix was taking me on a charity date to do something he wasn't into. What I know to be true is that an Art Museum is a lot more enjoyable when you're alone unless you're with someone who appreciates it at least as much as you do. Felix told me, "I recognized that painting print you have in your kitchen when I saw the ad for this exhibit and thought you'd like to see it in real life." I have a framed poster of Mark Rothko's "Untitled 1949" painting hanging in my kitchen. I squealed, "Rothko?" Felix laughed at me and said, "Yeah." He handed me the flyer. "Figure to Field: Mark Rothko in the 1940s". "Baby, you did good," I told him, "Get me to the Museum at once!"

As Felix and I stood in front of the actual live creations of one of my favorite artists of all time, I could feel his eyes on me. I looked away from the art and directed my attention to him. He was staring at me in a way I hadn't seen before and I said, "Are you enjoying this? Or no?"
He smiled mischievously and said, "I like what I see."
"Oh, you do?"
"Yes."
He pulled me close to him and said, "I think you should move in with me." I leaned back so I could look at his face but stayed in his arms and said, "I would love to move in with you."
"When can you?"
"My lease is up the end of July."
"Oh, really? That's so perfect. Do you need to give a notice?"
"Yeah, thirty days."
"Well, damn, I'm glad I asked you now, you would have had to wait an entire year."
"Yeah, you have perfect timing."

Then he kissed me. He kissed me again like he does, in a way that makes me forget the whole world around me. You might think people would stare but as far as I'm concerned I'd say there was no way it was the first time someone had stood in front of a timeless piece of art surrounded by the divine creative energy that you feel when you're inside an art museum, and passionately kissed the one they loved or just anyone for that matter. You never know. It turned out to be an unforgettable and pivotal moment in our relationship.

It was late in the afternoon and as we were leaving I saw museum staff and other people quickly moving in and out of the Reiman Bridge area of the Museum and lining chairs up all along the wall on either sides, all facing the same way. A security guard was watching me observing so I asked him, "What are they doing in there?"
"Setting up for a wedding tonight."
"In the bridge?"
"Yes, it's the best spot, in many people's opinion."
"Really? The ceremony?"
"Yes, ceremonies and receptions are held in there."
I gazed in and my mouth was open as the wheels turned and turned in my head. "Thanks." I said.
That's exactly where I want to get married. Exactly.

Everyone I told was extremely happy that Felix and I were moving in together even though we had only been dating for a few months. It was great validation to us that we got that much positivity from the people we cared about. Blayne kept joking that I was lucky I found a guy with a house. Felix said he would spend his spare time at my place that month helping me pack, move, and organize. He only had to do a few things to get his place ready for me and we had a whole month to do it. I was over the moon, as the say.

I'll never forget that the 4th of July was on a Thursday that year because Ben closed up shop for a four day weekend, which gave me lots of time at home for packing. We still went to a BBQ at Shawn and Johnny's for the Holiday and enjoyed beers and the company of friends. The most memorable part of the day was random and unexpected. Around noon I got a call from Blayne who was out of breath. It made me nervous so I quickly said, "What's wrong?"
"Nothing, I just ran to my car."
"Jeez, dude. You scared me."
"I have to tell you what just happened."
"What?"
"I'm in Roslyn, at moms for the 4th."
"Oh, cool."
"She sent me to the deli to get more meat, we are bar-b-qing."
"Yeah?"
"You will never believe who was in there."
"Uhm, who?"
"Amanda."
I gasped, "Really? What was she doing there?"
"She was getting meat too."
I laughed at his answer then asked, "No! I mean why is she in Roslyn? For the Holiday?"

"She just got a divorce and is staying with her parents temporarily until she regroups and figures everything out."

"Oh my God, Blayne."

"She looked good, dude. She was so happy to see me. I'm all messed up over it. I feel so weird right now, I haven't seen her in so long and it brought all the shit back to me, you know?"

"Oh, man. I can imagine. Did you get her number?"

"I gave her mine. I gave her my card. I said, "I hope you call me." Do you think that was a good idea?"

"Yes! I totally do! Wow, this is an interesting twist, no?"

He laughed, "Man, I'm so glad I saw her. I can't believe the timing."

"Wait. You're saying that you just met a girl in the meat section at the grocery store and gave her your number? I mean you already know her and used to love her, but still; you saw her in the meat section at the grocery store?"

He laughed, "What did I tell you! The meat section at the grocery store; that's where a guy meets the good ones. I knew it!"

We had a good laugh about that. I was on the edge of my seat wondering if she would call him too until finally he texted me and said she had texted him and now he had her number too. Of course mom who never gave up hope that one day they would reconnect, was sending me texts about how elated she was about the recent turn of events. Amanda Beth was back. My parents always loved her; I always loved her and never wanted them to break up. She was the one for him. I just knew it.

I didn't hear from Blayne again until Sunday when he texted me and said, "Amanda is back, dude. Psyched." I had fun telling Felix the whole story as we packed up all my music that afternoon. We got right back to talking about music when I was done. He said, "What concerts have you been to?"

"Lets see. Willie Nelson, the Black Crowes, Prong, Dio and Black Sabbath, Warren Zevon, Duran Duran, Phish, like seven times, The Grateful Dead, Bob Dylan, Shawn Colvin, Jackson Browne, Strange Folk. One time I saw The Spin Doctors perform that one song of theirs in a park for free."

"Uhm, I remember that."

"Little Miss Can't Be Wrong."

He laughed and said, "Yeah that's so random."

"It was. John Mayer, One Republic, Dropkick Murpheys, Bostones, Violent Femmes, Black Crowes again, Grace Potter and The Nocturnals, Ray LaMontagne, Rusted Root, White Stripes, Bone Thugs and Harmony. One time I was at a fair and Kid Rock was playing. I saw U2 at Mile High."

"Damn. That's a lot of concerts. Which was your favorite?"

"I have to say White Stripes. It was a relatively small venue and I was sitting stage right. People were on the floor but we chose to sit and watch. I was pretty sure I was in love with Jack White and that he was playing directly to me as he stomped through talcum powder or something creating a white fog at his feet. I've never ever felt more "players only love you when they're playing" at any other show I have been to."

"Wow. You ok?" He laughed and I pretended to snap back into reality and then laughed at my own joke. I asked him, "What about you?"

"I've seen Kiss, Iron Maiden, Anthrax, Megadeath, Testiment, Great White, David Lee Roth, and Treat."

"Whoah! That's all metal!"

"It was the Monsters of Rock tour in Schweinfurt, Germany 1988. I was about 13."

"13? That's crazy. Well, I would love to have seen those bands, I love concerts."

"I need to go to more of them."

I handed him my Joan Jett vinyl. As he put it on the record player, he said, "Cool. I like Joan Jett."

"This is one of my top five favorite albums since I was little. Four years old is as far back as I can remember being a Joan Jett fan. I played this album over and over and Crimson and Clover was my favorite track."

"Really?"

"Totally. I sang along and stared at this cover picture. I remember thinking she was so beautiful and trying to figure out what the "BA" spelled out on her t-shirt."

"Bad?"

"That's all I thought it said probably back then, but now I know it says "Bad Girl".

"Oh, yeah!"

"I idolized her. She was so fly. I also love The Runaways. Cherry Bomb? It was Shaun and my theme song back in the day. I used to tell my dad that I knew he really named me after that song and to just tell me the truth because it came out like three weeks

before my mom got pregnant with me and they saw them in concert. Cherry Bomb- that's me."
"Really? Yeah, I like that nickname."

When you're like me, music is important enough to you that it changes regular moments into unforgettable memories. If it's really good music it can even make you play the air guitar. I played the air guitar in front of Felix and he laughed. He said, "You're sexy." Imagine him thinking I'm sexy when I play the air guitar. That just means everything, doesn't it? My father used to play the air piano on the dashboard of his car during road trips. I guarantee you my mother thought that was sexy, too.

I moved on to the last box of tapes I own. "Look at this!" I handed him a mix tape called "American Girls Mix Tape". "Shawn and I made this for when we were going to set out on the road after high school. It has songs about different cities and states. We gathered them mostly from our parents and it took us months and the used records shop. It's so funny how complicated it was back in the day to make a mix. Now you just download whatever you want and make a playlist. I miss the blood, sweat and tears."
"Wow, cool. What does it have? American Girl, Tom Petty; No Sleep Till Brooklyn, Beastie Boys; Call Me the Breeze, Lynyrd Skynyrd; Me and Bobby McGee, Janis; Highwayman, Highwaymen; Proud Mary, Ike and Tina; Luchenbach Texas, Waylon Jennings; Going to California, LedZep; Mississippi Queen, Mountain; Don't Stop Believin', Journey; Ooh Las Vegas, Gram Parsons; Nothing But Time, Jackson

Browne; Tangled Up in Blue, Bob Dylan; Georgia, Ray Charles; Dirty Water, The Standells; I've Been Everywhere, Johnny Cash; Take It Easy, Eagles; Willin', Little Feat; Chicago, Frank Sinatra; and Boulder to Birmingham, Emmylou Harris."

"Oh, that's fun to hear you read after all this time."

"I know most of those songs. Pretty cool mix."

"Boulder to Birmingham, sung by Emmylou, is a seriously sad song. We shouldn't have put it on there but my mom told us a story that we liked about the album it's on, "Pieces of the Sky". It came out in 1975 and even though she loved it, my mom couldn't get into it because she was madly in love with my dad and really happy and Emmylou's debut album came right after Gram Parsons' death. She was originally his back up singer. She was touring with him. She and most everyone involved were all grieving this great loss to their lives and to music and moving on without him was done with a lot of heartache. That song turned into a tribute to him in a way. My mom gave away the album because she couldn't relate to the sadness at a time when she was so happy. After my dad died, she bought it again and embraced the sadness. The music helped her heal. I always thought that was a cool story. Music can have such a deep affect on us."

"It's cool to think about it that way. I don't think my parents are into music like yours. My mom likes Elvis and always wants people to dress up like him at parties. I think my dad listens to a variety like me. I love Journey, Skynyrd, Janis, and Johnny Cash. Everyone loves Tina Turner."

"I know I do. Tina was one of my dad's crushes. Best legs in rock n' roll. The Acid Queen."

"Yeah, she has nice legs."

"You're cute."

"You're sexy."

I had so much fun just hanging out and talking about anything with Felix. It was definitely special going through all of my prized possessions with him telling him all of my stories. He was genuinely interested in everything I had to say. What woman doesn't love that? Moving in with him was the easiest thing I ever did, literally and as far as my heart was concerned. I was also closer to Shaun and Johnny technically and that just made it feel even more right. I felt absolutely and completely madly in love and was looking forward to the next few months making his house our house and that is exactly what we did. Just as things were falling into place when it came to my love life, my brother was on cloud nine as he reported to me weekly about re-dating his high school sweetheart. Let's just say that love was definitely in the air.

Chapter 30 My Mother's Approval

December had finally arrived and Felix was like a little kid looking forward to Disney World. We were all packed up and ready to head east. That happened to be a year that Shaun and Johnny were spending Christmas in New York so they flew out with us. I never had so much fun on a flight, partly because we were all together and partly because we ordered drinks. I admit that I have never been much of a plane drinker, but on that trip I learned what all the rage was about. Shaun always drinks on flights so it was no new concept for her and Johnny. We were a source of entertainment for the flight staff that's for sure, though I'm positive every great flight attendant out there is sick to death of mile high club jokes.

We split a car service from the airport to Roslyn and it was a great drive, because it was late afternoon, so Felix mostly stared out the window at the city lights emerging as the sun was setting. Shaun and I smiled at each other in silence, both of us enjoying how excited he was. He had only been to the airport, he said. It was his first time in the city. He was really going to experience something because we pull out all the stops when we host a new visitor.

As we drove into North Hempstead, Shaun said, "Almost to the Village!" There was a little bit of snow on the ground and as we headed to the heights to drop Shaun and Johnny first, we ooed and aahed at the Christmas lights. I told Felix as we pulled up to the house, "Shaun's house is like Cameron's rich kid house in Ferris Bueller and mine is like the normal house that Ferris lives in, except smaller and even more normal." Shaun laughed and as she got out of the car she sang, "When Cameron was in Egypt's land…" Then, in unison, be both sang, "Let my Cameron gooooo."

Felix asked me question after question as we headed toward my house. I loved seeing him so animated. When we arrived, Blayne came out and helped us with the bags and appeared even more wound up than Felix. He hugged me so hard, I asked him in my father's voice, "What are you drunk?" He laughed and fake pushed me out of the way to move on to hugging Felix, "Hey, man, glad you could make it out here. We're psyched to have you."

I had butterflies; I was so excited for my mom to meet Felix. We walked into the house and she was standing in the foyer with Amanda. I saw my mom size up Felix and I hugged Amanda, "Amanda Beth! You look great. I'm so happy you're here!"
"Oh my God, Cherry, it's been so long, over 10 years!"
I squeezed her even harder and I looked at Blayne. He had an enormous smile on his face, "Blayne! I haven't seen that many of your teeth in a long time." I introduced Felix to Amanda and then switched my attention to my mom, "Felix, this is my mommy, Susan, mom, this is Felix Santoro." My mother has the kind of smile that demands a smile back from anyone lucky enough to witness it. She reached out to

hug him and said, "Hi, Felix, I have heard so many wonderful things about you."

"Nice to meet you, ma'am, I have heard a lot about you too."

"Listen to you; very polite and respectful. I like being called ma'am, but you can just call me Susan, ok?"

"Yes, ma'am."

She laughed at him calling her ma'am again and took his arm, "Please escort me to the kitchen, sir, dinner is almost ready. I bet you're hungry."

Blayne, Amanda, and I smiled at each other as we watched them walk into the kitchen and I remember how seeing that made me feel. As we joined them in the kitchen, mom was telling Felix, "I should have always known that Cherry would end up with a tatted man. I bought her that Red Hot Chili Peppers tape in the 90s, the one with their tongues out? Blood Sugar?" I piped in, "Oh my God, mom, Blood Sugar Sex Magic."

"Yeah, that's it and on the inside of the tape were all those pictures of their tattoos. Remember? She stared at them for hours."

"Mom, really? Hours?"

"Yes and you bought metal magazines, ripped out the pages and plastered long haired half naked rockers all over your bedroom walls."

Amanda burst into laugher, "You did have the coolest bedroom, Cherry. It was art."

I nodded in agreement, "Remember when "Point Break" came out? I lost my mind over Anthony Kiedis." Felix rubbed his bald head and joked, "I don't look much like Anthony Kiedis."

"You sure are sexy though." I squeezed him and saw my mom smile at my brother.

Mom finally broke the intensity of us all just smiling and looking at each other for an awkward amount of time and said, "Oh, I forgot to tell you, Ann is on her way over to visit for a while." Blayne and I both yelled, "Tante!" which means Aunt in Yiddish or German. Ann is our mom's best friend and she is our favorite New York Jew on earth, like an Aunt to us, hence her nickname. I explained this to Felix and told him, "You'll love her, she is one of the funniest people I have ever known and she makes mom laugh hysterically when they are together and brings out her inner New York Jew." It's really one of my favorite things to witness, the two of them. It's also probably the reason why when I imitate my mom or hear her voice in my head she sounds like Ann.

We finished dinner and had just given Felix the grand tour of the house when Ann arrived. It was almost seven and Felix and I were yawning so my mom put on a pot of coffee. Ann said to Felix, "So, Felix it looks like you spend a lot of time at the gym. Did you see his arms?"
"Yes, ma'am."
"Ma'am? Honey, no, you call me Ann or gorgeous, those are your two choices."
Felix laughed and Ann continued to talk, "Speaking of the gym, Susan, do you have any ice cream?"
Mom answered, "Yes, I sure do, want some?"
"No, I'm fine."

Amanda and I were laughing so hard and trying not to laugh as Blayne got up and starting making Ann a bowl of ice cream. Ann switched her attention to my mom and started talking about one of their friends. Felix sort of just stared at her smiling, obviously entertained. Blayne handed her the ice cream and she acted surprised and said, "Thank you, Blaynie, you're my favorite son. Is this Bryers Vanilla? I ate this like it was going out of style when I had my breakdown." She looked at me as if to reassure me and continued, "It happens to all of us, you know. You just start crying and then suddenly it's three days later." We roared with laughter, all of us. She just looked at us expressionless and took tiny bites of her ice cream. "Susan, I like those tiny espresso spoons, can I have a tiny spoon?" As my mom got up to get Ann a tiny spoon she said, "Reminds me of dad. He would drink his beer out of a juice glass. He made it look like he was only having a little bit but after 6 glasses it was a moot point. You're still eating an entire bowl of ice cream, Annie, even if your spoon is tiny."

Through the laughter, Felix asked me, "Your dad?"

"Yes."

"I like to do that too."

"I know, I think it's cute."

My mom put her hand on Felix's hand and said, "Willie would have liked you. You have a great laugh." Ann said, "Yeah, I never trust a man who doesn't have a good laugh, just like I never trust a woman who doesn't have raw garlic in the kitchen." Felix burst into laughter again confirming to us all that he did, in fact, have a great laugh.

As it got later and later, Felix and I were entering delirium fueled by coffee, and since we decided we would sleep until noon on Sunday, we rallied. Felix said, "You just can't pass up great conversations like this." He could not have been more correct. Blayne, Amanda, and I told stories of our childhood and of growing up in Roslyn to attempt to give Felix a full picture of what it was like. Mom explained that my dad grew up there but that she came later and a lot has changed since Blayne and I were born. I told Felix, "Dad used to always say this town was great to grow up in and be single in the 70s in." My mom nodded her head, "He hung out at a little club called "My Father's Place". It's not here anymore, it shut down, but it was *the* coolest venue for concerts back in the day. When we met all he was talking about was seeing "a guy named Bruce Springsteen" there and how good it was. The next year was when we met, 1974, and in November his cousin in Jersey got us all tickets to see Bruce in Easton, Pennsylvania. I'll never forget it. It was a college auditorium and we sat on bleachers. It was fantastic. I remember what they all were wearing."

I added, "Dad always talked about that gig in 1973 at My Father's Place, "New York City Serenade."

"Oh yeah, Bruce was amazing. We also saw Savoy Brown, and met them all. We saw Linda Ronstadt there, John Prine, Lou Reed, and Hot Tuna. We saw Tom Waits in 1977; I remember the year because it was the first time I felt like going out after Cherry was born. Oh, and we saw Joan Jett and The Runaways in '76."

Ann said, "I was at most of those shows too." She smiles at Felix, "Pretty cool parents, huh? I was the cool friend though, I never told when yous were running amuck in the village smoking cigarettes behind the tower or at the pond or whatever."

I gasped, "What? We never smoked!" Blayne and I laughed because obviously we did and everyone knew it. My mom laughed and said, "What do you think, I was born yesterday and dressed up today?" I looked at Felix laughing at her and told him, "Another thing my dad always said." Ann, agreeing, put her hand on Felix's arm and said, "You know the cliché that Jewish, Latino, and black and Italian moms always ask you when they see you, "D'ju eat yet"?"

Felix laughed knowing exactly what she meant and said, "Yes!"

"Well their dad, the crazy Englishman that he was, if anyone ever said they didn't feel good or when they were under the weather, you know? He would say, "D'ju shit today?""

Through all of our laughter and my mom laughing so hard that tears were in her eyes Blayne added, "He always said, "Take care of your feet and a shit every morning."

As the laughter ensued and tears squeezed out of ours eyes we were deep in nostalgia and memories. I said, "My father was one of the funniest people I ever had the pleasure of knowing."

Eventually, Felix and I couldn't stay awake another second. We were glad we rallied for so long. It was such an amazing first day back home.

I woke up the next day at almost noon and realized that Felix wasn't in there with me. I had slept like a baby and looked like it. After I went to the bathroom I could hear Shaun and Johnny were there and Felix was laughing at something my mom was saying. I thought it was so cool that he felt comfortable enough to get up and go out to hang with everyone even though I was still asleep. I consider myself outgoing, as you know, but I don't think I would do that. I think I would have woken him up to come with me if we were at his parent's house for example. Felix was different than any guy I had ever dated. He was perfect for me and seemed to fit right in with the most important people in my life. I stood around the corner listening to them all laughing and talking and heard my mother say, "I had a friend back in the day who was a Hare Krishna, you know, he would go to the airport and pass out little poppies for money." Everyone laughed and I thought, "What the hell are they talking about?" but it made me so happy. I just could not have been happier.

I walked in casually and everyone greeted me, happy to see that I was up and I reveled in the moment of seeing Felix with my family. He was smiling and sipping coffee and reached out his arms for a hug, "Morning, baby!" I squeezed him and kissed his ear like I always do and Shaun said, "They've been telling us how much fun last night was. I wish we had been here. We just ate dinner and went to bed." "I know. I wish you had been here too. Ann was making us cry laugh."

"Are we all coming here for Christmas Eve?"
"Yes, definitely. We can party here as many times as you need to, Shaun. The world is your oyster," My mom laughed and then she got serious and said, "Cherry, Ann really likes Felix, I told him that she said he was a keeper." I looked at Felix who was blushing and I said, "He is a keeper!"
My mom patted his hand and said, "Yes, we all love him."

Well, mission accomplished. He had my mother's approval.

Chapter 31 A New Year

For the next two weeks we really impressed Felix with the tour of New York at Christmas and at his innocent insistence, Blayne, Amanda, and I agreed to take him to Time Square for New Years Eve. We usually skip it, you know, it can be kind of a hot mess in the Square but he just had to witness it with his own eyes, he said.

Shaun and Johnny had already headed back to Colorado as they sometimes do before the New Year and every day Shaun would text me and tell me how sad she was that she was going to miss seeing Felix in Time Square for the first time. She kept telling me she was sick and that she had brought East Coast germs back with her. The East Coast bug she called it. I told her she was just homesick. We loved living in Colorado but it was always hard to leave Roslyn after Christmas every single time.

We went to Blayne's place in Manhattan, early on New Years Eve. We ordered takeout and took naps all day so we would be physically and mentally rested before we ventured out. The average temperature on the night of the grand ball drop is like 30 degrees so natives and those who have mastered preparedness know not to wear sequin mini skirts and heels. The best outfit for a girl like me is boots, jeans, and layers under the warmest winter coat in my closet.

I admit I was excited. I wished Shaun would be there; she always had been in the past. We had this idea that whatever you are doing at midnight on New Years would sort of represent what the rest of the year would be like for you. If you are throwing up and crying in the fetal position then that might be an indicator of trouble ahead. It also might mean you need to make some life changes but who am I to judge. It really just means, are you happy? And, are you with people you care about? That night if you had asked me those two questions I would have easily answered, "Yes!" I told Felix, "Just be ready for anything." He winked at me and said, "Oh, I am."

We headed down to the general area to arrive at about 5 PM, which was the earliest we could stand to get there. In the movies people just grab a cab, pull up to the middle of the square, and get out to watch the ball drop. That, my friends, is make believe. Some would describe Time Square on New Years Eve as a shit show. There is no place to go to the bathroom, no place to eat, and you can't take in bags with supplies. Once you enter the barricaded area, you get searched by the police. For Shaun and I the search was sometimes the best part of the whole night. We used to play spot the under cover cop, because they are everywhere. You can often pick them out of the crowd by their shoes. When we were younger it annoyed us, because we wanted to be drinking but the older you get the happier you are that they are there. Also, it is a scientifically proven fact that undercover cops are hotter than Sriracha on a jalapeño.

We slowly maneuvered through the crowd, site seeing for Felix, and people watching. We talked to people from all over the globe and laughed and sang with countless strangers. That's really all there is to do to kill the time, mingle and jingle, as my father would say. You really have to be an outgoing, social butterfly type. Being surrounded by a million people can be overwhelming just because of the energy alone. I happen to dig it.

By 8 PM we were standing closely together at about 7th Ave. and 46th Street near the Marquis. We felt really lucky to have secured that spot because it's a perfect view of the ball and not so close to the stages that you suffer the crowd frenzy. Unless you are there for the shows steer clear, trust me. I remember Melissa Etheridge sang "Imagine" that year.

As the hours passed by we entertained ourselves and the anticipation built up. Felix was snuggling me, keeping me warm, Blayne snuggled Amanda, and I became suddenly aware of how incredibly romantic it was. It wasn't just the snuggling; it was the cold air, the streets of Manhattan, the energy of the crowd, the anticipation of a new year, and the very beating of our hearts. Now, picture this: It was 11:59:50 and the entirety of New York, most specifically the million standing around us began chanting the count down, ten! Felix and I stayed in each other's arms, my hands in his coat pockets; our eyes fixed on the ball, nine! He smiled at me and then looked back, eight! I looked at Amanda and Blayne happily yelling, seven! Then I focused on the ball again and the warmth of Felix's arms, six, five, four, three! Felix took his eyes off of the ball and focused on my face, two! Blayne

336

reached out and handed Felix something small, one! As the world around us cheered and screamed, a muffled sentence came from Felix's mouth. I looked at Blayne and Amanda and then back at Felix who spoke again, "Cherry, will you marry me?" At the same second that paper confetti poured over us, he showed me a diamond ring, quickly closed it and handed it to me. I put it in my deepest pocket, reached my cold fingers up to his face and squeezed as I looked directly into his eyes. "Yes!"

We kissed forever and the whole world was silent. I heard only the pounding of my heart.

They had it all planned from the first morning that I slept until noon. Before Shaun and Johnny got there he showed mom and Blayne the ring and, as I was told, he said, "I'd like to ask Cherry to marry me." Mom teared up and Blayne hugged him and shook his hand, giving him the permission he was asking for in a way, but Felix stared at my mom who hadn't spoken up yet and handed her the ring. Finally she said, "I'm verklempt. You have my permission." That's when they quickly planned Time Square and that Blayne would hold the ring so I wouldn't find it or see it. Turned out to be a perfect plan because I had no idea, not even an inkling.

It was 2014 and we had entered it with a dramatic bang. We waited for the morning to share our news with everyone. We called his parents first and Ben and Margo second. I texted Shaun seven times and complained that she must still be sleeping even though it was 7 AM in Colorado. No one was allowed to post anything on Facebook about it until Shaun knew and she was the last person left to tell out of most of our closest friends. Finally almost an hour later she called me.

"Hello?"

"Cher, I'm sorry, I had a hard time waking up this morning."

"It's ok, are you ok? I have big news?"

"Well, I'm fine, I've been needing to talk to you too. You first."

"Ok, last night, at midnight, in the square, Felix proposed!"

She screamed, "Oh my God! I didn't know! Did Blayne know?"

"Yes! They set it all up on the first Sunday we were there."

"Oh man! I'm so happy! I wish I had been there."

"Me too, Blayne got a couple pictures though."

"Holy shit! I'm so excited. How cool that you got engaged on New Years, Cherry!"

"I know. It was perfect."

"I'm planning the wedding."

"I want Denver Art Museum."

"You do!?"

"Yes, dude, that bridge."

"I'm going to try to get June!"

"Really?"

"I bet I can."

"That would be crazy."

"It's going to be so fly."

"So, what's going on with you? Are you still sick?"

"Oh, well, yes, and no."

"What does that mean?"

"I don't want to mess you up on your first day engaged, but I don't have the East Coast bug or the stomach flu, dude."

"Ok?"

"I'm pregnant."

There was a long extended period of silence that followed those two words because, of all people, they came from Shaun. Finally, I said, "I literally *never* thought I would ever hear you say those words." Blayne sat down next to me and kept mouthing, "What? What?" so I said, "Can I tell Blayne? I'm with Felix, Amanda, and Blayne."

"Yeah, go ahead."

"I think I'm in shock."

"Yeah, I'm not. Puking every morning for a week will slap the shock right out of you."

"How did you get pregnant?"

Everyone gasped and Blayne started laughing hysterically yelling, "'Kid's are a bad plan" is pregnant?!"

Shaun answered, "Dude, a medical miracle because I changed nothing and missed nothing. I have no idea!"

I screamed, "Oh my God, Shaun! You're pregnant!"

"Yup, sweet Jesus, tell them all to keep this shit off of Facebook. I have enough problems."

"Shaun! What did Johnny say?"

"He's in shock, wants a boy."

"He's happy, I know it."

"Jesus, I know."

"It is Johnny's baby, right?"

"Shut up."

"I can't believe it! You're gonna be a mommy."

Later that morning, Felix and I said our goodbyes to my darling brother and Amanda and headed back to mom's for one last night before heading to Denver. We spent quality time with mom just the three of us and talked the night away about the engagement, life, and seemingly the most shocking news, which was Shaun's pregnancy. No one was expecting that, not even God. I laughed as I flashed back to all the times since we were 7 that she said, "Kid's are a bad plan." It could not be more entertaining.

When Felix and I went to bed that night, we lay in the guest bed in what used to be my bedroom and I just stared at him. He noticed and said, "What?"
"You're a beautiful man."
"You're a beautiful wifee."
I laughed at being called wifee and told him, "Not yet! But, at the earliest, six months."
"June?"
"Yeah, maybe, Shaun thinks she has connections."
"Are you happy?"
"Yes. I'm so happy. What did your parents say?"
"They were happy."
"You like me, huh?"
"I love you. You comfort my soul."
"Awe. You're the sweetest thing. I love you too, baby. I'm glad you love me even though I'm a weirdo?
"Yeah, you're definitely a weirdo."
He laughed and I said, "I know! Like, I never felt confident that I knew how to pronounce "Legumes" correctly, so, I avoid saying it."

"I don't think I have ever had the need to say legumes."

"Well, you're lucky."

"You're sexy."

"Let's stay together forever."

"I'd lose everything before I'd lose you."

Chapter 32 My Fiancé?

Felix and I spent the next few days infinitely aware of
how happy we were and how happy everyone was for
us. That Saturday I had plans with Shaun and Sarah
for lunch and to my surprise, Chris showed up too. It
had been a while since I had seen him. We were
having a fabulous girl's lunch going crazy over my
news and Shaun's news. Chris said, "It really is
precious that you two would end up knocked up and
engaged in the same year. Does this mean I have a
wedding and a baby shower to attend?" I answered,
"A baby shower yes, but we haven't decided on a
date for the wedding yet." That was when Shaun
laughed her fake evil laugh and said, "Actually, you
have, which is why we are really here today. I got
you Denver Art Museum, June 28th, it's a Saturday
night."
"You're shitting me."
"I shit you not."
Chris screamed, "Oh my God! Cherry Bomb! You're
getting married at DAM?"
"Well I though it would be so rad. Don't you think?
For me?"
Sarah piped in, "Hell yes! It's perfect!"
I took both of Shaun's hands in my hands and looked
directly into her eyes and said, "Thank you. You are
the greatest best friend I have ever had."
"I'm THE best friend."
"Yes, Shaun, you are like the entire cast of The
Divine Secrets of the Yaya Sisterhood and I am
Ashley Judd."

We laughed and clinked our cocktails, and Shaun's water together and celebrated our happiness. Chris asked Shaun the burning question, "So, sister-in-law, what does a girl like you do at her baby shower?"
"Well, I don't want any of those dumb games."
We all laughed but weren't surprised in any way. Sarah asked, "So, you don't want to melt candy bars in diapers or play pin the tail on the baby?" Through our laughter, Shaun answered, "Absolutely not."
Chris got very serious and said, "Now, I hope none of you ladies mind but I would really like to plan the shower." We all completely agreed that he should especially since he was the baby's fabulous uncle. He corrected us and told us he was actually the "Guncle" which made us laugh for another ten minutes. Then Shaun sad, "Yeah, no clowns and no drop the hot dog in the bottle games, Chris."
"Uhm, sister, I believe that is a bridal shower game or something someone like Tanya Harding does in her spare time on the weekends." I almost spit my drink out laughing but I was able to finally regain composure and Chris said, "Cherry make sure you use that word fiancé as much as you can! You only have six months. I know I said it as much as I could when I was engaged."
"Oh, yeah! I don't think I have even said it once."
"Say it now!"
"My fiancé."
They all smiled and Sarah said, "I've never been able to say it before. I'm jealous."
I laughed, "Don't be jealous. When it's time, it's time."

"I know, you're right. I'm not really jealous, I just love me some Corey. I really want to marry him."
"Well don't compare the time to us. We haven't been dating very long and some people think that isn't smart. It will be a year in March, though and for us, that's good enough. Everyone is different."
"That's true. Felix must really like you."
"He knows what's good.

Chris held up his glass again and said, "To Felix loving our Cherry Bomb." We all clinked together and I added, "And, cheers to Shaun giving it the old college try on the baby making thing." Shaun laughed and said, "Yes, yes, you're welcome. It will be a boy." I winked at Chris and Sarah and said, "She's having a girl."

My fiancé. I liked the way that sounded. Especially when I heard Felix say it. I was actually engaged. I had spent the last few years of my 30s grooming myself for the proverbial perfect man that doesn't exist. I've seen and heard things I could have lived without and more pictures of the male anatomy than the Banger Sisters. Would I do it again? Yes. I think the point is arguable because you can live your life in solitude with a set schedule and nary the spontaneous act, yet still you may find the love of your life, however, it is my opinion, that when you are looking for something you should go out and engage yourself in such a way that you are guaranteed you will find it. I was not taking for granted that I had found this man who was apparently so perfect, for me.

Would I miss being single? Would I miss texting pictures of my date's license plates to Shaun "just in case"? Would I miss having sex with a man that I may or may not ever talk to again? Would I miss being asked to have three-ways, orgies, do foot stuff, food stuff, wear strap-ons with men, and things so scary they would turn you white? (That is my last Ghost Busters quote, I swear, courtesy of Ernie Hudson.) Probably not, is my answer. I wouldn't miss awkward encounters, conversations, or mornings after. I wouldn't miss being a girl with condoms in her purse. I wouldn't miss the "thrill of the hunt". As the previously quoted Billy Crystal said in "When Harry Met Sally", "You meet someone, you have a safe lunch, you decide you like each other enough to move on to dinner, you go dancing, you do the white man's overbite, you go back to her place, you have sex." Just like Harry, I had grown "tired of the whole thing".

By March, Felix and I were celebrating being in love for a year and Shaun and I were in the throws of wedding planning. We decided to wait and take our honeymoon the next year. We had so many plans for travel and he wanted to go back to Europe one day. We just hadn't decided where to go or if we were financially prepared for a wedding and an extra trip. I always quoted "True Romance" and said, "We're minimum wage kids, you know?" when people asked me why we weren't honeymooning after the wedding. Felix told everyone our life *was* a honeymoon. I have to say that things were a lot easier to afford with a dual income. That is one thing people don't really talk about much when they mention the perks of shacking up. I really loved paying my bills with someone, saving money with someone, taking care of a house with someone, and making sweet love whenever I wanted.

In no relationship that I had ever had before, no matter how short lived, was I actually being my true self. I thought I was, of course. I never thought I was muted or diluted by any man I spent my time with. I thought of most of my old flings and boyfriends with fondness as I have said before. It's just that I discovered a certain amount of absolute freedom being with Felix. It reminds me of riding a motorcycle, it's risky, it's dangerous but it is freeing. My parents let me take my first motorcycle ride on the back of their friend's bike when I was young. We didn't go far, but I remember the wind on my skin, and whipping and tangling my hair. I don't know what it is about that, along with the two wheels beneath you, that makes you feel so free. Committing to one person is risky but when you're synced up and moving forward together, you're bound to have a great ride. I was actually my truest self. The self I am with Shaun, my brother, my mom, or when I am totally alone. That turned out to be an impressive accomplishment. Shaun said, "When you find a spouse who is a supplement to yourself, a best friend, and a teammate, you have struck gold."

Many women think they aren't really women until they find a man to marry. Have you ever heard what Cher said about the subject? She said, "A man is absolutely not a necessity. I adore men. I love men. I think men are the coolest, but you don't really need them to survive. My mom said. "You know, sweetheart, one day you should settle down and marry a rich man." I said, "Mom, I am a rich man." What an outstanding thing for a girl in her teens to hear. Either way, though, I found a diamond and no matter how much fun I did or didn't have while I looked for him, I had him now.

The most maddening thing that had been going on over that time period was that Shaun and Johnny, in their infinite wisdom, had decided to keep the sex of their baby a secret…from everyone…even their own parents…even me! I was completely annoyed by it but understood that they thought it was fun or funny or something. I chose to assume that the baby was a girl and call it "her" every chance I got. They referred to it as "baby" to be sure they didn't slip. Needless to say when Shaun, Johnny, Felix and I hung out, there wasn't a single human in the room *not* being called baby.

I tried to lose myself in wedding preparations so I could ignore the utter suspense of the whole incoming baby situation. I told her, "How the hell are we supposed to buy baby shower gifts?" She said, "Easy, Chris and I are selecting perfect "could be a girl could be a boy" nursery décor and baby gear. You just don't worry your pretty little engaged head about it." I watched the registry like a hawk too for any one single clue. It was fairytale themed. Everything from clouds to forest to space to classic books and any single baby out there from any land and of either sex would just love the hell out of all of it. So, I decided to move on and let her play her weird baby game without being harassed. I always knew that if she did ever have kids she wouldn't be the average mother with pink or blue painted walls and baby clichés. I related to that attitude. She was just going to be a mom who never used terms like play date. She was a little more old fashioned. I knew she would take a lot from the way my parents were to influence her own ideals just like I would. As the potential God Mother, I was ecstatic and I knew it was going to be a girl.

Chapter 33 We DID

Shaun and I had planned my wedding for almost six months and as the final hours counted down everyone who could make it were trickling into town. We had people staying in Hotels, at our house, and at Shaun's. I found myself being very reflective in the hours before my wedding. I thought mostly about my favorite people who would be in attendance and about the relationships that would be represented at our wedding; best friends, siblings, parents. They were people from every decade of our lives and they were in Denver getting ready to share this moment of ultimate commitment with us. The venue was small so I felt guilty, of course, not being able to invite all of Felix's favorite family members. He assured me, "We can't afford that anyway, don't feel guilty, they understand." That was one thing I knew, I did not want to offend my brand new family. I couldn't afford to invite all of my favorite family members either. I have a lot of cousins. I love them all like siblings. Whenever I meet anyone from Jersey I say, "Oh, you probably know my cousin then." How do people afford every single person in their life to be at their weddings anyway?

I remember it very well, it was Friday night, I was at my home, the one I was so lucky to have inherited when I fell in love, and I was with this man who loved me so much that he just couldn't wait to spend the rest of his life with me. I enjoyed being lost in my thoughts the night before my wedding.

On Saturday afternoon I headed to Shaun's to meet up with the girls, and the guys congregated at our house with Felix. Everything was ready for me, Shaun said, "All you have to do is get dolled up." What we did was relax, laugh, and tell stories all day while we did each other's hair and makeup. I never felt nervous at all, I felt excited, but never nervous. I waited as long as I could before I put my dress on. That dress, I will have you know, was purchased from the online home shopping network and it was a gorgeous ¾ length sleeve, semi-snuggly fit cocktail dress. Bateau necked and came to just above my knees. I wore it with navy heels, a hair clip made of navy netting, rhinestones and grey feathers, and embellished the whole situation with rhinestone jewelry. My hair was worn down, as usual, and instead of having a bridal shower my mom collected new and vintage jewelry, broaches, rhinestones, and bobbles from every girl I knew on earth until she had enough to make a vintage style, glam broach bouquet. People lost their minds over it. It was stunning. She made Felix a lapel pin to match it too and since he was as non-traditional as me, he pinned it to his shirt instead. He wore a black un-tucked dress shirt, black slacks, and black leather high top Chuck Taylors. He said he was a little bit Johnny Cash and I said he was a little bit Beastie Boy. Either way, he was a whole lot of sexy. I trusted that he was going to show up with his crew of boys, my brother included, in his limo looking as fly as possible. I knew I would.

We both arrived at the same time and walked in together, flirting every step of the way. Shaun tried to handle everything for us as our wedding planner and pseudo matron of honor. We didn't have a formal wedding party but we did have two of our favorite friends stand with us as witnesses and to help with the ring. Everyone took their places in the rows of seats that lined the bridge walls. The walls are white-zigzagged beams and windows that look over Denver at 13th Street. In the day you can see the mountains and since our wedding was in the evening, we had the extreme pleasure of watching the sun set. Everything was white, the chairs, tables, and a long white runner rug that Shaun had gotten. When the sun was almost down, the white was illuminated in pink aspenglow. It was magnificent. It was very contemporary and urban- exactly what I wanted.

I had decided months earlier that Felix and I would walk together instead of me being escorted to him. Honestly, I am obviously not as much of a traditionalist as I thought I was, so this decision was easy to make. You see, I couldn't bear the idea of my father not being there and no one, not even Blayne, could fill that void. I was ok, you know, I wasn't upset, it's just one of those things that can make a daddy's girl cry her eyes out on her wedding day if it isn't handled correctly. You know, when other girls dance with their father to "Butterfly Kisses" at their receptions? That's when I go have a smoke in the alley with the staff.

I talked about it in great length with my mom and her words were wise, as usual. She said, "Cher-bear, you found a good man. He was raised right. We all know with absolute certainty that your father would have loved him. The tradition of a father walking his daughter down the isle is old school and from the days when men accepted a dowry from the groom. It's a strange old custom that we have obviously turned away from. Now we simply have the most important man in your life hand you over to the new most important man in your life, with love. Your father will be with us on your wedding day in spirit and I have no doubt that he would have gladly handed you over to Felix. Let Felix walk you down the isle and stand with you. It's beautifully symbolic." I shared her words with Felix and he said, "I wouldn't have it any other way.

We entered the bridge from the reception side and walked along the white runner toward our guests and the Justice of the Peace. Everyone looked incredible, I noticed, as they stood to watch us. They were dressed like New Years in Las Vegas in sequins, gold, silver, pink, black, and white. It was as visually appealing as the venue. I tried to make eye contact with every one of them as we passed. The ceremony itself was short and packed full of love, adoration, and a little bit of God for the Catholics. I looked out at everyone a couple times and they were crying and sniffling and beaming from ear to ear. Mostly, my eyes were fixed on Felix standing there next to me. He was really so beautiful, from his heart, to his soul, to his big sexy body. I just loved him so much. I could barely focus on the words being said. Felix smiled at me and occasionally winked at me as if he knew I was zoning out.

Then, we DID. Our guests cheered and clapped and stood up and hugged each other. We were married and I had officially become Mrs. Cherry Santoro.

Chapter 34 What a Beautiful Wedding

Everyone eventually settled into their reception seats. Blayne spoke up and thanked everyone for being there. He said, "Thank you all for being here for Felix and Cherry. It's beautiful, no? You all look great too. I think I would give Chris and Felipe the best dressed award if we had one." Everyone whistled and clapped in agreement. "Don't take any pictures of me with them tonight, I'll end up looking like a bum!" We all laughed and watched as Blayne walked up behind Ben and Margo. "Can I get a round of applause for the guests of honor? Without these two beautiful people Cherry might not have ever met Felix!" I blew them kisses from where I sat and they smiled and waved at everyone. Blayne walked over to my mom who stood. She was teary eyed and holding a tissue. She said, "I am so thrilled to be related to the Santoros, they are a beautiful family. Felix, I'm proud to call you my son in law." She sat down and extended her arm to Felix's parents. His dad stood up and with a crack in his voice he said, "I love you, son. We are all so happy you found Cereza."

Those little sentiments from my mom and Felix Sr. made Felicity and I burst into tears. We laughed at each other crying and I attempted to save my make up from demolition. The positive energy around me was invigorating, I could feel it like a million hugs. I yelled out to everyone as I laughed, "I'm overwhelmed." That was when Shaun stood up. I will never forget a single word of her speech.

"Ok, ok, everyone, lets just take it down a notch."
Everyone laughed and took a deep breath. "Now,
exhale." Composure was regained and she continued,
" Cereza. I like that, don't you? Say it with me,
Cereza. It means, "crazy girl" in Spanish." Through
the laughter she told the truth, "I'm kidding, it means
Cherry. Well, this wedding sure has been gorgeous so
far. I have business cards if anyone- it was Cherry's
vision but I made it happen, ok? I'm so happy today
because my best friend just got married and I'm seven
months pregnant, but we'll deal with that in August
so they tell me. Whether we want to or not right?
Since we were little, we have talked about this day
and my day years ago and now that we are here I feel
so grateful and thankful to be a part of it. I feel
grateful to know all of you. When we were young,
Cherry would say we could be anyone we wanted
when we grew up. We had no idea who we were then
and imagining who we would be now was
exhilarating. Are you happy, Cherry?"
I answered, "Yes!" and my chin started to twitch. She
was going to make me ugly cry.
"Cherry has always been this cool, I'm into Rock n
Roll and cult classic flicks like Heather's and True
Romance and I can recite Goodfellas word for word
kind of a girl, but, don't let her fool you, she went
through a hardcore obsession with Legally Blonde for
like a year and all she wanted to watch when we were
like 10 was Smokey and the Bandit." As everyone
laughed I was able to get a grip on that impending
ugly cry.

"She never needed a man and made sure everyone knew it but deep down I think she always fantasized about finding her bashert, just like I did. Bashert means soul mate in Yiddish, thanks, Ann." Ann waved and I saw that she had tissues in both hands in an attempt to control her tearing eyes as well. "She could act tough and aloof when it came to menfolk but really, she had a Felix shaped hole in her heart."

Everyone in the room awwwed and I looked at Felix. He was emotional and trying desperately to keep it together. I looked back at Shaun and she continued, "I love you, Felix. We all do. You are perfect for our Cherry. She needed a man who would be strong, understanding, supportive of her independence, of her creativity, and of her love of adventure. He would need to be loving, tolerant, outgoing, and funny. Does this sound like an online dating profile?" Everyone, on the verge of crying laughed hard at that joke. I pointed at her and said, "You wrap this up, you." She smiled big at me and looked around at everyone until they were quiet again.

"I'm kidding. Most importantly, Cherry needed a man who was kind." Then SHE became emotional. I hadn't seen that in a while even though she was pregnant, and I knew she would blame it on that. I looked at Johnny who seemed deeply moved as he just stared at her and again, I cried.

"You are one of a kind, Felix. Thank you." She nodded at his family sitting there teary eyed and sniffling. She raised her champagne glass prompting us to do the same.

"Cheers to great happiness, peace, and a love that lasts forever. Felix, one more thing, as Cher's dad would say, "You break it, you buy it."

Through the laughter and tears, we cheered, for Shaun and her great speech and for each other. What a beautiful wedding, it was.

Chapter 35 What Happens Next is Just Gravy

People told Felix and I for weeks how wonderful the wedding was and that it was the best wedding they had ever been to and we just loved hearing it. You spend so much time thinking about getting married and then months preparing for the day so after its over I can imagine that people spend a lot of time coming down after a wedding high. I didn't feel that way, I felt like it was a climax for the beginning of our love story. Love stories are up and down, like hills and valleys. They peak in the beginning when you fall in love, they peak when you get engaged; they peak when you get married. My mother is the kind of person who wants to know what happens *after* the wedding at the end of the movie. I used to make fun of her for it. Not anymore. After the wedding is the best part. It's the rest of your life part.

On the same Saturday as Shaun's baby shower in July, I got a call from Blayne really early in the morning.
"I have to tell you something."
"What."
"Do you remember when we went to Cony Island when Amanda and I were first dating?"
"Yeah, totally."
"That was where we first kissed."
"Really? Aww. I can't believe you remember that."
"I do. So, we are going there today. I mean she doesn't know we are going but that is where I'm taking her today."

"Fun! I wish I could go."

"I'm going to propose to her."

"What! Oh my God, Blayne!"

"I got a ring last week. I kept wanting to show you but I kept forgetting to take a picture of it. You want to see it?"

"Yes! Are you kidding?"

As we were on the line with each other he texted me a picture of probably the biggest diamond I have ever personally known anyone to have. I said, "Blayne! That's gorgeous. Sweet Jesus. Did you steal it?"

"I paid for it, fool. That's how I do."

"It's unbelievable. She is going to freak."

"She is almost out of the shower, I don't want to give it away. I'll call you later and let you know how it goes."

"Oh, my God, make sure and tell mom."

"I did."

"Ok, love you! Have fun!"

"Love you too."

He must have been inspired to lock it down with Amanda this time especially after my wedding. I knew he wasn't going to wait long. They were destined to be together and we had to focus on the happiness of the fact that they reconnected instead of dwelling on the lost years between then and now. I think stories about people rekindling the love they shared with people from their younger years are incredibly romantic. It sure made my mother happy. Shaun and I always wished they hadn't broken up in the first place, so this was just what should have always been in our opinion.

I spent the rest of that day with Shaun, Chris, Sarah, and almost every other girl the two of us knew in Denver at her house. She invited a couple people I didn't know so it turned out to be a great mingling party as well. Everyone, including my mom, and Shaun's parents out of town, got her the majority of what was on her registry. She definitely scored big. Whoever came up with having baby showers is really a genius I mean, she got everything. I was excited to decorate the nursery with her. The baby was due in the middle of August and we were only a single month away.

She was perfectly pregnant. One of those girls who has a basketball under her shirt, you know? Except her boobs and booty were filled out like never before. Johnny told her he wasn't complaining when she would bitch about what the "baby was doing to her". I could tell that she had begun to bond with it back in June. She was becoming more and more excited. I kept telling her, "You can't turn back now, she is almost done."

I brought my gifts in pink gift bags and purple polka-dot ribbons. My message was received because everyone else did yellows, greys, whites, and natural bags and wrapping paper. I stuck to her registry of course, but I also included two books, "Girls Will Be Girls" and "How Girls Thrive" by JoAnn Deak, PhD. It was my last dig while being fake mad at her as payback for keeping the sex of the baby a secret from us. I knew people would think it was funny.

Especially if it really was a boy she was having but if not, they were good books. I wrote on the inside of one of them, "You're welcome. Love, Cherry" When she opened them she said, "Well, thank you, best friend. I am sure no matter what kind of baby this is these books have good information in them. I will be sure to pass them on to someone with daughters when I'm done reading them."

I winked at her and said, "Mmhmm. Whatever you need to do."

It was a great shower. Chris decorated with white and very light pinks and blues. We all had fruity summer cocktails made with Prosecco. There was music in the background and an enormous spread of appetizers and finger food. Chris arranged for no games, but two ways to win prizes. When everyone arrived they were instructed to write their name and address on envelopes, you know, for the thank you cards, and later Shaun put them all in a bag, shuffled them around and pulled one winner's name out. The other prize was given to the person who's birthday was closest to the due date which was August 20th. Sarah won that one because her birthday is in August. It was absolutely fun and not lame at all. I gave Chris a pat on his back. "You really pulled this off, Chrissy. I'm impressed."

"She's a tough cookie to crack, Cherry, but just look at her." We looked over at her talking to a couple girls while she snuggled a new teddy bear that someone had gotten her. "She is happier than she leads us to believe."

"Oh, I know, trust me." I downed my drink and said, "But, still, let's not leave any Lamarca behind for her to drool over."

He agreed and we finished off the last bottle together with a toast. "To the baby, let it be a girl, and if not, let it be a boy just like me."

"Cheers to that, Chrissy, cheers to that."

I heard from Blayne late that night when he sent a Thelma and Louise selfie of him and Amanda and her diamond studded ring finger in the forefront. "She said yes1"

I wrote back, "Of course she did, I'm so happy for you both. Love you!"

Chapter 36 It's A Baby!

In the beginning of August I had a good talk with Ben and asked him to please let me take off if Shaun went into labor during regular business hours. He promised me, "Unless we happen to be at court, you're good to go." By the week before the due date Shaun was beyond miserable and kept telling me, "I feel like this baby is going to jump out of my vagina any second, dude. I don't even trust that I should be walking."

"Did your doctor say that he still thought the due date was accurate?"

"He says yes but what the hell does he know? I keep having these false labor contractions."

"Braxton Hicks?"

"Yeah, Johnny calls them Toni Braxtons."

I laughed and told her, "Well, it will literally be any day now. It's just one week away."

"I know. I'm ready now."

"I know."

On Thursday, August 14th, which was the very next day after we had talked about her Toni Braxton contractions, at about 7 PM, I got a call from Johnny. I answered quickly, knowing exactly what it must be about, "Hello!"

"It's happening! Meet us at Lutheran." He hung up the phone before I even answered him, which made me laugh and I yelled, "Baby! Get dressed! It's happening!" Felix had just gotten out of the shower after coming home from work. He laughed and said, "We have to get food on the way!"

"Ok, let's do this!"

I drove and Felix ate. He also texted Ben for me and told him what was going on and if I could have Friday off. I may or may not have hauled ass to Wheat Ridge but I refused to miss anything. I remember when we got into the lobby of the hospital we saw Chris first and he led us to the right part of the hospital. He was saying, "I just know it's a girl. I just know. Aren't you freaking out? I can't believe my brother is going to be a dad. I'm going to be an Uncle!"

"Guncle."

"Yeah, I'm going to be a Guncle!"

Felix laughed loud enough to cause people stared at us as we walked briskly toward the nurse's station. We told them who we were there for and they told us that Shaun was in imminent delivery mode and where we should wait. I could not even stand the waiting. The suspense! At any minute Johnny or the Doctor or someone was going to show up and tell us the baby was here.

About thirty minutes into our wait Felipe showed up and Chris was so happy. "Oh thank God you're here. Hold me." Felipe looked alarmed as Chris ran up to him and hugged him. He said, "What's wrong!" Felix and I laughed and I said, "He is just being dramatic, everything is fine. We are still waiting."

"Oh my God, Chris. You queen."

Chris looked up from Felipe's chest and said, "I just now realized this, Cherry, you and I both have sexy Latin husbands." Felix laughed again harder than the last time and I said, "That's because we know what's good."

He high fived me, "Yeah, girl!"

Chris and Johnny's parents ran in minutes later and Chris screamed, "Mommy!" We all roared with laughter and the nurse said, "Now, y'all are going to have to stop being so happy or I will have to call security."

"Ma'am, please forgive us", I said laughing, "Do you maybe have some valium for this one?" I pointed at Chris and he said, "Girl, please."

We spent the next hour staring at everyone who walked by until finally Johnny came in with a big smile on his face. He paused briefly and looked at all of us staring at him on the edge of our seats and then he said, "It's a baby!" His mother stood up and said, "Young man! You tell us if it's a boy or a girl right now!"

He smiled at us all mischievously and after a long pause he said, "It's a girl."

We all screamed that time. Everyone was elated and I sat back and thought about my sweet victory. She was going to need those books after all. Man, was I smart. Johnny continued, "Her name is Jessica Erin after our mother's mothers." His mother cried and cried out of pure joy. I went over to her and hugged her. "You sweet thing. You knew it was going to be a girl too."

From behind her tissue she whispered, "I did."

About an hour later I went to see the baby and then I went to see Shaun. She looked up at me with sleepy eyes and in a crackly whisper voice she said, "Did you see my baby?"

I sat down in the chair next to her. "Yes I did. She is totally cute."

"I know."

"You know I would tell you if she wasn't. Most babies look like artichokes."

"I know, but she is cute."

"Jessica Erin is a beautiful name, Shaun. Johnny's mother was moved to tears."

"She told me. My mom and dad will be here tomorrow."

"Good. Was your mom happy that you named her after your Grandma Erin?"

"Yes, she cried."

"She did!?"

"Yes."

"Wow, this is really cool isn't it?"

"Yes, I like babies."

"You're high as a kite aren't you?"

"Yes."

Johnny came in and she fell asleep again. We giggled at her being so out of it and at how sweet she sounded in this moment. He said, "I'm really lucky."

I hugged him and said, "Yeah, man. You seriously are."

Chapter 37 Bells Will Be Ringing

Life after Jessica Erin was born was different for all of us. She was a big point of focus for us over the next few months and we all spent a lot of time together at Shaun and Johnny's because of it. As it turned out, her favorites to be held by, other than mommy and daddy, were Chris and Felix. She had no idea yet how lucky she was.

Right after she was born Blayne and Amanda had announced that their wedding would be on Christmas Eve night, which was a Wednesday that year, in the Camelot Room at the Swan Club in Roslyn. Lucky for Felix and I, we were already going to be there but I was nervous at first that Shaun and Johnny wouldn't be able to go. It was a "stay home for Christmas" year and they would have a 4-month-old baby. I was relieved, however, when Shaun told me that they would be going and that she was actually going to stay for a few weeks at her parent's house this time so they could spend time with the baby. Shaun and her mother really bonded when her parents were there the weekend after she was born and Shaun was missing her mom more than ever. She said it would be the first time since Jessica came that her and Johnny would be able to get dressed up and go out anyway, her parents could babysit and were right down the road from the Swan Club.

It would be a Christmas wedding. I had never ever been to one of those before. I imagined snow white wedding pictures and poinsettias. My mom was beside herself with excitement and sang, "Camelot!" from the musical every time we talked about it. In the beginning of December right before our trip we went shopping for outfits for the wedding. Amanda told us it would be cool if we wore rose red or emerald green dresses. She and Blayne were doing the same thing I did- which was not having a wedding party, and hoping everyone dressed in a way as to compliment the general look and theme of the wedding. She said she had been telling everyone, black, emerald green, rose red, or winter floral keeping in the same color pallet. Both Shaun and I thought it sounded amazing and it was easy for me to choose green and her to choose red so to the Park Meadows Mall we went. Leave it to us to procrastinate so long that we needed to pray to the shopping Gods that we would find something there and not have to buy it on line so close to the deadline.

Shaun had dropped the baby weight, but still had bigger boobs than she did pre-Jessica so we joked that everyone in Roslyn would think she had them done. We spent hours at the mall but we both came out of there with perfect dresses and faux fur to boot. Anyone who was there from the Heights would be in fur anyway so why not us too.

 Shaun and Johnny flew out with us again that year and we all took turns entertaining the baby during the flight. Three months to one year old turns out to be my very favorite baby age because they are so squishy and cuddly. One thing I learned, being in public with her, was that people always want to touch babies and that's just gross and rude. I understand that it is hard to resist squeezing their hands and feet but you're a stranger. Try to control yourself. As Shaun would say no matter if she was holding her or not when it happened, "Get your own baby!" Seriously.

The first ten days of that trip were a blur, other than drinking a lot of hot cocoa, honestly, but none of it mattered anyway until Tuesday the 23rd. Amanda went to her parents house for the night and Blayne stayed at mom's with all of us so they could experience the "keep the bride away from the groom in the hours before the wedding" tradition. I thought it was fun and I was glad to have him with me on his last night as my single brother. Mom made our traditional Potato Soup for Christmas Eve, a night early, of course. As we sat around the table as full as can be and as warm and cozy as we ever were in mom's kitchen, she said, "I can't believe the two of you will be married in the same year." It was strange, I had not even thought about it. She said, "The two of you have always been in sync, though, your loves stories are very, very different, I'm not surprised by this at all."
We just looked at each other pondering what she had said. She continued, "Are both of you happier than you have ever been?" I looked at Felix who was smiling his cute bashful smile and I said, "Yes." We all looked at Blayne and he said, "I have never been happier." Then mom asked, "Two Christmases ago did you think you would be this happy? Or that you would be married and engaged?" We both answered no and then she said, "It has been an amazing couple

of years that is for sure. But, here we are now. Cherry is sitting here with her wonderful husband and Blayne, you are getting married in twenty four hours."

Blayne was getting married!

Chapter 38 Happily Ever After

Christmas Eve sure was cold that year. I was wrong about the snow white wedding, it rained instead and as we headed to the Swan Club, we knew that soon Nassau County would be covered in a sheet of ice. I was quiet as we drove slowly across the Heights, deep in thought about what my mother had said the night before and how quickly things seemed to move in the last couple of years. She was right; it had been amazing. You know, I don't think there is anything wrong with moving fast sometimes. I think when you're young you should try to slow down a little and really spend a lot of time observing, learning, experiencing, and finding yourself, but I think when you're in your late 30s things are very different. Especially when it comes to love and babies. You will definitely not be surprised that this idea reminds me of the quote my mom recited to me when I was freaking out about how fast Mark was moving after we got back together that time. Remember? Billy Crystal as Harry in "When Harry Met Sally in the second to the last scene of the movie. It's New Years Eve and he is alone eating Mallomars. He suddenly realizes that he is madly in love with Sally and he isn't willing to let her go. She is across town suffering through a New Years party as a single girl who is technically in love with someone who isn't there, Harry. He tries in vain to catch a cab and instead has to run down sidewalk after sidewalk desperately hoping to make it to her before midnight. When he finally gets to the party she is ironically about to run out at the same moment to avoid dealing with the clock striking twelve and not having anyone to kiss. So, she unintentionally meets him standing there just inside the door. He tells her he loves her and she argues with him telling him "it doesn't work this way" so he says, " How bout this way; I love that you get cold when it's 71 degrees out. I love that it takes you an hour and a half to order a sandwich. I love that you get a crinkle above your nose when you're looking at me like I'm nuts. I love that after I spend a day with you I can still smell your perfume on my clothes and I love that you are the last person I want to talk to before I go to sleep at night. And, it's not because I'm lonely and it's not because it's New Years Eve. I came here tonight because when you realize you want to spend the rest of your life with somebody, you want the rest of your life to start as soon as possible." I believed that this is exactly how Blayne, Felix, and I felt this year. With Mark, bless his heart, it was like I picked up a melon, squeezed it and it just wasn't right, but with Felix, the sweet aroma of the fruitiest melon on earth captivated me enough to get me to put it in my cart. When you know, you know. Time means nothing.

The Camelot Room was beautifully decorated with white table clothes, red roses, and poinsettias. The guests were wearing their best duds and every single one of them fit the Christmas Eve theme that Amanda had hoped for. Shaun, my mother, and I cried as Blayne and Amanda read vows to each other and spoke about being in love for decades, being lost and being found. I remember one part of Blayne's vows he said, "You know I have always loved you, since our first Cony Island kiss and you're just as beautiful and mysterious to me as you were when we were 17." Man, I cried like a blubbering idiot when he said that. My mom and Shaun were no better. Johnny and Felix laughed together about it later that they were "distracted by their weeping wives".

Later on during the reception I stood by the bar panning the room, watching the guests and revelry and I noticed Felix across the room talking to Ann and my mom. I smiled a big smile as Blayne came up to me. He handed me a new glass of wine and said, "What are you smiling at?"

"Felix." I pointed toward them and Blayne looked over as Johnny was joining them in conversation. "He's a great guy for you, kid."

"I know." We watched as Felix and Johnny laughed hysterically at something my mom said and Shaun joined us. "What are you guys talking about?

I pointed again, "Look at our husbands, Shaun. Aren't they funny?"

"And sexy damn. I told him today, he looks so good he'll be lucky if he doesn't get me pregnant again after this."

"I know. Felix too. We almost didn't make it actually, Blayne. I must have put this dress on three times before we got here."

We all laughed and continued to watch as Amanda joined my mom and Ann, putting her arms around them and laughing with them at something Felix was saying. Eventually Blayne raised his glass to toast us. He said, "Ladies, we are the coolest three kids to ever come out of Roslyn, New York and the coolest yet, to leave it. All grown and married up, cheers to our single days behind us." As we clinked our glasses I said, "Let's hope we never have to be "out there again".

And, as far as I knew, we were all going to live happily ever after...

THE END